I0690948

DEAD SURROUND
THE JULIA POE
VAMPIRE CHRONICLES

CELIS T. RONO

Cover Designed and Illustrated by Tariq Raheem
http://www.tariqart.net

This book is a work of fiction. Any resemblance to actual events or persons, living or dead, is entirely coincidental.

"Dead Surround – The Julia Poe Vampire Chronicles," by Celis T. Rono. ISBN 978-1-60264-795-4 (softcover); ISBN 978-1-60264-796-1 (electronic) . Third printing.

Published 2011 by Virtualbookworm.com Publishing Inc., P.O. Box 9949, College Station, TX 77842, US. ©2011, Celis T. Rono. All rights reserved. No part of this publication may be reproduced, stored in a retrieval system, or transmitted in any form or by any means, electronic, mechanical, recording or otherwise, without the prior written permission of Celis T. Rono.

Dedicated to Joseph & Emily Celis

CHAPTER 1

RED AND DRIPPING, THE girl known as Poe struggled to maneuver the weather-beaten dinghy close enough to the foamy beach without getting sandbagged. The last thing she wanted was to lose sight of the shoreline and drift into the maw of the tumultuous Pacific waters.

The orange life preserver milked the last of her perspiration, and the black Clash t-shirt underneath was drenched. She didn't dare reach for the bottle of purified Santa Monica well water in her pack out of fear of losing one of the paddles mounted loosely on the tiny craft. Whether from dehydration or perhaps sunstroke, Poe's head throbbed excruciatingly as if an ice pick had jammed into the soft folds of her brain. Headaches and migraines were becoming more frequent companions of late.

She'd only been rowing for fifteen minutes, and the little excursion was proving more complex than she'd imagined as the taut, five-inch scar on her flushed face attested.

"Don't know how to paddle. Don't know how to swim," mumbled a disgruntled Poe. "Not very bright for trying to row to Venice. Just look at the size of the piranhas surrounding this bum contraption."

In response a ten-pound mackerel with cobalt-yellow fins bobbed up in salutation. Its theatrics elicited a guttural bark from Poe's sole companion, a tongueless, dirty-looking terrier half-buried in a blanket of tarp.

"Don't remember these things swarming this close to the shore when I was a kid." For her fishing excursions all she had to do was sweep her net into knee-deep water and capture a week's worth of food.

Nature in general had regenerated to the point of excess after a toxic miasma had mysteriously eradicated most of humankind. From Poe's now-and-then little hitching post on the Santa Monica Pier, the waters swarmed with noticeable sea life worthy of the infamous Nice and Monaco shores where the rich and uncomplicated had deemed it beneath them to interrupt a perfect tan to fish. Overly friendly fishtails slapped the shores without trepidation, and they were as commonplace as deer window shopping on Rodeo Drive or coyotes cavorting along the Pacific Coast Highway.

Poe had never been fitter or healthier since the Gray Armageddon, but she was finding rowing a hard task to master.

The dog mute-barked twice and wagged her tail under the warm tarp, startling fish surrounding the boat. Her halved tongue bathed in thirst like her companion's mouth. Two years ago vampires had broken the mutt's legs, cut her tongue, and left her for dead.

"We're almost there, Pen. Water and goodies will be waiting for us," she told the dog in her strikingly husky voice. She tugged at the edge of the tarp covering half the dog. "Too hot for this, Penny."

Poe had a terrible habit of talking to herself and the dog. Living underground for over a decade would do that to anyone. Ever since the murder of Goss and Sister Ann, her best friends and gurus, life had turned completely around. After the Downtown fiasco there was little chance for socializing again. She was a wanted woman.

"Unbelievable these vampires," Poe said out of habit, gritting her teeth. She made a point to blame all devastation and misery on the bloodsuckers that ruled Los Angeles – and most likely the rest of the world.

She wondered what happened to the Vampire Council, the most powerful branch of the vampire hierarchy that brought order to the master vampire fiefdoms. Three out of five Council members had been killed during the most ambitious cattle rescue ever executed. More so than the Council, the fate of Quillon Trench, the master vampire whose handsome face she'd marred with garlic water, worried her. If anyone were to track her down, Trench and his crooked LAPD goons would be the hunters. He hadn't joined the showdown at Union Station that ended in the liberation of hundreds of human blood cattle.

"Kaleb Sainvire, may I never see your dead eyes again," Poe said half-heartedly. It always ended that way. Every stray thought through the course of these years transmuted into a Sainvire rumination. There wasn't a day she didn't think about the master vampire with a conscience. How many in his position would give up his privileged life to rescue human cattle bled for the consumption of the vampire masses? At the end of the day Poe shrugged her shoulders and wished Sainvire well. This was the new Poe, the one who forced herself to meditate and

3

practice yoga to control her rage. She was growing up.

Ever since escaping the deadly politics of Downtown, Poe had tried to live life to the fullest in a vampire-free setting. She moved – or was chased away – to her childhood digs in West Los Angeles, a few miles from the Santa Monica beach. Nearly crippled from the multiple beatings she'd received from vampires and their spawn for assisting in the cattle rescue, an eternity had passed before she was able to stand without sharp, debilitating pain.

Nightmares of beatings plagued her more frequently than dreams of ravenous undead sucking her dry. Vampires had immense strength and heightened senses. Some, however, packed more than run-of-the mill supernatural power. A few had the ability to fly. She'd witnessed certain dead who lifted boulders and automobiles like they were loaves of bread. A particular vampire by the name of Maple grew mallet arms in battle that could pulp limbs. Poe shivered at the remembrance of a particular dead with a tentacle for a tongue. Then there were the sun-immune not-quite-vampires, the halfdead, who sometimes patrolled her neighborhood for signs of life. Poe was sorely outmatched, and she knew it.

There was nothing for it. She had to grow some calluses. Developing tolerance to pain was a must.

Only one form of martial arts came to mind: Muay Thai. She knew from her late friend, Goss, a bit about the street fighting skill that utilized devastating kicks and elbow strikes. But since he had been decapitated short of two years ago, Poe had to continue a grueling training of Thai boxing on her own. She looked to the movies, *Ong Bak: The Thai*

Warrior and *Breaking Bone: Volume 1-3*, for much needed tutelage. As providence would have it, she found such titles ripe for the picking at her neighborhood rental shop aptly named A Video Store Named Desire.

The punishing training included squatting and flipping car tires for over two hours to strengthen the hip, thigh, and arm muscles. Poe also routinely smashed her head, fists, and shins against blunt objects, preferably wood or brick, for the generation of calluses. A quitter by nature as evident by her lengthy stay underground after her parents' deaths, Poe nevertheless persevered as best as she could.

Never let them drink you dead became one of her growing number of mantras.

It was the first time in her life that she'd stuck to one objective without whining or making sorry excuses. She trained for no less than six hours a day, rain or shine. She leapt and jumped like her butt was on fire to increase her range and toughen her tendons. She clouted and kicked innocent trees, pretending they were creatures of the night. She awoke at dawn to run eight miles a day for stamina, packing various firearms in case she encountered some peskies.

For years she'd endured the life of a corpse hidden away in an underground bunker, afraid to surface above ground. Not so long ago vampires and their underlings had nearly broken her back. "Never again," she repeated with each punch to a sand-filled bag before going to bed each night. She repeated that mantra during meditation to wind down her day.

Rowing to Venice was the first time she'd actually attempted such a bold feat away from the safety of her parents' house. Even before setting foot on the sand, it was a nearly four-mile walk from Sawtelle Boulevard to the once popular tourist destination, Santa Monica Beach. Although the City of Santa Monica and the Venice neighborhood of the City of Los Angeles were adjacent areas and had been completely accessible from one location to the other in an easier time, the vampires had since disrupted the arterial and feeder roadways with impassible debris.

Perhaps months of strict regimen had taken their toll and brought out the girl's impulsive nature. A vise as powerful as a vampire's had taken hold of her reason. She saw only pink and blue.

"This will test my courage," she told Penny. "The fluff we're risking our lives over better be worth it," muttered Poe, slightly seasick from the choppy waves.

The Pacific Coast Highway and general street access to the famous beach town had been demolished. Roads concaved into deep lacerations, leaving gaping sink holes and broken concrete. Cars and trucks stacked like dirty dishes as far as the eye could see acted as a bulwark against stragglers like Poe. Cemented fences with broken bottle and razor wire made them a chore to scale. These smelled like human defenses to Poe.

Venice, so close, so freaking far, was trouble. And she was hungry.

Poe swiped at her nose dotted with sweat. "We might see some people, doggy. Cross your paws that they're not super jerks. They don't like me because of my tendency to get them killed."

Her eight-year involvement with other humans hooked her forever more. It was great to actually talk to someone other than the TV. During the previous decade Poe had been under the illusion that she was the last person on earth until she met the near-giant-size Goss.

She was now better off in the company of one mute, scruffy mutt in the long run, but what she would give to be able to talk to her old comrades Megan, Morales, and Joseph again. Then her mind returned to Kaleb Sainvire, the master vampire with unnerving gray eyes. How could she forget the love of her life? The vampire who chose protecting his people over her?

"Blast!" Poe burst out, maneuvering the dinghy to shore. "My arm hurts, Penny, and we're getting nowhere. I'm a lousy boat person. We'll have to walk the rest of the way."

First she checked the Glocks and Walther PPKs, her guns of choice, on the various holsters found under her dark windbreaker. She had other guns in her pack, but they were all Ziploc'ed in the event she fell overboard. She slung a hefty Ruger Mini-14 assault rifle around her neck. If placed on the floor vertically, it rested just barely under her breast bone.

"We can scale the sand bars, doggy. No more water," she explained to her pal, hating that her shoes sloshed around in sand and seaweed. Poe folded her sodden olive army pants to the knees after forgetting to hitch them up. Penny, who yelped her happiness at being off the tiny boat that resembled a canoe, ran gleefully like a young elk around her one true friend.

You'd never think two of her legs were ever broken.

"Please, don't let them get us," Poe quickly prayed. It was her usual prayer to her parents, her intercessors.

To be outdoors was a welcome change. Poe was pleased to see her dog kicking up sand and racing here and there to encourage her to hustle.

Venice, the fun land of her youth, was a destination she'd dreamed of visiting for a while now. The land of dollar hot dogs, yummy ice cream, cheap socks and t-shirts, and no-neck muscle men showing their oiled wares to the gawking public simply had to be intact. Multi-story sand mazes on the beach pumped her doubts, however.

"Somebody took the time to form these," Poe said quietly. "Graffiti's everywhere." She studied the words spray painted repeatedly on concrete walls, fallen billboards, and pieces of cement mounted on sandbars.

DOGTOWN

Somehow Poe didn't think the tagging referred to the infamous Z-Boys who had elevated the art of surfing and skateboarding in the mid-1970s. Even Penny seemed to realize that something was amiss as her pep dissipated suddenly. She sniffed the air suspiciously.

"It's okay, Pen," she assured the dog who kept close. She naively added, "We're almost there. Don't worry. This place remembers me. It knows how much my family and I loved it. Nothing bad can happen."

In silence Poe climbed the last five sandbag walls with her dog by her side. Each ascent and descent magnified her ever increasing heart rate.

Crustaceans on the sand sidling every which way, their antenna eyes missing nothing, fascinated Poe.

"Face paint and candy apples," she mumbled once then continued on.

Methodically Poe bent down to tighten the double-knot on her dark blue Adidas. Her obsessive-compulsive shoelace problem had been tamed to three incidents a day.

"Let's have our lunch first, shall we, Penny girl?" Poe said and reached into her pack. She tossed Penny three dry slabs of jerky. Poe munched down on two apples and crackers and took a swig of water. The rest of the liquid she placed in a plastic bowl for the dog.

"What do you know? People are actually living in Venice," Poe pondered. "Ballsy."

CHAPTER 2

TO SAY VENICE WAS no more would be a dry joke.

The famous Ocean Front Walk that bore the weight of artists, bizarre street performers, and pierced denizens covered in tattoos stood cracked and baking under the California sun. It wasn't a noble end for such illustrious concrete. Bleached and wind worn, the hostels and businesses in the vicinity had a look of sagging carnival floats a hundred days after Mardi Gras.

No muscle men or boisterous vendors selling velvet paintings and braided hemp bracelets harassed the girl and her dog. Nor were there rollerbladers, skaters, bicyclists, unicyclists, or pedestrians to be seen.

At least it smelled the same – fishy ocean mist and mesquite with a hint of excrement. *Correction*, she thought. *A lot of excrement. Folks certainly still live here.*

"Should'na come," Poe told Penny in a tight voice. "Now I'll only remember the graveyard feel of this place."

Expecting a predator to rush out and ambush her any minute, Poe positioned the assault rifle with her index finger ready to fire. Poe sweated copiously, especially on the tip of her nose. She was suspicious of every swaying palm tree as if monkey-vampire-men straddled them with ill intentions. She always felt that way when the nagging voice in her mind warned her and turned out to be correct at every galling turn.

"Hello," Poe cried. "I know folks are living here. It's way too clean. Not even bird shit on the ground." As she spoke, her shoe stepped on fresh pretzel-shaped poo, soft enough to be a few hours old. *Disgusting!* No bird crap, alright, but dog shit aplenty decorated sand and concrete like flies on key lime pie. *How could I have missed them?*

Penny curled her lips and bared her sharp yellow teeth.

"Even my dog can smell you all," Poe continued, wiping the sole of her wet sandy shoe on sharp, uneven concrete. Revolted and sweating in her dark windbreaker, Poe focused her eyes on building windows and ledges for possible trigger buggers. She was nevertheless pleased with herself for not stuttering, an embarrassing problem she'd finally conquered her last few days in Downtown Los Angeles.

"I'm no stooge. I'm nobody's Igor. Just wanna check this place out since my folks liked to take us here. Got my face temporarily tattooed here Maori-style by a one-armed holy man. Ate tons of cotton candy and caramel apples with my brother and sister right at this spot." She banged the rust layered storefront with the rifle nozzle for emphasis. At the moment Poe looked more like a sixteen-year-old than her creaking old age of twenty-four.

She pointed the rifle on a metal slab that used to be a bench. "And it's really rude to ignore me and my dog. I know people live here. I have a sixth sense about these things," she lied. "I'll have to check each and every one of the buildings, I guess."

Not two seconds after Poe's less-than-poetic soliloquy, a shrill whistle pierced the roar of surf crashing on four-ton K-rail cement barriers once used to divide freeways during construction. Before Penny could bark a warning, dogs of all sizes and breeds swarmed from every beach house and storefront. The mass of growling canines streamed endlessly, backing Poe and Penny into the nostalgic bench of happier days. *There's more than three dozen of them. We're Alpo!*

Not a bite did they receive. Though demented guttural sounds emitted from their drooling chops, the dogs refrained from barking. Poe could see engorged ticks hanging brazenly on fur-lined skin and tiny fleas jumping to and fro on matted fur. The little hairs on her arms rose and looked hurriedly at Penny. *You ticks better not infect my extremely hygienic dog. I'll have to waste my bullets on you all!*

"This is kinda unfair, don't you think?" Poe screeched, climbing vigilantly up the bench and lifting Penny's 24-pound bulk along with her. With a shaky voice she recited another mantra, "I am Bruce Lee's daughter, Muhammad Ali's niece, and Xena's clone, and I'm not gonna get eaten by dogs today."

Thinly spread doggy muscle and tendon flexed in her hand. Tense Penny was about to snap like over-wound fiddle string. Poe could almost feel those yellow teeth chewing on her bones. She didn't have enough bullets to exterminate the packs of mastiffs, bulldogs, and dotted, mutated mutts. How many could she realistically kill before one of them clamped down her throat?

"This is the last time we go exploring, Penny," Poe whispered to her uncowed and growling dog. "Really sorry for mixing you up in this."

A Doberman twice removed and a couple of his Rottweiler friends were especially annoyed by Penny's sass. Poe's medium-sized companion wasn't at all daunted by the larger dogs' scars of seasoned street fighters. Masticating, Penny continued to snarl at them. She tried to leap at the growling creatures three times her size but was held back by her friend. *They're waiting for some kind of command,* Poe thought. *Otherwise we'd be lamb stew by now.* Lucky for Poe and Penny, the rest of the bunch took a step back. Before the words "we're dead" crossed Poe's mind, the pissy Rotts with pink herpes mouths lunged at the punier Penny.

Bedlam hit and Poe found herself shooting at dogs at close range and having a miserable time of it. The rifle proved to be too long and inconvenient for the melee. The blunt end bludgeoned implausibly thick skulls that seemed to get denser with each thwack. Within seconds Poe's windbreaker looked like shredded wheat. Her arms dripped blood and saliva as she reached for the Glocks in her shoulder holster concealed beneath her quickly disappearing jacket.

An ankle buckled, held captive by a motley dotted creature that could possibly have belonged to the collie family. Sharp teeth obstructed by bone dug deeper. Like a spit laden chew toy, Poe was dragged nastily to the ground.

It was like off-roading. Instead of a sturdy jeep, there was Poe's sweaty back. Tail-waggers that had merely stood watch suddenly angled in to join the frenzy. She fired at those closest to mangling her flesh.

What vampires couldn't accomplish the past thirteen years, the flea bags put to rest in a span of seconds. Dogs snapped their jaws at Poe, embedding crusty teeth into her skin. The older ones lost rotten teeth in their haste to take their share. Their breath, akin to freshly squeezed dumpster surprise with a dash of sewer, made her want to faint.

Before the shrill cries of a whistle put a halt to the melee, the dogs managed to bite Poe more than a dozen times, an amount greater than her kill tally. Fresh lines brimming with blood covered her arms and legs and overlaid old scars.

At least they didn't get my face, Poe murmured thankfully. The deep, five-inch scar running from forehead to cheek courtesy of a vampire's slash when she was a kid was quite enough decoration. The slightest more would have been overkill.

Penny, to her knowledge, remained uneaten. Around her silent friend several dogs lay dead or twitching, their necks and bellies oozing. Poe was amazed for a medium-size dog to still be standing after such a skirmish. Penny's mouth trickled with blood and bits of flesh from dogs she'd thrashed. Not quite done, Penny continued to gnaw on the convulsing body of a mangy Spitz, its blood like pungently thick sangria sprinkled indiscriminately on tangled fur.

"Hey, enough of that, *perro*!" Poe gently kicked Penny in the rump to get her attention. Poe hopped backwards when her own dog snapped on instinct. "Hey! Dog's dead, Pen. Calm down. No need to eat him to boot!"

Penny eyed her as if irritated by the interruption.

"I'll have to check you out for injuries later, Pen," she said unevenly, trying to catch her breath. "After I kill the whistle-happy jerk that set the Cujos loose."

It took exactly three whistle commands for the dogs to stand down. A delay would have found Poe sprawled on the floor, her major veins spraying the hot cement of the Venice boardwalk.

What kind of chupacabras could command hundreds of killer dogs? It can't be a vampire. That's for sure. Dogs can't abide the dead.

Dainty of step and supple of hips, the creature Poe wondered about materialized as if in answer to the girl's question. Mouth slack from surprise, Poe watched the most exquisite woman she'd ever seen in her life slowly strut to where she stood. Her movie-memory pegged a glimpse of Sofia Loren at her most fetching with rounder flesh and wider hips. Excitable dogs drooled and danced around her. They, too, seemed hypnotized by her presence.

Her face was immaculate, brushed with burnt rose rouge, bronze powder, and other beauty essentials that brought out the fine panes of her cheekbones and the slight opulent puff of her lips. The woman's skills were surely lifted from Kevyn Aucoin, make-up artist extraordinaire whose books she had happened upon at the West L.A. public library.

As the woman drew nearer Poe noticed the dark lashes that curved around her tremendously wide brown eyes. Her russet skin emitted a floral smell that clashed with the dizzying stench of dogs. Poe couldn't help but feel like a bug trapped in a spider web, waiting for the final puncture to do her in, but for the life of her she couldn't stop looking.

She has so much hair – triple mine at least. And she's so tall! Amazonian goddess in the flesh.

The woman was all curves. And height. Her body was a number 8 with emphasis on the lower half. Her tiny waist blossomed into size 44 hips. Without shoes she stood over six-foot-two, roughly the same height as Sainvire. With the yellow open-toed heels that hugged her feet, she would easily tower over him. The gold whistle about her neck brought Poe back to reality. It was twice the size of the silver one Poe wore around her neck. The altitudinous woman's shrill whistle could order dogs to kill at her will.

"Um, you're human right?" Poe asked tentatively. She breathed hard from the beating she had received from the woman's dogs. "If you're one of those leech caretakers for vamps, then I'll need to shoot you."

"Yes, I'm human. Passionada Cruz is the name," she answered with a secret smile. "I'm supernatural in looks, so I've been told. But I'm no vampire puppet."

Poe remained guarded. She ogled the yellow high heels that kept the voluminous woman upright like stilts supporting ornamental Hollywood Hills homes.

"Tried wearing a pair of those a couple of times. Just playing around," said Poe as she nodded at the shoes. "Both times I injured my ankles."

"Hmm. Well not every woman can handle heels. It's an art. You must be Poe," the dark woman proclaimed lightly.

Poe, having swallowed spit the wrong way, coughed.

"How the heck do you know that?" she asked when her throat finally cleared. She could feel the veins in her eyes throbbing.

"No offense, girl, but the missing earlobe and the scar's a big giveaway," she said with amusement. "And people didn't exaggerate about your raspy voice, either. Oh don't look so shocked. Everybody knows about you on the Westside," she said jovially. "And quite possibly all of California."

"H-how? Who told? I thought I was alone," Poe blurted all at once, tugging self-consciously at the ear with a flap eaten by a wiseass part-vampire halfdead infatuated with capoeira, a laughable martial arts dance in her opinion.

"Girl-child, who do you think planted those fist-sized tomatoes you love to take? And the nice yellow squash that plump up like a man's arm two blocks from where you live?"

"I, I thought they were wild," Poe said, her voice wavering.

"No inkling, really? Even when you found a perfectly suspect skateboard with shiny Swiss ball bearings two houses away where you pick up fresh eggs?"

"Um, no," Poe shook her head, paling. "I thought it was a gift from my brother. From the grave, you know. He was into skateboarding."

"You're serious?" the towering woman asked. Seeing the girl's mortification and finally accepting that Poe was probably not quite one hundred percent in the head, she nodded. "Right. You mean it."

"How come nobody tried to contact me?" *And why didn't the reliable voice in my head let me know I wasn't alone?*

The woman shook her head and tapped the gold whistle resting closest to the mound of her left breast. "Because you have a bad reputation, girl. Granted you've saved lives, but you've also taken a few to the grave."

Poe swallowed. The woman's reminder released an unpleasant stink in the armpit of her memory. She'd killed innocent vampires in a fit of rage, and they had been loyal to the cause of Plasmacore, the alternative food source Sainvire had been trying to introduce until the Vampire Council put an end to it.

"Don't worry about it, Poe," the woman said with kindness. "You've been allowed to stay because you've more than made up for your mistakes."

"H-how?" Poe asked. Her old stutter had resurfaced. In case the words 'torture' and 'revenge' factored in the woman's explanation, Poe tightened her grip on her guns.

"You've helped extricate hundreds of human cattle from blood farms and most significantly, from that bastard, Trench. It also helps that you had a hand in decimating the fascist Vampire Council in L.A. with your sharpshooter skills."

Little Penny snarled a warning to the sweet-smelling woman that she was getting too close to Poe.

"Easy there, Penny," Poe ordered wryly.

"Interesting dog you have there," the woman remarked. "Likes to eat dog flesh, does she?"

"Sometimes, I guess," Poe said distractedly. "I don't usually let her, but more times than not she scouts ahead of me—" Clearing her throat, she stirred the conversation back on course. "Sounds like I have quite a few neighbors. They must've peed on the produce I took." She shuddered at what they might have used as fertilizer.

"Maybe. But they never forgot that you were off limits, even when you penned their chickens and ate all the eggs."

"Hmm, the chicken. Nice of them," Poe said with derision, wiping her bloody arms with the bottom of her t-shirt. The protein from the albumen and yolk kept her well fed. "I guess it didn't matter that I never ate the chickens."

"Nope."

"So who threatened to grind their bones and eat their kidneys if they lay their hands on me?"

"Can't you guess?"

She could think of only one powerful enough to keep her breathing. He had gray eyes, and he was dead.

"Is the cotton candy machine still inside that store?" Poe asked, evading the answer. She pointed with pursed lips at the dilapidated shack behind the tall stranger.

Once the pulse of the boardwalk, Dino's, a hot dog and junk food dive, looked weather beaten and diseased with its tagged metal roll-up door. Over a decade after the death clouds had poisoned most of the population, the storefront looked affronted but alive.

"I'm not sure," she answered with a shrug. "I don't think I've ever been in there. I keep away from boarded storefronts because of the rats."

"Can you step aside then?" Poe asked brusquely. She swallowed her disgust. She had her unwanted share of rats and their droppings. Limping, she studied the door.

With careful aim Poe fired three shots at the medium-size lock corroded with age to bust the lock loose. She couldn't help it. She peeked at the reaction of the woman in a yellow dress. The lipsticked diva's smile never floundered.

"I have a craving," Poe explained, "for cotton candy."

"Ah. So that's why you've braved spiked fences and a sea of dogs."

"Can't fight PMS."

The lady thinks I'm nuts.

"So I take it you get your menses pretty regularly?" asked the woman bluntly.

Reddening, Poe shook her head. "Um, no," she stumbled. She never had the opportunity to talk about that stuff with her mother or Sister Ann. "I'm lucky if I get it once a year. I substitute 'PMS' for 'craving', I guess. Stupid thing to do."

"Language confusion is common nowadays. The younger ones are switching and substituting meanings of words because no one was there to educate them. Sister Ann had the 'talk' with you, right?"

"Huh?" Poe said. She was astounded at the candor of the built woman she'd barely met. Sister Ann had taught Poe how to shoot with precision among other things. She and a giant black man named Goss had completed her education and more. The mention of their names cast a gloom in her mood. Following Goss' sober instruction, Poe had decapitated him when she found him bled to death. Dear Sister Ann had been stabbed in the eye fighting Trench's people, and Poe dreamed about exacting revenge on the foppish master vampire every waking hour.

"I mean about your monthlies and other delicate things."

"Um, I saw the movie *Carrie* when I was ten, and it was pretty much self-explanatory. The rest I learned through trial and error and watching videos and DVDs."

Instead of continuing with awkward pleasantries, Poe pushed up the metal barrier and limped inside the dark store smelling of rot and staleness. The contact left bright orange rust on the palm of her hands.

From her pack she took out two solar powered lanterns, the kind that needed to be pumped ten times an hour, and placed them in convenient locations to illuminate the store.

"There it is," she said with relief at spotting the cobwebbed cotton candy machine. The blood on her arm stopped her from touching it. She attacked the wounds on her body first, dousing them with alcohol gel and smearing them with Neosporin. Next she pulled cleaning rags and paper towels from her pack. Poe took a good hour to clean the Floss Boss, a compact cotton candy machine, as it was crusted with crystallized sugar and rat droppings.

All this time the dog woman hovered over her shoulder, watching with interest and sometimes bringing a fresh bucket of water from her private well and charcoal filtration system. Occasionally grungy dogs padded up for a petting. Poe wondered if she trusted the woman enough to keep from stabbing her in the back.

"All the sugar seems to have morphed into amber. That's going to be a problem," said her curious audience. Passionada inspected the melted chip bags and pebbly slush machines with a frown.

"I have some in my pack," Poe said, proud at her foresight. "Got some pink and blue food coloring, too."

When the electricity didn't spark to life, irking Poe to no end, the woman wheeled in her own mini-generator.

"Thanks."

"I want a piece of the action, girl. You've whet my appetite."

Lumpy pink clown-hair monstrosities that weighed about a pound were produced to the disappointment of all. Poe finally got the hang of maneuvering the stick clockwise in unhurried circles while hot air blew strands of sugar on the side. Sparing drops of color and loosened sugar did the trick, and Poe was able to replicate perfectly decent cotton candy.

The fluffy snack put Poe in a sociable mood enough to ask, "So has anyone figured out the gray miasma since I retired?" The poison that had wiped out almost the entire human population had never been solved. It had struck like the hand of death itself, suffocating the nonimmune with their own blood and mucous.

"I don't know what to tell you, girl," shrugged Passionada. "No one's left that's smart enough to figure out what happened. The usual germ warfare-slash-hand of God theories still abound. Who knows why so many died and we didn't? It doesn't matter now. We've got bigger problems, like keeping ourselves from becoming cattle for vamps to feed on with their straw attachments. Downtown vamps now resort to drinking minority blood since all the white blood cattle have been rescued. We're considered prime rib, Poe."

"I guess you're right. More important things to worry about than what killed my mom and dad," she agreed. "I hate racist vampires who made non-whites into janitors to clean up their shit. I hate them even more now that they want to eat us, too."

Dimples showing, Poe proudly handed the woman a fluffy cotton candy head the size of a basketball. She bagged about a dozen for later consumption. Poe made extras for herself and for the stranger, but she spared the food coloring. She didn't like the bitter taste it left on her tongue. The goof-up batches she gave to Penny who already had her fill of dog corpses.

In silence Poe and the woman stuffed their faces with quick dissolving sugar and grunted in satisfaction while sitting on a bench facing the electric blue Pacific. The sun combined with ocean wind had an uncomfortable blow dryer effect on their skin. Poe's scalp tingled from the heat. Her conductor mass of black hair didn't help her, either. Their view was obstructed by billboards and rolling dunes and distracted by frolicking, fornicating dogs which didn't seem phased by them one whit.

"It's been bloody, these retaliations," Passionada Cruz told Poe as she licked her thick but strangely delicate fingers clean without marring her perfectly glossed red lips.

If I had that lip gloss I'd look like I'd just gnawed on a pile of greasy pork chops, Poe thought. *Not sexy at all*.

"Like for instance last month thirty cattle were retaken from a rehab farm," Passionada continued, daintily dabbing the edges of her lips with tissue. "The ones the master vampires didn't take, the elderly and the sick, were slaughtered along with Sainvire's people. They were gutted. Their insides were yanked out and used to spell messages like: A RECKONING AT HAND; STEALING WILL GET YOU KILLED; SAINVIRE YOU'RE NEXT."

"Man, that's so medieval. Imagine how many yards of intestines they needed to spell a long message like that," Poe contemplated quietly as she watched Passionada bust open another bag of cotton candy, her third. "Really brutal the way they killed the old folks. No respect."

"They have orders to leave no cattle behind. What they can't carry or eat they kill," the woman said. She shook her head. "It's all for Sainvire's benefit, of course. He's a Judas to them for turning his back on the vampire way of life. They think Sainvire's a greedy thief, and they'll do anything to get him back."

Despite the warm day Poe shivered. Although she was loath to admit it, she still had feelings for the vampire. He was her first, after all, and the best person she'd ever met, vampire or not. The thought of every vampire in California pledging to tear his flesh into fish bait for stealing their food source frightened her. *All this trouble because Sainvire freed up hundreds of human cattle from vamp farms. Doing the right thing sucks!*

Her large dark eyes followed a miniscule dust devil skipping across the sand as it teased a grungy Penny into chasing it, and she only looked up when Passionada Cruz' feminine and musical voice spoke once more. Penny still didn't trust the substantial woman though they'd shared dessert on a bench.

"The new Vampire Council will give whoever destroys him master status and fifty heads of prime cattle. Two hundred if they bring him in alive. For human traitors, a mansion in Beverly Hills, free supplies of human food from Valley farms, and lifetime immunity from predators. Instant royalty," Passionada explained. "Sainvire's followers are to be beheaded, disemboweled, and dried in the sun like jerky for one whole year like the Brits did to Captain Cook when they caught up with him."

"That'd be you, I guess," Poe said, trying her hand at comedy.

"And you," Passionada snorted. "You're second on the most wanted list. You aided him and killed off a few Council members. Worst of all you marred Trench's beautiful face when you threw garlic water at him. Plus everyone has a theory that you and Sainvire were…close."

"Well they're nuts."

It was one night. Saying it was a mistake just wouldn't cut it. So she shifted the subject slightly off center. She thought about Joseph, Sainvire's ever ebullient tattooed best friend who shared the same name as her brother, and thoroughly felt ill. Sainvire and Joseph did not deserve to be hunted down. If only there was a way of protecting them.

"Is Joseph alive?"

"As alive as a dead man can be, no thanks to the Council."

"That's good. He's an okay guy. He's Pinoy like a quarter of me. Practically my brother." Poe sighed.

"You look it with your can't-put-my-finger-on-it ethnic background," said Passionada. "What are you again?"

"My dad's Scot-Irish and Mexican," said Poe proudly. "And my mom's Filipino and Japanese. They were the best sort of people. Really fun parents. No complaints on that score." She took out a battered Bad Badtz-Maru Velcro wallet encased in three zip bags and pulled out a picture of her parents flanked by her older sister, Sirena, her brother, Joseph, and Poe. "That's them."

"Good looking family you have there."

"I think so," she said proudly, tucking the picture away with infinite care and placing the wallet in the Ziploc bags once more. "I guess it's no surprise the Council went haywire after the mass exodus of their cattle." She wondered again about the five most powerful undead in the city. She and Sainvire had decimated their ranks.

"They have a new set every few months. Just for show, you know."

"So who's the leader now?" Poe scratched her sunburned scalp.

"No one really," Passionada sighed. "There is no more Council as you knew it. They're mere decorations of days gone by. It's just one vampire now from San Francisco named Peter Newbitt and his lap dog, Quillon Trench. Rumor is you made Trench so ugly he doesn't leave his lair anymore. The two of them are running the show."

"His face wasn't so bad," said Poe. She remembered his craggy face at a Council meeting two years before.

"Well you know how egotistical he is. And the head cheese is Trench's Obi-Wan. His objective is to take back the stolen cattle and kill Sainvire."

"I should've killed Trench when I had the chance," Poe said as she stabbed the sand with her stick. Deep down it gave her goosebumps to think Quillon still harbored a grudge against her. She didn't think he would easily forget the incident. "I hope he never gets his hands on me 'cause I'm really gonna get it. Vanity's a top motive for violence."

"So I take it you don't know about the bounty on your head."

"Bounty?" Poe swallowed with an audible gulp. "You said I was number two? You're serious?"

"Yes, but never mind," Passionada waved the business away. "Anyway, last year Sainvire put out an APB on you to his people throughout SoCal and the Central Valley. We've been hard at work making sure you don't get into any trouble."

"You're kidding, right?" Poe gave the woman an annoyed glance. "I didn't even know there were any of you around. And for the record I never got into any trouble."

"Despite what you think, it's hard being invisible while keeping you out of a sticky muck," said Passionada. She pursed her lips as the last cloud of oh-too-sweet cotton candy melted on her tongue.

"Burning down a house on Iowa Avenue, I'd call that trouble."

"What?" Poe shook her head then remembered the charred bungalow she'd looted for can food and towels a few days ago. "I didn't burn that house down."

"Well somebody was roasting a can of cream corn on the stove and forgot about it."

"I, I—" Something nagged in the back of her mind. "I didn't mean to do it."

"Still, a team of us had to leave our comfy hideaway to extinguish the blaze. Couldn't have smoke signals for greedy vamps and scavengers to notice."

"Um, I didn't know," was all Poe could say.

"Then there was the incident with the cars parked along Armacost Avenue. Did every single windshield have to meet with the thick end of a baseball bat?" Passionada droned, her large eyes in slits. "You know, some of those cars are operational. They're laboriously kept up for emergencies."

"Look. If I had known, I wouldn't have done any of those things," Poe said, wincing. "I was super-depressed that day."

"Fair enough," Passionada acceded. "I've told Sainvire from the beginning that keeping you ignorant was a stupid idea. Truce then. Let me properly clean your wounds and give you a set of rabies shots."

"Oh no. Sister Ann gave me those shots four years ago," Poe said, letting out a long breath. "If we're going to be friends, Passionada, you gotta know I can't handle needles. To me they're worse than rotten vamp teeth."

28

"Very well then. I see your point. I don't like flat shoes." Passionada shook her head with disgust. "Even though heels make me look like a female Paul Bunyan, I love them to death. If you can believe it, I can run with three-inch heels without breaking a sweat or injuring myself."

"Nice. With or without heels I'm clumsy. No chance of looking graceful or classy there."

She followed the giantess to one of the clothing shops on the boardwalk that had been converted into a plush dwelling. Porcelain poodles in different shapes and sizes occupied every table, bookshelf, and cranny while posters of Clive Owen, Christian Bale, and Matt Damon covered the walls. Meeting Passionada gave an extra lilt in her step.

Before she could think of magic carpets, cloud cities, and the healing power of friendship, her happy mood quickly turned to shock. Passionada thwacked Poe on the head with a weighty granite pestle. Poe collapsed into confused oblivion.

Something stunk.

Like Roquefort cheese with veins of blue mold. *The kind Mom and Dad chomped noisily while watching* Conan O'Brien. *Why did the floor heave? The liquid sugar in my belly is troubled.*

The wet and sandy thing that touched her face had a faint smell of decomposition. She had no desire to open her eyes. Only bad things could come, but Sister Ann's voice persisted in her brain.

"Lord, child," the nun said in a voice of irritation. "You have an intrinsic gift of hitting the bullseye, no

29

thanks to me. I only handed you a gun and told you to hit the red circle. The rest was all you. That's a gift if I ever saw one, especially in these perilous times. Now cut the bullshit and open your eyes!"

With a start Poe's eyelids fluttered open.

Bright blue sky stabbed her eyes. Her watery gaze eventually focused on her molester, Penny the half-tongue. *Why does my dog have wavy auburn hair? And she smells.*

Shaking, she pushed the dog at arms length and entangled her fingers in something spidery in the process. Once her clearing eyes saw what had snagged in her fingers, Poe belted out a shriek, too embarrassingly girly in her opinion, which pierced even her own ears.

"Get this off of me!" she screamed as she thrashed about. "Help!" The colors processed by her dark eyes were just too stark.

Cold metal held her wrists and ankles. Her eyes registered what it was, and she had to fight back panic. *I'm clapped in irons like a goon in pirate movies!* Penny inched closer to her. The dog had on a makeshift collar and leash that was tied to an anchor. *Anchor?*

"I'm on a boat?" she croaked, her parched lips cracking. Queasiness assaulted the center of her belly. She was surrounded by ocean that painfully reflected the sun and made her squint.

What she had thought was Penny's new hairdo was auburn tresses of a nylon rope. It was hung out to dry and held suspended by laundry clips along the rails of the boat edge where her chains coiled against. Drying carcasses of salted fish, abalone, and squid dangled to be cooked by the sun along the same laundry line. Interspersed with the seafood, more of the spidery fibers in different shades of color were pinned to dry out like salted fish.

"What the hell is this?" Poe asked in disbelief. She noticed the few dozen monstrosities that looked like human scalp. She pulled herself as far away from the grit and blood drips that collected on the edges of the deck.

Poe had a headache like she'd been stepped on by a monster pachyderm. She wanted to belt out another girly scream that would last for days. But vampire killers and cattle rustlers were supposed to be made of tougher material.

"Fuck!" she cried as her fingers combed through a livid lump on her head. Seasickness had taken hold of her throat and midsection. "Jesus, Mary, and Joseph! That loca clobbered me, and now I'm gonna get scalped!"

"The notorious Poe, awake at last," said a voice from below deck. It was a voice full of gruff and sarcasm. Penny, the ballsiest dog Poe had ever met, crept closer with her tail between her legs.

Poe spotted deeply tanned bare feet a stone throw from where she huddled in chains, uncomfortably near bloody drips, scalps, and seafood. Her dark eyes crinkled around the corners to reveal fire building within. Ferociously Poe flicked her eyes up to brown legs bursting with little black hairs. Her gaze rose higher until she saw a savage tree of a man in below-the-knee shorts, tattered from sea water and exposure to the elements. He had a grizzly beard that was slightly shorter than Moses'. His head must have gleamed in all its bald glory a few weeks ago but now sported an inch thick of dark growth.

She blinked a few times to uncloud her thoughts. Most of his skin bore puncture scars as if he'd been the fresh slab of tuna to go with the dinner party's sake.

A jinn's got me. Or maybe an end-of-the-world loon sniffing for a disciple. His fierce, deranged eyes the color of green rhinestone supported at least one of her theories.

"Whoever you are, I don't got a religion," she said shakily, her mouth dry. "My parents made sure of that, so forget about converting me into your scalp-happy sect."

The man continued his hard stare. His eyes and strong cheekbones jutted out in halleluiah glory from the nest that was his face.

"Who the hell are you?" Poe asked uncomfortably.

"I'm the poor sod who's been duped into bearing you to an undisclosed location two days from now," he answered dryly. He took a half-smoked thin cigar from behind his ear and lit it with a pink disposable plastic lighter. "So I'm supposed to take the long way round."

"Long way around? What?"

"Kill time," he spit out an invisible curl of tobacco on his tongue and ran his eyes lazily over Poe. Awkward and insecure, Poe surreptitiously checked if her brassier was in place. She often had nightmares about throngs of humans and vampires ridiculing her for being on the bounce during her growing years. Her discomfort was due to neglecting to wear a bra until she was twenty-two, and she took up the practice at the behest of a few of Sainvire's allies.

"Oh I get it now," Poe said, massaging a wrist that itched to punch a hole in the man's chest. "This is about the bounty on my head." Without mirth she accused, "You and Passionada will split the reward, right? The upstairs mansion in Beverly Hills for her and the pool house for you?"

Instead of answering, the bearded man trained his searing, no-nonsense eyes on Poe until she looked away, burned. *He has no sense of humor, this guy.*

"Think what you will," he finally said. "Just don't do anything idiotic. I've been quite short-tempered these past ten years."

"Mister, I can't do shit with these things clamped around my limbs," she said between coughs. Her throat was sandy from lack of moisture. "Can I have some water?"

Maybe you need to take another tactic, she told herself. The society of today was one misstep away from Thunderdome and complete chaos. Before her ability to speak forsook her, she added, "Do I detect Scottish in your accent?"

She was again given "the look" and had to bear it until he broke contact by handing her an Evian bottle filled with foggy water. "You have a reputation," he said and let it sit.

Poe prodded him after she'd downed her water. "Yes? What about my reputation?"

"Took me a while to get used to this boat, and I'm not keen on losing her because of something foolish you do." He was shirtless, and his skin stood darkly against the light color of the floor as he sank down cross-legged in front of Poe. "We have two days to funnel away. Two days to kill. That's the official time they're expecting you."

"Them?" she asked calmly.

"Them," he confirmed.

Infuriated knowing he would feed her filtered and twisted information, Poe took deep yoga breaths to calm down. *Anger will accomplish nothing. Take another approach*, said the voice, the rational one in her head that had saved her from so many scrapes.

With sufficient air in her lungs, she began a negotiation tactic. "Mister, I don't know how to swim or drive a boat. I can't tell north from south for that matter. East and west could be straight to the moon or Mars. I don't know," she exhaled, proud that she hadn't stuttered at all. "My skin is burned. My skull is throbbing. I've no choice but to do what you say 'cause it's between you or Orca the killer whale."

She turned her arms and pulled up her sleeves. Her red and browning skin starkly contrasted with her light upper arms.

"My face is pretty badly off, too. I can feel it," she added. "And there's no shade where I am. Could you take off these metal thingies? Or at least consider moving me below deck?"

He didn't speak, but his eyes never left her face. His doggedness was a takedown, a humiliation. Poe was rattled and for once was afraid. *All those fang bites must've made him callous*, she thought. He never turned. When finally he did speak, it was with a smile. But his words froze Poe's heart.

"I have no sympathy with humans who consort with vampires," he said slowly. "Intimately, that is. To me that is lower than being a ruddy vampire."

34

CHAPTER 3

BLUE.

She was surrounded by water that could drown or pickle her for the sea life. The bearded man had tossed her an umbrella, the type that doubled as a walking stick with a sharp point. She seriously contemplated skewering him with it, but she wanted the sunscreen and lip balm he offered her. He had also freed her ankles from their metal bonds and as a bonus handed her a bucket. *How generous. Now I can do my business right under his nose.*

She hadn't said a word to him since he'd told her that she was a stained traitor to the human race for sleeping with a vampire.

Does the whole world know my life story? It happened only once.

She didn't know why his words affected her so much. He was a dirty fisherman and bigoted against good vampires and who knew what else. Occasionally she would turn her head to watch him throw a line or snag wriggling fish. But his words continued to echo with each wave lashing against the bow of the boat where she was chained. The implication that she was a whore and a traitor tore her up.

I'm not any of those things. I've only slept with Sainvire. That one day. Don't my scars prove I'm no traitor? I've done my part. I really have. And besides, in my book Sainvire's a hero.

"Heroes don't fall for nobodies like me," she gritted.

She checked her pockets. A spool of floss, an ink gel pen with a dull metallic tip, mouth guard in case of a fight, and breath-mint spray. In those dentist-free times she had a fear of cavities and a well timed punch in the mouth that could render her toothless. *Thank goodness*, she sighed, discovering the spray contained marinated garlic. It was like acid to vampires, and Sister Ann used to refer to it as holy water. She rewrapped her battered Bad Badtz-Maru wallet. The lurching Pacific Ocean made her nervous.

She felt him watching her from the stern where he steered the boat. He was no doubt sucking on a stale cigar he kept extinguishing every few puffs. Tobacco stunk, and she imagined the smoke floating toward her despite the wind. Foamy spray baptized her face with liquid salt. Her headache subsided to a more tolerable level though her entire body shook imperceptibly from exhaustion and seasickness. She sat rigidly staring at the horizon for what seemed like hours. It was a protest. It was also a way to stave off vomiting.

She'd thrown up four times over the handrail. When her head hung in the effort, she noticed the exterior color of the 60-foot power boat. It was iridescent blue, fluctuating shades of colors as frequently as the sky and ocean. *Chameleon of the sea.*

Penny lay sprawled on her lap, blinking lazily at the salty water that occasionally misted her goateed face. Now and again Poe massaged the coarse milk tea coat of her companion. Penny, quite perceptive for a dog, sensed trouble. The girl who had carried her off instead of leaving her with broken legs for the undead to finish had her everlasting devotion.

From where Poe perched, legs dangling on the triangular tip of the bow with her chin resting on the lowest guard rail, the sinking sun looked enormous. Deep red-orange, the orb spit fire, protesting its banishment from this side of the hemisphere. Poe made a fist as sunspots flickered in her eyes. The man's words still resonated and frustrated her. Sometimes she was just too inarticulate to defend herself. Growing up in solitary from age eight on didn't exactly help.

Her formal education had ended around the second grade, and she went on to the tedious affairs of dodging the undead. The rest of her lessons had been supplemented by a shotgun-toting white nun on the verge of mental collapse and by a six-foot-six black man bent on avenging his murdered lover. Films, books, comics, and old magazines had filled in the cracks. This attack on her morality was new and confounding, and it made her want to crawl inside a conch shell.

Two years ago her neck had carried rope necklaces that would have made Mr. T nervous. She'd whittled them down to two. She tugged at the nylon ropes holding a thin silver whistle and her house key. They indicated change, empowerment. Calluses she'd worked hard to develop also counted as armor yet they weren't strong enough to withstand insult. Baking under the setting sun, Poe wished she had some of her old gadgets to get her out of this jam.

The bearded man's bare feet made very little noise. Penny, her long body strung like a bow, whimpered softly and alerted Poe. *What the heck did he do to my dog?*

"Dinner," he said. He plunked the bowl of fried potatoes and fish and a box of soda crackers in front of her. When she didn't make a move, he squatted to almost eye level with Poe. "It'll get dark soon, and we can't have any lights. There are eyes that never close even in these substantial waters. You've got twenty minutes."

She contemplated a huge strike along the lines of Gandhi and Cesar Chavez. She could have shoved the fried fish up his kazoo. But her cause was not deep enough, and she was fairly empty from hurling cotton candy. As soon as he headed back to the wheel, she began munching on the crackers as they were the safest food for her condition. The meal she gave to Penny who inhaled the food in no time. She poured some water into the empty bowl for Penny to lap up.

He returned ten minutes later with another bottle of murky water and a blanket which he brusquely dropped to the floor. "Wind can be fierce at night. Tuck in that blanket."

Poe took a long look at her captor. She took in the deep scars found even on his rough knee. His body, corded like a fanatical surfer, must have suffered mightily. Whatever beauty those limbs had boasted was forever disfigured by missing flesh. Bite-sized flesh had been chunked off in several places like half-eaten fried chicken. *They didn't just suck his blood. They ate him, too. And he didn't turn.*

The bearded man was no vampire who could function under the sun. She'd met plenty undead, like

Sainvire, that weren't bothered by UV rays. But he wasn't one of them. His chest took in air and exhaled. And unlike Sainvire, this man sweated in the heat.

"Take this," he said, retrieving a bottle of anti-nausea pills from his pocket. "It says take two, but the bottle's expired. I'd take about six if I were you."

When she remained motionless he shrugged and put the bottle down next to her Adidas. Everyone has a trigger, a button that alarmed when pushed enough. Poe's nostrils flared.

"Hey!" she said rather loudly and startled her own ears. He turned around with a strange expression in his green eyes.

"I, I've b-been thinking," she began, kicking herself mentally for stammering. *Speak slowly. Breathe deeply. And don't embarrass yourself.* "Been stewing for hours about what you said. I realize you're the last person whose opinion I should care about since I don't know you. It didn't help that you've chained me up like a sacrifice to some hungry sea creature." *You better stick to reality, Poe, and not* Clash of the Titans*!*

"I figured you out. You're not here to turn me in to the vampires you grumble about so much," she said, her already throaty voice raspier from repeated vomiting. "So maybe you're taking me to Sainvire's people."

"How perceptive of you," he said drolly. "Passionada cashed in all her favors. She asked me to risk my neck and smuggle you out of Venice."

He laughed dryly. "My instincts are right on when it comes to danger. You see, the wee voice in my head told me to skip Venice, one of my routine seafood drops, but I didn't listen. I know there's trouble in the forecast."

"Bummer for you, but worse for me," Poe griped as she lightly felt the lump on her head. She rattled her chains worthy of the Count of Monte Cristo while she was at it.

"They were supposed to go to your house tomorrow and force you away. It was getting too hot for you there, especially since you nearly burned a house down."

Poe stilled herself. *That stupid house again. It was an accident!*

"Word is, a contingent of Newbitt's people is going to thrash the area for renegades, runaways, and chiefly a criminal rustler like you with a price on your head," he said without inflection, though with a hint of accent Poe would still have bet worthless money to be skewed Scottish. "Passionada was set to retrieve you but was warned you would refuse. You made her work easier by going to the boardwalk. Some sweet tooth. The hitch – your guide is expecting you two days from now. So that's why we're drifting."

"You're doing this as a favor," Poe said with a shake of the head, her jaw muscles working. "And they told you to chain me up."

"Listen. My motto is to stay as far away from vampires as I can. And their little helpers. I hate them all equally," he said, his deep voice acquiring a thicker accent. "Hate" sounded like "het."

"Yeah, I can see that," Poe ran her eyes over his chunked body. "Especially since you were the hors d'ouvre at some swanky vamp art opening."

The increasingly dusky skies couldn't hide the livid look on his face. He reached for the dark shirt tucked in his back pocket and put it on self-consciously.

"I'm a fisherman. This is a favor for a friend," he said with ire.

"The gray poison that killed most everyone sure is something, isn't it? It morphed fish into growing hair like John Lennon. What do you do, scalp 'em before you cook 'em?"

A slight crookedness took hold of his wide mouth alone in a sea of beard. "Loads of patrols in the water nowadays. Pirates everywhere—"

"Maybe you'll need my help," Poe said while she extended her wrists. "You wouldn't know it by my size, but I can kick butt."

"That's what I'm afraid of," he said gruffly. "I've bloody seen you flipping truck tires around the neighborhood and abusing trees."

He lives near my parents' house?

He walked away irritably. The bearded man paused to look at the orange-tinged horizon. With what sounded like a grunt of displeasure, he fished out an assortment of keys from his pocket. "'N ddrwg ddrychfeddwl," he said under his breath. "I've gone daft in my age. This is how trouble starts."

I guess I'm not the only one who talks to herself. Or himself. And in a weird language, too.

The hirsute fisherman kneeled before her. He took her left wrist and unlocked the shackle. His large hands felt rough against her skin as he examined angry scratches and bite marks from the dog attack in Venice. From the wrist his gaze traveled upward, quietly locking with Poe's.

"One fetter for tonight and the other one tomorrow morning," he said matter-of-factly, dropping the chains to the floor. He ended the prickly staring match that colored Poe's face like Mercurochrome in cotton. "I need a good night's sleep, and I won't get it with you prowling around concocting ways to toss me overboard like one of your damned Goodyear tires."

Before she could protest, the bearded man added, "Take the bloody seasickness pills before you spray my boat with more of your vomit."

With one hand freed, a smiling Poe lunged for the man's throat, toppling him back.

"You Cro-Magnon Neanderthal son of a bitch!" she hissed. "You think you're doing me a favor by unlocking one of my chains?"

Somehow another trigger had been tripped, and she was pissed. Poe had no intention of spending the night with one wrist chained to the railing. Seeing nothing but caveman, Poe grasped a fistful of beard and punched her captor in the throat, taking the wind out of him. The wheezing man struggled to breathe.

Temporarily losing her fear of the man, Penny began biting indiscriminately.

The bearded man gasped and clutched at his throat, his bushy beard getting in the way. He kicked the dog when it sunk its teeth into his calf muscle and was rewarded with a yelp.

Poe straddled his waist and clouted him on the side of the head saying, "You kick my dog again and I'll end your miserable existence."

Taking advantage of the large man's pain, Poe ruffled through his pocket for the keys and managed to retrieve them. There were at least a dozen keys.

She couldn't for the life of her guess which key fit the lock of her shackle. She was seeing double. The man began bucking, throwing her off balance. Unexpectedly the sudden movements and the rough undulations of the ship further hampered her equilibrium.

The man, coughing violently but with the advantage of longer arms, snatched the keys from her hands. Her stomach sloshed as they wrestled.

"Let go, you fucking caveman!" Poe cried. She tried her best not to spew on both of them. "You have zero rights to chain me up!"

With a roar the caveman snagged the key ring from the five-foot-three-and-a-half lightweight and tossed it toward the stern, a good many feet from Poe's reach. She'd grown an inch from yoga stretches. His longer limbs and stronger upper body strength won the day. It wasn't lost on him that Poe could barely keep her balance from extreme nausea as she seesawed on top of him.

Returning the favor, the bearded man snuck a hand to Poe's insignificant neck and slammed her, back first, to the floor. With one move they reversed positions. His heavier bulk pinned her body and stifled her respiratory tract.

"And you question why I prefer you chained," he rasped, his throat still sore from the well aimed punch.

"Well I don't trust you, either," said Poe with bitterness. "How can I when you chain me up and rant that vampires and all the people that work with them can't be trusted? Barring your retardation, you must know by now that not all undead are evil, right?"

"I know that they shouldn't be ruling over us," the equally bitter bearded man said. "Nor should they be eating us."

"Sainvire and his people are against those things. That's why he's trying to spread Plasmacore among vampires instead of the usual death-bite on human victims." *Or the bite that drives people catatonic for nearly a year and turns them into cattle.*

His eyes twinkled in the diminishing light. He was amused.

"Plasmacore? The synthetic blood?" He smiled and his clean, slightly crooked teeth showed. "Do you know how many vamps scoff at drinking that plasma concoction? It's emasculating to them, and it's nothing but a joke."

"Joke or not, vampires are taking it, and that's good enough for me. Besides, P-core's more potent than blood, and some dead can go without food longer. Some even acquire sun immunity and such."

"So you're Sainvire's trooper 'till the end, eh?"

"Yeah, Caveman. I'm a trooper for Plasmacore, a new food source for vamps," she said, shaking. "If you're implying more than that, I'll slit your cave-dwelling neck tomorrow. I promise."

"You refute the rumor circulating about you two lovebirds? So nothing happened?" he asked, his strange accent reappearing.

Poe could smell the salty perspiration and earth on him. His hairy face was inches from her, and a brawny hand pinned both her arms above her head. His free hand left her neck, and the fingers edged their way to the valley between her breasts down to her hip – to where the top of her panties showed.

"W-what happened between us is none of your business," she said. Her voice dropped deeper in her nervousness. His hardening crotch seemed to be grinding deeper into her olive military pants.

"It's everyone's business, Julia Poe. You should know that by now," he said with a smirk. He slid his free hand under her shirt and felt the underside of her breasts. "When a woman allows herself to be fucked by the dead, she forfeits her reputation forever."

"Chain me up or whatever. Just get your ugly, hairy face away from me!"

His expression sobered, and the palm of his hand ceased its exploration. He realized how close he was to committing something he would never have done under normal circumstances.

"Self-check, boy," he muttered. "Ach a gwyrdro awron?"

"Quit your gibberish, you dirty fucker!" Poe nearly screamed. "I know about the Stockholm syndrome. I've seen Patty Hearst and a dozen other kidnap movies. There's no way I'm going to fall for my captor. So you can just go to hell."

Shamed, he rose off of the girl.

"I apologize for my behavior. I've behaved like an animal. I, I haven't been with a woman in quite a while."

"Don't frikkin' tell me about your love life! I don't give a shit," Poe said with a shaky voice. She pushed herself to a sitting position. "Unlock my wrist, and I might just find it in my heart to forgive you."

Looking dog-eared, the man slowly walked away. Without a word he swooped down to retrieve the keys and coolly placed them in his pocket.

Poe glanced at her dog accusingly.

"Where were you, you stupid mutt? One kick and you let him at me," she said woefully then stuck out her head over the rail and puked.

Shivering and ill from the acerbic taste in her mouth, Poe reached for the bottle of Dimenhydrinate pills and popped ten of them.

"It's simple, child," a stout Sister Ann sighed, sitting precariously on the railing with sawed-off shotguns held in each arm, her habit stained. "You can break your thumb and slip your hand out of the clasp."

"It's the only way. Or you could gnaw your wrist free," Goss agreed, his long dark legs draped over the stern. He maneuvered the wheel with one finger.

"You guys are insane. I'm not going to hurt myself like that."

"Julia, your problem is that you're a quitter," the nun intoned in her Tennessean accent, her wimple blowing in the wind. One blundering seagull bumping into Sister Ann and down into the water she'd have fallen.

"When the going gets tough," Goss said, pole vaulting to the bow. He landed his size seventeen shoe on her chest. "You give up."

The pressure on her torso took her breath away.

"Uh," mumbled Poe. "I've done my share. Rescued hundreds of people," she said, attempting to wrest his foot away.

She could barely breathe.

As another blow landed on her chest, she opened her eyes and awoke. Penny's little feet pounced on her chest a third time. This time she pushed the dog off of her. "Cut it out, Pen! What're you trying to do, kill me?"

Her head hurt, and the nightmare had worn her out. *Must've been the motion sickness pills.* Only the salty tang in the air and the usual fear that invaded in the dark felt familiar. Unearthly green reflectors from her dog's eyes made Penny seem spectral. Poe could hardly suppress a shriek.

Fortunately she didn't make a sound, for somewhere off the boat, near the bow, Poe glimpsed what appeared to be a flash of light. The small conflagration could have been from a lighter or a quick flick of a match. She instinctively knew that Caveman was asleep in his bunk.

"Shhh now, Penny," Poe said almost inaudibly. "You've done a good job waking me up. Now be quiet." She massaged the scant flesh under Penny's chin. It was the dog's second favorite spot after the area behind her ears.

The chain allowed Poe a leeway of about four feet. For assurance she took out the pen, uncapped it, and turned it back pointy-side-down in her pocket. *This is the Old West, and I'm the best shot there ever was.* Julia Poe was not the type to boast about her skills, but she was a natural-born sure-shot.

"I might've taught you how to load and shoot," Sister Ann had once told her, "But the rest is innate. You can hit the target instinctively. You've got a gift, girl. Never seen anything like it."

Her heart sank when she saw her umbrella clear across the starboard, nearly ten feet away. The strong night wind had not only removed her blanket, it had also taken away her best substitute for a weapon.

Quickly Poe extracted the breath-mint spray containing holy water. It would have to do. She positioned herself behind the tarp that covered two barrels of dried fish. Whoever was trying to shimmy the ship was no good. Her gut told her so.

Mom, Dad, don't let them get me and Penny, she said fervently. It was close to the only prayer she knew. *Let me live through my twenty-fifth birthday. If you gotta kill off somebody, the caveman's ready and waiting.*

Gasoline hung thickly in the air, exacerbating her headache.

There were two smaller swift boats sidling against either side of Caveman's vessel she'd taken to calling the Chameleon. The pirates were near enough to thump against the boat if the waves so inclined. Poe could scarcely see, and she prayed the quarter moon would provide more light.

Where the heck is he? We're about to get boarded, and he's more asleep than the dead.

Whoever tried to pirate their way onto the boat didn't try to be quiet. *Do they assume this is just another boat that's out of gas?*

Voices carried in the wind. Ribbons of conversation floated like the lightest of feathers to tease her ears. She heard fragments of curses, snorting, and unpleasant squealing. *Lots of snorting and grunting.*

"I'm hungry," a jocular voice said from one of the boats to the other. "Don't you start without me!"

"Don't worry, I will," answered an amused voice from the portside.

"You better not, man! I want the pick of the litter this time. Lemme drop these babies on the 60-footer.

Then we can chow. I'm sure it's a ghost ship anyway."

"No shit. I've yet to see a live one," the other chortled. "And I've been doing this for six months."

"Stick around. You will," he chuckled. "'Course, all of the action is up north with L.A. upside-down."

The sound of clicking and clumsy tripping filled the air. *They must be ready to board. If I only had my guns*, Poe beefed. Each bullet had been fortified with garlic oil, fatal to vampires. Active chemicals in the pungent cloves prevented regeneration of flesh and caused a severe allergic reaction to the vast majority of vampires. Garlic was undeniably the most effective weapon against the undead besides blunt damage to the heart and decapitation.

She patted Penny's head, sticky from the salty ocean spray, and looked painfully toward the stern where the bearded man reposed below deck. *Wake up, you hairy idiot!*

From the portside she saw something shoot up in the air, limbs extending like a ballerina and landing noisily on another boat. The moon illuminated the shadow of movement, and she thought the acrobatic leaper looked to have the figure of a man. Poe blinked the confusion away only to see the same stunt repeated again and again. Somebody was jumping from vessel to vessel with dramatic flair and dropping objects on her boat.

"Let there be light," a crackling voice said. Several powerful spotlights from both watercrafts popped to life.

Poe staggered and quickly covered her eyes. Explosions of lightning and color stabbed her vision.

She was blinded. She made herself as small as possible, putting Penny before her.

"I know it's cowardly, Pen," Poe whispered in the dog's ear. "But they can't see me right now."

When she was able to open her eyes without tearing up, Poe observed the Trampoline Man scooping what looked to be bodies from the two pirate tugboats and depositing them onto Caveman's boat. The unloading was done quickly and efficiently. The mound on the floor grew.

Please, Caveman, throw me my guns! At times like these Poe felt how vulnerably human she truly was.

The mound, only several feet away, began crumbling and fractioning into individual entities. Clicking noises overwhelmed the night. Trampoline Man had dropped four bodies which were systematically raising themselves from the deck as their damaged bones reassembled in a pattern of clicks. The creatures had holes for mouths that opened and closed as if deprived of air. Their clothes hung like oversized curtains. To say they looked emaciated would be an understatement. They were positively skeletal. Leathery skin and shadows under their eyes enhanced their ghoulish appearance.

"Oh shit," said Poe, unable to control the fear in her voice.

She'd never seen nightmarish creatures like these before. Even her dog could sense that they were sinister, and she whined in fear.

"Go ahead, Revenents," said Trampoline Man. He dangled a piglet by its neck fat. "Sweep up while I have my supper."

"Still think those things can understand you?" scoffed the other man who followed Trampoline Man. "They're worse than dead. They're not sentient."

The Revenents' rubbery legs were as unaccustomed to the seas as Poe. Slow in every way, these creatures walked like they had elephantiasis of the nether organs, and their bones poked out under stretched leathery skin like branches set wrong on a Joshua tree. They weren't quite right.

Their thin frames rattled like bags of marbles as their bodies mended the bones that had broken from their graceless landings. *Rancid bacon, that's what they smell like*, Poe thought as she caught a whiff. Again she fought the bile shooting up her esophagus. *Can't get sick now. Or I'll be dead for sure. Where are you, Caveman? I need my gear!*

One of the creatures couldn't quite rise like the rest for it had but one leg. Instead of skulking the little beast crawled to where Poe and Penny crouched. It was the first to notice Poe. Her breathing became labored as she watched what looked like bony matter with loose, spotty skin gain ground. Poe could almost feel the long, curling nails that looked as if they had been cultured in a Petrie dish with special gangrene sauce.

"Hey, Caveman! Wake the fuck up!" she screamed at the top of her lungs, not caring about being seen anymore. Her call was loud enough to alert the Trampoline Man who popped his head from his associate's boat. He carried two squirming piglets in each arm this time. His chin dribbled blood.

"Herbie," Trampoline Man said with amusement. "Check her out. Can you believe there's a chick on that boat? There's never anyone alive on transports we find."

"Too bad we had us a few pigs already," Herbie said in an Eastern New England accent, his chunky face disappointed at his gluttony. "Ah well. We can share her tomorrow night. Let's see how she goes against the Revenents first. This ought to be exciting like ESPN meets American Gladiator."

"I don't have your dainty, pussy appetite, Herbie. I have a hardy palate. Besides, I haven't sucked on a human in twelve years," Trampoline Man growled. "Seems there's another one in the cabin. I'll go check it out."

"No way, man," cried Herbie. He rubbed his engorged belly. "This is our chance to see a live fight. If you haven't noticed lately, the world is sooo boring, and we're patrolling in the dark. Let them at her."

"She's chained, you fat bastard."

"Only one hand," grinned the bulbous-faced vampire. "A few chunks won't kill her. Then we can have her later. How about it?"

"I don't know why I listen to you. You're a moron. But okay. Just a few nibbles here and there, and then I'm pulling her up."

Poe had no time to spare for her eager spectators. She was too busy stomping on the hand that took hold of her Adidas. She used enough force to break digits. Milky dead eyes looked up at her, and the turkey neck of the androgynous creature shook like Jell-O. Oily hair parted in the middle revealed a skull with onion paper skin, and Poe could see the veiny outline of a grayish-puce brain within. The eyes reserved blinks for once a minute.

"I've never seen anything like this before," Poe said aloud to no one in particular, her old habit too deep-rooted to die. "It doesn't feel pain."

With much aplomb Poe kicked its head like a soccer ball, cracking the neck bone from the spine. By all rights it should have been a goner, but its eyes continued to blink as if nothing untoward had happened. The clink clank of fusing bones sounded almost immediately. Behind it a hoard of three sluggishly walked toward her. One of them had a useless stub for an arm.

Please, Dad, don't let me throw up!

The terrier-mix gnawed on the forearm of the crawling thing on the floor. The one-legged creature was trying to get on its one foot. Surprisingly it succeeded and bounced to balance with every ocean wave.

"Screw this!" she cried, every hair on her body standing up.

Poe extended her unchained hand as near as her attacker's mouth as she could stand. Showing off its three-inch fangs, it snapped at her. She sprayed the holy mint into its mouth and prayed that the wind would not scatter the garlic essence.

"Sheeekeeee. Sheeekeeee!" the cadaver screamed in an expression of agony.

The one-armed clunker, ahead of the others, slipped once in its haste to embrace Poe. Her lipless face bore a permanent vampiric smile that disturbed Poe more than the other.

"That's right, you," she said to Legless who was choking on the spray. Her chest rose and fell at a rapid pace. Poe sprayed it again just in case. It screamed noiselessly and clutched at its throat. Its eyes spelled out PAIN. "Die already."

Poe grabbed a slimy arm, and using leg strength she hurled the body to the edge of the gratings. The dog tore at the skeletal mess on the floor. Poe shooed her pet and dragged the squirming body to the edge of the rails. She kicked it off the boat with her double-knotted shoe as a bon voyage. The big splash did not lighten her spirits.

One by one the clicking bodies approached. If ever there was a time she needed to use the bucket, it would have been then. Armed with a pen and breath spray, Poe took her stand. Three others locked their unblinking opaque eyes on her.

"Hello, bearded guy! If you're not dead yet, you will be soon be if you don't give me my guns. Creeps are headed your way!" Poe yelled. She noticed newly lowered cadavers making their way into the cabin-kitchen area below.

Their bones may have been brittle, but they reformed quite impressively and were as solid as oak as Poe found when she snuck a punch into Plain Ugly's jaw. Her vaporous eyes looked momentarily cross-eyed, but that was all while Poe's fist screamed murder. Not so far behind Plain Ugly was a female in an oversized muumuu unfit for her skeletal frame. She had a mop of greasy red hair and lacked any teeth except for one drawn out fang. Her mouth smacked open and close in anticipation of dinner.

Then there was No Nose who proved to be more limber than the rickety rest. He made a grab for Poe's scarred forearms. Sharp undulations of the boat bided Poe some time as every wave made the creatures pause for balance. Whatever they were, they were shoddily put together.

"This is just a dream. Any minute now Penny and I will find ourselves sitting on our couch watching *Office Space* or *Caddyshack*. Something hilarious," Poe said stupidly to boost her courage.

"Use only your legs, or they'll get you!" she told herself while kicking at the knees of whichever came closest.

No Nose was a grabber. His raw fingertips slid out its last slivers of blackened nails in the process of clawing Poe's shoulder for the second time. He had a way of absorbing blows, even Poe's focused attacks, without complaint. The swifter the blows, the quicker he mended as the clicking sounds demonstrated. *Even Sainvire couldn't fix himself up this quickly.*

"Why don't you just keel over, you dumb goon!" cried Poe as she watched No Nose's friends join the revelry. "Go get 'em, Pen!"

Lathering at the mouth, Penny unleashed more damage. She tore tough chunks of sinewy meat off of the creatures and swallowed them. *Beef jerky treats!* The dog focused on ankles and knees until the undead literally fell on their faces.

"Attagirl, Pen," Poe encouraged. Deep inside Poe was disgusted that her dog had eaten at least two pounds of jerkied flesh. "Try not to gulp them down this time."

Poe kept the undead at bay by tucking her arms close to her body, utilizing round and side kicks. One false move and she'd have been snagged and wrestled on the deck. Chained and vulnerable as she was, she'd have been defenseless once down. A few times she saw her kicks damage ribs, knees, and hip bones to the point of paralyzing the creatures, but they would glue themselves back together.

Bones fused under thin, kite paper skin right before her eyes. *No wonder Trampoline Man dumped them on board to do his dirty work while he had a snack of piglets with his buddy.*

There were too many, and she was getting tired. Her head felt like a giant vacuum was sucking it clean. Eventually the muumuu-wearing automaton figured out that the chain limited the girl's reach. A tug of war arose leaving Poe with boxed-in kicking range and without the use of one arm.

"Shit!" Poe screamed as the wind scattered garlic spray useless. "Come closer then!"

She was near tears. A real honest-to-goodness migraine had crept up on her, and the swell of the seas hindered her footing.

Muumuu had Poe's chain wound around her arm, her long face blank but nonetheless determined. Poe let herself be dragged. "Calm down. Or she'll get you," she said aloud.

The moment Poe's extended right arm was within shooting distance of the creature's face, Poe let out a squirt, catching the long-faced dead in the white of the eye despite the wind. For good measure Poe sprayed the mouth, too. She didn't get to relish the hissing or the smoke indicating that part of Muumuu was melting and sputtering. The dead converged at once on an overwrought Poe. The lack of food and continuous vomiting the past day had left her weaker than usual and ill prepared for the assault.

Can't cry about it now! Gimme some adrenalin, Xena!

She swung around, stuck a pen in No Nose's eye, and followed up with a fist into Plain Ugly's concave chest. Poe, breathing laboriously, kneed No Nose on the side of the head. Despite holy water damage, the redhead creep crawled blindly toward her.

They kept getting up to Poe's dismay. She wanted so badly to cry.

The harassed dog fought bravely alongside Poe. Bereft of the ability to bark, Penny took her courage from biting, but like Poe the mutt was tiring. The silent freaks that occasionally made a sound halfway between a Chewbacca snarl and a humpback whale feeding call were gaining on them.

It was no surprise when Plain Ugly reached down and picked the dog up by the tail like a rat. Penny tried to take a chunk of jerky from her awkward position but failed. The noise that escaped from the dog's mouth injected Poe's thudding heart with dread. The tail, after all, was connected to the spine. Her dog was in pain.

"Penny!" Poe yelled with trepidation. "Hold on for me!"

Left with no choice, Poe turned her back on No Nose, her pursuant whose eye popped back to normal. She made a grab for Penny before Muumuu could sink her teeth into her scruffy neck. The dog tumbled to the floor and banged her head along the railing.

"Thank you, Warrior Princess!" she said with a gasp and picked up the pen she'd lost. Poe grunted angrily and plunged it into No Nose's heart. Blinking in wonder at the force of the pen that was now buried into the undead's chest, she stared as its body spasmed.

"Oh no you don't," she said, nearly in tears. She pulled out the pen and heard a sucking sound. Stooping low on the ground, Poe squirted holy water into the wound. To her wonderment the thing on the floor twitched, beating the deck with his feet and arms until he expired.

Before she could exhale with relief, Plain Ugly tackled Poe to the ground. Her screams were furious in the night.

"Get off of me!" Poe shrieked.

A blinded Muumuu, who still had Poe's chain curled around her arm, yanked Poe's right hand painfully upward. With only one limb free, Poe aimed the holy water into the mouth of Plain Ugly who sat on her like a couch. He sputtered from instinct, but the spray was empty.

"Oh no!" Poe said in despair. She pressed the spray button once more, but only air gasped out. Hoping a piece of garlic clogged the spray, Poe tried again. She got more of the same.

Plain Ugly, seeing no immediate threat, backhanded Poe with a rotting hand. Without further ado he lowered his gray half-stacked teeth down to Poe's cheek. Before the fiend could partake of her flesh, Penny the dog lunged on Plain Ugly's Sequoia tree bark neck.

Plain Ugly battled the dog. The chain entangled, the slack tightened, and each movement bruised Poe's wrist. It was like being weighted by an anchor during a boxing match.

Muumuu wrestled Penny from Plain Ugly, tearing off the dog's collar and tossing her into the water. Poe cried as she witnessed her dog fall overboard.

Poe was dizzier than ever.

Muumuu captured a leg. No matter how much she fought, Poe couldn't free it. She closed her eyes tightly as the monster opened wide, her one yellow fang doubling in length for a piece of thigh. Her olive army pants gave the ogre a struggle, however. Plain Ugly bit her cheek and proceeded to suck. His reeking breath made Poe want to cry.

It hurt. She could taste her death in the drizzle of rain she'd only just noticed.

Like watermelon-flavored shaved ice in the summer, a most pleasant thing occurred. Poe heard gunfire, albeit shrouded in a silencer.

And the archangel swept down to her rescue.

Equipped with a gun muted with a silencer, he shot Poe's cannibalistic friends in the back, destroying their moldy organs until they slumped dead on top of her.

"Sainvire?" Poe asked disbelievingly while half-submerged in the bodies of the truly dead. *Is it him? Same height and dark coloring.* Her migraine was making her see double.

He didn't say a word.

Completely undone and nearly weeping from gratitude, Poe mustered a smile for the dark-haired seraph with a glowing face.

"How's your cheek?" he asked, gently wiping blood from the one-fang bite.

Poe's smile vanished. His voice pricked her ears. Without the halo of hero veneration, she studied the face that seemed to shine as if a candle was directly lit under his nose.

"Well are you alright then?" he repeated, sounding irritated. Since she didn't answer, he dragged the bodies near the edge of the railing. The man took a clean swipe off of their scalps and gave them a kick until they rolled off the boat.

"Clear your head, woman. I'm not bloody Sainvire," he grumbled, offended.

His voice. That odd accent. He sounds like…

"Caveman?" asked Poe incredulously.

Upon closer examination of fresh shaving nicks, she noticed that his face glowed. He appeared unearthly because everything about him was dark, except for his cheeks and chin, unbleached by the sun.

"That would be James Maclemar to you," he said with a frown. He selected the correct key and unlocked her restraints.

"Where the hell were you?"

"Sorry. I'm a deep sleeper."

Poe was speechless.

"I've brought your gun," he said, reaching for the Ziploc'ed Glock tucked behind his back. Almost everything in her pack was sealed in plastic. The light drizzle was threatening to turn into rain.

Before he could hand it to her, Maclemar found himself zooming thirty feet up in the air and tersely dropped into the chilly water by a sour-faced Trampoline Man. Within seconds the jumping wonder returned with his pig-eater companion in his arms. Both glared furiously.

"Lucky for you. We have a few more Revs in our boats," said Trampoline Man.

Just looking at the pair of thugs wearied Poe. She'd had enough. She was starving, worn out, highly confused by James Maclemar's make-over, and devastated by her dog's watery death. Before the two vampires could hurt her, Poe spoke.

"Hold it, boys," she said steadily. "Hold off trying to chomp on my neck. I'd like you both to take a good look at my face. Look familiar?"

If Passionada hadn't been lying about her fugitive status, then Poe thought she could bide her time until she was strong enough to take on the two bozos harpooning her with their eyes.

"You're killing time, gel. I got your numba," the roundish undead with a New England accent said, batting away the fish and scalp found hanging slapdash on the boat. The mound of recently sliced head parts he booted into the waters.

"You will be our dessert after all," seconded Trampoline Man as he took a step toward her. "Like it or not."

"Hold up. This is the face that can make all your dreams come true," she said quickly as he took another step closer. "Recognize this scar?" She traced the five-inch scrape job from forehead to cheek. "Beverly Hills mansion, unlimited cattle…"

"Oh shit, Herbie," Trampoline Man exclaimed. He smacked his forehead with an open palm. "This is the cattle rustler everyone's been looking for. For like two years. The one who disfigured Pretty Boy Trench and stole our Downtown food reserve."

"We can't be this lucky. No way." said Herbie with a slight hesitation. "The elusive Julia Poe, cattle thief and Sainvire's whore? We're going to be master vampires, man. No more boat patrol for us!"

"Um, excuse me," Poe interjected, seething. She massaged her bruised wrist slow-like. "I'm not Sainvire's whore."

"Whatevah you say, gel," Manitoba giggled then turned to Trampoline Man. "Ain't she small? Thought she would be a six-footah at least."

"It's all propaganda so Trench won't look like a pussy."

"Yup. And she don't look so bad even with the scah," said Manitoba as he examined her with a critical eye. "Sainvire could always spot the diamond in the rough. I hear his new girlfriend's a looka. A masta vamp from Nevada. This girl's hootas ain't bad."

Poe's eyes narrowed from the conversation. Fatigue exited her body the more insults they threw her way. *And what's this about Sainvire's new girlfriend?*

"Um, excuse me, but don't talk to me," she said, grinding her teeth, "like I'm not standing in front of you."

"Oh yeah? What are ya gonna do about it? You're gonna do more of that kung fu shit?"

A spiteful uppercut from Poe and a delectable kick in the groin quickly erased Herbie's smug grin. Judging by the pain registering on his chubby vampiric face, Manitoba wasn't as gifted in healing as the Revenents.

"Yup! That kung fu shit."

Trampoline Man she attacked in the knee with enough force to break a cement block in half. By the third pounce Poe heard the sweet sound of cracking.

"That's how I like it," Poe said happily, her smile dwindling.

She gave it all she had, succeeding in pulping faces and breaking limbs. But since she had no holy water handy, Trampoline Man and Manitoba, the piglet-eating duo, were far from dying permanently. Her blows became stunted as her anger and adrenaline dissipated and the new batch of Revenents assembled themselves. Every bruise, cut, and sunburn screamed "time out."

Such was just the moment Trampoline Man was waiting for: A chink in the glass. As Poe prepared to deliver a blow to his good leg, Trampoline Man squatted low, launched into the air, and disappeared.

"Oh shit," she said testily, looking up into the dark evening sky. The boat flanking hers seemed to be empty.

A haze of movement teased her peripherals. A great hand grabbed a fistful of hair from behind and lifted her the few feet in the air the slack of her shackles allowed. It was a rocky ride as Trampoline Man balanced on one leg.

"Bad move, girl," he said, his face contorted in antagonism. "Now I'm going to have to hurt you." He threw her against the anchor and enjoyed watching her squirm from the pain of hitting solid metal. "Manitoba, you alright there, man?"

Manitoba's face oozed with tar blood where Poe had targeted his veins especially well. He had trouble getting back on his feet.

"Fuck this, man," he said. "Trench ain't getting her. I'm going to personally drain the little bitch."

"You're willing to give up a life as a master vampire? Cattle of your own?" Trampoline Man asked his hot-tempered friend.

"Yup, easy. Politics is so fucked up on the mainland anyway. Don't wanna be no part of it. 'Sides, I'm a quarter black, and you know how shitty we get it in the new realm. Janitor, incinerator, ass wiper," Manitoba said with a wince. He wiped his eyes clear. "Guess you can say I've taken a liking to swine blood. There's nothing like vampires that don't burn in the sun and the open sea. We've got more choices than some." He shoved the Revenents out of the way.

"Let's do it then. Heads or tails?"

"Heads."

Trampoline Man took a shiny half dollar from his pants pockets. Poe didn't know if there was any fight left in her. She was so tired and bruised that all she could do was watch with detachment as the two vampires flipped for the first suck. She licked ocean, rain, and blood from her lips.

I'll fight them when they get near me. Maybe by then I'll get my grit back to beat the shit out of them.

The tall jumping frog tossed the coin and caught it in his palm. Poe's full lips trembled as Trampoline Man slapped the coin onto his left hand, palm down.

"Shit. It's heads," he announced not so happily. "Better make sure to leave enough for me."

"You know me, buddy," Manitoba laughed. "I'm accommodating and generous to a fault." He met Poe's eyes as she crouched tiredly on the floor. "I'm talking about my buddy here, not you, gel. You. I'm gonna need you to strip to your skivvies now. That G.I. Joe dyke look isn't to my taste."

Herbie's words wound her mettle into gear. With as much dignity as she could, Poe rose to her feet, her nostrils flaring.

"The only one stripping around here is you, Stay Puft man."

"Timid words. Too bad I can't take them seriously, pink pants."

Poe, shaking from the horrendous evening, made fists. "Get ready to die, worm. And you, too."

Both men cackled at her threat.

"And how exactly are you going to do that?" Trampoline Man asked with a snort.

Poe had no idea how to answer, but a solid object thrown between her shoulder blades caused her to curse uninhibitedly.

"She loves me, this gel," said Manitoba. "Wants me to give her a lap dance or sumfin."

The two vampires continued to guffaw and titter. They didn't see or hear the object that the ocean had spit out.

A smile slowly formed as Poe noticed the object that hit her. Between her legs lay her salvation.

"I'm going to waste precisely two bullets on you both. I'll shoot you smack in the center of the heart. Then I'm going to lay to rest the walking jerky chained up on your boats."

The sniggering duo slapped their knees at the girl's statement.

"And how are you gonna do that, gel?" asked Herbie.

"Maybe she's mentally ill or something," said Trampoline Man heartily. "Are you going to use your fingers as a pretend gun?"

"Nope," Poe said with a sunshine smile reaching down. "I'm going to use my very own 9mm Glock."

With a smug smile Poe reached for the sopping object on deck and tore it out of the Ziploc bag. Quickly but with precision she pierced the hearts of both Trampoline Man and Manitoba. Bullseye.

———

She awoke nestled between a piglet and a dog.

Poe would have dismissed her bed partners as figments of her dreams but for the rather low cabin ceiling that looked like it was getting vodka shaken. She reached for the expired anti-nausea medication conveniently placed on the bolted bed stand. Swallowing a few tabs with only her spit to help them down, Poe clamped her eyes shut and waited for the uneasiness to dissipate.

"Come here, Chops," Poe said in a raspy voice. She hoisted the rosy piglet with a single perfectly round black dot on its rump. She'd named the little critter in her dreams. "You, too, Pen," she added when her dog complained of favoritism. The dog nearly ate it. If it weren't for Maclemar, Penny would have been lost at sea.

Both critters stank.

She ached all over and suffered from motion sickness. Two days since she'd had her last mouthful of cotton candy. Her stomach was empty, and last night's debacle was no dream.

After flushing the two boats filled with chained up Revenents, she and Maclemar had discovered a snorting piglet with a curly tail hiding under a pile of life preservers. The moment Maclemar had transferred gasoline pilfered from the two boats, he fired up his engine and headed for their destination. Maclemar, immovable, ordered her down to the cabin for some shut-eye. Poe had been too tired to protest.

"Where is that weirdo taking us?" Poe asked the pig who had taken quite a liking to the rip on her mom's Clash t-shirt. "I gotta get off this boat. I don't know about you two."

Within fifteen minutes Poe was up and about, examining the tiny cabin-slash-kitchen. On a redwood shelf were dog-eared books consisting mainly of classic American writers.

"Vonnegut, Thoreau, Conrad, Hemingway, Steinbeck, Faulkner, Twain, Wharton…wow," read Poe. "My folks have the same stuff on their bookshelves at home. Maybe Caveman's not such a Neanderthal after all."

"Much thanks then," said a dry voice from the entrance. "Suppose I ought to be flattered."

She colored, and she watched the man warily as he walked down the steps. He carried two freshly gutted sea bass. As coolly as she could, Poe put on her damp sneakers.

"Breakfast will be ready in about twenty minutes," Maclemar pronounced.

What do I say to someone who chained me up and molested me? Something neutral, I suppose. He's the only one that knows how to drive a boat. And he did throw me a gun while doing butterfly strokes in the choppy ocean.

"Do you want me to go on deck?"

"You can do what you want. If it gets too smoky and fishy down here, I suggest you do," he said with a shrug. Poe watched his long, well designed fingers dice up a small red onion and five hefty potatoes with their skins intact and throw them in a deep iron pot. In a large skillet he poured a generous amount of olive oil and arranged the two fish comfortably side by side. He squeezed some lemon on top of the nicely browning fish and covered them with a handful of dill. The fisherman had quite an array of potted herbs scattered about the cabin.

The smell made her eyes water, and her empty belly began speaking in tongues. There was nothing Maclemar could do to force her out of there. To occupy her mind she decided to harass the cook.

"Are you Irish? Or English?" she pursued once more.

"Nope and nope," he said while moving the potatoes around with a wooden spatula.

"Well?"

"Hmm? Well what?"

"What are you? You're not American. Your accent's a little off."

"That's nice of you to notice, but I've met plenty of Americans with more varied accents." He turned his head to give her a meaningful look. No matter where she went she seemed to get a civics lecture of some sort. He was correct, though. Her grandfather had a slight accent, and he was an American. "If you must know, I'm Welsh. From Wales."

"Oh. Where's that?" Poe asked, self-conscious about her ignorance in geography and her tendency to generalize when it came to touchy personal questions.

"That's part of the UK. The 4th slice they hardly talk about. It's west of England."

"Would there happen to be mines in Wales?"

"Yes, there are. I'm afraid we're known for that. But let me assure you that my country is magnificent with unforgettable landscape and people. "

"Yeah? Well can you name me some world renowned Welsh people then?" "Right," he said. He pulled at the beard that was there no more while pondering the girl's question. "There's T.E. Lawrence."

"Dunno him."

"He's Lawrence from *Lawrence of Arabia*."

She nodded. "I saw the movie. Extremely long but good. Who else?"

"What about Dylan Thomas?"

"What about him?"

The fisherman expelled a heavy breath. "He was just one of the greatest poets that ever lived."

Poe shrugged her shoulders.

"Bloody Americans," he mumbled under his breath. "Pissing on heaven under their feet."

"What did you say?"

"I said, how about Richard Burton?"

"Oh I know him," Poe said. "I've seen sixteen movies with him in it. Go ahead. Ask me about movies and movie stars 'cause chances are I've seen most everything they ever made. Including their early smut stuff."

"I beg your pardon?"

"Nothing. Never mind." Poe waved his question away. She wasn't very discerning with movies. She watched anything she could get ahold of. *Anything*.

"Well I thought you sounded a little like the cast of *Trainspotting*," she changed the subject as Name-the-Welsh was going nowhere. She perused his jaw which looked almost greenish from emerging stubble.

"You wouldn't be wrong there, either. My parents immigrated to Glasgow when I was twelve. They were both professors at the University. Then for a time I lived with my grandparents in London so the accent's a tad screwed."

"Um, yeah. So what were you doing in America when the world got poisoned?"

"I was getting my Doctorate in American Literature."

"So that's why all the books," she said, waving her hand at the shelves. "I hardly see any Shakespeare or Dickens in your collection."

"The British could be a bit snobbish about literature," Maclemar said, wiping his hand with a rag. "But I'll tell you something. The most sincere, most poignant novels I have ever read are those penned by American writers. Less bullshit and fluff. Give me Steinbeck, Hemingway, and Vonnegut anytime." His eyes shone with the joy of defending his course of study.

"Well I read a couple of English stories that made me cry. They were so good."

"Oh? What were they?"

"*Silas Marner* and *Goodbye, Mr. Chips*," Poe offered with a lump in her throat. She had read them because they were two of the thinnest books in her parents' collection.

"Aye. Those are good books," he concurred. "They squeezed a good amount of liquid from my eyes as well."

"I agree with you, though. Steinbeck and Hemingway rule," said Poe who shook her head at the surprise in Maclemar's eyes. "Yes, Mr. Caveman. I read, too. Whatever I get my hands on."

"Good for you then."

"So where are you taking me, Maclemar?" Poe asked. She cleared her throat.

Maclemar scraped the steaming potatoes onto four plates and likewise divided the fish. With care he plunked down a plate where Penny sat, still distrustful of him. The piglet rested her little bottom in a corner and waited for her own plate. The third plate he handed to Poe.

"Tabasco?" he asked Poe, who shook her head in the negative.

She watched him douse his plate with over a dozen hits of soylent green hot sauce. He paused before taking a bite of the somewhat raw potatoes and answered, "Right. We're going to New Brighton State Beach south of Santa Cruz. Sainvire's people are hiding out there for now. And oh, your backpack and guns are under the bed."

"Thanks," she said.

After the first bite of the plain but delicious meal, Poe couldn't help slide the last of the food on the plate into her mouth. She didn't mind that some of the bits were still underdone.

Like nothing had ever happened between them, Poe and Maclemar acted like old mates on a ship. It was easier to shut out the unpleasant past rather than bring it up to mutual disadvantage. As a peace offering Poe pulled out a bag of colorless cotton candy from her pack to share for dessert. She snuck looks while he ate fluffy sugar. *Maclemar's pretty good looking. If Sainvire has a girlfriend, I wouldn't mind sailing with Maclemar for a time.* The thought wrenched her heart.

"What were those things last night?" Poe asked, surreptitiously rubbing off grease from her fingers on a beaded Indian pillow.

"They're called Revenents," answered Maclemar, who was in the grips of an unofficial staring contest with the piglet. "They were once blood cattle, dying from iron and vitamin deficiencies from excess blood tapping. Eventually they stopped eating. Because they were no longer useful, newly turned vampires that had never had a go at a live human were allowed to finish them off by ingesting whatever was left of their blood as rewards. Keep in mind that some of these younger undead had never bit through anything but straws to suck on refrigerated bottled blood. It was a rather big production. Then some of these bodies started coming back to life, brain dead and completely untrainable. They died hungry, and they came back ravenous. They'll eat any living flesh before them."

He tossed the cotton candy stick to the wriggling pig. "As you saw last night, they're only good for sweeping and flushing out. The whole thing's quite blood curdling, but there we are."

"They were effective enough," Poe shivered, remembering how close she came to being consumed. "If they had two or three more on deck, Penny and I would've been chopped liver."

Maclemar's brow furrowed, his gaze lost in the small porthole with a view of the aquamarine ocean. Poe took the opportunity to study his profile. His prominent cheekbones gave his face character while his eyes, jewel green and intelligent, disqualified him from being a Cro-Magnon throwback like she'd once accused him of being. If ever the bottom half of his face followed the same brown hue as the rest of his body, Maclemar would have been considered good looking.

His lips, though wide, weren't as full as Sainvire's.

They were both tall, dark men, but they couldn't have been more different. Sainvire had a broken body and a scar on his upper lip that disfigured the nobility of his face. His shoulder was misshapen from a wound he'd attained trying to defeat Franco in Spain. Maclemar was a perfect specimen of a healthy male with the exception of bite chunks on his flesh.

"Julia," he said, still looking out of the porthole. "If you want to see a school of dolphins, you had better go on deck at once."

"Dolphins?" Poe said stupidly. "Flipper? I'm there!"

She paused mid-step and looked back at Maclemar who was in the process of gathering the dirty dishes. "Um, Maclemar, call me Poe. I don't much fit the name Julia anymore."

CHAPTER 4

SHE KICKED WITH HER feet as nobly as she could in such an unflattering position. Poe, down to her skivvies and supported by an orange inflatable tube, tried to keep up with both Maclemar and her expert water trotter of a dog. Even Chops, occasionally paddling in circles to show off, did a better job. It was the price of never learning how to swim. Her pack contained a few guns and knives, decade-old candy bars, two packets of squished cotton candy, night vision goggles, junk, toiletries, and spare clothes dryly ensconced inside two plastic garbage bags.

The unhealed bites and scratches on her body stung. She felt the sort of pain she hadn't practiced for, the sort of pain that proved to be vastly different from pounding a tree.

Buck up. At least they'll heal quickly from the salt water, said the voice in her head.

Maclemar swam effortlessly, his marked arms cutting the water in powerful strokes. Occasionally he would tug Poe's dawdling floatie along, and the break gave her time to hawk out remnants of salt water accidentally swallowed.

"We can't dock at any pier. Someone would see us," he had told a sour Poe earlier. He chose a secluded cove with more trees of different species than sand. "We've got to drop anchor a mile then swim the rest of the way."

And the mile seemed like swimming the English Channel tenfold. "The hell with this. We've been going for thirty miles, it seems," Poe grumbled. "I'm dying from hypothermia."

"We're nearly there, woman. Can't you see how close the trees are?" He tugged at her tire floatie more aggressively.

They finally reached the narrow shore. Poe lugged the garbage bag behind her in the pebbly sand, and she coughed the salt water out of her lungs. The ground stung her pruned feet, proving the northern shore to be harsher and colder than its southern counterpart. She was winded and out of breath, and the vibrant tire float still hung about her waist. "That felt more like a billion miles," she said to Penny.

Poe was so tired and heavy-limbed that she'd forgotten about her state of undress. Like most of her clothes, her underthings were predominantly black. The cotton panties contrasted sharply with skin untouched by the sun.

She pursed her lips the moment she felt eyes watching her. Poe wasn't exactly ashamed of the bruises, lacerations, and gun shot scars that marked her body. But she wasn't proud of them, either.

"Hey," she said. She turned to Maclemar who stared his fill of her shivering body. "Could you not look at me? Because you're pissing me off."

"Right. Can't blame a guy," he said without guilt. "Haven't seen a woman half-naked since I was taken." He shook his head from the vision of Poe in black bra and panties dripping in sea water. Her tapered waste, full breasts and luscious posterior called wildly to his celibate body. He'd never seen any woman so cut and so deliciously supple at the same time.

"Why don't you bother Passionada then? She seems partial to dogs."

"No need to get testy," he said, raising an eyebrow. His eyes continued to inspect her. "Passionada's a sweetheart."

"For your information, Passionada slammed me over the head, and I still got the bump and the headache to prove it. If you don't quit eyeballing me, I might just have to beat the shit out of you to teach you some manners, you damn pervert."

"If you're self-conscious about the scars, don't be," Maclemar said matter-of-factly as if he'd read the girl's mind. "They're quite alluring."

Poe touched the deep scar above her bra and remembered a vengeful vampire's hook lifting her by way of her breast. "Glad you think so, kilthead, but there was nothing alluring about the way I acquired them. If you want to talk about scars, then let's talk about yours."

"You can change here," Maclemar said. He pointed at a clump of cypress trees, and his dark blue boxers dripped seawater. The scars on his body shamed him. An awkward silence fell between them. He tore his own garbage bag and pulled out some items. "Here's an extra towel for you and the dog."

His eyes politely stayed on her face

"Thanks," Poe said. She accepted the towels. For once it dawned on her that she might have a smidgeon of sex appeal. Or Maclemar was just desperate for warm female flesh. Never really taking her looks seriously, Poe had assumed she was boyish and quite possibly cute, but that was all. Her facial scar prevented any hopes of entering post-apocalyptic beauty contests. What she didn't know was her ignorance of female enhancing items like make-up, blow dryers, and curling irons endeared her to Sainvire and to men like Maclemar. She was a natural beauty, understated and humble. Her body had filled out with relatively healthy food and plenty of exercise. Rigorous training sculpted her body into something strong yet womanly.

"I'll dress over there, I guess," he said with a nod toward a grove of birch trees.

"Hey, Maclemar," she said, sounding curious.

"Yes?"

"Are you going back to your boat after you drop me off?"

"Yeah. That's as far as my debt to Passionada goes," he answered. He was drinking in Poe's near nakedness one last time.

"Okay then. See you in a bit," Poe said with a sardonic smile that showed her thoroughly flossed and fussed-over white teeth. He turned away but not before she saw him redden. *Imagine. A grown man like Maclemar blushing because I smiled at him.*

Every rock, leaf, and piece of bark her Adidas trod on perturbed her. She credited her paranoia to being a city girl lost in the wilderness.

It's Sainvire. He's got you so jumpy. Don't think about him anymore, and focus on not getting ambushed. Think of the lives in your hands. Penny, Chops, and the Welshman.

"This is a lucky sign," Poe said with forced cheer, fishing out two sticks of gum from the pocket of her blue straight-leg Dickies. She handed a stiff piece of Orbit Wintermint gum to Maclemar who crouched tensely behind a sage bush.

"Thanks," he said with a nod. "This'll take me a while to chew. Just to get it soft."

He'd changed into dark jeans and a green t-shirt. After hunching over for an hour, they felt the weather in the shady forest turn chilly. He slipped on a black hooded sweatshirt and warmed his cold palm against his thigh.

"You look super-grim, Maclemar," Poe whispered, refastening her shoulder holster and rechecking the firearms she had positioned on different parts of her body. She slid out both wrist sleeves that held small but lethal throwing knives slick with garlic oil. Once satisfied she put on a black zippered pullover, and she looked like a smaller version of Maclemar. She left it unzipped.

"I don't like when guides are late." He gazed at her chest then looked away. "In my experience it bodes nothing pleasant."

"He's only half an hour late," Poe shrugged, looking down at her shirt. *Really, there's nothing to see. I'm wearing a bra for Pete's sake.* It was the second time he'd looked at that part of her anatomy. *What's up with that?* Peevish, she tied up her damp shoulder length hair with one of the many black bands around her wrists. They had walked over a mile to get to that spot. "Probably lost in the forest. Must be thousands of trees here."

The thought of getting left behind in the vast forest didn't sit well with her at all. Her sense of direction, though poor to begin with, was Kryptonited by verdant nature.

He didn't say a word, just pressed his lips together then snuck another look at her chest.

"Do I have bird crud on my shirt or what?" Poe asked rather severely.

Maclemar's mouth twitched on the sides. Shaking his head, he quickly explained, "Ah now. Don't misunderstand my lingering admiration for your t-shirt as something predatory. Just wondering if you actually listen to the Ramones or you just found the shirt somewhere."

"I grew up listening to the Ramones and a bunch of other bands like the Pixies and Pavement," Poe said, insulted. The fire in her eyes ebbed, however. "They're my mom's favorite bands."

"I assume she liked the Clash as well, seeing that you wore that shirt yesterday."

"Yup. These t-shirts were hers." Poe gently smoothed the front of the Ramones shirt that was far from black from frequent wear.

"She had great taste in music," Maclemar said. His green eyes were sincere.

"Thanks. I always thought so," Poe said. "She was a terrific artist, you know. Neon sculptor. That's what she was."

Poe gripped her Walther PPK and pressed it against her cheek. *Please, Mom and Dad, look after the four of us. Yes, I've changed my mind about Maclemar. He's a bit of a perv, but he's alright.* She took a deep whiff of fragrant forest air until she felt a calm descend like meditation for vicious killers.

Violent yoga she called it. Her seven chakras were long past purifying, tainted by her past kills and future destructive behavior. Her soul was too craterous for saving. She knew this, but she didn't want to give up on salvation.

So Sainvire has a girlfriend, Poe thought. The news hurt like lime juice on broken skin. *But what the hell*. It had been two years since they'd made love in her underground bunker. The vampire had probably forgotten about her.

She eyed Maclemar who looked tensely about him. He was leaving her after the guides picked her up. For some reason she didn't want the man to go. He was a good cook and a lover of literature. *You get attached so easily*, the voice in her mind told her. Poe didn't know what came over her, but she asked the Welshman the same question she'd asked Sainvire who'd slipped from her. "Maclemar, do you think I'm pretty despite the scar on my face?"

Maclemar turned to her with a frown on his face. "Are you serious? You're asking me this now when we're supposed to be in silent mode?"

Her dark eyes wide, Poe nodded. She was feeling insecure. "Well, Sharren, I think you're one of the most attractive women I've ever met in my life. The scar on your face doesn't take away from your unique features. You have nothing to worry about."

Poe expelled a breath of relief. "Thank you, Maclemar. Would you, um, mind kissing me since, um, you're leaving and all?"

Maclemar couldn't believe what he was hearing. Though danger lurked, he cupped the back of Poe's neck with his large hand and kissed her sensuously parted lips. His tongue delved inside her mouth, coaxing her inexperienced tongue to dance with his. Poe remembered Sainvire's cold kiss and couldn't help comparing the two experiences. Maclemar's warm tongue left her breathless.

Her eyes remained closed long after Maclemar ended the kiss. When she opened them James Maclemar was smiling down at her. "How was that, my love?"

Poe rolled her shoulders and shook her head. "It was nice. Been a while."

"Since your lover, Sainvire?"

"He wasn't my lover. It was one day," Poe sighed. "We made love exactly three times. In one day. That was the extent of it."

"Sainvire's a fool," said Maclemar, and he continued scanning.

The fallen cypress where they took cover was double torsoed and quite intact, a genuine twin tree downed by disease and its own heavy weight. Brambles and bushes sprung out along its limbs, giving it a second life. It was the pre-arranged spot.

Poe's trigger finger was poised, anticipating. Maclemar calmly peeked between mint-colored shrubs that leaned lazily against the fallen tree, an Arminius Windicator revolver in his hand and Poe's rifle on the floor within easy reach. The American Lit scholar was no munitions expert. She could discern that fact without any effort. Granted he had shot those Revenents the night before, but he had been not five feet from where they stood. And they had moved terribly slowly.

A six-shooter? What's he thinking? We have tons of guns to choose from. Just ransack every other house, and he'd find something that can shoot more than six rounds.

The rectangular barreled gun was attractive and powerful but useless against a dozen vampires. *He'd have to carry two or three of those things to have an even keel with swift-footed undead. He and Morales should get together.* The rustler, her friend, was also fond of useless guns. The thought of the time it took to reload those things brought on another migraine. She made a mental note to educate the scholar about firearms when it was safe to talk again. *But the man sure can kiss.*

A heavy bout of apprehension, the kind that came with a tummy ache, fell upon her.

"Put that thing away and use this," Poe whispered as quietly as she could. With brashness she peeled the six-shooter from his hand and stuffed it in the band of his pants right above the zipper. Flicking the safety off, she placed her reserve Beretta into his palm.

His leaf-colored eyes narrowed and spit negative sparks her way. The man was doubtless irritated. "Gah, Sharren! Hasn't anyone told you that it's not polite to handle a man's gun without asking first? And it's rude to shove it where it could de-man him?"

Who's Sharren? Before she could ask or explain herself, Maclemar put a finger to his lips. Penny's throat emitted a low growl. Poe tapped the dog's nose to keep it from making any further noise. The traumatized piglet sat quietly munching on bark next to the mutt. Chops had become their shadow and was never far from Poe or the dog.

Crunching leaves and the rub of trodden earth alerted both humans. From the sound of it, more than one set of footsteps was approaching.

Quietly parting the curtain of vines that knitted itself on the dead tree, Poe held her breath. Two men and a woman casually strolled their way. Poe squinted to get a better look through the shadow of the opulent tree canopy.

The one in front, a short-necked, deeply tanned man in skin-tight bicycle shorts, took vigilant steps. He carefully avoided trudging on any overlarge protrusions on the ground. With a number 94 tacked on his Kevlar vest, his tour de force outfit made him an easy target. His tadpole belly stretched over tight green spandex that didn't quite blend him into the natural landscape. He held two 9mm Browning pistols with the barrels pointing skyward in his sweaty hands like they were knives.

Behind loomed a taller man with a whoosh of blonde hair that looked as if it had never mated with the bristles of a brush. Though quite slim, he had a belly of one who enjoyed regular doses of Chivas Regal and Johnnie Walker. His searching eyes never missed even a fallen acorn. His hairy paws clutched a shotgun, nicked and discolored from use. From the way his brows drew together like two check marks, the man appeared angry at the world.

The tall woman in the rear kept a few paces back. Her slow, assured steps broached a confidence only a person in her later years could cultivate. She was the type a smart bloke would like to have on his side. Despite a fawn-colored Stetson that kept her profile in the dark, Poe's stomach muscles clenched.

Do I know her?

The woman's manner of walk, self-assured and easy, nagged at her memory. Unlike her tense companions, she exuded calm. Not until the woman tipped back her hat and trained her serene brown eyes to the island of ivy where Poe peeked from did the light of recognition flicker.

Maple.

This was Maple, the middle-aged vampire with arms that transformed into powerful mallets at will. Her unassuming, schoolmarm façade had been the death of many a foe. She was one of Sainvire's most trusted comrades. Maple loved the human scientist called Perla who had helped develop Plasmacore.

With one dignified wave Maple smiled at the figure hiding behind foliage. *X-ray vision*? Poe slowly blinked three times then stood up.

"Whaddya think you're doin', Sharren?" asked Maclemar roughly, his accent thickening. He captured her wrist bulging with knife and sheath and pulled her down. The two men pointed guns in their direction.

Poe resisted Maclemar's hold. She looked down at her companion whose face registered anxiety and gently tugged her hand free.

"The name's Poe, not Sharren. Maple's a friend," she said confidently. "We're safe with her."

Unsure, Maclemar didn't move and pointed his gun from behind the small bush at the two men.

"Maple," Poe said with care. She scrambled over the tree trunk and walked with a quiet smile to where Maple stood. Penny and Chops quickly shuffled up to join them.

"Poe. It's been a long time," Maple said affectionately. She held out her arms and Poe walked into the warmest embrace she'd had in a long time.

"Thank you for bringing her, Maclemar. It's good to finally meet you," said Maple, squeezing Poe's shoulders one last time. "You're a legend with your catch and for carrying hot cargo."

Maclemar nodded but kept silent. He looked at Poe who was rubbing Penny and Chops on the belly. Poe felt his stare and stood up."

"So you're leaving now?" she asked. She kicked herself for sounding melancholy.

Maclemar shrugged, but before he could answer, Maple said, "You should go. Otherwise you won't have enough light to swim back to your boat." His eyes stayed on Poe and memorized her face.

"Bye then," Poe said, holding out her hand. The bruise on her wrist from the shackle glared at him. "Thanks for everything."

He didn't extend his hand and turned away to face Maple. "I'm going with you."

Maple looked at the Poe then at the Welshman who stood with resolve. "It's a dangerous time, Maclemar. We could use all the hands we can get, but it's not a fishing trip."

"Don't worry, Maple. I'm in desperate need of vacation," he said, and he smiled at Poe. "Too long on a boat can stir a man crazy."

"You lost quite a bit of weight since the last time I saw you," Poe commented as she followed her guides through the heart of the forest. The woman had been as stocky and thick-bodied as a sack of grain. "I didn't think vampires could change their appearance so drastically."

"Well it's been a difficult two years, Poe," the vampire explained patiently. "It's no pleasure cruise having every vampire in the state hunting us for reward. You'd be surprised how many would try. The promise of a cattle farm can goad even the most cowardly of vampires to come after us. I think you'll find many of us much changed."

Even Sainvire?

"What about the cattle we rescued?"

"Many have died on us," she said with a strained smile. "They couldn't handle the constant change of venue. Some turned Revenent and were terminated. Quite a few were stolen back during skirmishes. And the survivors needed time to revive and had to be hidden from place to place."

Most victims succumbed to a year-long stupor, and while in this pliant drugged state, vampires harvested their blood. Poe had helped some of these unfortunates escape from Downtown L.A., and their release proved to be a trial, indeed. It was like prodding a mannequin to take a first step.

"Is everybody okay? Joseph, Morales, Megan, Perla?"

Poe couldn't quite say his name.

"Most of us live," she said, her lips tightening. "But like I said, many of us have changed."

"Guys, I think we should cut the talking. At least until we're out of the woods," Jorge Lechuga cautioned, his vigilance comically upturned by his green spandex.

"Still think we're being followed, Maple?" asked Romulo Gutierrez, pushing his wheat-colored bangs off his face. He was a vampire who could walk in daylight, a talent Plasmacore made possible after prolonged intake. "Ya sure it ain't deer or squirrel? 'Cause there seems to be an explosion of them out here. There's four of them now," he said while pointing at a buck and his three girlfriends.

The wilderness fauna seemed to have exponentially burst the egg sack. The results were a new generation of deer, squirrels, coyotes, and critters little afraid of humans whom they scarcely encountered the past decade.

"There's no doubt about it. They've been on our tail probably since we got here," she answered with a nod. "They're just waiting for a ripe time to get us. We should maintain silence like Jorge said."

"No reckless shooting, kid," Romulo cautioned Poe, his permanently angry brows drawn. "Remember to shoot them, not us."

You should be telling that to the Welshman, jerk. She was about to verbalize something emphatically rude when Maple spoke for her.

"She's the best shot I've ever seen, even among vampires with superior eyesight," Maple said with grave seriousness. "Lay off her."

"So it's not all myth. The blurb on her wanted poster," he said with a smirk.

Most every California city had a barrage of posters glued on walls and street lights. The computer likeness of her face, no doubt put together by Trench's police henchmen, bore an exaggeratingly thick centipede scar that would make Poe's ego seethe if she were to see it. There was even a

87

sentence that said: *Perp is riddled with scars and is very very dangerous.*

"I mean, she's human and so puny to be the second most wanted after Sainvire. Even over you, Maple. You're number four! It just seems like a joke."

Poe could stand many things, but not a crack about her height or frame. Her height was a sore point because both her parents were taller than average. Her growth had no doubt been stunted due to malnutrition and from years of eating expired canned foods. Living in constant fear since she was eight years old didn't help her bones stretch vertically toward the sun, either. Her hands shook. She had a feral urge to dropkick the vampire with alcohol breath and brownish yellow teeth. Already in tune with the girl's mercurial moods, Maclemar put a restraining hand on her shoulder. He stared pointedly at Romulo and said, "Y coc oen!" Literally it meant the pubic hair of a llama. Or wanker for short.

"Jorge is right. We should all zip our cakeholes and be vigilant," Maclemar finished in a stretched voice.

"You should tell the pig and the dog," complained Romulo.

"They won't make a peep," assured Maclemar.

Silence fell immediately. They held their weapons closely and followed Jorge, the human guide, as quietly as possible. His stealthy ways and knowledge of the woods impressed Poe and especially Maclemar who earlier had dismissed the spandex-wearer as a bloody poof.

The forest dimmed the longer they trekked. They had another two hours of light and they had to put distance between them and the state park. It wouldn't have been smart to drive on unpredictable highways and backroads in the dark.

Jorge paused and raised his arm to halt. With a look he beckoned Maple over. On tiptoes he whispered in the taller woman's ear. Maple nodded without expression and headed to the small meadow ahead.

Jorge gestured for the group to huddle. Poe decided she liked his open, beardless face. In the softest voice he could muster, the man whispered, "Sorry but some vamps have Jaime Sommers hearing. For you young ones who've never heard of her, she'd be the Bionic Woman. Anyway, the glade coming up is the perfect place for an ambush. It's ten minutes from where our van is parked. Lots of overgrown bushes, hedges, and juts for cover, but we could still be easy pickings. I'm pretty damn sure this is where it's going to happen. Maple's climbing for a better view. Prepare yourselves. Keep to the trees. They're banking on picking us off in the clearing. And Poe, I've got an extra Kevlar in my bag. It's huge but better than nothing."

The motley crew heeded his advice, and they clutched their weapons of choice like winning lottery tickets. It was a sinking feeling to know that in ten minutes all five of them could die. Jorge tossed the extra bulletproof vest to Poe.

She silently mouthed a thank you to Jorge who she later learned had founded two organizations dedicated to getting more bicycles than cars on the road in Oakland. The more benign of the two was Bike Not Car that mainly participated in pro-bicycle rallies and costumed bike rides on Sundays. Later he put together a clandestine die-hard group of cyclists that randomly punctured automobile tires to make a glaring point. It was called Pedal or You're Cheddar.

Instead of putting on the vest, Poe handed it to Maclemar. She figured he'd need it more than her.

"No way," he said inaudibly. "You wear it."

With a hard stare Poe grabbed the neck of his sweatshirt until her lips were next to his left ear. She whispered, "I have experience. Put the damn thing on. It's too big for me anyway." Impatiently she took his arm and began shoving it in the arm hole of the vest. Ticked, the Welshman pushed her hands away.

Once Maclemar suited up she removed the two guns from her shoulder holster. The left hand clutched the Walther PPK she had nicknamed James after 007, and the right one held a lightweight Glock that carried 17 rounds per magazine.

The girl was ambidextrous and a pretty steady shot with both hands. *My only talent*, she thought wryly. *And sometimes I miss*." She thought of the human cattle she had shot accidentally out of misplaced confidence.

Never shoot unless you're sure, Poe, she told herself. *You're 24, and you can't use your youth as an excuse for screwing up anymore.*

Followed closely by Chops, Penny sidled up to Poe and scratched her leg with a paw. The mute dog, looking worried, blinked up at her. She bent down and kissed the mutt on the forehead and patted the rosy pig on the rump. As if the animals could understand, Poe put a silencing finger to her lips.

A flurry of bullets erupted ahead of them, jolting each one to action. Maple was in the crossfire. Jorge deferred leadership to Romulo who stepped up to the plate. He had more experience being Sainvire's top henchman and head of security in the Bay Area.

"Split up," he ordered. "They can't box us in that way. You and the girl go left. Jorge and I will take the right. *Entiendes*?"

With a hiss Poe answered with viciousness brought on by the moment, "*Sí, cabrón!*" She didn't like the way he omitted her name and referred to her as "the girl." In fact his pheromones didn't click with her essence, period.

She heard Romulo's nasal chuckle as she and Maclemar sped left. Poe was a quarter Mexican and her knowledge of Spanish was limited to numbers and swear words. It felt good to practice on a prick like Romulo.

"Lay low," she ordered, and she told Maclemar to take cover behind two-ton boulders that ensconced trash and recycling bins for the park. How her words rang true as bullets nearly decimated his head. His height and build were distinct bulls-eye signs for the opposition. Shots continued sporadically at the once popular meadow that had brimmed with park visitors.

"What's happening?" he asked Poe who seemed to be locked in a trance. When he didn't get an answer, Maclemar nudged the girl with his shoulder.

"Trying to figure out where the shots are coming from," Poe answered with exasperation.

"And?"

"And I think two of them are firing from the clump of cypresses ahead. Three are hiding near the ranger cottage. A couple of vamps are zigzagging super-fast by the stubs near the pond. You can see their blurry images against the water at the edges of the pond. And there are at least two more crack shots in Jorge and Romulo's side of the clearing."

"You got all that from listening?"

"Don't be annoying," Poe gritted her teeth. "Maple drew them out. We'll need to take down the goons up those trees. They're closest, and their vantage is bad for the five of us. I'm gonna run real fast to that fat tree over there." She pointed at a thick redwood that must have been a few hundred years old. "Get to that boulder near the redwood and cover me. Don't run! Crawl on your belly 'cause you don't camouflage."

She handed him two clips and quickly scrambled from tree to tree, barely dodging bullets. Maclemar blew out a breath and followed her lead, throwing himself on the floor when needed and crawling like a Marine under barbed wire.

From the other side of the clearing, a furious Romulo announced his location to the world by hurling a string of curses per shot fired.

"Fucking turds!" he yelled as he squeezed the trigger. "Ball lickers!"

Stupid asshole, thought Poe at hearing the commotion he was making. *They're going to plow him down because of his potty mouth! And he might just take poor Jorge with him.* In her book the cycling fanatic was more than alright.

Her eyes darted to the crop of diverse tree species only a few hops away. In the center were pretty cypress trees familiar to her from her dad's collection of colorful California crate labels from the 1920s.

Poe paused behind an overturned picnic table to better gauge where the bullets were coming from, usurping a hare that dug its hole alongside the crumbling artifact of days gone by.

Know how I know that you two are up there? 'Cause you're firing at my ass and you're not even changing trees! She leapt behind the nearest redwood. Bullets grazing the earth exploded into dust as they pursued Poe's heels. Despite the peril, the dog and pig doggedly continued to trail their leader.

She crouched inside the elbow of an especially leaden tree root and waited for Maclemar who made every effort to hide his broad body from the snipers perching on the tree.

"The unfortunate chump looks like he's going to need a defibrillator," she muttered under her breath as she recalled the oft used term in medical dramas she'd ingested over the years. "He can't be more than forty. He hardly has any white hairs," she said. "C'mon, Welshman. I need to get to where that squirrel is," Poe complained. "Duck for fucksake! That tree won't cover your hand!"

Maclemar reached the boulder near enough to take a good shot at the dubious trees, and Poe took off running in a crisscross manner.

Never run in a straight line under fire, or you'll be road kill, Sister Ann had inculcated in her brain.

Maclemar shot at the tree tops, drawing fire his way. Poe bit the bullet and dropped and rolled to the nearest tree that provided an improved underside view. "Close enough," she said in a whisper and waited.

Within seconds she spotted movement from a lanky cypress. She fired twice. A distended body fell with a wound around the shoulder and neck, and an obese daywalker in fatigues lay permanently dead not too far from where she kneeled.

Poe cast her eyes to the other vamp sniper perched overhead and waited.

"I know you're up there, brother," she said calmly. "I'm not going anywhere."

As predicted, a succession of movement shook the top branches of a nearby tree. With lightning movements, a creature jumped from tree to tree. Maclemar nearly emptied a clip without grazing the enemy. Poe seethed.

"Hey, Welshman," Poe said loud enough to be heard over the din of gunfire. "Don't waste bullets 'cause they don't grow arm hairs!"

"Right you are," he articulated with contrition.

Poe focused on every shaking branch and wobbly tree with the barrel of her gun but did not shoot. "Go slow, Poe," she whispered to herself. "Don't shoot unless you're certain. Can't waste bullets. The Welshman's already used up most of 'em."

She watched him leap to an engorged oak ten feet away and back-flip toward a eucalyptus. He was barefoot. The monkey vamp was wily. With a deep breath Poe allowed instincts to take over. *He's going to fake a right but will land on the cypress sculpted like a woodpecker*, the ever reliable voice in her head told her.

Twisting her lips, Poe uttered, "I knew it." Her prediction proved wise. But not wise enough, for the orangutan undead swung back on the branches and launched himself thirty feet to Poe's tuckaway. A vicious sleet from heaven, his dirt-caked feet landed savagely on Poe's chest.

The pain, virulent and convulsive, took the fight out of the vampire killer. Her upper body burned like skinned flesh drizzled with unbleached sea salt. *Possible breast cancer in the future.* With her eyes tightly shut, the squeal and whines of her animals became vague mournful sounds, overshadowed by the sobs that escaped her own lips. *Let me not get cancer.*

No calluses ever developed in that part of her anatomy.

Her faithful dog tried to block access to the injured Poe, and the dotted piglet stood indomitably next to the mutt who had adopted her as kin. Penny's yellow fangs, slick from overactive saliva glands, didn't even faze the reeking vampire with incisors triple the length of the canine's. With scorn the vampire kicked Penny in the underbelly. The dog shot up a few feet in the air and hit the ground with a thud. Chops imitated Penny's protective stance and was quickly given the boot as well.

"No more animal blood for me," the predator declared to no one in particular. "From now on it's high-grade stuff or bust. Ha, my very own farm! Patience pays off. It don't hurt to be loved by the sun, neither."

Able to draw a piddling, careful breath again, Poe pried her eyes open and stared into the sneering face of the vampire with stringy, oil-matted hair.

The fucker's a girl!

"Better stay the hell down, Julia Poe," a sharp, twangy voice suggested while confiscating weaponry and pack from the downed vampire killer. "You're my ticket to ride outta obscurity. After tonight I'll be a fuckin' master vampire. Me, Missy, the dissing girl.

Can't wait to see those jerks' faces when they see who reeled in the big bad fish. Guess living on trees for 64 days straight paid off."

The skinny vampire with bunny teeth and protracted incisors giggled like a hysterical three-year-old. She kicked Poe soundly in the shin and wrenched her pack away before launching herself on Maclemar's boulder. Her shins didn't hurt. Poe was used to abuse where her legs were concerned. Her chest was killing her.

"I hope I don't get cancer," she prayed once more to her parents.

Wheezing, Poe crossed her arms over her upper body and hugged herself. She couldn't rise up just yet. The pinhole ducts on the corner of her eyes pumped out tears that flowed unbidden down her cheeks. A second later she heard gunshots followed by yelling.

Stand up, you! the voice in her head said with urgency. *The monkey girl's wrestling with the Welshman right now. Can't you hear him yapping?*

Poe took an excruciating gulp of air until she was satisfied that no ribs were broken. *Only my boobs*, she thought wryly. Biting her lower lip, she took the first step toward the fisherman that seemed a long stretch away.

"Dos i ffwcio dy hun y cont!" Maclemar cursed. He spewed saliva threads in vehemence.

"I don't know what you're saying, but I know it ain't nice," the congo bongo girl said, smiling at the blows he was raining on her cheeks and chin. The hundred-pound girl didn't even bother to block the punches that skinned Maclemar's fist and left blood blush on the vampire's face. The girl appeared as

96

though she was sunbathing on the boulder instead of being pinned down and clouted by a large man twice her size with muscles in the right places.

"I said, 'Go and fuck yourself, you cunt,'" Maclemar ranted, disgruntled that his best punches had barely an effect on the vampire with a flat figure and blonde hair browned by filth and oil.

"Hang me now, Lord. I've just been insulted by a cute guy," she said. She looked to the sky in exaggerated injury of pride. "What kinda language is that you're insulting me with anyway?"

"That'd be Welsh, you slag."

"Never heard of it, handsome," she smiled, and her thin, colorless lips curdled Maclemar's blood. "Such a shocking way to behave in front of your future mama master. If I were you, I'd be kissing my ass right about now. Your future cattle status might be upped a notch."

"Och. Sorry, no. I don't kiss flat asses," he said with wry grin. "I like my women to have a bit of padding, top to bottom," he bleated. "Slatternly anorexic girls are positively a turnoff."

The woman's close-set eyes narrowed as she felt truly insulted at last. She obstructed his forearm diving down for a jab with one sweeping block. In a breath the vamp flipped positions with the man, effortlessly pinning his larger body. A delicate hand, thick with grime and translucent veins, captured the wrist of the sturdy fisherman who'd just disparaged her. Ill intentions on her face, the vampire forced his fist to her lips and sniffed the rusty blood like it was ice cream. And like the creamy ice cold dessert, she licked his wounds clean to the horror of the crass-tongued scholar.

Her lengthy teeth, grimy with rot, remolded into a form more lethal and micro-sharp.

"Oh shite," escaped from Maclemar's suddenly dry lips.

"You don't insult your executioner, foreigner," she said, her pithy knuckles landing strikes to his face and succeeding in slicing skin. "She might just kiss you to sleep and violate you for a year."

"I'd rather," Maclemar began, set on dying with class, "do myself in first, thanks."

"Then get ready to die," she said with the fire of an ugly woman who had been scorned most of her life. She grabbed an ear and yanked it back, exposing his brown, fisherman neck. Within seconds the vampire's three-inch fang dug into Maclemar's jugular, and she thirstily ingested the Welshman's blood.

Poe walked into the grizzly scene in time to witness Maclemar's green eyes roll up the sockets. A limping Penny and twitchy Chops flanked her sides. She picked up a rock and aimed it at the vampire's spine.

A four-pound rock was the interruption needed to stop a bloodletting, and it landed crisply on the vertebrae of the feeding vampire.

The succubus bailed her greedy teeth from Maclemar's neck, not bothering to wipe the thick and salty juices from her mouth. The vampire was pissed like nothing else, and she glared noxiously at Poe who grasped another hefty rock with her hand.

"I was aiming at your skull, but I didn't want to smash my friend's face in," Poe said with a perverse grin that didn't quite reach her dark eyes. *I just shared a memorable kiss with the Welshman, you bitch!*

"I squashed your ass," the dirty-nailed vampire griped. "You should be crippled on the floor."

"Um, no. You dropkicked my boobs," Poe corrected, her wing-tipped brows drawing closer together. The particular spot was a sore point with her. "But I guess I'm tougher than I look."

"Don't give me cheek, girl." The vampire stood to full height, a half an inch taller than Poe. "I might get fifty less heads of cattle, but it would be worth it to kill you."

"Bummer then, you future master fanger, you!" Poe said lightly.

She kept her eyes trained at the vampire with dirty hygiene, but her peripherals followed Maclemar's shaky trek from the boulder to a nook out of range from Poe's granite projectile.

"Your guy ain't going nowhere unless you carry him outta here. My venom will drug him like a crank toy for a year. He'll be like the other cattle, squirting blood into a milk bottle."

"And I was just beginning to like him," Poe sighed with regret. "But changing the subject, are you allergic to garlic?"

The flat-chested vampire hissed. She angrily located the girl's pack and guns by her own feet. Satisfied that Poe was weaponless, she answered, "I'm a goddess. Of course I'm—"

Thwack!

Quick as a cough, Poe's left wrist released a knife slick with garlic oil. With an expert flick it embedded into the vampire's heart. Two seconds later another four-inch blade from the right wrist pierced the same dead organ.

The vampire hunter bridged the ten yards that had separated her from the fallen body. Hair and dirt clung to her head like Christmas ornaments.

"Bye now," she waved to the woman foaming at the mouth and twitching by her feet. "Black sludge ooze equals dead vampire, right? Well so long, slim." Like one who dreamed of revenge frequently, Poe kicked the woman's head and pounced on it Bruce Lee-style and with a neck snapping twist.

"How in heaven's name did you do that?" Maclemar asked with fevered eyes. Poe was taken aback as she had thought the Brit had turned bovine.

"Holy!" Poe exclaimed. She darted to where Maclemar massaged his bruised neck. "I thought you turned cow already."

"No chance of that," he sighed tiredly, looking into Poe's dark-lashed brown eyes. He enjoyed the feel of the girl's toughened palm against his cheek. Her concern touched him more than he could articulate. "Ever wonder why I have so many bite marks on my body?"

"'Cause you were the champagne fountain at vampire functions?"

"You're astonishing," Maclemar declared with a lazy smile. He reached out to pluck leaves from her hair. "Right you are then. I was their cocktail drink that never turned vamp or cattle however many bites."

"Lucky you."

"Not when I was in their service for eight years," he said, caressing her face with his eyes. "I'd rather have been asleep forever with an ass goiter than go through that business."

Poe nodded and studied the fresh bite on his neck. She couldn't take the way his gaze suddenly made her feel.

"Can you get up?"

"I think so."

She helped him to his feet, glad when she no longer touched him. His sweat stayed in her nostrils like mint after brushing.

"Really, how did you do that?" he asked. He nodded to the vampire body.

"It's in the wrist, I guess," Poe shrugged, picking up her knives and wiping them on the dead vampire's shirt.

"Did you replace your clip with a full one?" Poe peevishly asked Maclemar. The sporadic gunfire where Maple was drawing fire reminded her to get her shit together. Drinking slimy Gatorade and lollygagging over their bruises and bites was excessive to say the least.

"No," he answered, discomfited. "Not yet."

"If you want to die so badly, don't replace the clip," she said meanly. Instantly feeling guilty about her stern tone, Poe touched his arm. "Sorry. Replace the clip so we can join the others. They can use our help."

Awkwardly Maclemar fumbled with the release and fueled Poe's ire further when he tossed away the empty clip.

"Hey. You don't throw out magazines like used tissue," she lectured, moving Chops out of the way with her foot. "Give it back to me."

Emasculated, Maclemar bent down to pick it up and narrowly missed an arrow aimed at his heart.

"Shit! Get down! " Poe bellowed. She tackled Maclemar behind a tree. Another arrow skimmed low on the ground, piercing the little pig cleanly in the rear flank. Chops squealed like she was getting the hack. The dog, traumatized by the murderous cries of her new friend, emitted a low whine. Being a sharper-than-average dog, Penny clamped her teeth into the pig's fatty neck and dragged her to Poe's feet.

Tears stung Poe's eyes, and her jaw worked in anger. Chops was her pig now.

"Hold her down, Maclemar," she said with haste.

With a steady hand Poe unsheathed the knife in her left wrist and cut the arrow to the quick. Wincing at the cutting screams of the piglet, Poe pulled the arrow out. She resheathed her knife and looked into Maclemar's pained eyes.

"Lemme borrow this," Poe said as she slid the rifle from his shoulder. "Do me a favor and stick out a body part. Then yank it back quick." She'd once asked Morales to do the same thing when trying to pinpoint a sharp shooter at Trench's Bonaventure Hotel.

Maclemar exposed his right arm and quickly snatched it back. No arrows came. He looked down at Poe kneeling on one knee with the rifle cocked and ready, her eyes squinting into the scope. Furious determination etched her face. *Such a small person for such a large, messy world*, thought the Welshman who resigned himself to undertake the ultimate sacrifice. *It's for a girl and a pig. What else could be more chivalrous?* He thought right before leaping to the next tree cover.

Thwack!

A whoosh of air grazed his neck, inches from skin. Before he could finish saying, "Bloody hell," Poe's index finger pulled the trigger, and she dropped the rifle.

"Penny, stay here with Chops!" she instructed. And she was off running in a half-crouch with a gun in each hand. Maclemar, once reoriented and on his feet, followed without delay. His courage was so dented by the near miss, he could hardly keep up. Chops' shrill cries penetrated his spine like a shot of extra concentrated Liquid-Plumr clog remover. The furious gunshots in the background proved the saboteurs hadn't been subdued.

Maclemar cursed the lightheadedness that kept him lagging behind Poe who had shorter limbs. Blood loss or not, he needed to catch up with the girl. But he ran on, keeping low on the ground and making himself small.

"She's heading for the damn awful wailing to finish the job," he said under his breath and shuddered at the thought. *What if the injured vamp had more than one friend hiding in the bushes?*

The shooter was alone, and he wasn't a vampire. He was human. *A leech!*

Maclemar wasn't fast enough. With one knee pinning his arm and shoulder, the girl clonked the human stooge on the forehead with the rounded grip of the Walther PPK. These leeches, willing servants of vampires, pissed off Poe as much as skinhead vamps.

"Oh does this hurt?" Poe asked with false concern as she inserted two fingers into the bleeding hole in his stomach.

"Stop! Please! Jes – jes kill me," cried the man whose flesh looked and felt like the clammy insides of carp. His balding head, slick with sweat, shimmered like the surface of a pond in the moonlight. "It hurts so much."

"Oh yeah. You should've thought of that before trying to kill your fellow humans and their pets," she said. Her teeth grated together like a knife sharpener on rock. "What did they promise you?"

She slapped his face with hands wet from his stomach juices. "Answer the question."

"Some respect," he gasped. "So I wouldn't be no lackey no more."

"You sniff glue, lick vampire assholes to keep your neck bite-free, rape and impregnate cattle? And you want respect?"

If she could smell gastric juices and foulness emanating from his wound, in most probability so could he. She had read somewhere that dying people's sense of smell sharpened the nearer they were to death. Blinded by a sadistic streak that hadn't surfaced in years, Poe proceeded to yank out his intestines foot by foot like ingredients for menudo. She was completely unfazed by the man's terrible screams even when the little voice in her head chanted for her to stop.

All your hard work to try to Zen yourself into a decent human being amidst all this dankness is gone. Wasted.

"Get off of him, girl!" yelled Maclemar who looked suddenly pasty even with his fisherman tan.

"He shot my pig," she accused, justifying the torture with a voice deep in umbrage. Poe stared the dying man in the eye. "I'm going to leave you out here with your sausage casings on display. Something gourmet for the animals tonight!"

"Please. Please, no!" the man begged, searching an iota of compassion. He found none in Poe and mere disgust in Maclemar.

Before Poe could properly savor the look of horror in the dying man, she was roughly pushed down to the dirt by a weak and sick Maclemar.

"You're fucking mental, you are," he cried. "This is wrong," he told himself. "*1984* meets *Lord of the Flies*!" He pointed the Beretta to the man's head. With his eyes closed Maclemar shot the leech until he couldn't hear the sickening screams any longer. One. Two. Three.

Her stained hands smelled putrid. The little lapse of morality shook whatever foundations she'd cemented the past twenty years. It left craggy, seismic veins in the concrete. She felt cracked and shaken.

She only had to look at Maclemar's tortured face to know that she had appalled him.

I compelled him to murder.

He refused to look at her as they walked the edge of the clearing to reach an exchange of gunshots.

All his tough words about hating human traitors and vampires were just words.

The scholar was a romantic, after all, who ultimately believed in the effervescent soul and its ability to transcend filth and injustice. He had never lost faith in the Joads, the Prynnes, or the Huckleberrys of the world. But with three shots of the Beretta, Maclemar's humanity was suddenly compromised.

CHAPTER 5

"DOES ANYBODY KNOW HOW to drive stick?" asked Maple as she set a groggy Jorge in the middle row of the roomy van.

"I can drive a Vespa," Poe said. She cringed for voicing her unhelpful thoughts out loud.

"That's nice, Poe, but we need a driver. I can't do it. I have to attend to Jorge."

"I know how," answered the bike enthusiast, his speech slurred from the anesthetic he'd been injected with earlier.

"Anyone else besides Jorge here?" Maple asked urgently.

"Aye, me," volunteered Maclemar who cradled the injured piglet in his arms. He set the shivering pig on the floor of the vehicle nearest the front where she was joined by a concerned Penny who immediately began licking Chops' wound. "Cars with automatic transmissions are scoffed at where I come from."

"Good. You better get started, Maclemar. I hear coyote baying out there," Maple nodded distractedly, tearing off Jorge's No. 94 cycling jersey. "Romulo will guide you to the safe route. And this might help." She handed Poe night vision goggles to pass on to Maclemar.

"You'll have to drive with those things on, I'm afraid. We don't want headlights to attract any hostiles this evening."

"Right," Maclemar said as if stunned. "This is a new driving experience for me, I guess. At least I can drive the British side of the road if I want. Traffic willing, of course."

"Poe, kneel here with me. You're going to clean Jorge's shoulder wound, and I'll handle the stomach. Let me know if bullet fragments are in there."

"But my hands are filthy," protested Poe. Patching up another human after torturing another didn't feel right.

"Then use gloves, dammit!" Maple burst her façade of calm. "Listen, just do the best you can."

"Alright, Maple," Poe said. She scrubbed her hands with rubbing alcohol and hydrogen peroxide and put on latex gloves from the emergency kit. Placing a tiny flashlight between her teeth, Poe cleaned the wound as best she could. She inspected the hole. A probe with tweezers located the bullet lodged near the solar plexus. The copper bullet containing no lead expanded upon impact into four petals with sharp edges. With much difficulty as it was dark and the road bumpy, Poe succeeded in extracting the bullet. Poe swabbed and dressed the wound for the last time, and she shined her light at the cavernous wound Maple labored to patch up.

Poe's back was damp. Little beads of sweat appeared on the tip of her nose like clear glue. Breathing deeply, she tried her hardest not to throw up. Maclemar's driving was making her carsick.

Maple, still looking for the missing bullet that stretched into a flower with lethal edges, kept on delving with unstinting focus. Poe averted her eyes from the surgery happening right under her nose. She breathed through her mouth.

When Poe and Maclemar had reached the others, everyone was still standing. Maple and Romulo had flushed and destroyed the mercenaries that had fired on them in hope of claiming a reward. It was Jorge who shot the last of the vampire snipers in the head. No one could have expected that the undead would raise himself up and retaliate because he had merely been grazed in the head.

The scummy vampire whizzed Romulo in the temple from where he lay dying and hit Maple's powerful forearm which spit out the bullet seconds later. He fired a few more shots before Poe shot him in the heart. She thought Jorge was simply resting on a log. The junkyard smell of blood alerted her differently.

"Jorge's a goner," said Romulo sitting shotgun with Maclemar and swigging cheap whiskey in a flask. He didn't bother lowering his voice. "It's that damn faggoty outfit of his that did him in. No. 94, my ass!"

"He said it was his lucky number," Maclemar said defensively. He hadn't even met Jorge before that day, but he felt compelled to defend the quirky man fighting for his life. "I know the world's wasted and fucked, but we should really try to keep homophobic slurs to a minimum."

"Sure, it's his lucky number alright," Romulo snorted. He took a swig of whiskey from a small container. "And what are you about with this PC crap? Wake up, man. This is the Apocalypse.

Anything goes. What're ya anyway, an English fruit?" He corked his flask.

"No, I'm not a poof. Nor am I English," Maclemar corrected, squinting at the indelibly black road ahead of him. It was like driving through the insides of a Ding Dong. "But my dad was."

"Was what?'

"Gay," Maclemar said matter-of-factly. "He came out when I was in primary school."

"So that's why you're so bleeding heart about that fashion disaster fender bender back there?"

"Jorge is not homosexual," Maple interjected. "He had a wife and two children before all this Armageddon madness happened."

"When does being married ever stop a queer from getting it from behind? C'mon," Romulo laughed with derision. "I mean look at this for chrissake," he said. He tapped a cassette into the tape player and the lively "Oh L'amour" rang out. "Fucking Erasure! I rest my case."

"This is Megan's van, Romulo," Maple said testily, meticulously feeling for projectiles in Jorge's stomach with only the light held by Poe and by the overhead light of the van. "That's her music."

"Maybe, maybe not," Romulo said insolently. "Either way, that bootie pirate's outfit speaks for itself."

"Oh fuck off, you alcoholic son of a bitch," Maple carped, startling Poe who'd never seen the gracious and normally tranquil woman unravel. "I'm trying to concentrate here. If you want to insult anyone for their sexual orientation, pick on me."

"I have nothing against lesbians," Romulo shrugged, "I rather encourage them, especially if the ladies are young. No offense."

Maple ignored him. She found a small piece of cartridge. She sighed with relief.

"Romulo, you're a vampire," began Maclemar, changing the subject. "Why are you still downing that stuff?"

"I like the taste of whiskey, still do. Reminds me I was human once."

Poe cleared her throat and asked, "Is Megan gonna be where we're going?"

"Yes, she is," Maple said curtly as she concentrated on her task. "They'll have to suture the ruptured intestines at the HQ. I can't see very well here."

"Megan ain't going nowhere," Romulo snickered, twisting to look at Poe. "She's about to burst."

"What?"

"He means she's pregnant," explained Maple. "She's due in a week's time."

"She's Sainvire's grandniece," explained the vampire with whiskey breath to Maclemar. "The two of them will get us all permanently killed."

"What are you talking about?" Maple asked, frowning.

"We're getting hunted like criminals. And like criminals we move from place to place like goddamn gypsies," he fumed. "We ought to wage war and kill Trench's henchmen and Newbitt's people instead of running away all the time."

"There aren't enough of us," Maple explained tiredly. "And we have the ex-cattle to think about."

"I say we ditch them. They're all cured. They can fend for themselves, by damn!"

"They are our people now. We've got to take care of each other. Besides, more than half have already been placed into their new communities."

"Bullshit!" he spat, and he hit the dashboard with a fist. "They're liabilities. And whatever cows we have left are weak and useless to us. If Newbitt ever gets a whiff of where we're hiding those fuckers, we're all everlastingly dead. I'm hopping on the next ride outta this shithole when we get back."

"They're needed more than you think, Romulo," said Maclemar, winding his way out of a maze of trucks and cars. Some vehicles had been deliberately pushed onto the opposing lane to clear the road, but some remained to give Maclemar a solid pain in the ass. "There aren't many daywalkers in your outfit, I hear. There're the two of you and a handful of others, but the rest haven't developed the 'skill' yet. The humans who guard these vampires during the day are in essence part of a symbiotic relationship, integral to the group's survival."

"That's crap," dismissed the vampire. He shooed Penny who'd stuck her head where the emergency brake poked up between the front seats. "Sainvire's gone soft. Every time some dick gets recaptured, the master vampire falls into a depression. Well I say, 'don't cry over spilt milk.'"

"If you're so gung ho about this, Romulo, how come I never hear you voice your concerns to Sainvire directly?" Maple asked tensely while disinfecting Jorge's wound with fizzy oxygen peroxide. "You always rant at people who can't do anything about the state of things. He's an easy one to talk to and even easier man to find."

"Maybe I will tell him. One of these days," Romulo muttered, clearly displeased at being called out. To change the subject he turned to the van's driver. "Why did you decide to come ashore, Maclemar? I thought you were strictly drop and go, even with your cargo of fish." Maclemar's fresh and dried fish were usually kept inside five-gallon plastic drums and left along docks or attached to buoys. Gasoline, clean water, and produce were left as payment for the seafood.

Poe narrowed her eyes. Maclemar didn't have to come ashore with her.

"Figured it was time to look around," he answered. He looked at the rear view mirror through his goggles.

"Look around, my aromatic asshole," muttered Romulo. "You did it for a piece of ass!"

Maclemar's brows connected in vehemence, but he waited a few seconds to compose himself. "Maple, does this guy have Tourettes or something?"

"Never thought of that, but your theory would explain a lot of things," said the vampire who finally settled in the seat behind Jorge's.

"Whatever Tourettes is, I still think you've got the hots for Sainvire's girlfriend. That's why you're following her to Gilroy, the garlic capital of the world, where every new sock ends up smelling like last month's moldy cheese," Romulo said, throwing in his two cents. "Can't wait for you to meet Sainvire." He rubbed his hands in anticipation of conflict.

"Nice one, pal," Maclemar said. He scratched his closely cropped Roman hair. "However, I've already met the bloke. He asked me to guard cattle and sleeping vampires who couldn't take the sun."

"What did you say?" Poe asked from the back.

"I said that after eight years of incarceration, I preferred to go fishing," he answered in a deadpan voice.

"Well then I can't wait for the little girl to meet Sainvire's honey. She's a pretty master vamp from Nevada with the heart of Mother Teresa that melds perfectly with Sainvire's missionary ego. The broad left her position to proselytize about Plasmacore to anyone with an ear. She's a cute blonde with legs up to my neck, little girl. She's going to break your heart."

"Romulo," said Maclemar in a threatening way as he looked at Poe's tense face in the rear view mirror. "Shut the fuck up!"

It was a tiring ride that seemed to go on forever. Because of the congested streets clogged with stranded automobiles and over a decade worth of waste, the journey east to Gilroy proved to be a creeping one. Hours had passed, and they'd yet to hit the land of the potent bulb. And through it all, Poe and Maclemar held their hunger at bay by eating energy bars replete with squirmy weevil and the last of the cotton candy batch she had been saving for a rainy day.

"I don't know about you lot, but my bladder's engorged," announced Maclemar. I need to stop and whish the plants."

"That's a good idea," noted Maple who was checking Jorge's vital statistics once more. Even under the deficient light Poe could tell that the man had a waxy look about him. The van smelled of body leakage and rot. The middle-aged vampire peeled open a new syringe and filled it with morphine. Poe took the opportunity to go outside with the dog. Maclemar had carried the piglet with him for a "wee" as he called it. She left Penny to her own devices and searched for a place to relieve her own bladder.

"Jorge's going to die," Poe whispered to herself as she did her business behind an upturned truck. "The poor man. Seemed like a nice guy, too."

A twig snap followed by a loud thump jarred Poe to finish sooner than expected.

"Who's there?"

"The moon is fickle," somebody said startlingly near. "It shows itself once in a while, but mostly it hides behind the clouds. Don't worry. It's well veiled now. I can't see a thing."

"Romulo, you fucking pervert!" she hissed. Her hands shook. She had no love for night, but she respected it enough for the privacy it offered.

"Just making sure nothing creepy jumps out at you," he drawled. "I've seen creatures weirder than Revs around here."

"Are you sure you didn't see your own reflection, asshole?"

"Nope. This is what I saw, pretty girl," he said. He threw something creaky her way.

Poe stepped back and shone a small penlight on the crumpled bones before her. They were no bigger than a small dog.

"Not exactly a Rev, but it's close enough. Better turn that light off before you attract any more of 'em."

Poe could almost see the shit-for-fangs smiling. The bones of baby vamps replete with teeth and pointy hands definitely gave her the creeps.

"Now aren't you glad I peeked?" he said, rubbing it in.

In her haste to reach the van, she nearly mowed down Maclemar.

"Whoa there," he said, placing a restraining hand on her arm. "You alright?"

"I'm fine," she said. She brushed away his concern and ducked inside the van with the dog following closely behind. She filled Penny's Tupperware from her pack with water. She gave the dog and pig some jerky. "Maple, am I allowed to blow Romulo's brains out for being a pervert?"

"I don't see why not," Maple answered after two seconds of deliberation. "Seeing that he's the most annoying person here, I'd say it's a good idea."

"Hilarious," said Romulo who strapped in his seatbelt in imitation of Maclemar. He fluffed his flaxen hair and tried to part it in the middle. The jungle of hair stayed shrub-like and unmanageable. "I'm indispensable. You said so yourself, Maple. I'm one of the few left who can sunbathe during the day. It's not my fault enemy combatants have weeded the rest."

Half an hour into the drive, Jorge's heart gave out. The passengers, even the loquacious and obnoxious, were shocked into silence when Maple broke the news. Wracked with guilt at the torture she'd committed that afternoon on a leech, Poe bit her lip to keep from bawling. The man with the shiny head had died from the same stomach wound as Jorge.

I shouldn't have pulled his intestines out. I shouldn't have made it personal. Bad karma.

All traces of grief ended when the van hit something bulky. Maclemar brought the van to a stop.

"What was that?" asked Maple.

"An animal maybe?" supplied Poe hopefully.

"No animal, girlie," said Romulo Gutierrez. "My little eyes see a very hungry wilderness vampire brushing dirt off himself. And he has tag-along friends, so I suggest you drive as fast as you can, Maclemar."

The Welshman didn't need to be told twice. He revved the old van and swerved whenever he encountered automobiles. Poe put on her night vision goggles and saw five undernourished undead running next to the van and banging on its sides. She pulled an Astra automatic from her pack. Before she could crack the window open, Maple stayed her hand.

"No, Poe. Use a gun with a silencer. We don't want any more of them following us."

Poe nodded and rummaged through her bag. She found a silencer for her Beretta, but before she could screw it on, a hand punched through the driver's side window and grabbed Maclemar's shirt.

"Fer fuck's sake!" he yelled, his accent deepening. "Geteroffme!" The van banked left and banged into a car. Maclemar did his best to straighten the van and keep driving.

Poe screwed in the silencer, leaned close to Maclemar's head, and fired at the undead. She adjusted the Star Wars-like goggles and with her green sight pulverized the vampire in the head. Maple rolled her window down a few inches and fired at a leathery undead, insane from lack of food. She hit him in the stomach. The creature fell on the ground screaming like he was getting autopsied alive. "There's three more, Poe."

One appeared before them and threw a heavy fender at the windshield. It startled Maclemar so much that he crashed into a jackknifed produce truck. The engine died.

"Do something, sheep-shagger! They're coming!" said Gutierrez harshly.

"Listen, boyo, I'm trying," said Maclemar. He turned the ignition, but the engine merely coughed. "I don't see you helping the women out."

"That's because I don't have a silencer," he sneered.

The fender-throwing undead punched holes in the windows. Glass scattered inside. Poe said, "Excuse me" to Jorge's body before she hopped over his extended legs. The van shook amidst Maclemar's cursing.

"Thank you, my beauty!" said Maclemar when the engine hummed back to life. "Get the bastard that broke my windshield, please." "I'm on it," said Poe. She lowered the window and aimed at the leather critter holding a second fender in his hands. *Now*, said the voice in her mind. Poe pulled the trigger and hit the blood-deprived vampire in the heart. To its left side emerged another vampire throwing rocks at the van while running to keep up.

Poe squinted and fired, catching the undead in the head.

"One more, Poe," said Maple who wasted most of her bullets hitting nothing. She was taking pains to kill the fastest vampire of the lot.

Poe saw it, naked, bony, and hung like her neighbor's ratty Marmaduke pooch. He was walking toward Maclemar with a tire iron. Poe launched herself toward the front of the van, vaulting over Jorge's dead body and landing on the emergency brake between Maclemar and Gutierrez. She aimed through the hole in the window and fired twice. Glass scattered as Poe hit the dead in the eye and heart.

"That's my girl," said Maclemar with relief. He pulled Poe by the shoulders and landed a deep, grateful kiss on her cheek.

"So that's why Sainvire wants you back. You're a superhero," said Gutierrez sarcastically.

"And don't you forget that, Jorge," said Maple.

"Yeah, or I'll shove my Welsh foot up your alcoholic ass," seconded Maclemar.

It was dawn when the van pulled into an impressive barn, the red kind used in Superman films but four times the size, with haylofts and animal stalls. Instead of horses, however, sleeping bodies occupied the hutches and cubbyholes. Several trucks and buses were parked neatly in two straight lines. The air was crisp but tolerable with the redolence of acrid garlic blossoms. The scent made everyone's eyes water with the exception of Maple. It was like sniffing freshly sliced onions.

"I may be an intrepid daywalker, but I gotta confess that I can't abide the smell of garlic. It makes me weak-kneed like my Johnson's about to get shaved," said Romulo. "To build tolerance to garlic, I'd have to get inoculated by its essence and fight permanent death until my body gets used to it." He tied a yellow bandana bandito-style to cover his nose. The vampire looked like a train robber.

Nobody acknowledged him. Any odor was better than the smell of the liquid oozing out of the dead man's mangled intestines. Maclemar and Poe had been fighting off nausea the last hour of the drive.

Poe recognized the small man who closed the barn door behind them. It was Ed whose height and weight defied all stereotypes. She'd seen the five-footer who weighed less than her plunk down hefty railroad tracks ahead of a train like a scene from a Wallace and Gromit flick and toss two-ton boulders as if they were beach balls. The man could probably lift an elephant with one hand and drink cappuccino with the other.

"Hello, Poe," he nodded politely. "Good to see you again."

"Hey there, Ed," Poe smiled guardedly as she stepped down from the van. She wondered whether the man would have the dubious honor of lifting the body out of the vehicle. The folks rubbing fluorescent lights from their eyes made her queasy. Most people didn't trust her. She'd killed perfectly good vampires because she thought Sainvire and Joseph had betrayed her. "Nice to see you, too."

His impassive eyes focused on the body inside the vehicle and paused. She didn't hear what Maple told him for Maclemar, carrying Chops in the nook of his elbow like an infant, draped an arm around her shoulder and led her away. A few curious folks padded toward the van.

Penny darted to the side door. Her tail was wagging, but she was reticent because of bodies scattered around the barn. She joined Poe. The dog sat on her haunches and stayed close to her companion.

"Should we go outside? Maybe people will feel more—"

Words failed her as the barn door opened and he came in. He was followed by a long-limbed vampire with shortly shorn blonde hair. Her curious blue eyes caught Poe's, and she smiled. *She's beautiful in her confidence and obvious kind heart,* thought Poe.

By this time a crowd had congregated around the van. The stark fluorescent lights on the high ceiling hid nothing.

They didn't hide the dark circles around his eyes or the stubble that sprouted from his face. No feature about him was welcoming. His gray eyes rimmed with black glanced her way for but one second. That was all. Jaws working, the master vampire made his way to the van.

Maclemar's pity squeeze embarrassed her. She shrugged off his arms still about her. She vaguely heard Romulo say, "Well, boss, the good news is you got your other girlfriend back but at the cost of—"

Poe felt claustrophobic and headed for the door. She didn't want to stay to hear Romulo's ranting. Letting herself and the dog out of the suddenly stifling barn became job one. Before she could reach the door, however, Romulo's scream of surprise echoed ferociously until his body slammed onto the highest parapet of the barn wall. Then like a bird that struck a window, he sluiced down and lay on the ground with a groan next to Poe's foot.

Poe couldn't help it. She stared back at Sainvire who looked murderous. Their eyes met. His spitting gaze dared her to judge him. She couldn't and looked away.

"Aw. What the fuck," moaned Romulo on the ground. "It was only a joke."

Wordlessly the master vampire carried Jorge's body from the barn with the aplomb of a broken king.

———

Some of them couldn't speak properly from residual effects of at least ten years in an induced coma. Pregnant pauses and stammering were common among the ex-cattle. A mere two years of freedom barely cured them of stiff muscles, phobias, and nightmares. Tossing and screaming were common nightly occurrences in the barn. To be allied with vampires and halfdeads who liberated them from Downtown L.A. blood factories was still a strange concept.

Two of them took her to the sprawling farm house in the vicinity. Hansel and Gretel, she referred to them secretly, as they didn't offer their names. She was lucky to get as much as a grunt. Both Scandinavian blondes in their forties, they provided her with a half-filled tub of cold water and a pail of hot water.

Word had spread about Jorge's passing. Poe was certain from the rude way shampoo and soap were tossed into the tub from the door instead of being handed to her. Poe had been sitting in a curtainless tub half-full of water for five minutes. The bar of soap landed on her foot and bruised a toe.

She bit down a string of curses. It was a day of mourning.

No such thing as locks in the countryside, I guess. She wrung the face towel until no drop of water could be extracted to manage her rage and degradation. Jorge, after all, had died trying to transport her safely to the temporary headquarters.

"They probably peed in the bottle," Poe said out loud and sniffed the bottle of Herbal Essences. Her habit of talking to herself had returned. "I more than deserve it, too. Jorge was a good guy."

She blamed Sainvire.

"Why did he have to bring me here?" she asked the air. She lathered her hair with her own travel-size shampoo. "Why if he's just going to ignore me and get somebody killed? And then there's his girlfriend. She's beautiful, and she looked at me with pity. That's not right."

Two successive knocks forced her out of her reverie. "Hey. I'm not, um, done in here."

"Don't care. I'm coming in," a muffled woman's voice announced. "I got some more hot water for you."

"I'm fine. I don't need—"

The door swung open, and a very pregnant Megan came in with a steaming pot. *Whoever heard of a bathroom without a lock and shower curtain?* Poe covered herself with her arms and a face towel as best she could.

"Poe! At last," said Megan. She got down on her knees to give Poe a hug and kiss, unmindful of her friend's naked state. "I've missed you, girl!"

"Hey, Megan. I missed you, too. But can you please shut the door?"

Her heart dropped to her knees when she saw Maclemar and Sainvire walking past with somber expressions on their faces. Both looked her way in time to see Poe turn crimson and slip lower in the soapy water.

"Oops. Sorry," Megan said quickly. By the time the redhead managed to heave herself up and reach the door, Poe imagined half the household had seen her. "I hope your trip wasn't too bad."

"Um, you know. It was great," Poe answered. She poured the hot water into the tub herself. Her hand shook a little, an aftermath of seeing Sainvire and Maclemar outside the door. "I was clunked in the head by a gorgeous giant I shared some cotton candy with then kidnapped by an American Lit grad student turned fisherman who shackled me to his boat as Revenent fodder. Today we landed on Endor, and instead of meeting up with over-the-top Ewoks, we were attacked by tree vamps with bad hygiene. One of the men Maple brought along died a painful, drawn out death this morning. Really, I had an absolutely stupendous time."

"I'm sorry, Poe, but we had to do it," Megan explained. She pulled up the lid of the toilet and sat down. It was more comfortable that way. "Our sources informed us that certain sections in West L.A. and Santa Monica would be razed. Some rat blabbed that a bunch of squatters were living there. Including you, Public Enemy Number Two."

"I'm only number two because of Trench's conceit," said Poe.

"You did melt away his movie star good looks, the pride of his life," she concurred. It was the first time she really looked at Poe, half-submerged in the soapy water. A gasp escaped her lips. "My God, Poe. What on earth is that on your chest? Are those fresh bite marks?"

"I got kicked by a simian. You can see the imprint of its toes right here," Poe said as she pointed at a bruise shaped like a foot. "The rest are scratches and dog bites courtesy of Passionada's posse. Oh, and this wound on my cheek is from a Revenent tooth.

"Getting back to the subject, if I had known about the demolition, I would have headed for Malibu and avoided all B.S.," she added. She thought about her parents' things she would have liked to preserve. The thought of them burning made her sick. "I rode my bike there a few times, up the PCH. Trench wouldn't have destroyed a glitzy neighborhood like Pacific Palisades or Brentwood. Not that my neighborhood sucked. It was small but full of character."

"Sort of like you?" Megan smiled.

"I'm not small. My real height is 5'8" – the same as my mom's," said Poe. She dunked her head underwater. "I'm camouflaged right now 'cause I'm wet."

"Wow. You're not as touchy anymore. You can take a joke, I see." Megan grinned. "I remember how sensitive you were." Nevertheless she didn't dare correct Poe's overestimation of her height.

"You'd be surprised how much I've evolved, and how much I've stayed the same."

"You look healthy and not sickly thin anymore. And you still don't have any hair to shave. How I envy you."

"Who shaves nowadays? A waste of time. And who are women trying to impress anyway?"

"You're absolutely right. Every follicle is needed this coming winter. What are those things on your legs?"

"Calluses," Poe answered. She took a towel from Megan. "Long story. But tell me, who's the proud papa?"

"That'd be my darling Joseph."

"Joseph?" asked Poe, her eyes huge with questions. "Dragon tattoo Joseph? Sainvire's best friend? Fellow Filipino Joseph? Vampire Joseph?"

Megan giggled and nodded happily. "Yes, yes, yes. He's the one."

"But I thought vampires are sterile in general. And the ones who do have kids have ugly ones with lizard tongues," Poe said in confusion, shaking her head. She still dreamed of the babies that walked the ceiling like geckos. They had formed a chain and attacked her in the Los Angeles subway tunnels so long ago.

"Don't worry, Poe," Megan reassured. "I'm pregnant via turkey baster."

"A what?"

"Through a human donor who donated his sperm?"

"Who was it? And a turkey baster, really?"

"Remember Morales? And yes, a turkey baster."

"Morales?" She got it now. "Wow."

"I thought you liked him."

"I do. He's a super-great guy. One of my favorite people," she said. She recalled the man who had accompanied her in the tunnels and helped carry her after injuring an ankle. He was a flirt who wore an infinitesimal amount of cologne that made her groggy, but Morales was an all-around swell guy.

"He and Joseph are taking a third of the group to a secure location near Monterey. These are the people willing to try homesteading on their own. Once they decide on a place, Joseph and Morales will make their way back to Gilroy."

Megan caressed her smooth boulder of a belly and added, "I know it's nuts, but despite all this craziness I find myself so happy. I'm 38, Poe. I have to take major leaps to make things happen. And what's better than creating a new life to make this earth a little less rickety?"

Poe nodded. She kept her thoughts to herself. "I'm glad for you."

Less rickety? Most people I've seen in this compound are already dead. Arthritis. Degenerative bone diseases. Psychologically frail and physically ridiculous. These are the soldiers in charge when Sainvire's fellow vampires slumber during the day. Like Romulo said, only a few can call themselves daywalkers. Megan, the baby inside you will be Trench's blood supplier someday. There's nothing happy about that. For once she was thankful she didn't menstruate. A baby was the last thing she wanted.

"You've seen Jenna?" Megan asked, looking at Poe through her reddish eyelashes.

"The vamp standing next to Sainvire when I came in this morning?" said Poe. "Sure. She seems lovely. Looks like a model."

Megan rubbed her belly. "She's very nice. Sainvire met her before your time, Poe, when he was hawking Plasmacore in bordering states. They were on and off."

Poe wanted to end the conversation, but she wanted more answers. "Does he love her?"

The girl's naïve question put a smile on Megan's lips. "Maybe. They seem more like good companions to me."

"Isn't that the best kind of relationship?"

"I suppose. But I think he had passion for you. And I believe he loved you."

"Sure," Poe said. She rolled her eyes to the cottage cheese ceiling.

"Listen, he made sure you were safe. He knew you'd head to West L.A. because your folks were from there. He alerted the bands of humans who lived there to treat your right, to never let you starve, and to keep you from harm's way. He made Passionada write coded reports about how you were faring. If that's not passion and love, I don't know what is."

Poe shrugged her shoulders. If Sainvire loved her so much, then why didn't he send for her? Why did he renew his relationship with Jenna? "Don't kid yourself, Megan. He's just feeling guilt. He's good at torturing himself over nothing."

"I'm sorry. That's all I can offer you two," said Habib who hovered like an anxious hen while Poe and Maclemar filled themselves with buckwheat pancakes and spinach omelets he'd whipped up.

"Are you joking? This is the best food I've had in years," cried Maclemar who ingested everything put in front of him.

"Poe can tell you about the buffets we used to have at the library," he said, twirling the ends of his mustache. He looked melancholy.

"I remember very well, Habib," Poe said. "I think about those meals more than I think of my brother and sister sometimes. Whatever happened to your fellow chefs? Janice and—"

"They're gone, Poe," he sighed heavily.

She couldn't swallow the omelet bites in her mouth. *All those nice, generous people dead?*

Before she lost it, a muscular girl slightly older than Poe came in from the kitchen entrance and dropped a heavy sack of turnips on the kitchen floor. Even Poe doubted she could've lifted the sack. Her presence spelled 'tough' and 'badass'. She was not the sort to be crossed because she would certainly have retaliated with her fist. At least that was what Poe thought of the young woman who dogged her with intense eyes.

"What's this?" she asked. She tossed tightly wound brown curls out of her eyes and wiped the sweat from her forehead with a grimy hand. The girl had been hard at work in the scorching sun. With an icy hazel stare she looked Poe and Maclemar over. The young woman sported a body sculpted from hard work and equipment taken from gymnasiums. Her orange tank top was cut before the ends reached her pierced belly button. Poe balked at bruising around her belly. *She must've pierced it recently. Ouch!* "I thought there was food rationing. They get omelets and pancakes while we make do with lumpy oatmeal for breakfast?"

Most of the food was packed away in buses and trucks in case of emergency evacuation. Sainvire, Joseph, Morales, and camp leaders decided that in order to survive, the larger group had to be divided and tucked away in places where no vampire would dare look. Four groups had been settled so far.

"Now, now, Michelle," Habib began. "These people have come a long way and suffered greatly."

"Suffered greatly?" she laughed. "They're still alive, right? The only one who I see suffering are Jorge's grieving friends. And let's face it. He's dead because of you, Public Enemy Number Two."

The pointed stare full of barbed accusation would have wilted the strongest of men.

Fortunately Poe wasn't a man but a girl who'd learned a painful lesson about torture and ready violence not so long ago. Poe pushed her plate away and stood up. "Thanks for breakfast, Habib. It's awfully nice to see you again."

"And look at the spoiled little princess, leaving half her plate full while we starve around here."

"Oi, Sharren!" Maclemar bellowed. He wiped his mouth with a disposable napkin. "How can she finish her food with you taking the piss?"

"You're the other boyfriend, aren't you?" she wrangled. Her heart-shaped lips twisted into an ugly line. "Why don't you finish off her plate and mind your own business?"

"Nice one, Sharren," he said and gripped the fork like he wanted to stab her. "It is my business if she gets harassed by a bunny boiler like you. Can't you people understand that I brought her here against her will and that I shackled her up on the railing of my ship? She was nearly done for by Revenents for chrissake. Who'd want to face hostile gibbons like you willingly?" He cleared his throat and added, "And she's nobody's woman as far as I can tell, so geroff her!"

Poe needed some fresh air and let herself out. She tuned out Maclemar's guilty rants and the girl's insults. Nearly puking, she spit out the barely chewed egg to the ground. A mother hen pecked at the food until it disappeared into her beak.

"Gross," Poe said aloud then was startled to see that various people were working not too far from where she stood. Some shucked corn, others ground different kinds of grains, and a few opened cans to see if the contents were still edible.

Torturing the balding human in the forest had done something to her, especially since Jorge ended up dying from the same type of wound. About a dozen circled a wooden table, pressing and casting bullets. Fire was roaring on the ground to melt metal. The people at the end of the table dropped garlic oil on the finished bullets.

The wry faces that greeted her with punishing silence were in no danger of harm from her fist or her guns that she'd worn openly in holsters like she was in the viperous streets of Los Angeles. She noticed that the ex-cattle also carried guns tucked in their belts and night vision goggles hung somewhere on their person at all times. Some even wore Kevlar vests in the sweltering outdoors.

At least they won't go quietly when the enemy comes for them again.

She suppressed a smile. *Karma's got me by the throat. And at least I didn't sock that obnoxious girl with thick muscles. If anyone could intimidate me, it'd be her.*

"Chickens will eat anything," said a squelchy eight-year-old. The girl with solemn eyes and dark hair looked up at her. She wore a stained Princess Mononoke shirt and equally filthy jeans cut off at the knee. Flies were having a picnic around her skinned brown knees. "Even each other."

Penny sauntered over, tail wagging, followed by a limping Chops. Many eyes were on Poe, and she knew it. *There's no way I'm going back inside with that toughie girl in there. And I'm not gonna run away.*

"I guess so," she answered. She pet Penny and inspected Chops' leg. Her wound was swollen but no infection had set in. "Chickens are like the flies buzzing around your bloody knee – not very particular. They'll take what they can get."

"I remember you."

"That's nice," Poe said. She expected an insult from the kid who'd probably been sent by a cowardly adult.

"A baby vampire had me dangling on the ceiling of that smelly tunnel, and it was going to eat me, but you shot him," she said without expression. "I fell to the ground and sprained my arm, but it's all fixed now."

Poe cleared her throat and took a deep breath before answering. She did remember a child, the first she'd encountered since the Gray Armageddon, dressed in a potato sack. "I'm glad to know that. I try not to think of the subway anymore. Not a pleasant memory."

"Yeah, it sucks," the kid agreed. She reached down to tentatively pat Penny's head. Once. "When I have bad dreams about the evacuation, I think about you, and I don't feel so scared anymore."

Poe nodded. She was unable to speak. She reached into her pack, kneeled in front of the girl, and procured globby antibacterial gel and two Band-Aids. Without asking, she cleaned the skinned knees with gel and tissue and covered them. The girl's expression remained unreadable.

"Um, I'll see you later, kid," said Poe. She couldn't take her audience of ex-cattle any longer. Their eyes were much too pregnant with judgment.

"I'm Percy," she said, nodding gravely.

"My name's Poe."

"I know," said the girl. She watched Poe walk the gauntlet of stares with brisk strides. The terrier mutt and the limping pig followed behind, loyal to the last.

———

Country air suited her after the initial sneezes that came with unfamiliar pollen and dust. The stench of garlic was tenacious but didn't register after a while. In her haste to escape the company of people, Poe followed the two-lane highway that used to be known as Pacheco Pass, overgrown with dandelions, sage, and the ever present garlic bulbs and the closely related family of shallots, lilies and onions. It was gratifying to bend down and grapple a handful of keeled green leaves to bring up bulbous gems. Their liquid potency could cause a fatal allergic reaction to most vampires.

However, she refused to walk through the fields. She believed them to be infested by snakes and strange animals. A city girl's peculiar nightmare.

"It's like *Little House on the Prairie* around here," she said to her animal companions. "I hope they don't have rattlers and such."

All the same she basked at being alone at last. Now that she'd found the companionship she'd dreamed of the past years, she seemed to have changed her mind. She wanted solitude and peace from passive-aggressive ex-cows. And from over-aggressive Michelle.

"Careful what you wish for, Poe," she chided. "Your wishes might come true. And in the future you might just say 'fuck off' to cotton candy cravings. Stick to reading, watching films, and kicking trees."

The golden colors of untended fields and farmhouses in disrepair tugged at her heartstrings like excessively saccharine nature calendars. "If they could just combine this scenic prettiness with urban concrete living, then it would be something."

Three miles of musings later, Poe's wanderings led her to Casa de Fruta, the world renowned local produce stop just off the highway. The billboards along the side of the road were a mix of history lesson and fodder for the imagination. One in particular said: *The historic intersection of California State Route 156 and 152 was once called "The Don Pacheco Y."*

Several billboards advertised tempting gastronomic allurements with images of peeling produce and train rides to ensnare the hungry.

Hollister's Own Casa de Choo Choo!

Need Casa de Bathrooms? How about Casa de Petting Zoo?

Casa de Buffalo, home of three generations of Bison.

"World Famous Cup Flipper at Casa de Fruta," read Poe, admiring the sign and unconsciously licking her lips. "What does that mean, cup flipper? Maybe I can find some food around there for Habib. That'll shut Michelle up."

The need to earn her keep and provide food for the group gripped her. It was a fantasy of one who enormously yearned for acceptance. She couldn't eat if somebody tapped his foot to check how many ounces she'd ingested already. "And I've got a terrible appetite these days," Poe said to the clouds. "Maybe running less will slow down my metabolism."

Poe cautiously inspected the grounds before going inside the dilapidated building with open walls and empty stalls crusty from calcified produce.

"What a great place. It would be even better if there was some food left," Poe grumbled after two minutes. *There really is a train here*, she grinned, noting a miniature train in the back that could seat up to twenty passengers. Wagons, carousels, and a pond filled with happy geese peppered the site. "No bison or dwarf horses," she frowned. She brightened up when she spied a sweet shop a few yards away.

"No nuts, honey, jam, dried fruit, dried anything," she complained after finding the inventory looted and disintegrated after so many years. The candy shop proved to be as barren, and she felt depressed. As Poe was stepping out, her flashlight shone to a corner where Penny was sniffing. The dog sorted through a pile of old drinking straws, and her behind swayed to and fro with animation.

"C'mon, Pen, let's go."

When the dog gave her an I'm-not-ready-yet look, Poe grew impatient. "Don't make me get a leash," she threatened. Then upon closer examination she noticed that the pile wasn't made of drinking straws at all. They were honey sticks.

"I love you, Penny dog!" Poe shouted, and rained her pet with kisses. "I love you, too, piggy!" She patted Chops' head in case she felt left out.

She doubled up a brown paper bag and threw nearly a hundred honey sticks in it. High from discovering such a goldmine and the three straws she'd sucked with greed, Poe didn't stop there. Honey wouldn't impress them as much as fresh meat.

Poe sat on a tiny tot bench and followed the fat carefree geese with her eyes. She'd killed plenty of vampires but never an animal for consumption. In fact she'd mostly avoided eating meat, canned or otherwise, since forever. Eggs were the only animal products that she ate. An incident with a can of Spam from the One Dollar Store had turned her off meat for life. The gun in her hand shook.

"I don't think I can do this," Poe told Chops who lounged by her feet beside a box of triple-action garbage bags. "I'd have to use a silencer. Wouldn't want to attract the wrong sort." *I'm a frikkin' vegetarian. What am I doing?*

Four fat geese lay dead inside heavy-duty bags. Combined they weighed more than Poe. She had placed them in a rusty shopping cart that left her palms orange. It had two wayward wheels that constantly hung right along the splintered highway road. Chops, tired from walking, napped in the child seat.

All happiness derived from finding the honey straws vanished and left her ill and miserable. Twice she vomited on the side of the road. The smell of game and blood sickened her. It was like being on Maclemar's boat again.

"I don't know what came over me," Poe told the geese jiggling like gelatin inside the bag. For the hundredth time she apologized. "I'm sorry. It's sick what I did to you, especially for a really lousy reason."

I'll never do anything like this just to fit in, she vowed silently. "I'd rather be a hated loner for the rest of my life."

Penny barked, looking up at the sky. From the corner of her eyes, Poe saw a speck quickly approaching in the horizon. Poe dabbed her eyes and blew her nose to compose herself as much as she could. In no time at all, Kaleb Sainvire floated down to the ground. The vampire had many talents that few creatures of the night ever attained in the second life. Flying was one of them. He didn't speak. He merely met her hard gaze with his curious one.

"Hello, Poe," he said. He looked solemn in black t-shirt and black Dickies. "I see you got some game for Habib. He will appreciate it. I don't think the people have had much meat in a while. You see, most refuse to eat the chickens. They're saving them for when they get a more permanent home."

"What do you want?" Poe asked frostily. She didn't appreciate his coldness a few hours ago when he looked past her like she was invisible. *He may not care about me, but a little respect wouldn't hurt. At least in front of his people.* In her mind his slight made it okay for ex-cattle to treat her like shit.

"I wanted to ask if you'll be going to the burial," he asked. His voice was pleasant but tempered. "It will begin half an hour from now."

"As much as I'd like to, I don't think so."

Sainvire didn't force the subject, and Poe assumed that the master vampire was relieved. He scratched behind Penny's ear.

"You still remember me, little Penny? You're a good girl. Goss would've been proud of you."

He looked worn, like someone sleep deprived. The stubble on his face and his twisted shoulder that showed through his shirt made him look less than a master vampire. His misshapen right shoulder, a memento from extracted shrapnel during the Spanish Civil War where he had volunteered for the Popular Front, reminded Poe of the scars she'd touched when they made love two years ago. The Chicago native was a pushover for aligning with the losing side.

Sainvire's gaze flickered and met hers. His fathomless silver eyes, holding memories that only Poe shared, disturbed her. She focused on the vertical line under his nose that met his upper lip. Many automatically assumed that the scar was a hare lip, but they were wrong. It was from tiny mortar fire shrapnel. Being an idealist had a price.

That's why I liked you, Sainvire. You're damaged like me.

"You look really good," he said with a nod. "I heard that you've been eating well and training like the devil, kicking trees every day."

"Passionada told me you had spies look in on me."

"Of course. Sister Ann and Goss would haunt me if I didn't."

"There's no such thing as ghosts. Only vampires."

He cracked a smile that disturbed Poe to the core and frowned.

Who am I kidding? I love this vampire. That's the more reason to head back home.

"I need to go home," she blurted. "I don't appreciate you having me kidnapped and roughed up. I don't want to be here. There are too many people here, and I'm not, I'm not used to them anymore," she paused, breathing deeply. "And I need to save some of my parents' things before the old neighborhood gets destroyed."

"I'm sorry, Poe, but you can't go back there," he said, patting the dog's head once more before straightening out and looming over Poe. His startling gray eyes bothered her. "I wanted you safe, and I'm sorry if it was an unpleasant trip. The dogs were an accident. Passionada couldn't control them."

"Remember *Superman 2*?"

"Vaguely," answered the vampire with a look of confusion. "What's that got to—?"

"Superman ditched Lois Lane right after the kinky lava lamps and fortress of solitude sex romps," she said while raising an eyebrow. "You never cared these past years. Why now all of a sudden?"

"Believe me, Julia," he said. "I had to fight tooth and nail not to leave the cattle we rescued to follow you to West L.A. I've never wanted to retire and be with someone so badly."

Poe's lips trembled. *It didn't take you long to find someone to replace me, did it?* "You're telling me this two years too late, Sainvire. You don't know the pain I went through retrieving Penny with vampires scouring the entire city. You left me alone!" Her dog had been recuperating in her underground bunker in Little Tokyo, a stone's throw away from vampire lairs. Poe, with all the damage to her body, had risked death to rescue Penny despite the odds against her.

"I asked you to stay with me," he said somberly. "You said no."

"You could have hog-tied me if you wanted to," she said almost inaudibly. "You'd rather be with your people, Sainvire. That's just the way you are."

Before she could say anything more, he raised a hand to stop her accusations. "Our caravans have to move every twenty days to keep Trench and Newbitt off our scent. It's damn hard on all of us, even the vampires. In the beginning four hundred of us moved together, but that took a lot of space and resources. We were ripe for conflict and disorganization, especially when the cattle could barely walk. We've divided the group to give us a fighting chance to survive. Many of us have been picked off over the months by amateur bounty hunters.

"It's a hard life, so hard that even the most loyal choose to sell us out for a permanent home and a handful of cattle," he said. His face hardened. "As you can see, our numbers have dwindled from the days of Downtown. This life isn't exactly easy. But I'd rather see you live in this environment than be tortured and killed in West L.A."

"I'm an adult and not some stuttering little girl anymore," she declared. Her nostrils flared. The tip of her nose and upper lips were beaded with sweat. "Even you can't tell me what to do. I was never a blood cow or one of your people. If I choose to live alone, then that's how it's going to be." *And do you really expect me live with you, to see you with your woman everyday?*

"Megan wants you here to see her give birth safely. If you can stay another week after that, I'll make sure you're taken home safely if I have to fly you all the way there myself. But if your home is gone, you can choose to live here with me or another safe place of your choice."

"This whole thing is about Megan's pregnancy?" she asked incredulously. Her red-haired friend used to be in love with Sainvire who happened to be her great-uncle. "Is my neighborhood really in trouble, or did you make that up?"

"They will eviscerate the Sawtelle neighborhood right up to the Los Angeles-Santa Monica city boundaries. Kawana assured me of that," he explained. Kawana was one of Trench's cops and Sainvire's loyal spy. She was black but was rescued from the drudgery of being a janitor because of her unwavering beauty. She also had the strength of a hundred men. "The fire you set created great interest, trickling up the ranks and eventually reaching the ears of Downtown players like Trench and Nesbitt.

But, yes, part of this has to do with Megan wanting you near her. She's been wracked by nightmares since conceiving. Joseph and I aren't enough protection for her. She specifically wants you to protect her child."

Poe couldn't speak. She could rant endlessly about the brutish selfishness of Megan or how easily influenced Sainvire was when it came to his last remaining kin. Despite her need to return to her childhood home, Poe felt in her gut that staying there was the right thing to do.

"I'll stay until the birth," she said. Her brown eyes challenged his gray. "After that, don't try to contact me again. I'm through with all of you."

CHAPTER 6

"I'M NOT SUCKING UP anymore," Poe told Joseph who looked as carefree as he did the last time she had seen him. He, Morales, and a half-dozen vampires returned to Gilroy with a bang, their dodgy looking police chopper landing haphazardly on the barn roof. By the time the much nicked helicopter nose-dived and spun before finally eating the ground, a gaping hole on the roof was left and debris showered those asleep below. The pilot apparently had learned his flight skills from flight simulator games. Luckily no one was seriously injured. Rufus, the fly man, was the halfdead who had eaten her left earlobe for revenge. She had ripped out his ear in a sham fight Joseph threw to gauge her fighting skills two years ago.

Joseph sat in the kitchen snapping green beans in halves. His ponytail was immaculate. Who would have thought he was a vampire? Morales, always dressed for a date, lounged on the seat across from him and peeled shells off of boiled eggs. The smoldering ex-real estate agent with bow legs and solid upper body strength listened to Poe with rapt attention.

"Whatever I bring, be it game or firewood, everyone harrumphs and gives me the evil eye. They think I owe them meat and work for getting Jorge killed."

"They're afraid of you," Joseph shrugged. His chiseled face looked neutral. "You were never cattle. And some vamps in this camp still haven't forgotten that you killed their friends in a fit of rage. I mean, you even shot me in the balls!"

Poe reddened. She remembered the day she had mixed up an address and ended up going to the shady side of Downtown Los Angeles warehouses where ancient undead anted up humans for poker. She had shot up Sainvire and Joseph and killed five good vamps when she saw them again.

"And for someone as puny as you, you sure kicked some vampire butt and not to mention rescued a changeful of ex-cattle," added Morales, as handsome and charming as ever. "That's humiliating to some."

"I saved your hide a couple times, Morales. Do you hate me?"

"Nope. I love you!" he said. He kissed his fingers as if admiring a gourmet meal. "I've always said so, and I always will."

"You still have that cheesy Vegas tongue of yours, I see," said Poe. "But you know, you'd have a fighting chance if it weren't for your grody cologne." She waved at the air under her nose. "As it is, I can only be in your company ten minutes or else I'll get a migraine. So anyway, I better be off on my run. Oh, Joseph. If your woman pees, send Sainvire to pluck me quick and deposit me to her bedside."

"Will do, sis," Joseph grinned. "And correction. It's not pee, but 'break water.' Amniotic fluid to be exact."

"Whatever," Poe said and headed outside. She detested sounding ignorant, but she'd relied on movies, comic books, and music for education.

It had been four days since she'd had a talk with Sainvire. If it weren't for Joseph and Morales coming back, she would have gone batty. A very plump Megan had given her some nice Adidas sweats and encouraged her to go running. And she was ever so glad to listen to her friend.

Poe tried to phase out people in general when she was about the grounds. She focused on her own breathing and the condition of Penny who always seemed to tail her once she left the farmhouse where dogs were barred. It was easier that way. She followed the highway then looped back after a couple of miles. For a finale she lashed out at a stumpy oak tree across the road from the farmhouse and used it as a kicking bag.

No matter how her running schedule varied, she always encountered Michelle running in the opposite direction, tank top and short shorts showing off her unmarred, densely muscled body. That day was no different. The girl with the curlicue hair and navel piercing squinted her hazel eyes at Poe.

"That girl keeps dogging me," Poe gritted, and she refocused her energy on abusing the tree with her shins and forearms. She and her dog were joined by Chops who still limped. The pig would undoubtedly have followed Poe's jogging route had she been a hundred percent.

She'd see Michelle sparring with a sixty-year-old ex-boxer in the morning and practicing judo with a few former cattle in the afternoon. *No wonder she acts so tough. People who take a martial arts course or two suddenly believe they're ready to kick Jet Li's butt.*

"I've seen the judo club doing Tae Bo in the barn," Poe said under her breath and shook her head. "How embarrassing is that, Penny? Billy Blanks as a fitness guru? Sounds like a porn star name to me."

On the way back to the farmhouse, Poe came upon a familiar figure she hadn't seen since arriving in garlic land.

"Hey, Maple!" Poe waved and jogged to the middle-aged vampire standing with a bowl of porridge in her hand. "I've been looking for you, but nobody seemed to know where you were. Or at least they didn't want to tell me."

"Hello, Poe," Maple smiled. "Sorry about that. I've been busy this past week."

"No problem," Poe said. She wiped the sweat off her nose with a sleeve. She had overactive sweat glands on the very tip of the proboscis. "Yeah, I sort of wanted to see a familiar face, I guess. I was meaning to ask you about Perla, too. I know she's busy being a scientist and all. I've been wondering since I got here if she still wears pajamas seven days a week."

Maple kept up her smile, but her composure was tight at best. "Ah well. If you'd like to see her, you can follow me to that Winnebago over there." Half a dozen RVs could be seen parked about the farm grounds.

"Perla hasn't been herself, Poe. You can only stay for a minute."

"Sure. I just wanna say hello," Poe said nervously without knowing why. The plump scientist was one Sainvire's invaluable knights. She was a grand woman who had treated Poe with kindness during her stay at the Los Angeles Central Library where Plasmacore had been researched and produced.

She ascended the set of stairs that led to a door. With a catch in her throat, the girl turned the knob and entered. Softly tinted floral wallpaper decked the narrow interior. In the corner opposite the lace curtained window was a couch where her old friend sat.

"Hello, Perla," Poe greeted, walking toward the woman wearing Mr. Potato Head pajamas. "I see you're still wearing neat PJs."

The Mexican American scientist with meticulously brushed hair did not stir. Vacant eyes looked out the window. No smile touched her normally energetic face. For the longest time Poe stared at her.

"M-Maple? What—" stammered Poe.

"She was bitten six months ago during a raid," Maple explained calmly. "She's become cattle."

"I'm sorry," apologized Poe. Her usually steady hands trembled. Overcome by melancholy as clinging as fly paper, she began to cry. Silently. However hard she tried Poe could not stop herself.

"It's alright, Poe," said Maple whose brow was lined with worry. "We'll have her back by early next year."

Instead of consoling Maple, Poe needed cheering up of her own. The lover and tender nurse to Perla gave Poe a reassuring hug that made the girl cry harder. Perhaps it was the pressure of the past week, but she simply couldn't stop herself.

"I'm s-sorry, M-Maple," Poe managed to say. "I d-don't want to upset her, so I'll just go." With one last forlorn hug, the girl left the Winnebago.

She hadn't taken five steps when Maclemar crossed her path.

"What's wrong, Poe?"

"N-nuthin! Outta my way!" she said, embarrassed by her irrepressible crying.

"Did anyone do anything to you?" he asked. His green eyes looked stormy.

"L-leave me alone, Maclemar," Poe cried, and she pushed him away from her. She saw faces turn their way, agitating her further. "I swear I'll d-drop you if you don't shove off."

Maclemar, who'd been keeping busy servicing cars, trucks, and buses the past week, rested his grimy hand on her arm in concern. He was like an annoying pest asking a crying kid what was wrong. Of course constant egging would make a kid bawl louder and longer. That was the last straw for Poe who didn't like being the center of attraction for ex-cattle with mouths agape.

"I said leave me the fuck be!" she shouted clearly without a stutter. Anger seemed to keep her articulate. A quick sweep of her right leg under Maclemar's much longer ones and a shove to the chest left him sprawled on his back. In a wink the muscular fisherman was on the floor staring incredulously into Poe's callused fist itching to strike his face.

"I'm sorry, but you just won't let me be!" she said. She was already wracked by guilt as she ran toward the farmhouse. She sped past a blur of faces and heard a buzzing of voices. It wasn't until she passed a sneering Michelle and her judo partners that Poe's mind cleared.

The girl wearing a snug tank top ignited Poe's already incendiary mood.

"What the fuck did you just say?" asked Poe. She wiped her snot with the sleeve of her jacket. She was glad her stutter had called it quits. Sounding tough with a stammer wouldn't have been very effective.

"What a mouth. What a mouth. I said," Michelle taunted, "some tough chick vampire hunter you turned out to be. One look at cattle and there you go. Snotfest."

Poe's nostrils flared, and her fist was keen to connect with the girl's petty jaw. *Remember the guy you disemboweled? No revenge fights, please. Karma never forgets,* said the officious voice in her mind. However hard it was to turn her back and swallow the elephant that used to be her pride, Poe walked away.

"And some of you still say she can save us," Michelle scoffed, fiercely proud of her audacity for stumping the legendary Julia Poe. Her normally pleasant lips were now a twitching line. Unlike most freed cattle after the mass rescue, Michelle had worked on strengthening her body and mind by learning about self-defense with dogmatic single-mindedness. She refused to be intimidated ever again. If she appeared thuggish, the attitude was born out of defiance. "I say we can save ourselves! We shouldn't look to vampires and their sluts to get us out of this rut."

The hell with karma! I'm going to kill that smug bitch. Pivoting around, she approached the bodacious curly-haired jerk who had been yanking her chain.

"Michelle, right?" Poe asked with barely contained energy. "Let me tell you a fact about me. I saved you and your friends. And you know what? It was a fucking thankless gesture, and I nearly broke my back for it. Dangerous work for a kick in the ass. I don't intend to put my life on the line again."

She glared at Michelle, dressed in an outfit as provocative as a cheerleader's, and raised a perfectly arched eyebrow. "Nope. First sign of invasion, me and my animals are outta here with a 'see you later, suckas' sign glued on the back of my Death to the Pixies shirt." She always packed at least two of her favorite t-shirts in case of emergency. Leisurely she looked at the crowd that had gathered expecting entertainment. Besides living in fear of being retaken, most survivors hated living in constant boredom. Repetition reminded them too much of their days as vampire food.

If they want a show, I'll give them a pay-per-view worthy spectacle. Girl-on-girl action. We'll duke it out to see who's the baddest chick in the roost.

"As for your insinuation that I'm Sainvire's slut, I could snap your head for that."

Maclemar's tense face towered over the crowd. For an instant Poe lost her train of thought. She'd glimpsed a very pregnant Megan standing by the second floor window of the farmhouse. Joseph and Morales flanked her spherical form with beatific expressions. Jenna, the beautiful vampire with pixie hair, stood not a few feet away.

"Beat the crap out of her and get it over with," Megan told her more than once.

"Just try to snap my head, why don't you. I'm no tree to just take your kicks without retaliation. You're not the only toughie in these parts," Michelle dared. She took Poe's silence as a cue for her to say something ironic.

"Oh don't worry. I will," Poe said, and she smiled for the first time. "'If they can make penicillin out of moldy bread, they can sure make something out of you,'" she said with a pretty fair Kentuckian accent, eliciting some befuddled noises from the crowd. Her naturally throaty voice lent credence to the quote.

"What the hell did you just say?" Michelle asked. She was as confused as those in the crowd, and she turned to her silver-haired boxing coach. "Is she comparing me to mold?"

The man named Ted who acted as her mentor shrugged his shoulders, and his rosacea-prone face looked hot. "Dunno, but it sure sounds familiar."

Suddenly all worries and insecurities left Poe. A genuine chuckle escaped from her throat. Her tears had dried in the heat, and Poe did not particularly care about offending the crowd that had treated her with incivility ever since she had arrived. With the Champ on her side, she couldn't help but feel elated.

"'Only the nose knows, where the nose goes, when the door close'. Now, where was I? Ah yes, the slut question."

A little cruddy girl that pushed her way to the front waved at her. It was Percy, her one fan. Poe winked at the girl. "I'm nobody's slut," she said with intent. She looked briefly at Jenna who stood out in the crowd of wobbly-kneed ex-cattle still recuperating from years of forced bed rest.

She spotted Sainvire, elbows resting on both knees, hunched on the scallop roofing of the farmhouse. She wondered how long he'd been sitting there. Apparently he wanted a box seat to the spectacle of the week. *If it's entertainment you want, vampire, then sit tight.*

She removed her damp hooded jacket and handed it to Percy, who looked mighty pleased to be singled out. Arms crisscrossed, Poe grabbed the ends of her Clash t-shirt and pulled it up, exposing her unmarred belly, tight from years of hard training. Her lean and nicely muscled body usually hidden by outsized clothing was presented to over seventy-strong observers. Many a fly could have darted in and out of the mouths in the crowd that had slacked open at seeing the full cleavage of her black sports bra.

"Psyche!" Poe sniggered. She tugged her shirt down and ended her brief career as a stripper. "Michelle, that's what I call slutty!"

It was a cheap shot, but even some hard asses cracked tightwad smiles.

"Oh please. Let's get this on already," cried Michelle, gesturing with her hands.

Without the jacket, Poe's strong arms revealed myriad scars. Her damaged face scratched by a vampire nail when she was eight and a missing earlobe made it obvious to onlookers that the girl had fought the fight.

Poe tightened her ponytail and began dancing with fancy Muhammad Ali footwork, shadow boxing a confused Michelle. "'Float like a butterfly. Sting like a bee. Your hands can't hit what your eyes can't see.'"

"That's it," Ted the coach said. He clapped his hands together. "She's been reciting Cassius Clay stuff."

"Who?" asked Michelle. Her eyes were wide from the pageantry.

"Muhammad Ali, the boxer!" the old man explained, tsk-tsking the girl for not knowing about the legendary fighter and poet.

"He's only the best boxer that ever lived," piped in Maclemar in his strange accent that was growing on Poe, "and possibly the most charming athlete there ever was."

"Don't forget the bravest," added a distinguished black man named John who used to dabble as a San Francisco lawyer when the world was normal. The man did his share of work around the camp with aplomb. He was gracious but meager with words. "Mr. Ali defied the draft board in the 1960s. The great man said, 'I ain't got no quarrel with them Viet Cong. No Viet Cong ever called me nigger!'"

The quote stung the spectators into silence with its reference to Vietnam and the ever present topic of discrimination carried on by the ruling vampires. Many blacks in Downtown L.A., San Francisco, and other cities toiled as custodians or incinerators of dead cattle. Vampires considered their blood suspect and lower grade. John Danby had never been cattle, but he had mopped floors, cooked, and incinerated people for nearly a decade at the bidding of the empowered blood class.

The prickly quiet was sapping her strength, so Poe ended it. This was her moment after all.

"Now, girl, put 'em up. I'll beat you so bad you'll need a shoehorn to put your hat on."

John Danby crossed his arms and shook his head at Poe who still kept on with Muhammadian grace. The lines on his face crinkled, and he laughed. The other old timers laughed with him and eventually infected even the youngest of the crowd.

"Can you believe it?" he said after the noise had died down. "A girl this young quoting Ali?"

"He's my hero, mister," said Poe as an aside.

"Mine, too. Mine, too," Danby agreed. "Now are we going to see a fight or what?"

Voices echoed his sentiment.

"Hurry up. I've got duck to roast," complained Habib, wearing an immaculate white apron.

"Michelle, if you even dream of beating me, you'd better wake up and apologize," paraphrased Poe, her voice deep. "I'm not the greatest; I'm the double-greatest. Not only do I knock 'em out, I pick the round."

The girl with technically sculpted abs looked bewildered. The desire to wrest the championship belt away from Poe had dissipated somehow. The scarred vampire hunter was a comedian whose jokes Michelle didn't understand, and she had expertly brought the crowd on her side with laughter. Michelle stood unsure about what to do. Poe was the real thing judging by the fancy moves. A killer.

"Whatsumatter?" Poe asked. Ali danced around her with impressive foot speed and threw fake jabs at her face. "Scared?"

Michelle frowned deeper. She still had her pride. Too many people were watching the drama for her to nod in the affirmative. Every human and daywalker suddenly seemed to be around.

"Silence is golden when you can't think of a good answer," Poe said. "Hit me," she ordered, "and don't just use one hand!"

Michelle jabbed left which Poe easily avoided by taking one step back. The reddening girl tried again, and this time she swung with a right hook.

"And it was an air ball, ladies and gentlemen," Poe said, taunting Michelle to pound punches which Poe artfully dodged. Her neck extended back to avoid a punch, and a quick duck followed by a side swipe confounded Michelle.

Angry now, Michelle showered her with close calls blocked by forearms laced with calluses from banging them against bamboo and bricks. Poe could see that contact with her elbow and forearm hurt Michelle's ungloved fists and decided to cool it off.

"And that's why Superman don't need no seat belt." Poe danced backwards. "Hey, you wanna know something, Michelle?"

"What?" the girl said. She was breathing hard.

"Since you've been such a sport, I'll let you know a trade secret." Poe pointed her index finger at the martial arts club.

"I'm listening."

Deliberately dropping her Ali accent, Poe answered in a serious voice, "I gotta let you know this, Michelle. You're a decent boxer, but you need to keep your chin down with one fist protecting the face at all times. "And most importantly, you gotta stop looking your opponent in the eye. It's distracting and a major handicap. Look at the neck. The muscle there will tell you which side the next punch will come from. Look at my collarbone. See the subtle movements when I jab? That's how I was able to guess which fist you were going to use and get safely out of the way."

Michelle nodded slowly, listening. Her coach nearby pulled his Colonel Sanders beard in contemplation and whistled. Apparently he hadn't known of the simple trick, either.

"You're a natural athlete with a seditious body. I'd be jealous if I thought about it too much," Poe grinned. "I've been watching you. You're pretty good at judo. But let me tell you something, and this is very important. Judo will kill you and your tag team buddies over there." She waved at the six men and two women looking wilted.

"It's pretty hard to slam and trip an undead on the pavement no matter how powerful you are. Who's to say they'll stay down? And believe me, you don't want to get that close."

If the curly-haired girl was offended, she didn't show it. Michelle was paying attention, and Poe was encouraged. "I gotta say judo isn't as useless as capoeira. The guy who ate my earlobe cartwheeled himself right into my extended foot."

"Hey, don't make me sound too ridiculous," yelled the culprit, Rufus, the chopper pilot who nearly destroyed the barn with his bad landing.

Poe gave Rufus a guilty, dimpled smile and shrugged.

She had no problem with capoeira as a form of expression. But as a form of in-the-trenches martial arts, she'd have to put her foot down. "If you want to last, you need to harden your body not just with muscles. It's not pretty, but you need to start developing calluses. So when they hit you, you won't be distracted by pain. And it's best to use the legs. They're farther away from the reach of a stronger opponent."

Poe showed Michelle how to block a punch and kicks with the knee folded close to the body, Thai-style.

"Like I said, always keep a fist against your chin for protection. It's a perfect time to land a punch after blocking someone's kick, so have the other fist ready at all times," Poe explained.

One by one the spectators left to their tasks, bored by demonstrations that replaced the promised fight between two attractive young women. Even Megan and her men had left the window long ago.

"This is no fight," said a sour-faced geezer.

"Yeah, this sucks balls," another complained.

"Where's the violence?" a man with a cane said aloud, prompting Danby to answer, "You've lived it for over ten years, Matt."

Only Percy, Danby, the judo team, and Maclemar remained to learn some basic street fighting skills from Poe.

One other watched from the roof. His silver eyes followed every move Poe made with fierce pride. He didn't know right below him Jenna scrutinized his face.

———

Only tolerated and ignored before, Poe moved among the camp and received tepid nods at best.

Better than nothing.

Devoting two hours a day to training the judo and boxing club reduced her listlessness. Megan, as big as a house, had yet to birth her child. According to Miriam, the octogenarian midwife who had hands and limbs as brittle as a bird's, childbirth would have to be induced soon.

"Four days overdue in this heat," Poe muttered as she left Maple's Winnebago. She dropped off a basket of apples for Perla that she'd picked from a neighboring farm. The past few days had seen an exodus of buses full of vampires and humans leaving for their new homestead. Those left behind sweaty in the heat looked listless and fearful.

You'd do anything to avoid going inside, wouldn't you? the voice in her head mocked.

The camp had begun to disassemble, and a pall had fallen among those left behind. It was a breezeless, hellion of a day. The dregs who hadn't left with the respective shuttle buses to their new destination escaped to the coolness of the barn or the water hole half a mile south of the farm. Like garlic broiled in an oven, the smell assailed the nostrils and left an indelible stench on everyone's sweaty clothing and skin. The cracked highways produced a winding mirage of gasoline-infused images that played with the mind's eye.

"It's so hot, hell's knocking on the soles of my feet," complained Maclemar. He was half-hidden as he read a paperback copy of *Fahrenheit 451* under the droopy arms of a willow tree that stood in the middle of the farm. "How's your friend, luv?"

The sight of the Welshman put a smile on Poe's lips.

"Good. They're both fine," she said and tossed an apple his way. "Picked some apples for Perla in the orchard next door for their trip. Haven't climbed a tree since I was a kid." She was shadowed by Penny and Chops who rested their rumps under the tree. "Trying to squirm out of working?"

"No, Sharren. This little quiet moment is reward for completing the look-over of the vehicles, including your friend's Winnebago. They might leave tonight. Hence the black nails." He held up his sooty fingers for Poe's inspection.

"Eesh! That's nasty stuff there, Maclemar."

"Next to Habib, I believe I was the only one who did not shirk from duty this day," he said, patting the cool spot on the ground next to him.

"Who can work in this heat but crazy people? And what the heck does Sharren mean?"

Maclemar smiled, and slightly crooked teeth showed. Her mom did say that perfect teeth were a complete turnoff. Porcelain smiles of beauty pageant contestants irked her like nothing else. The Welshman's teeth were pleasant enough. The chance unevenness added character to his smile.

"Sharren means a woman who thinks she's tough," he answered with a roguish glint in his eyes then quickly took a bite of his apple. He'd no intention of offending the girl and curtailing the pleasant moment.

"Huh. That's interesting," Poe said and squinted with distrust. Since she didn't want to spoil the nice day by being catty, she took a huge bite of her apple. "What's the male equivalent then?" she asked after she'd swallowed the mush in her mouth.

"Darren, if you must know."

"Well I don't know how that word translates in Japanese, Tagalog, or Spanish, but I can teach you the word, 'gago.'"

"Gago. What's that?"

"It means stupid man in Tagalog. Gaga is the female equivalent."

"Nice one."

"I think so. One of my all time favorite words."

They finished off their apples in silent companionship. Poe couldn't help notice how long his legs were in comparison with hers.

Maclemar could really pound somebody if he wanted to with those big fists and that intimidating torso. At least what I saw of his half-naked body on the boat. If we live through this, I'd like to train him. If he'd let me.

"Watch me litter," Poe said. She threw the core a few feet from where they sat. She didn't feel so bad because most had gone indoors to avoid the heavy pelting of the sun.

"The pod people will boil you alive for that."

"My meat's tough and wiry. It's only good for soup stock," she said, studying his dark face sprouting new bristles. His skin was almost completely the same shade now. "I've been thinking, Maclemar. You could've just dropped me off at the cove. You didn't have to come here."

"No, I didn't," he answered after a lengthy pause. His green eyes bore down into her own.

"Why?"

He combed his dirty fingers through his buzz cut and shrugged. "I nearly got you killed by chaining you like a criminal on my boat. The Revs could've made Christmas pudding out of you."

His answer disappointed her, and she didn't know why.

"That's water under the bridge," Poe said, proud of her idiom. Both her grandpas used to recite them like mad.

"And to be completely truthful at the risk of raising your ire," he continued. "I wanted to get into your pants."

The wide grin on his face cooled the blood that rushed to her cheeks. She laughed it off, punching his arm in the spirit of a light and cozy afternoon.

"You've been had then, mister," Poe said. She wiped the perspiration on the tip of her nose. "There's nothing special in my pants. You'd get a better deal wooing someone like Michelle who has interesting body piercings."

"Nah. I think I'll wait until you come round."

Poe sighed in admission to herself that she liked Maclemar a lot. She tried to strike the emotion, but he had grown on her. *I can't see myself stuck in a camp like this all my life. But I can see myself on his boat, possibly happy. Except for the seasickness part.*

"Don't count on me too much, Maclemar. I could break your heart."

"You already have, Poe," he said with a grin. "I know I can't compete with a master vampire with a conscience to rival Mahatma Gandhi's, but I'll take what I can."

Without thinking, she pulled his head down for a kiss, surprising both herself and the fisherman. She had forgotten how tongue could be so moist and delicious. Sainvire's kiss, though wondrous, had been arctic compared to Maclemar's.

She tasted apples in his mouth.

The sinewy feel of his arms made her shiver. When his hands explored her back, shoulder, and waist, Poe nearly forgot that she was in the middle of the grounds where anyone passing their way could see their frenzied embrace. Without knowing exactly how she ended up on his lap, straddling his arousal, Poe panicked. *Stop! Don't give him false hope. He's too nice a guy for that!*

"No more," she entreated huskily. She pulled away. "I'm sorry, but I must be starved for physical contact. I don't want to use you."

"Please do," he said. His eyelids were heavy. "Luv, I'm here for you 24/7."

"I know that," said Poe. She stood up, and she was visibly shaken. "I'm not sure what's going on with me. I just can't see myself staying with them. I don't belong here. I'm leaving after Megan gives birth and is safely transported out of here. Maybe you can to take me back to Santa Monica to retrieve some of my parents' things. Then we'll see where this goes."

"Beauty, I'll take you wherever you want to go. And no, I don't expect you to forget about him. I'm very patient. One of my best traits." He pulled her down to the spot next to him. "I won't take advantage if it's going to push you away."

"Um, I think I was the one taking advantage, mister," said Poe. She pulled on the abbreviated flap of her damaged ear. Sometimes she could swear she felt the missing nub throbbing.

Maclemar sighed and leaned against the tree. His hand rubbed his tummy. "Ah, lassie, what can I say? Women just can't take their hands off of me."

Poe chuckled. "What can I say? You're not a bad looking man."

"Ah, music to my ears," he said, sitting Poe back on his lap. "I won't take advantage this time." She swatted his hand away when he pulled the rubber band holding her ponytail together. Too late. Her black hair cascaded just below her shoulder blades.

"Hey, stop that!" Poe complained. She attempted to retake the band from an exuberant Maclemar. She would never have believed Caveman had evolved into such a charming man.

"Nope. Not yet. Just wanted to see what you look like with your hair down.

Poe looked at him and made a face. "Satisfied now?"

Maclemar laughed deeply and captured Poe's face in his hands. "May I kiss you again because you're so damn gorgeous?"

"I don't know," Poe grumbled. She scratched her nose. "What do you think?"

He brought her face close to his and kissed Poe's plump sensuous lips. It was a deep and extended kiss that left both panting in the afternoon heat. When their lips parted, Poe's eyes met Maclemar's green gaze. "Mac—I mean James, I'd like to—" Before she could finish her thought, a thought that would have made the Welshman immensely happy, she noticed movement in the corner of her eye. She turned in time to see Sainvire and Jenna walking by. The vampire's gray eyes swept hers then quickly looked away.

Poe squared her shoulders and turned back to look at Maclemar. "As I was saying, would you like to take me to your trailer right now?"

163

"Are you asking me because of those two?" he asked and stared at the backs of Sainvire and Jenna who'd just reached the homestead.

Poe twisted Maclemar's ear in annoyance. "Listen. I was going to ask you before we saw the lovebirds. If you don't want to do it then fine!"

Maclemar hooked his arm under her knees and lifted her up in his arms. "Believe me, Julia. I want to do it and more with you."

He carried her light form to a small four-person trailer parked under a tree and kicked open the door. The air was cloyingly hot as he set Poe down on a small bed. He turned on the lights and the small fan by the headboard.

"Shouldn't you turn off the lights?" asked Poe uncertainly. She had suddenly become nervous.

"No ma'am. I want to see you Botticelli-style," he said. He removed his shirt followed by his jeans and underwear. He stood there sweaty, tanned, and so like a Greek statue that Poe couldn't look away. His erection frightened her. "Now it's your turn."

With a deep breath for courage, Poe shed her clothing slowly, not to titillate but because she suddenly felt shy. "Do you know how beautiful you are?" he said as he joined her, caressing her hips, raining slow kisses on her neck and myriad bruises. "You taste so good, and you smell even better."

"Irish Spring," Poe offered. "Maybe a hint of garlic."

"You're practically bald, you know that?" he said as he drank in her sex and her limbs. She mumbled, "Must be my Asian genes." His hand spanned her flat abdomen, and his fingers dipped lower. Poe put a stop to that. "James, your hands are filthy. There's no way you're touching my whatchamacallit."

"Fair enough," he said. He captured a nipple with his mouth and filled his hand the opposite breast until the girl was moaning her approval. His tongue licked the valley between her ribs down to her firm stomach. Poe tensed, anticipating his next move. She remembered Sainvire doing the same thing to her.

"James?"

"Um hmm?"

"Could you just skip the foreplay? It's really hot in here, and I'm ready for you."

Maclemar looked up from where he had barely begun toying with her clitoris with his tongue and growled. "Woman, one of these days when my nails are clean, you're going to let me do what I want with you." He cracked his neck and hovered above her. His triceps bulged. Poe reached for his throbbing organ, thick with veins, and put her hand around it. "Ah, Sharren," he said.

She could smell his sweat and inhale his musk. Sainvire or no, she wanted Maclemar. She let go of his manhood and explored the hardness of his ass. "Um, you can put it in my mouth if you want. Hover it over me."

Shocked, Maclemar asked, "Did you do this for Sainvire?"

"No. I've seen it in films," she said. "And don't mention Sainvire to me again. This is between you and me." At that the Welshman groaned and floated his erection above her face until she led his throbbing organ into her mouth. Cautiously he dipped deeper into her lips which closed tightly. The young woman sucked and pulled like it was the only Popsicle left in the world. He tasted salty. When he couldn't take it anymore, he pulled out of her mouth and parted her legs. "I'm gonna come if you don't quit that," he said breathlessly, kissing her mouth until both could breathe no more. "I, too, want to give you pleasure, my love." With one swift move he entered her slick opening.

The moans that escaped from Poe's throat as he thrust into her were music to his ears. "Fuck," he grunted, startling Poe.

"Am I doing something wrong?" she asked.

"No, beauty, I'm just about to have a heart attack. You're so tight that I'm dying."

Poe met his hips, clamping her mouth down because of the racket she was making.

"It's alright, luv. You can make as much noise as you want. Everyone's at the watering hole." He wanted to please her more than he'd pleased any other woman in his life, so when a knock interrupted their lovemaking, he cursed. "Go away," he said harshly, but the knocking continued.

"It must be important," said Poe. She pushed the angry Welshman who refused to disengage from her. "Go see what they want." To Maclemar Poe had never looked so beautiful. Her black hair, billowing about her and framing her large eyes and much kissed lips, made his heart skip a beat. He punched the bed and reluctantly pulled out between her legs.

Maclemar stepped into his boxers and jeans then looked over his shoulder. Poe was safely hidden under the sheet. He opened the door only to see the master vampire himself leaning against the door frame.

"Sainvire," Maclemar said with disgust. "Of course it had to be you."

"Sorry to interrupt," Sainvire began. His voice was calm, too calm for the awkward moment. "But I need to talk to Poe for a minute."

"You expect me to leave this trailer, do you?"

"Yes, I do," said Sainvire. He met the Welshman's dark gaze.

Not wanting to be alone with the master vampire in near nakedness, Poe quickly said, "Um, whatever you need to say to me, you can say in front of Maclemar here."

"No need, luv. I'm not the jealous type. I'll wait outside," said Maclemar. He let the vampire enter. He shut the door behind him and walked outside barefoot to join the patient Penny and Chops sitting dutifully under a redwood tree.

Poe peeked out from under the blanket. "What is it?"

Sainvire, seeming to compose himself, bore his gray eyes into hers. She wished Maclemar had turned off the lights. "They're having problems inducing the birth. Megan will need to have a Caesarean soon or her life and the child's will be compromised."

"What can I do?" Poe asked. She sat up quickly and forgot about her nakedness. Sainvire caught an eyeful of perky breasts before she could cover herself once more. It dawned on her, despite the gravity of the situation, that Sainvire had seen her nude before. No time to be shy. She flung the sheets away and reached for her clothes. Before Sainvire she dressed herself. She could feel the vampire's eyes following her every movement.

Do you still desire me, Kaleb?

Sainvire stood motionless in the sweltering trailer, but his sharp eyes never missed an inch of skin, curvature of the neck and thighs, or toss of hair that drove him to hunger. At that moment he despised Maclemar for having what he couldn't.

"Okay, so what now?" asked Poe, breathless. She could barely contain her lust for him. *Two beautiful men in the span of twenty minutes? What a slut.*

"The hospitals within a thirty-mile radius have been ransacked many times by our people. The supplies the midwife needs are depleted. Three of us will go north to San Jose to borrow medical provisions. The hospital we're targeting lies in Peter Newbitt's jurisdiction. There might be some trouble, and we'll need a sure-shot like you on the team." The vampire spoke while his predatory eyes watched Poe carefully. Her long black hair and tousled appearance drove him to ball his fist.

"When are we leaving?" Poe asked. She draped her black bra on and hooked it from behind. There was a time when Poe didn't even consider wearing such luxuries because no one had told her to. Sainvire remembered the days all too well.

"Right away. You may want to know that this is a night job. We need to operate on Megan as soon as possible. We'll need anesthetics most of all." His eyes drew together in anger. The girl was standing in front of him in her underwear like a goddess. She'd just coupled with Maclemar, a warm-blooded man of decent character. Sainvire could smell their scent in the heat of the room. He had never felt such jealousy in his long life as a man and vampire.

Poe pulled on her dark shirt and stepped into her olive green pants. Sainvire watched her double-knot her Adidas. "Let me get my gear," she said. She walked briskly past him and let herself out of the oppressive trailer.

More than half the camp had been deployed to their new locations. The 400 had been split to ensure a better rate of survival. Sainvire quartered the 175 remaining survivors and ordered them to stand ready for deployment. Mechanics worked around the clock on buses and RVs. They gave each vehicle the Mad Max treatment by applying gratings and metal sidings coated with garlic oil to deflect bullets and hungry vamps. The allies understood that the destinations would be kept secret from each group in case of capture. No one could give up vital information under duress or torture.

Buses and trucks stuffed with bug-eyed passengers traveling alongside barnyard animals that could fit through the door evacuated when Joseph and Morales deemed it safe. Moving had never been easy for both ex-cattle and vampire escorts, and the last trip was no exception.

Roughly thirty-five warm-blooded people and ten vampires, those willing to wait for Megan to have her child, were still in Gilroy. To Poe's surprise Michelle and her club members were the first to volunteer to be among the last. Many others stayed because they could only feel safe with Sainvire and Joseph, who represented tangible power and fealty to human plight.

The mood in the desolate camp was of high-strung fretfulness, as if they expected to be the fattened veal sacrifice for the new head honcho. Men and women carried their duffel bags and luggage with them at all times, and some had corralled their animals in case of a quick exit. A monster was coming. It was in the air. It was in their arthritic bones.

Megan was ensconced in the sick room. She was ashen and pinched by the infant that refused to leave her body.

"If Miriam doesn't perform a C-section, Megan will lose her life and her baby," Morales whispered outside the makeshift birthing room. His face had taken its toll from many a wakeful night anticipating the birth that refused to happen. "The trouble is the midwife has never performed one in her life."

"She'll do fine. We'll get the supplies. No problem," said Poe.

"Yeah. We'll be back in a jiffy," said Michelle who was wearing fatigues.

The team consisted of Sainvire, Poe, and Michelle.

Jenna, who had never once spoken to Poe, turned to Sainvire. "Why can't I come? I would be better at this than these two regulars," she said in an offended voice. She looked at Poe. "And I don't mean any disrespect by that, ladies."

"None taken," mumbled Poe.

Sainvire steered her away from the group and draped an arm around her shoulder. "I told you, Jenna. I never leave my people without a strong vampire to look after things when I'm away."

"There's Joseph," she said, and she gazed at Poe once again.

"Joseph will be with Megan. Listen. Just please do this for me," implored the master vampire with his hypnotic gray eyes until she nodded her assent. "Sometimes," Jenna said, "It feels like you're using me. I'm a master vampire, too, if you remember." Sainvire cradled her face and gave her a brief kiss.

Poe, who'd been watching the exchange between the two striking vampires, felt ill from unrequited passion. Hard as she tried to forget him, Sainvire still weighed heavily in her heart.

"Joseph and I appreciate your help, guys," said Morales to Poe and Michelle. His voice cracked. "He's in there with her now. Won't leave her side."

Poe got on tiptoes, kissed Morales on the cheek, and gave him the warmest hug she could muster. "It'll be okay, dear friend," she whispered in his ear.

"Let's go," said Sainvire who stood behind Morales. He placed a hand on the man's shoulder and said, "All will be well, my friend."

Michelle took the helm of a black Mini Cooper that proved too small for the three of them. Poe was surprised that Sainvire's legs fit inside the vehicle at all. The compact car, serviced by Maclemar, was the perfect size to zigzag through the stranded cars on the Pacheco Pass and onto the crowded 101 Freeway to San Jose. The confident young woman drove with ease even when the sky turned dark and she had to don night vision goggles.

Sainvire sat in the passenger seat and was monosyllabic to say the least. He only spoke when a direct question was asked. Michelle shrugged and began interrogating Poe.

"So you hid out all those years since you were eight?"

"Yeah. Until I discovered an underground bomb shelter. Then I lived there until a couple years ago."

"Were you shitting your pants?"

"All the frikkin' time," said Poe. "I used to stutter, too. I was a mess. Scrounging for food was the scariest. But hey, being cattle is no picnic, either."

"Nope," Michelle agreed, bobbing her curly hair. "Being drugged-out was horrible. I was aware of leeches up on me, but I couldn't snap out of the fog to defend myself. It was like I was being held underwater. Thank God I never got pregnant. I don't think I could get over that."

The conversation ended. Something crunchy slammed into the tiny car and cracked the windshield.

"What was that?" asked Poe. She massaged her forehead after hitting the back of Michelle's seat. Jolted, she put on her seatbelt after the fact. She prayed that it wasn't another half-starved country vamp.

"Keep driving, Michelle," said Sainvire. "It was a Revenent who won't be getting up anytime soon."

"Revs? That's bad news."

"It's the third I've seen," said the vampire.

"That means Trench is close, doesn't it?"

"Yes," was all Sainvire said. He calmly laced his fingers together. The enemy commonly dumped Revenents as a tactic to clear the way in advance of a main assault.

Poe adjusted her goggles and shivered.

"I hate those things," Poe said.

"Never got too close myself, but they're creepy fuckers alright," said Michelle. "You've had dealings with them?"

"Yes. On Maclemar's boat. I was chained up, and all of a sudden they were dropped on the deck and started attacking me. What a nightmare."

"Maclemar chained you up?" asked Sainvire in a curious voice.

Poe cleared her throat. "Well yeah. He didn't trust people who—"

"Who what?" he asked. He turned his head to look back at her.

"You know. Who are friends with vampires and all that."

"Friends?" Michelle asked. "You mean—"

"Yeah," finished Poe. "He was a real asshole to me."

"Glad to know you're on kissing terms now," said the vampire with sarcasm.

Michelle guffawed, and she narrowly missed a motorcycle spilled out on the road. "Oops. So you and Maclemar are an item."

Not liking the thread of conversation, Poe said rudely, "I'm with nobody, Michelle."

"I thought you don't lie, Poe," said the master vampire.

Poe seethed quietly. She resolved never to speak again during the journey, but she soon couldn't help herself. "It was only sex, and we didn't even finish because some jerk interrupted us," she said and added, "Not that it's any of your business."

Michelle's eyebrows rose, but she kept her mouth shut. The drama unfolding before her was too good to interrupt.

"You're right," Sainvire said. "It's none of my business, but I just have to emphasize for you to use precaution. This isn't the time to be having children, Poe."

"Don't worry about me. I don't menstruate. That means I'll never have babies." Her nostrils flared. "You ought to think about you and Jenna instead of bothering with me and Maclemar. You're more likely to spawn little dead babies than me."

Their argument ended when the Mini ran over two Revenents that had thrown themselves in front of the car. After a few bumps the car was stuck. "Make sure your guns have silencers," said Sainvire while getting out of the car.

He lifted the Mini by the fender and pulled out the mangled bodies underneath. The Revs were already in the process of clicking back together. The nail on his forefinger shot up twelve inches long, and with brevity he cut off their leathery necks. From the darkness a flying vamp swooped down and hurled Sainvire onto a rickety van, and his body left a deep imprint on the metal.

Poe and Michelle got out of the car at the same time. They looked up in the air and around the vicinity for others but found none. They couldn't help Sainvire. The two vampires fought like feral cats in fast forward mode.

Sainvire grabbed his nemesis by the throat and slammed him against a concrete road barrier. "I'm going to kill you, Sainvire, if it's the last thing I do!" screamed the vampire like a ridiculous cartoon charter. He was half-a-head shorter than Sainvire. "I used to be a Council member. Now I'm a fucking scout for Nesbitt and Trench!"

"You should've joined us, Umberto. You can sniff out lies. You know Plasmacore is the best thing for the vampire race."

Umberto Dali kicked Sainvire in the crotch and hurled him to the ground. His handsome face contorted and ugly from rage, he bitterly said, "We don't want science, you fool! We want power. We want the old ways!"

Dali, an old-fashioned vampire in every way, procured a dagger from his belt and threw himself at Sainvire who quickly rolled out of the way. Sainvire got on his feet and faced Dali. "The old way's empty. And it's dead."

"It's dead because you killed it, you of an insignificant bloodline!" Umberto Dali lunged at Sanvire again, but this time the gray-eyed vampire stepped quickly away in time to sever the ex-councilman's left hand, the one holding the dagger. Sainvire's worker hands stoppered Dali's curdling scream.

"That's the kind of prejudicial thinking that's going to wipe out your kind, Dali," said Sainvire. "The antiquated notion of Euro birthright is all in the past. In the new world we're creating, humans will have the same rights as vampires no matter their background."

"Your fucking idea—" The master vampire cracked Umberto's head and quickly sliced it off before he could finish his thoughts. "Fleabag," said Sainvire.

Poe watched Sainvire sling Dali's body over his warped shoulder and pick up the head. He stuffed Dali into the back of the van he had dented minutes before. He threw the dead Revenents in there with

175

him to hide any evidence. Her heart pounded painfully. No wonder she had been pining for him all these months. He was the real thing. He lived his truth, and she loved him for it.

"Are we still going to San Jose?" asked Michelle who was a little shaken by the vampire deathmatch.

Sainvire ran normalized fingernails through his short black hair. "Nothing's changed, Michelle. We're getting the supplies Megan needs, and nothing's going to stop us tonight."

Poe had seen Sainvire fight before, but this time it was like watching a movie. Rumor was that he and Dali used to be friends. Without thinking, Poe placed her hand on Sainvire's broken right shoulder. She was surprised when his cold fingers briefly squeezed her own before letting go.

The ride to San Jose was surprisingly without incident after Dali. Michelle, the chattiest of the three, kept her mouth shut and so did Poe out of deference to Sainvire who had the weight of the world in his hands. He had changed the course of vampire rule, and he would suffer for it until Trench, master vampires, and Council members from other cities finally caught up with him.

They parked the car two blocks from Good Samaritan Hospital in a spot hidden by overgrown trees with gigantic roots that had uplifted concrete. From the information Sainvire's advance team had gathered, the hospital was located in an area least populated by leeches, halfdeads, and vampires.

Placing the hood of his jacket on his head, Sainvire looked like any other leech scouring the streets of San Jose for contraband. Black hooded jacket and brown Dickies weren't exactly the usual ensemble for a master vampire. He put his arms on either side of the women.

"We've got to make this look normal," he explained.

"A guy with two hot chicks, normal? Why not?" said Michelle. She wound her arm about his waist. "Put your hood on, Poe. They'll recognize your scar. The moon's pretty bright."

Poe did as she was told and likewise put her arm around Sainvire's hips. She felt strength in the vampire's wiry body. She trembled in the warm night. Old feelings were hard to suppress. They walked toward the hospital as a happy-go-lucky trio by all appearances, and they met no one along the way.

Like wilted fiesta flyers, Sainvire's mug covered street lamps, houses, and every conceivable nook. He was the most wanted vampire in town. Not far from his photographs were wanted posters of Poe, accurately drawn by a former police sketch artist with the exception of two glaringly exaggerated details.

"Shit. Look at my scar. It looks like a goddamn banana millipede. And my lips! C'mon, they aren't that puffy!" complained Poe.

"Face it, Poe," Michelle chuckled quietly. "You have porn lips."

Once inside the doors the women took out their flashlights and their lists.

"Pharmacy's to the right according to the sign," said Michelle. "Let's go."

The hospital was stark black but for the illumination of flashlights. Poe's imagination ran away with her. All those movies about hospitals and ghosts.

Like Sainvire said, there are no ghosts. Only vampires.

The small pharmacy had been looted. Practically every prescription medication had been taken, most likely by leeches that were legendary for their drug addiction. These wretched people looked after humans and drew their blood for vampires in exchange for their freedom.

"All out of pain killers," said Poe. She bit her lower lip.

"Grab the sutures and medical instruments," instructed the vampire. "We'll figure out another way to make Megan comfortable."

Michelle filled her pack with gauze, antibacterial fluids, and liniments she'd never heard of.

"I'll look around," said Sainvire, and he disappeared down the cold hallway. Unlike the women he didn't need night vision goggles.

"You better not go anywhere, Poe," said Michelle. "This place is creepy. Japanese horror film creepy."

"Are you kidding me? I'm sticking to you like glue."

Poe looked at the crevice between two shelves hoping for a find. She nearly jumped with joy. Two half-filled plastic I.V. containers plopped in the corner. She fished out the plastic bags and showed them to Michelle.

"Hope this stuff's still good," said Poe, stuffing them in her pack.

"I don't know if those things expire. Hopefully not."

The women squealed at the sound of a knock on the semi-open door. Wearing night goggles stood two leeches who had come to raid the pharmacy.

"Well hey there, ladies," said a bean pole with 'Player' written on his shirt. "Hope you left some good stuff for us."

"Hey, Larry, these ladies are fine. And young!" said his goateed companion with a beer gut. "Haven't seen girl leeches in years. Where you from?"

Both packed rifles slung across their shoulders. Leeches were fond of shooting at random things to stave off boredom.

"Thanks, boys. Don't stop with the compliments. We're actually from down south a ways. Looking for some scintillating pick-me-ups for our ward," said a quick-thinking Michelle. "They got shit here, but we've got kush you might die for. Chita and I are more than willing to share." She inched her hand behind her back where a .45 was lodged.

"Hell yeah, leech girl!" yelled Larry. "Me and Bogart are gonna get you and Chita all fucked up in all different ways for your generosity."

"You said it, bro. I get the hot curly-haired one. You get the hooded one," said Bogart.

"Um, hold it, guys," said Poe. "What's the news this side of town, eh? Anything exciting happening? Any new plots hatching?"

Michelle ribbed her on the arm. The girl was being too obvious. "What my friend wants to know is any new developments with the main event? You know, the search for Sainvire and his people?"

"Oh sure. Most of our vamps have joined with Newbitt's crew. Rumor is Sainvire's real close."

"How close?"

"Like tomorrow close. Newbitt's coming down from SF himself. And Trench, who knows? That guy always misses the big fights. Remember how he didn't even bother stopping the mass cattle stealing in L.A. 'cause he was too busy nursing his burns. The guy's a wuss."

"Yeah, that little bitch with the scar doused him with garlic water and shot him in the chest. She's one mean hellion and as ugly as my dead toenail," added Larry. "Now come here, baby, and let me see your face."

Poe looked at Michelle and shrugged. She went toward Larry who had called her the b-word. Obediently she stood in front of him and waited for the unveiling.

Michelle sashayed over to Bogart.

"This is like Christmas," laughed Larry, rubbing his hands together like Mr. Burns from *The Simpsons*. He pulled down Poe's hood and yelped. "The fuck! It's her!"

Poe smiled and pressed her wrist knife against his throat. Michelle pulled out her piece before Bogart could whip out his rifle.

"Now now, boys. Don't make any noise because Julia Poe here, Public Enemy Number Two, will not appreciate it. You don't want to eat your own testicle sandwich, do you?"

Real fear gripped the glue-addled minds of the men.

"Any more of you coming?" Poe asked.

"There's only us. W-we snuck out hoping to find the good stuff here. Somebody stole our stash, and we're desperate."

"Oh that's too bad," said Michelle, and she rested the barrel of her silencer on Bogart's head. "Do you have any idea how much I hate leeches, Bogart?"

"N-no."

"I hate you all. I promised myself that when I got my senses again I would kill every single leech I encounter. And here you two are."

Bogart shook his head. "Please, miss. I'm a good leech. I never torture or rape anybody. Really. I just smoke out."

"Whatever," Michelle said before pulling the trigger. Bogart slipped on the floor like soggy pasta, his brain Pollocking the walls. "You just serve vampires who make cattle out of your brothers and sisters."

"Geez, Michelle," was all Poe could say. She'd killed before, but watching somebody else do it at close range unnerved her. Larry was crying, and he embarrassingly peed his pants.

Sainvire chose this time to make an appearance. He looked at the body on the floor impassively. On his hand was a tank of old school laughing gas, nitrous oxide.

"Slice his throat, Poe. So we can get out of here."

Poe shuddered. "No. I can't. Not like this." She looked at Sainvire for help, but he just shrugged.

"If you let him go, he'll rape, beat, and continue to serve a corrupt system," he said. "You know this, Poe."

"I won't. I'll run away. Just let me go," blubbered Mac.

"You kill him," said Poe. She sheathed her wrist knife. "I don't want another nightmare to add to my thousands." She pushed Sainvire out of the way and headed for the front entrance.

She'd sliced so many leech throats before this night. But she couldn't do it. Maybe if Larry and Bogart had threatened her with guns or assaulted her, she could have killed in cold blood. No problem.

Perhaps it was the bald man she had disemboweled in the forest without mercy that got her so shook. Killing like that took its toll.

The drive back to Gilroy was dead silent in the eerie darkness of night. Each questioned their own motives, and they fortified their stances on the cause. No matter their excuses, their humanity was shaken that night.

CHAPTER 7

"WHAT DID JOSEPH DECIDE?" Sainvire asked, surprisingly calm. He had found the time to shave and make himself presentable to the imminent yet fickle birth of his newest family member.

"He's talking it over with Megan," Poe answered as she finished off a bowl of oatmeal and honey in Habib's kitchen. She hadn't eaten since they had returned from San Jose. *And from the sound of it, she's going to need all the strength and energy to survive the long night ahead.*

"What about Miriam? Is she ready for this?" Sainvire inquired. Though the woman seemed competent enough, the midwife's age and frailty bothered the master vampire. She'd had a minor stroke two days prior. If anything were to happen to the old lady, no one was qualified to take over.

"She's inside with them, reading medical books and some natural birth and herbal encyclopedias. Really hairy situation," said Morales. He rubbed his sleepless eyes with his fist. The sperm donor via turkey baster sympathized greatly with Joseph who had become a good friend the past two years. Megan he'd known the longest, and the thought of losing her tore at his insides. Whatever family was conjoined in this post-apocalyptic madness, he wanted to keep.

"She should operate soon while the baby's heartbeat is strong," Sainvire said more to himself.

"Can you hear the baby's heartbeat from here?" asked a surprised Poe.

"If I concentrate enough," he said grimly. "Julia, are you assisting with the operation?"

Poe shook her head. "No. Megan said I make her nervous. Miriam thinks I'm a klutz just because I dropped a couple of things accidentally."

"Joseph and I will be helping Miriam," Morales said to Sainvire. "Michelle and John Danby will be coming later to lend a hand."

Poe raised an eyebrow but lowered it right away. She had nothing but respect for the young woman driven to defeat those who wanted to make a slave out of her. The Thai boxing lessons had been coming along smoothly until the evacuation had begun. Michelle had a sponge for a mind and a rock for a body. *But she executed a man inches away from me that night, and she's going help deliver Megan's baby?*

"So Poe and I won't be needed this evening?"

"No. Habib's got a cauldron bubbling to last the entire night. Why don't you guys take a walk or something so I can sneak a quick nap before they call me in?" said Morales.

The two got the hint and left the kitchen reeking of alcohol and herbs. Before Poe could take a step downstairs, Sainvire placed a hand on her elbow and led her up the attic stairs.

A voice stopped her progress. "Poe." She looked down to see Jenna beckoning her downstairs. The undead threw Sainvire a cold look.

"I'll be waiting right here," said Sainvire from the third step of the attic ladder.

Jenna led her to a sitting room decorated with floral wallpaper and motioned for Poe to take a seat. She obeyed, but when the vampire kept standing, Poe clamped shut her jaw. Jenna's arms folded like an impatient school teacher.

"I'm sorry we haven't talked these past days, Poe," Jenna began. "I've been busy getting busloads of people organized and transported to their new homes. I've heard so much about you. In fact you're all I've heard about these past years from Morales, Megan, Joseph, Maple, and so on. The only one who doesn't talk about you is Kaleb. Don't you think that's strange?"

Poe placed her palms flat on the couch. "No, I don't. He doesn't talk about a lot of things. He's practically mute. Besides, why would he talk about me? I only knew him a week back then."

"Apparently you made quite an impression," she said. Her lips thinned as she spoke. "He was looking after you these past years through his people in West L.A."

Poe didn't like getting interrogated. "He was friends with Sister Ann and Goss, my mentors. He promised them he'd watch over me if something happened to them. I'm sure you know they died. Really, Jenna, I don't know what this whole thing is about, but I don't appreciate all the questions."

"Oh I think you do," she said, staring down at Poe's dark eyes. "He hasn't taken his eyes off of you since you showed up."

Poe looked down at her hands. "I don't know what to say about that, Jenna. I can't control where his eyeballs fall."

"I just want to know if you loved him so I can get on with my life," she said. "If you've moved on to Maclemar, then I'll stay with Kaleb. If not, I'll be on the bus out of here tonight."

Poe stared out the window at the willow tree where she had attacked Maclemar. She had no future with the master vampire. "No. I don't love him. Never have," she lied. "It was one day of sex, Jenna. After Megan gives birth, Maclemar will take me on his boat along with my dog and my pig and we'll get as far away from you vampires as we can. You don't have anything to worry about."

———

Poe nervously tugged down at her shirt and went up the trap door into Sainvire's room. As if attracted to one of the few light sources in the room, Poe stood by the window away from the unmade mattress on the floor. Quietly he watched her.

"You heard everything, I suppose," she began. She squinted at the vampire.

"Most of it, yes."

"She loves you, and the fact that I'm in this room right now is killing her." Of the character types from the thousands of movies she'd seen over the years, homewreckers bothered her the most. She did not want to be the other woman.

Sainvire smiled sadly. "I've told her from the beginning not to care for me too much. Our relationship is symbiotic. We both need each other to spread Plasmacore into the hands of every vampire in the world."

"Then you're a selfish son of a bitch. You can't ask that from someone who already loves you."

He remained quiet, and his eyes never left hers.

"Is there something else you want to say?" she asked after a long bout of prickly silence.

"Yes," he said after a pause. "There is."

"Can you tell me what it is? I'm gonna start sneezing if I stay up here another minute."

"They're coming this way," he said evenly. "We've placed barricades to block the highways and country roads, but they've got someone with Ed's strength. A few hours from now, five of our people will lead the rest of the group somewhere safe. I want you and Maclemar on that bus."

"What'll happen to Megan?"

"A few of us will stay until she's well enough to travel."

Too many thoughts converged at once, leaving her speechless. When she finally found her voice, Poe shook her head and said no. "There's no way I'm leaving Megan. Isn't that one of the reasons you got me up here, to take care of her?"

"I wanted you out of the Westside, period. As for babysitting Megan, I've changed my mind," Sainvire said. He looked troubled. "It's every master vampire's prerogative."

"Well I haven't, Sainvire. And you can't—"

"They have bulldozers and Hummers to our measly school buses. They're better equipped," he said tensely. "While all of us are whittled away by constant worry, they're invigorated by bloodlust and greed for the reward on our heads."

"We've fought them before," Poe said. "We can take them, can't we?"

"Morales is leaving with the infant tonight." He avoided answering Poe's question and massaged his temple instead. "Habib will be going, too. He's preparing the baby formula as we speak."

Makes sense to take the baby away from the looming skirmish, but exactly how many will be left behind to face the assailants?

"Who besides you and Joseph are staying to protect Megan?"

"Ed and five of my closest friends volunteered."

"Eight of you against Trench's police force? Plus Newbitt's people?" Poe cried. She roughly shoved Sainvire in the chest. "That's a suicide mission if I've ever heard one!"

"The eight of us are mighty persistent, Poe," he said. He calmly caught hold of the girl's fist and pulled it against his non-beating heart. "Besides, the men are furiously repairing the chopper as we speak. You need to be on that bus, or I will not be able to focus knowing your scalp might be hanging on somebody's belt."

"Why should you care so much?" she asked tensely, glaring into his black-rimmed gray eyes that seemed to smolder in the half-light.

"It's the same reason I hear your heart pounding like a locomotive whenever you're around, Julia," he said wanly. "I care about you as much as you care about me."

Poe, taken aback, shook her head.

"Bullshit."

"Think what you will, Julia. The brief time we spent together has sustained me and kept me from losing it. If you think I'd rather be in the company of ex-cattle that fear me than in your arms, you really don't know me at all."

"Be quiet! The woman you've replaced me with so quickly can hear us!"

"She can't. She doesn't have my ability to hear from far way," he said quietly. "She's been a friend for a long time, and occasionally we sleep together to tone down the pressure of these times."

"Like I said, the woman loves you," said Poe, remembering the tortured vampire she left in the sitting room.

"Jenna knows how I feel about you," he said quietly. "I've been upfront from the very beginning. You ought to know by now when I'm telling the truth."

"What? I don't know you at all!" she burst out. "We've only been in each other's company a little more than ten days total. I delude myself by saying I'm in love with you, but what do I know about it? Maybe I've confused three pleasurable sexual couplings in one day as love. Who knows?"

"Stranger things have happened," he said while looking intently at Poe.

"Well let me tell you though, Sainvire. There's no way a refined idealist vampire like you can fall for an ignorant, scarred, and coarse girl like me. It would be like Cary Grant going ga-ga over the uglies in Mike Leigh films."

"For someone so strong and together, you sure have low self-esteem when it comes to your appearance," he said furiously. "Have you looked at yourself lately, I mean really looked at yourself? After a couple days you've got Maclemar drooling

189

over you. He's a good looking man, so it's fair to say he could have any woman or vampire in this camp. Does he take advantage? I don't think so. You know why?" he asked, bringing his heated face inches from Poe's. "Well?"

"No, you dick, I don't!"

"Because you're a goddamn beautiful woman with muscles and brain to match," he said a little less harshly. "Scars only add to your appeal because you're a damn survivor. And really, scars or not, who'd object with a body like yours?"

His face was so close she could almost feel the dead coolness of his skin. Her hand, still imprisoned in his, would not be dislodged.

"Let go, or I'll beat the shit out of you," she threatened as a last resort.

Fully cognitive of what Sainvire was about to do, Poe closed her eyes when he dipped his mouth into hers. His generous mouth left her shivery while his cold tongue coaxed itself into her tightly shut lips. He gave her goosebumps that led to a sigh which paved the way for a fully realized kiss. Like Maclemar, Sainvire's skill was devastating but in a quite different way. His cold lips were familiar and wonderful and had been part of her dreams for months on end.

She didn't know when he released her hand, but she discovered later that it had snaked around his neck on its own volition. His arms twined around her waist to bring her closer to him.

"Stop. Jenna—" Poe said breathlessly. She led his hand away from where it explored under her shirt. "This sex thing won't get me on the bus tonight, you know. I'm staying because my friend asked me to."

He tightened his hold on her waist and traced the round firmness of her behind. "Let's not talk about this. We only have a few hours together." Savoring her, he traced a trail of kisses from her neck to the makeshift vee of her shirt. "I've wanted to touch you for so long it's become an ache. When I saw you with Maclemar, I nearly tore his throat out."

"Was that why you interrupted our encounter?" she asked irately.

Sainvire shrugged. "Even a vampire like me can get jealous, sweetheart."

"You're just gonna have to keep your libido and jealousies in check, Sainvire," said Poe. She struggled out of his embrace. It was one of the hardest things she'd ever done. "I need you to let me inside the armory, the little closet downstairs."

The Y-shaped vein on his the edge of his forehead throbbed like the rest of his body. His dark mood could not be hidden by the shadows of the attic, but he didn't break his silence.

"Look, Sainvire. As much as I want to be kissed by you all over, there's this thing called fear that's taken over my lust. I want to survive. I want the people I love to make it. I want to see that the baby has a mom to raise him," she said. She trembled. Standing on her toes, Poe kissed Sainvire on the mouth for ages.

"We'll settle this thing between us later," she said in a husky voice. "Now please, show me to the gun room."

There wasn't much of a selection left. The little closet had a crate of bullets heavily saturated in garlic oil, a couple dozen Kevlar vests, assorted knives, and a few double-barreled shotguns. The firearms were limited to Smith & Wesson revolvers, heavy as hell with an afterbite.

"This is it?" Poe asked. She was flabbergasted.

"Afraid so," Sainvire answered, his face inscrutable. "Take what you need."

"Do you have any more clips?"

Sainvire pulled from under the vests a square cookie tin stocked with over twenty magazines. "Take as many as you want. Everything's been distributed. Get some for Maclemar, too. He might need it in case the bus is attacked. Some of the folks riding with you have terrible eye-hand coordination."

"Thanks, but I'm not getting on that bus," said Poe. She felt like they were saying a final goodbye. She filled the clips with the strongest and most damaging hollow-point, spitzer, and lead-ensconced bullets, stuffing as many as she could in her pack.

While she rifled through the arsenal, Sainvire excused himself then promptly reappeared.

"This might come in handy," he said as he handed her a Calico 9mm. "I've been meaning to give it to you."

"What is it, a sub-machine gun?" Poe asked with awe in her voice. The twenty-inch, double-grip firearm looked like a throwback from old World War II movie props.

"I think it's a Para pistol. This thing holds up to a hundred rounds, but once you're out of bullets, chuck it," he said pensively. "It's hell to reload. Also, this thing is for ambidextrous shooters like you. If you hold the grip too close to the trigger guard, there's a danger ejected cases will burn and damage your palm. Aside from being unpredictable, this gun should be useful to you."

"Maybe you'll need it more than me," she said. Her brown eyes were huge.

"If you can't fly and puncture metal with your nails, then you'll need it more than me," he said with a smile. "Don't worry. I have my own stash in my room."

"Much obliged then," she said. "Does this mean you're not going to force me to go?"

"Guess so," he sighed with exaggeration.

"You need to relax, man," Poe said. She shook her head then added with a grin, "Can't you tell I'm not going to live that long?"

Sainvire's face darkened. He didn't like Poe's lighthearted attempt at a joke. "Do you and Maclemar already have Kevlar?"

"He does. From Jorge."

"Ah. I better find one that fits you," he said, rifling through the vests. When he found a small one, he insisted she put it on without delay.

"Isn't it a little early for this, not to mention hot?"

"It's never too early for extra protection. As for the weather, it will cool down soon enough." Without much of a choice Poe donned the vest with Sainvire's help.

"Maybe you should wear your hooded sweatshirt over this vest. It will fend off the apprehension among the last batch."

"Satisfied now?" she asked peevishly after zipping up her black hoody.

"Very," he nodded.

"Just do me one more favor, Poe," he said. "Try not to die."

"I'll try to avoid it as much as possible," she said acerbically. "Anything else?"

"Yes. Just one." He traced the scar on her face with his index finger. "I love you."

With a what-the-fuck look Poe crumpled to the ground, unconscious from the blow to the back of the head. The vampire had clunked her skull with a rock hard fist.

"And because I feel that strongly about you, I'm not going to let you die," he said, finishing his thought.

Carefully he lifted her inert form and her pack and deposited her to the nearest unoccupied room.

"Such a small thing," he mumbled and glanced down her face. "Yet the amount of damage you can do is staggering."

CHAPTER 8

DEAD HEADLIGHTS ILLUMINATED NOTHING. The
school bus hummed and rumbled in the dark,
occasionally squashing debris and indiscriminately
mashing the odd creatures that crossed the road. The
vehicle, painted black, narrowly circumvented
thrashing its third bumper soldered by Maclemar for
extra protection. Though crooked and rusty, the
harmless metal could puncture tires and kick-start
headaches to those aboard the yellow bus. The driver,
a vampire named Sarah, did manage to mow down a
Revenent wearing a tattered evening gown to the
delight of extremely tense passengers.

"Good one, Sarah," a twitchy man from the back
complemented. Like most of the passengers, he
draped a protective arm around a crate. His contained
three miserable chickens deprived of sleep. Others
held rope leashes latched to the neck of small goats
that smelled as pleasant as foot fungus.

Wearing high-quality image intensifier night
vision goggles, Sarah was able to sideswipe a grime-
faced undead, half-raving from starvation. The
tattered beings seemed to pour out of the countryside.
No human traveled the Pacheco Pass much anymore.

"Shit," exclaimed Yawo, the co-driver and
companion of Sarah for the past two years. His thick
Ghanaian accent became more congealed as the

minutes ticked by. He, too, wore special goggles to see in the dark as did most of the passengers on the bus. "We've only been on the road for a little over an hour, and already two unfortunates have become road kill. That is sass if I ever saw it," he said with pride.

"That's right, baby," said Sarah. She patted his cheek and concentrated on the road beleaguered with decrepit cars. The countryside congestion was nothing compared to city traffic, however. Ed, the supervampire who could lift a three-ton boulder, had taken weeks to clear enough space for a bus without being too obvious. "Just keep your eyes peeled for me, and we'll be okay. Two pairs of eyes are better than one."

"Ahem. That would be three pairs if you count this old man," piped in John Danby who sat in the front passenger row with a calico cat curled on his lap. Goggles that gave him the look of a fly rested on his nose.

Sainvire had insisted they carry a pair along with an emergency travel kit at all times. The kit included two sets of guns, a few boxes of cartridges, a Kevlar vest, and food and water rations. After the raids had become more frequent with ex-cattle getting abducted and killed like game during the evening hours, each man and woman had to be taught basic self-defense. Sainvire decreed that his vampires were to ransack police stations and military outposts and bring in weapons and artillery to outfit the humans under their care.

Sarah laughed a little self-consciously. "Sorry, John. Of course I'll need all the help I can get." The pretty, pear-shaped driver was winding around an RV when the old lawyer and Muhammad Ali fan shouted,

"Deer!   Watch   out!"
It couldn't be avoided. The bus slammed into the animal barely sprouting antlers that rolled noisily under the tires at the same time Sarah hit the brakes.

Like most older school buses, seatbelts had not been installed. The heads of the passengers kissed the seatbacks in front of them before inertia hurled them to their seats. Those asleep near the aisle ended up tasting metal floor.

"Everyone alright?" Sarah asked as the last thud of tires rolled over the carcass of the animal.

Angry groans filled the bus. But having traveled in the dead of night every three to four weeks for the last couple of years had toughened hides. The passengers quickly settled down.

Except for Poe, certain animals, and an infant.

Poe pitched forward from the cozy spot between Maclemar's arm and shoulder. She dove head-first onto the metal aisle of the bus with a clang. A crescendo of clucking, bleating, meowing, oinking, and screaming became the symphonic soundtrack of the moment. Maclemar and Michelle, who had flanked her while she slept on the unsegmented couch in the last row, helped her up as soon as the bus settled down.

"Ouch," Poe cried, and she palmed her injured forehead. Running her tongue on her teeth and touching her nose for anything broken, she stood up. The sound of wailing drilled into her head, and it was the only sound that frenzily continued. "Shit."

"Poe, are you alright?" asked Maclemar. He rubbed her back to calm her.

"Maclemar?" she said, holding onto his waist. "Can you turn on the lights, please? I think I'm gonna hurl."

"You better not!" someone threatened from her right over the din of crying.

"Who the hell was that? Is that Megan's baby? Where's my guns?" she asked in succession out of nervousness. She could hear someone singing a dead-on imitation of Frank Sinatra. "Is that Morales?" she asked softly to no one in particular.

Someone squeezed her arm gently and said, "Here, Poe. I got your goggles from your pack. I'm going to slide then over your head."

"Michelle?" Poe shook her head, fighting the urge to hyperventilate. The darkness and crying were eating her up. "I think I'm dizzy." She ignored the pain caused by the elastic as it touched lumps on her forehead and the back of her head.

From the abyss of darkness came phosphorous-green reception. Faces like insects stared at her from their seats. Some looked grim. A few smiled. Certain ones waved.

"Why don't you sit down, dear?" a wrinkled woman by the window suggested nicely. "So we can mosey on."

As soon as Poe sat down, Sarah resumed driving.

"The son of a bitch clobbered me," Poe said. She gritted her teeth. Michelle handed her knives and guns to be sheathed in various holsters on her wrists, ankles, waist, and across her shoulders. "How long have we been driving?"

"A little over an hour," answered Michelle.

Poe turned to look at Maclemar who remained unusually quiet. "How long was I out?"

"Three, maybe four hours," he said staidly. "He asked me to tell you he's sorry and that Megan's glad to know you'll protect her child."

Opening a bottle of acetaminophen, Poe popped five tablets and swished them down with water. "They both sound as if they're going to die tonight," she said with a frown. "Any of you got a candy bar?"

"I do," piped in the voice of Percy who was two rows up to the left. She pulled out a bar from her Eeyore bag and scrambled toward Poe. Night goggles ate up three-quarters of her face.

"Twix. My very favorite," Poe said in a low voice melting with indebtedness. With the kid looking on, the vampire hunter wolfed down the candy bar alive with living protein. "Hey Percy, can you do me the biggest of favors?"

"Anything, Poe," the girl said with complete devotion that almost embarrassed Poe.

"Can you help Maclemar look after Penny and Chops?"

"Of course," Percy said in a high-pitched voice. "I'll look after them good."

"Thanks, Percy. You don't know how much this means to me."

She watched the girl go back to her seat.

"What do you mean by that, Sharren?" Maclemar asked. He clamped a heavy hand on her shoulder.

"Nothing, Darren," she answered glibly. After another swig of water she swung her pack on her back and followed Morales' voice that continued to sing to the crying infant.

"Hey look, little Piper," said Morales. He smiled at Poe and patted the seat next to him. "Here comes your Tia Poe. Come say hello."

Habib, who parked in the seat behind Morales, handed Poe a bottle. "Maybe she's ready to eat now."

"Go ahead, place it in her mouth," guided the baby's other daddy.

Poe looked at the shriveled little phosphorescent green troll in the dark and smiled. "Cute little thing. I hope her looks improve in the daylight hours, though."

"Don't make me pinch you, Poe," said an offended Morales. He took the milk from her and placed it gently in the infant's tiny lips. "Megan said to make you godmother. I'll have to veto her orders if you're going to give Piper a complex this early in life."

"I was just kidding," Poe explained as she watched the nipple jerk away from Piper's mouth after the bus galloped over a pothole. "So Megan really said I could be her godmother?"

"It was Joseph's idea, but the little redhead took to it right away."

"Wow. That's something, isn't it? Are you the godfather then?"

"Yup," he said with pride.

"What color's her hair?"

"Green," he said as he secured the nipple in the baby's mouth. "Why do you have your pack on? Did I just hear you ask Percy to babysit your pets?"

Poe shrugged her shoulders.

"Uh oh. You're not going to pull one of your tricks on us, are you?" Before she could answer,

Morales hollered. "Maclemar. Michelle. Get over here quick."

"What's wrong?" the Welshman asked. He took three giant steps to reach them with Michelle close behind.

"Guys, don't make this any harder," entreated Poe who held up the palm of her hand to deflect any naysayers. She stood and made her way to the front. Penny doggedly followed her, and the pig in turn tailed the dog. Penny was smart enough to know that something was up.

"Excuse me," she said to Yawo who stood by Sarah. When he didn't move she elbowed him out of the way and whispered something in the driver's ear.

"We've covered over ten miles, girl!" the bus driver exclaimed after a few whispered seconds. "There's no way you're going to make it there in one piece.

"I run an average of six to seven miles a day, and I'm not even close to tired," Poe said out loud, fully aware her friends were listening. She pulled at her lobeless ear in frustration. "Double that should be nothing."

"Right, but you've never tried sprinting in the dark, have you?" Maclemar butted in, making his way to the front. Excusing himself to Yawo who was bumped further back, he added, "Those are the nasty sods who want to have a go at your flesh. Your delicate blood is incidental to them."

"They're slow. I can outrun them."

"Bloody hell you can, crazy benyw!" He took another step until he hovered over her.

"Save me your Welsh compliments, Maclemar," she said. "I'd go back for you, too, if you were stuck in garlic land and weak from childbirth." She was shaking.

"I'm touched, truly," Maclemar said with sincerity. He draped his large hand over his heart. "But I'm a little unnerved that you see me not as a strapping man, but as someone female-like capable of popping out babies."

The fisherman's retort made more than a few snigger.

"Now, now. Lay off the girl," said Morales to the watchers-on. "She was only eight when they canceled school permanently. Poe didn't get to sit through sex ed slide presentations replete with graphic pictures of gonorrhea and the birth canal."

Poe, when she thought about her comment, grinned. "I didn't mean to say it that way, Maclemar." She turned to the driver before she said any more silly things.

"Miss, you're going to need to let me off. The more you drive, the more I'd I have to walk. My friends need me. Trench and Newbitt are on their way. I'm more than a decent shot," she said, not wanting to boast, but she had no choice. "Sometimes I can hit things with my eyes closed. Sister Ann, a friend of mine who's dead now, said it was an intrinsic gift."

"We need you here then," a woman about sixty years old said. "Especially with an infant on the bus. Anyway, they got that helicopter up there if worse comes to worse."

"Last I heard, the helicopter was smashed during the dreadful landing," Poe sighed. "As for Piper, she'll be alright with all of you here to protect her."

Sarah shook her head and pursed her thin lips. Harried, she threw out, "Help me out here, people. I'm kinda busy driving." She barely missed hitting an upturned truck.

"Folks may have given up on the eight left on their own at the farmhouse to face those blood slavers, but I haven't. I don't believe in many things, but I believe in Plasmacore. It will help depose those fascist bloodsuckers that want to act like royalty, like blasted Count Dracula, with castles, Igors, and slaves." Poe looked around at the green-faced humanity around her and made a fist. "I'm tired of asking. I'm going to get off this bus, stopped or not." So angry to the point of salivating, Poe yanked the lever that opened the door and prepared to jump out.

"Let her out," a familiar voice said from the middle of the bus. Poe scanned for the person and located Jenna's face looking impassive in the green haze of her night vision goggles. The woman had left Sainvire, and in some sick way, Poe's headache disappeared. She had never been so glad in her life. Jenna didn't speak again.

"This is madness," Maclemar uttered temperamentally. "Even with these bloody things on, your peripheral vision will be hampered."

Sarah sighed and stepped on the brake. "Alright. I think this is foolish and a waste of a good fighter. This group would be better served with you on our side. But good luck all the same. Remember not to make too much noise or flash a light of any kind."

"Appreciate it, miss."

"Can someone hand this to Poe?" Morales said from his seat as he tossed a roundish helmet to Yawo. "These are ANVIS-6 goggles. The helmet might look like it came right off Luke Skywalker's head, but it has perimeter control and it's handsfree. Plus it might protect that stubborn noggin of yours. I got it on good authority that fighter pilots wore them in battle."

"Thanks, Morales," Poe said sincerely. Sarah pulled the old goggles off and placed the new night vision contraption on Poe's aching head. "This thing is heavy but an improvement to my old gear."

"Don't thank me, loca girl," Morales harrumphed. "You can thank Sainvire. He told me to hit you over the head every hour. But too bad, I was busy. Seems he pegged you right that you'd pull a stunt like this when you came to, but was he was hoping we'd have put miles behind us by then. So there's nothing more to say. Just make sure to keep that helmet tight on your head."

"Yeah, I will. Thanks. Look after my little godchild." She turned to her dog. "Penny, you stay here and take care of Chops," she said to the dog while patting her head. "You're my bestest dog, and I'll be back for you."

Poe saluted to the driver and stepped down from the bus. The dog, not wanting to be left behind, followed.

"Wait, Poe, I'm going, too," Maclemar declared. He ran to the back of the bus to retrieve his things.

"No you're not, Welshman. You're staying with these people," Poe shouted. She began to run just in case Maclemar and others decided to tag along. "I'll come looking for you, Maclemar. You promised to take me back to West L.A., and I aim to take you up on that." She heard the rumble of the engine as the bus drove away. She stopped to look back only to see the face of Maclemar staring out the back window.

"Pad Thai, lasagna, clam chowder, garlic bread, chicken tikka masala," Poe recited to keep the darkness from overwhelming her. Terror latched onto her body like half-starved cattle. She reached back into her memory until the names of her favorite food fell from her lips like lyrics to soothe the mind. "Are you getting hungry yet, Pen?" she asked as she looked down briefly at the loyal dog keeping pace.

"Adobo, zereshk polo, bibimbap, udon and soba noodles, In-N-Out burgers, fresh cut Islands fries," she said. She slowed down and took a swig of water. Once the water bottle had been replaced in the netting outside her pack, Poe pulled out a second gun from her thigh holster. It was a homemade 9mm automatic pistol with a silencer. She picked up the pace to a moderate run.

"Whoever said they're not afraid of the dark is full of yak shit," Poe muttered as she jogged cautiously around a jackknifed truck. Her vision enhancer goggles showed a skeleton hugging the steering wheel.

He said he loved me right before he popped me over the head. Did he mean it?

Heat still emanated from the asphalt regardless of the drop in temperature. She was soaked under the Kevlar and hooded jacket. It was too warm a night to be so bundled up.

Don't go too fast. You might step on something unpleasant, the voice in her mind said bossily. *You'll need to protect your ankles or you're dead meat.*

There's no Morales or Maclemar to carry you. Or a Sainvire to give you a lift.

"Please, Mom and Dad, let our side be alright," she prayed for the umpteeth time to the only deities she believed in. "Trench and Newbitt can't win. They just can't."

The hooting of an owl interrupted her prayer and startled her enough to examine the sparse trees along side the road. She missed tripping on a tubular tip of a muffler peeking out behind weeds that sprouted from crags on the road. A shot fired accidentally as Poe tried to stop her fall with the hand that held the Sig Sauer without a silencer. The booming sound that echoed in the warm night nearly stopped her heart. Penny whined.

"Oh no," she croaked. "I hope nobody heard that."

Shaking the dust from the knees of her pants, Poe started running. She paced herself to not get too fatigued in preparation for whatever the blasted gunshot would bring.

"Yes, I should've stayed to look out for Piper. And yes, this a nasty suicide mission where I'll be the main dish, extra rare," she told the green darkness. "I'm so sorry, Penny," she said and bent down to pet the wiry terrier mutt. There was movement ahead. She zoomed in at the line of field mice crossing the road and shivered.

"Eesh! Mice." Her ears were hot, and her vital signs unstable. *Think of something to keep your mind occupied. Think of dessert.*

"Sticky rice with mango, pumpkin pancakes, marmalade crepes, sticky toffee pudding, warm pecan pie with a dollop of vanilla bean ice cream,

Hof's Hut chocolate wipeout cake, Big Man Bakes red velvet cupcakes."

She saw the first one dragging his bum leg behind him along the grassy road side. Even in green the Revenent looked positively fiendish with hollowed eyes and a scarecrow gait. *Keep running. He can't catch up. You were thinking of dessert.*

"Dessert? Are you kidding me?" muttered Poe. "I can't think of food right now." She spotted two more Revs ahead, a female and a child walking achingly slow.

The cretins must plant themselves within easy reach of the road, the voice in her head mused. *Your hands are shaking. Quit it. Keep your mind busy.*

There were more than a handful of them now pouring out from the countryside. And the Revenents had spotted her. *Remember, don't shoot. It'll attract more of them. Plus you don't want to waste your bullets. You'll need them at the farmhouse.* Poe resheathed one of her guns and picked up a crooked branch thick and long enough to inflict damage.

"Where are they coming from?" Poe complained to Penny as she caught sight of more Revenents. "When did these things start popping up? I don't remember seeing even one before on the Pacheco Pass."

Focus! Give me the names of actors who played Sherlock Holmes!

"Um, there's a—" Poe swung left to avoid a creature squirming itself out of a banged up Camaro. "There's Michael Caine and um, Vasily Livanov, Basil Rathbone, Ronald Howard. Oh shit!" Poe screamed, kicking the walking beef jerky that came from her blindside. She let out a shaky breath and looked down at the corpse with a broken hip still wiggling about thanks to a combination of Muay Thai kicks. "And let that be a lesson to you!"

She surveyed the area with a quick 360-degree turn. She urgently returned to a run, this time faster than usual. Penny bared her fangs.

"Um, there's Geoffrey Whitehead, Peter Cushing, and that kid – what's his name – James D'Arcy." Poe slowed down. "Where are they all coming from?"

There were over twenty Revenents looking like they were having a circle of togetherness. Some were too busy to notice her. A curious Poe swung a leg up the hood of a station wagon and climbed up to the roof. Penny whined in concern, and her tail withdrew between her legs.

"Oh no," escaped from her lips. The green screen showed Revs picking apart the remains of a deer. "That must've been the animal we hit. Oh shit!"

A skeletal hand clasped an ankle from behind her and was tugging hard to pull her down. Penny chomped down at the Revenent's foot until her companion was freed. The noise drew the attention of the Revs outside of the circle, the ones with no access to deer meat. Slowly they made their way to Poe by walking like the zombies in the Thriller video.

"Fuck this!" Poe cried. She jumped on the Rev's shoulder until it was reduced to nothing more than an accordion of bones when it hit the ground. She dodged, ducked, and skidded to avoid the outstretched hands that tried to grab her, running like the mouth of hell was opening wider behind her. "Penny, please keep up with me!"

Calm down or you won't be able to think. There might be more of them out there! Finish off your list.

"Right. Right," she said, and she exhaled shakily to slow her breathing. "There's Douglass Wilmer. And of course, hands down the best Sherlock Holmes there ever was, Jeremy Brett!"

Then she couldn't speak anymore. Ahead of her was a procession of twitching limbs and trembling necks too emaciated to carry their own skulls, and one or two crawling baby spawn beating the Revs to the finish line. They had surfaced for the deer and perhaps incidentally to investigate the gun shot. Or they had been sent ahead like robots to sweep the roads. No matter. The rascally bunch had seen her. She and her dog would have to walk the line of fire.

———

"This is like a patchy soccer match," stated Poe. "One person against the bleacher crowd."

Poe took a deep swig of water. "Sorry, Pen. No water bowl for you." Holstering the Walther PPK and gripping a piece of wood, Poe charged through the horde and whacked away. She hit brittle bone. She had no choice but to part the Red Sea so she could reach the other side. The terrier attacked ankles and baby arms mutely. Poe herded them toward the middle of the road then veered to the far right where activity was thin. If they could just avoid creatures popping up from the side, they would be fine. Her own intermittent breathing rankled her ears.

You were sitting on a goldmine of vampire diuretic, and you didn't bottle it up? the angry voice in her head complained.

Poe sniffed. She was mighty disappointed with herself. What was she thinking by not replenishing her spray bottles with garlic marinade?

You're too busy lusting after a vampire and a man, that's what. But getting back to the subject at hand, maybe this area is bleeding corpses because it's the demarcation line between garlic territory and the no-smell zone.

"I hope so. A couple more miles and it'll start stinking like garlic, and they'll be off our tail," she tried to appease the voice. "I'll get us there, but just keep off the subject of Maclemar and Sainvire," she said abrasively as she clubbed the nearest Rev in the neck. "If I want to lust after them, then I will. I don't have much time to live, and I aim to think about the top men in my harem."

She pointed the Walther PPK at a Revenent that was light on his feet and blasted his head off. Besides the tripping accident it was her second bullet of the evening. "Down you go. Pen, you okay?" The dog looked up at Poe and whined.

More sounds of gunfire shattered the quiet of the night and dissipated all thoughts of harems. "Shit. No. Please don't let it be Maclemar," prayed Poe to her parents. "I hope the dumb Welshman didn't follow me."

She looked back at all the Revs she'd clubbed out of her way for what seemed like hours. The thought of crossing paths again made her knees shake. Another shot rang. The dog whimpered as if knowing what her human friend was considering.

"There's no way they're killing one of my boys!" Adjusting the stick to a more comfortable grip, Poe turned back and charged.

It was surprisingly easy to run back. The Revs, nothing but reeking bones and leathery skin, had given up trying to catch her and headed like automatons to where the shots originated. Poe aimed for knees and necks. "They'll be crawling."

She thought of Maclemar and shivered. Poe was attached to him for good or bad. "We have unfinished business together, Welshman, so hang on!"

"Sorry for dragging you into this," Maclemar said as he swung a tire iron at the same Revenent he'd hit three times. The creature just wouldn't stay down. Since disembarking from the bus, Maclemar had almost regretted his decision to go after Poe.

"It was my decision to tag along, man. So you're absolved from guilt," Michelle said. She hacked tirelessly with her axe at the bodies that came at them. "Just thank your stars I brought this limited edition Gimli broadaxe along."

"Right. I thought I recognized the Elvish on your scabbard," he grunted while stomping the face of the tenacious little fiend.

"Fuck that, Maclemar. Your ignorance is glaring for being a countryman of Tolkien. It's written in Dwarvish. Can't you tell the difference?"

"Maybe by the fires of Moria," he said unenthusiastically. "There're more of them by the second. Slow or not, we better get out of here before they block us in completely." She walked in sweeping strides to keep pace with Maclemar. "I think they heard the shots I fired back there, and they got curious. I should slice off my left one for that blunder."

Maclemar winced at the woman's mouth not for the first time that evening. Her vulgarity, though interesting, hurt the ears. "Right. I'd a done the same thing myself if something jumped at me with deer stomach hanging from its mouth. Let's just fend off these accursed arse nutters and find Poe. And mind the muffler by the weeds there."

"You must like her a lot for you to risk gettin' eaten by these things," Michelle said. She tried out a Muay Thai kick Poe had taught her and smiled at the result.

"You can say that," he said gravely then spotted a baby dead hanging like a slug from the passenger door. "Oh fuckall! A baby!"

She would never forget the babies that had attacked her in the Los Angeles Metro tunnels. The babies were vampire spawn that had been thrown into the storm drain. "Mind if I waste a bullet by blowin' that thing's head off?"

"Bullet well spent, that would be," said Maclemar.

"Damn right. I saw a bunch of these in the subway tunnels when I was still braindead cattle. Swear-to-God-no-kidding, I peed in my pants and snapped out of my stupor," she said as she pulled the trigger and hit the demon baby in the stomach. Like Alka-Seltzer in water, the baby fizzled in its own sauce. "They crawled on the subway ceiling defying gravity and stuck out their lizard tongues at us. I remember Poe coming with Morales in the nick of time to spray those walking abortions until they sizzled. Seems like she always shows up in the nick of time."

"Let's return the favor, shall we? We can't let her go through this horrific muck alone. I can't imagine surviving this without you here. Watch out! To your right!" he warned as a fallen Revenent attempted to rise again and reach for Michelle's leg.

She hacked it with the axe. "So would you say you're head over heels?" she said.

"Michelle lass," grinned Maclemar in the dark. "I don't know. But it is some powerful sentiment nevertheless."

"Yeah, powerful enough to go through this shit," Michelle's voice cracked. Her badass persona had wilted. She was on the highway full of hellish grotesqueness, and it was getting to her.

Surrounded by such abomination that once only existed in books and film, they relied on their little conversations to keep them both from losing it. "And man, don't worry about Poe. She's a superhero," said Michelle. "The power in her arms and legs when we spar could take down even a big guy like you. Oh yeah, she already did in the courtyard." Her giggle sounded faintly crazed. "And the most outlandish thing is that she held back her strength."

Maclemar winced at the masses of ulcerous dead things headed their way. *Be safe, Poe*, he prayed. The creatures were half-a-block away. To keep fear from taking over, he focused his mind on making mincemeat out of the ultra-slow Revenents. "What about you? Why did you decide to go on this thankless mission?"

Michelle snorted maniacally to disguise her rising fear. "Dunno myself. Maybe I want to be a superhero, too." Her eyes worriedly swept the grounds behind the goggles. There were so many of the silent beasts. "So when did you fall for her? The second day or what? Rumor is you've only known her for a few days."

"The first hour maybe, when she was out cold from Passionada's crack on the head," he said. He sighed and shoved a limping creature out of his way. "I was set to hate her for having relations with vampires. But when she opened her puffy eyelids to stare into mine, I knew then that I'd follow her wherever she wanted to go."

"We better run, lover boy. There's too many of them, and my arm's getting tired. They keep getting up even after the hardest blow!"

"Right. Ready when you are," he agreed. He wiped the sweat on his forehead with the sleeve of his jacket. Their sheer numbers were staggering. It was as if all the hard-to-find Revenents had been dropped off and herded to the exact spot where the stench of garlic could no longer be detected. They combed the area strategically.

The Pacheco Pass had many obstacles besides dead jerky. Rocks, stones, pieces of metal and wood tripped Poe's would-be saviors many times.

"I think they were put here to keep any survivors from escaping during the impending raid," he conjectured with fear in his voice. "This is a large-scale production for so few. There are eleven of us now to be exact including the folks at the farm."

"The fuckers really mean business this time. They want the countryside swept," croaked Michelle. The axe in her hand felt as heavy as a sack of thirty Rev heads. "They've come all the way from Los

Angeles. They don't want to go home with a hot potato in their crack."

"I wonder who finked on Sainvire."

"Who knows? It could've been anyone. They have such an attractive offer. A human Benedict Arnold would get a villa in Beverly Hills with unlimited fresh food supply from North Hollywood. Beef, produce, and milk. And of course, the 'hands off, vampires' sign on the gates. A vamp would have a Bel Air mansion of his pick and at least a hundred heads of human cattle," she shrugged.

"It's hard to stay an idealist when everything around you is burnt to cinder. I met Sainvire about three years ago. He was full of plans and glowing with ideas. It's no wonder Poe fell for him. But now it's shocking to see his transformation. He is overworked, haggard, and violent. He's besieged from both ends by friends and enemies alike. The ultimate tragic figure of our time."

"Too bad there won't be anyone to write about his life," Michelle said sarcastically. "For someone so in love, you're real damned open-minded about your girl's lover."

Maclemar jumped a hurdle of child Revenents and shivered from disgust. They looked old enough to play soccer. "I'm not the jealous type. It's good to see a different perspective, in my opinion. Keeps me grounded. But enough about that. What do you think of your vampire knight?"

"Sainvire gets all our respect. He's kept us alive and needle-free these two years," she said while wielding her axe freely. "But people don't always show it. It's easier to yap and complain than say 'thank you,' you know. Hey, to your right!"

Maclemar massaged his sore arm after thumping a stiff over the head.

"But you know," Michelle continued. "Sainvire is so fucking hot. Too bad he's not the type to take advantage. I would've done a Poe, too, and jumped his bones."

"Nice one there," the Welshman grunted.

"Hey. Don't get me wrong, I'd do you too if Poe wasn't my guru and stuff." She laughed a little too violently. The girl was overwhelmed by the walking rot. "You're gorgeous, too, with your tight body and face—"

"Okay. No more descriptions of me, please," he said and cleared his throat.

"Oh fuck!" escaped her lips as the axe blade irretractably lodged in the spine of an unfortunate Revenent. Michelle was left clutching a wooden handle with a Made in China stamp.

"Mae hi wedi cachi arna i!" slipped from his mouth.

"Huh? What the fuck did you just say?" asked Michelle, pulling out an extra gun.

"I said we're buggered. For the chop! We'd better run for it!"

"Uh, we're already running nimrod."

"We've got to do better."

Maclemar took the lead. He struck left and right at the Revenents to create an opening wide enough for the two of them to pass through. The orbs weren't that mindless after all. They knew how to create barriers with their otherwise sluggish bodies. The rancid sheen on their skin was overpowering. *Power in numbers*, he thought wryly. The sound of clicking bones set his teeth on edge.

"What are you doing? Keep up!" Maclemar said acidly. The line held from the main road to the fringes, and it made him nervous. They couldn't escape from any side. They'd have to punch their way through. And Michelle, the fierce pierced, was dawdling.

"I'm looking for something to hit them with," she said in a panic.

"That's bollocks! We need to get ahead and outrun them. This is no time for shell collecting!"

He sheathed his gun and grabbed hold of Michelle's sleeve. He ducked and continued with the tire iron onslaught, shouldering cold, hard bodies out of his way. He did not expect the line to be four men thick.

"Ouch! You buggers!" yelled Maclemar as he clutched the tire iron tighter with his bleeding hand. A Rev took a bite of his forearm. After kicking the creature away from him, two more lunged at his throat. Each whack gave him ten seconds before the Revs would be clicking back into shape. These raccoon-eyed pests wrestled the weapon away from him after a third wraith bit him on the forearm.

"Bum gravy bastards!" he yelled. He punched every lurid corpse that came his way.

Michelle began firing incoherently and chanted, "Can't go back to cattle. Can't go back."

"Michelle! Don't waste your bullets, lass!" he ordered. "More of them will come. Shoot only the aggressive ones," he added to calm the girl down. "The Revs have nothing viperous in their bite. They were humans nearly dead when they were turned. They're weak"

The smell of blood from his wounds awoke the Revenents. Michelle had no choice but to shoot. Seconds later even Maclemar started using his piece. The line had converged to the middle of the street, surrounding the two humans in a thick circle.

"Fuck. Fuck. Fuck," Michelle intoned as she fumbled with a replacement cartridge for her Browning 9mm. Her hands shook so much that she dropped two cartridges before successfully loading her gun. "Shoot me clean in the head, man, if it comes to that."

A succession of shots spooked Maclemar and Michelle and momentarily stopped them from fending off the walking dead. The dense bodies around them thinned as each creature crumpled with a bullet smack center in their heads. 23 bodies lay sprawled on the highway like trodden-down gnomes. The two looked up to see Poe hastily replacing magazines and shoving the guns into her shoulder holsters. The faithful Penny, tail wagging, stood by her companion.

"What up, guys," she said in her funny looking helmet. "Stupid thing to do following me."

Maclemar wiped the water from his upper lip. "Yes it was, but we all know how useless you are in situations like these."

"Positively inept," agreed Michelle.

Still catching her breath, Poe shook her head. "You guys are freaks," Poe said, gulping much needed air and holding the stitch on her side. Once she took a swig of water and poured some on her palm for Penny to lap up, she said, "Let's go then," and broke into a run.

"She must've run back when she heard the gunshots," Michelle said to Maclemar and shook her head. "I don't know if I'd have the cojones to loop back to Revs congregating like Sunday church goers."

"That's my Poe," he said proudly. He leapt over the bodies of Revenents scattered around their feet and tailed Poe. Michelle, with a sigh, followed.

The two caught up with Poe. Again she told them how insane they were.

"You're the one to talk," Michelle mouthed off. "And I can't let my guru fly solo on a fucked up mission like this, right? Otherwise how would we earn our capes?" Feeling a little embarrassed that her words sounded like hero worship, Michelle mumbled, "I'll go check out what's ahead."

Poe scrutinized Michelle's departing back with a puzzled look. "What's up with that girl? A few lessons in kicking and I'm suddenly Yoda?"

"Well you obviously like living in the swamp because you haven't stopped smiling since she called you her guru," he said with a grin.

"Shut up there, Welshman. You read into things too seriously. Must be your useless university learning," she intoned. She fired at a Revenent behind Maclemar.

"You look like an X-wing pilot with that ridiculous helmet on," said Maclemar. He knocked on her head gear.

"Hey!" complained Poe.

"Dw i'n dy garu di."

"Did you just say I'm gross and sweaty?"

"No," he said and almost tripped over Penny.

"Aren't you going to tell me then? I mean you followed me all the way here?"

"Nope. It's a secret," he said and sprinted ahead to join Michelle.

CHAPTER 9

THREE THREADING THROUGH FUNEREAL darkness were better than one. Courage was an inestimable thing to lose in such a dire and unpleasant situation. With great relief Poe, Maclemar, Michelle, and the terrier found themselves jogging in a setting akin to a battle zone, but they were lighter of spirit and better prepared.

Mettle was tested, like the thin membranous façade that it was, when the sound of wreckage getting bulldozed crushed the silence.

"What the fuck's that?" Michelle queried.

"That's heavy machinery clearing traffic behind us," answered Maclemar. He and Michelle looked at Poe. "That means they've found the headquarters, and they're clearing space. I'm thankful most of us have been sent away."

"At least it's coming from the opposite side of the pass," said Poe. She thought about Morales and Piper.

"And we were all doing so well," said Michelle, breathing hard and stretching her calf muscles that seemed to have turned into balls of knotted beasties. "How long do you think we've been at it?"

"Eight or nine miles, easy," said the tall Welshman who was likewise stretching his legs. He felt the bites on his skin and they didn't seem to bother him. "They'll probably get all this cleared up for Trench's stretch limo before we get there."

"And when we do get there, we'll be hella dead weight to the folks we're trying to rescue," said Michelle, stating the obvious.

"Don't care," said Poe. "We keep running." Before her two companions could speak, she dashed away. Penny, who didn't exhibit any signs of fatigue, followed.

With tightly wound limbs Maclemar and Michelle ran as if Freddy Krueger was hot on their heels. The crushing of automobiles to clear the pass for more virulent vehicles was a constant reminder that the invasion was all too real. They didn't stop until they reached the tree Poe had practiced her kicks on just outside the farmhouse.

While her companions held the stitches to their sides and waited to regain control of their breathing, Poe shared a Kit Kat and a protein bar with an unpronounceable name with her dog. She finished off one of her three water bottles but still replaced the empties outside her pack.

"Do you throw nothing away, luv?"

"Not anything I'd reuse again," Poe answered. She scanned the quiet farmhouse. Not even a trace of movement could be seen. "You guys ready?"

———

"You've got to leave me, Joseph," Megan pleaded. Her blue lips barely moved. "I'm dying. I can feel it." She sought her great-uncle for help. "Kaleb, tell him. Convince him."

"I'll tell him no such thing, Megan," the vampire said matter-of-factly. He avoided the horizontal line of red along her bandaged middle. "The helicopter is almost repaired. A few more minutes and we'll all be out of here." The lie lay bitter in his tongue for he knew that the flying machine was in no state to hover a measly inch in the air. The remaining eight were stuck at the farm as the sounds of the enemy clearing the main highway became louder and more imminent. "You have a beautiful baby daughter to hold and feed. You cannot give up now."

"Hear that, Meg? Piper is with her godparents, Morales and Poe, and they're waiting for us," encouraged Joseph. His trademark mirth was absent from his face. Megan's hand was cold and limp in his. "You remember her tiny little fingers, don't you? She has fully formed bitty nails and everything."

Too tired to speak, Megan nodded. Her red hair was slick with ebony sweat. The color didn't suit her at all. "Poe won't let anything happen to her."

"No, she won't," assured Joseph. He caught Kaleb's hard stare. "You know our Poe. She's a fighter."

The two friends left the sick room as soon as Megan dozed off. There was no one in the room to attend her. Miriam, the elderly midwife, had succumbed to a fatal stroke after suturing Megan's Caesarean cut closed. Her body lay in the next room. Joseph was grateful that the woman had waited until her task had been completed before taking her last breath.

"Is it ready?" asked Joseph.

"Far from it," said Kaleb. He raked his black hair with his fingers in frustration. "It's my fault for betting on Rufus to fix and fly the helicopter. The man can barely read. He's only good at playing video games. Why didn't he study up on landing? Goddammit!"

"Too late for recriminations, Kaleb. The question is, what's the backup plan?" asked Joseph who tucked an errant hair behind his ear. "How are we getting Megan out of here?"

"If worse comes to worse and the helicopter can't fly, I'll carry her off somewhere while you and the rest fend off Newbitt and Trench."

Joseph nodded grimly. "That'll do. As long as Megan's safe."

Sainvire put an arm around his best friend's shoulder and squeezed. "She'll be safe, Joseph. She has you and the child to live for."

———

The four had been resting under the tree Poe had used for kicking practice the day before. They could see the farmhouse clearly though no light shone through the windows. The only source of light was behind the barn where major overhaul and repair of the battered helicopter was occurring.

"How much time you think we got?"

"Dunno, Michelle. Maybe half an hour?"

"All I know is I can't run anymore this night," said an exhausted Maclemar. "My last stumble back there did me in."

"Then we'd best find us some more guns and a better shooting position, right quick," said Poe, rising to her feet after petting Penny affectionately. The decade-old dog had followed her through hell and back. "I love you, Pen. And don't you forget it."

A volley of bullets besieged the ground the moment they crossed the fence surrounding the farm grounds.

"Whoa! Whoa, fuckers! Quit firin' on one of your own!" yelled Michelle who remained on her feet while Maclemar and Poe dove on the ground for cover. "Stop shooting, assknocks!"

"Michelle?" asked a voice from one of the rafters.

"Yeah, motherfucker, it's me! And I've got Poe and the Welshman with me, too."

"Hold your fire!" ordered the voice.

Before Poe could haul herself off the ground, Sainvire's size 12 Pumas landed in front of her. With uncharacteristic brusqueness he pulled Poe to her feet.

"What the hell are you doing here, Poe?" he furiously asked. His fingers dug hard into her arm. Penny growled her disapproval.

"I'm, I'm here to protect Megan," she answered with confusion.

"The hell you are! You're supposed to be taking care of Piper!"

Maclemar stepped forward looking equally dangerous. "Sainvire, take your hands off her."

As if realizing the heavy pressure of his hand on Poe's flesh, Sainvire let go and took a step back. He ignored Maclemar who positioned himself protectively to the girl's right. Sainvire said, "You've just complicated an already glum situation, Julia Poe. Not only have you left Megan's child unprotected, you have also brought more problems for us. There are only eight available seats in the helicopter. Now we have to worry about three more bodies."

225

"That's assuming the bird will fly," Maclemar commented. "You know Rufus doesn't know shite, don't you?"

"Painfully. Escape plan or no, we have eleven against a hundred well equipped vampires with bulldozers. The odds are pretty bad any which way we turn."

Maclemar remained quiet in contemplation. He broke his silence with, "I don't know anything about helicopters, but I'm pretty good with engines. I'll see what I can do."

Sainvire nodded. "Thank you, Maclemar."

"Don't thank me yet. If I get the bird running, I expect these two girls to get a spot inside."

"I can't promise that," Sainvire said direly.

"Then I won't even bother."

"Don't be a fucking idiot, Maclemar. This is no time to bargain," pronounced Poe. "I don't want a place that's not rightly mine. Besides, I have Penny to think about. So you better go help Rufus fix that helicopter. Now!"

Maclemar opened his mouth to protest, but Poe's determined face dissuaded him from even trying. "Right ya are, sweets," he said then walked toward the barn.

"Michelle, Ed can supply you with better firepower."

"Yessir. I know when I'm not wanted," she said and walked away. She yelled, "Ed, where the hell are you? I need me some guns!"

Poe and Sainvire glared at each other in stifling quiet until the young woman tore off her night vision gear. Wiping the sweat from her face with her sleeve, Poe locked in her death stare.

"I aim on staying here. No matter what," she said. "So don't worry about me taking up space in your precious helicopter."

"Don't make me sound like a monster," he sighed. "Those seats are reserved for those brave enough to sit it out while Megan recuperates."

Poe nodded. "I know. But I still don't appreciate you thwacking me on the head and choosing for me."

"Sorry about that, Poe," Sainvire apologized. He glanced briefly at the bright moon. "I'm sorry about a lot of things."

"Me, too."

"Maclemar's a good man," he began. "He seems to deeply care for you."

"So what are you trying to say?"

"He'll make you happy."

Poe wiped the sweat from the tip of her nose. "Gee, thanks for the blessing, you goddamn vampire. Do me a favor and don't tell me who I'm going to be happy living life with. Now take me to Megan."

She trailed him. He said, "I'm only thinking practical, Poe. There's no one else I'd rather be with, but my responsibility is immense, and there's no end in sight."

"Just zip it, mister. I don't want you anymore. I'm totally over you, so don't even flatter yourself. I'm into warm-blooded creatures now."

Sainvire stopped walking and grabbed the front of her shirt. His eyes were angry-silver in the moonlight. "I gave up a lot of things when I took up this dead-end cause. I've eaten about as much shit as I can swallow with a smile on my face, but if you think giving you up to a man that breathes is an easy feat, then I can strangle you right now. I want to fly us as far away from here as possible and live our own life so badly I can taste it. But I know that you'll never let me. Just like I know I need to finish this through." He let go of her shirt. "So don't poke fun of my efforts. They cost me dearly."

Poe's throat hurt. He'd thought about absconding with her and leaving all the mess behind. He truly cared for her, and the realization made her want to weep. Instead she swallowed her pride and quietly said, "Since I'm probably gonna die tonight, I need to say *mahal kita.*"

"*Mahal kita din,*" he said, catching her off guard. "Don't be so surprised, Poe. My best friend's Filipino after all."

"So I keep forgetting."

"Just don't forget what counts the most no matter what happens."

"I won't."

The sound of a bulldozer cutting through the perimeter barriers of old farm equipment and rusty automobiles rang.

"You can find Megan in the first floor near the kitchen," he said while taking her hand. "I've got to delay the shock troops a little while longer to give Maclemar and Rufus some more time. I love you, Poe. If I don't see you again, I pray you'll have a long and happy life."

He bent down to kiss her forehead and touched her lips with his thumb. He took to the sky before she could say anything back.

With a tortured heart Poe trudged on to the farmhouse. There really wasn't enough time to cry. Not when the end was so near. "You stay out here, Pen," she said. She bent down and hugged the dog.

228

Joseph opened the door for Poe. His youthful face furrowed with grief. The vampire had been watching them from the kitchen window.

"I told Kaleb it was a bad idea to bash you over the head," he said quietly. "I knew you'd pull a dumb stunt like this." He motioned for her to sit down while he poured her a glass of goat's milk intended for his child. "How's my Piper?"

"The babe's got Megan's lungs," Poe said before taking a sip of the milk. "She was crying something fierce when I got off the bus. I'm sorry for leaving her, Joseph. I was kinda thinking more about Megan, I suppose, because I haven't bonded with your kid yet."

"You better plan on bonding with her quick since you're her godmother."

"Yeah, I heard. I will when this thing's over with."

"You're a good friend to Megan and me. I appreciate your effort." He nodded, and his ponytail bobbed. "I'm sorry it's gonna get you and your friends killed."

"Hey. I knew my days were numbered when I was eight," Poe said with a laugh. "I'm surprised I've lived this long. Anyways, the bus was heading away from Trench's people. That's a big plus."

Wordlessly Joseph stood up and lifted Poe to her feet. He smiled with sad eyes. The vampire who couldn't excrete tears encompassed her in an embrace which lasted a lifetime. "She's dying, Poe," he whispered in her ear. "I can smell death on her."

Poe bit her lower lip until the pain made her forget the selfish urge to cry. "She'll be okay. She's strong."

"Infection has set in, and we don't have working antibiotics." He placed his hands on her shoulders and looked into her wide, fearful eyes. "I asked permission to turn her, but she refused. She doesn't want to live as a dead even for the sake of seeing our child grow up."

Like drowning alone in a dark lake, Poe struggled to keep afloat. There was nothing worse than witnessing the grief of friends. The process of turning someone into a vampire involved puncturing a hole through the cranium and spitting black dead blood in the brain. No wonder her friend was against it.

"Joseph, I'm so sorry. I feel so useless," she said. She pointed at the firepower surrounding her hip belt alone. "These goddamned weapons are useless, and they're all I know in life."

"Convince her, Poe," Joseph said tiredly. "Tell her she can't just leave us. This life is hell enough. But with her in it, it wouldn't be so bad."

She patted his back. He was the closest thing to a brother she had in this whacked world. Joseph even shared the same name as her fallen older brother. Megan's room was next door to the kitchen. With a trembling hand she touched the door handle.

Megan lay on a twin bed surrounded by kerosene lamps. Her cream complexion was pasty with a greenish hue. Her bluish lips and her matted red hair like clumpy seaweed gave her the look of a dying mermaid. Poe inhaled and exhaled dragon-style enough to flush the sadness from her system.

"Megan," she said softly from on the edge of the bed. She took her friend's cold hand. "It's me, Poe. I've come to tell you about Piper."

Blue-veined eyelids fluttered open. Her jewel eyes rested on Poe's face.

"Hey there."

"Hey yourself. You want me to put on *Freaks and Geeks* for you?"

"My favorite show."

"Yup. I see a box set over there. And I think I saw a laptop in the kitchen."

"Thanks, but I'd rather talk to you," Megan said with a cough, and she winced at the pain her cut stomach evoked. "How come you're here? Where's Piper?"

"She's safe with Morales. What a voice box that girl has!"

"You'll watch over her for me?"

"Of course. I'm her godmother for crying out loud."

Megan smiled and closed her eyes for a moment. Then with slow deliberation, she captured her friend's brown eyes trying so hard to be brave. "Poe, I will not be turned into a vampire. I would hate you, Kaleb, and my Joseph for it. Maybe I'd even take it out on Piper."

"But you can't just leave us."

"Sure I can. It'll hurt for a while, but it'll eventually get better." She faced the window where an outline of the moon was visible beneath the thin calico curtains. "They're almost here, Poe. Can you do me a favor?"

Poe sobbed. She clutched Megan's hand with both of hers. "Anything, Megan. Anything."

Megan smiled wanly, extricating her hand and patting Poe's disheveled ponytailed hair.

"I don't think I've ever seen you with your hair down, Poe. I bet you'd look mighty pretty."

"Sorry. I'm sweaty. I had to run wearing this to get back here," she explained. She held her night vision helmet.

"My amazing Poe. Such a good friend."

"What can I do for you?" Poe asked. She wiped tears from her face.

"You can lend me one of your pistols and leave the room." Megan's hand stopped playing with Poe's hair.

"Jesus, you can't ask that of me."

"You said anything."

"Not that. Never that!" she yelled. She got on her feet and backed out. "Joseph would never forgive me!"

Before Megan could utter another word, Poe exited the room. Once the door closed she sat on the floor and covered her ears. Her eyes and nose oozed.

"She asked for your gun?" Joseph queried. He was suddenly sitting on the floor beside her.

"Uh huh," Poe answered miserably. She took the tissue he handed her and blew her nose.

"She asked for mine, too," he said grimly. "I guess she has the right to die the way she wants. Especially with those bastard lions at the gates." Determination etched on his chiseled face. He stood up and pulled a .22 from his back pocket. "Say your goodbyes, Poe. Then go outside. We don't have much time."

CHAPTER 10

A SINGLE SHOT WAS all it took.

Poe heard it as she ran blindly toward the barn. The helmet bobbed unused against her legs. All she could think of were Maclemar's reliable arms enveloping her. He was the only solace left for her in such dark times.

With only the moon for illumination, Poe did not see the two vampire scouts that dogged her every step. Penny made a throaty warning noise, but Poe didn't pay attention. Finding the girl's tears apropos, the taller of the two reached out and yanked Poe's hair. Her run ended. Chuckling quietly, the vampire clamped his gloved hand over Poe's mouth. Penny clamped down on the intruder's boot but took a kick for her troubles.

"That's right, little girl. Cry away. The big bad wolf's here," he whispered in her ear.

The vampire, half-a-head taller than Poe, bared his fangs that sharpened as she stared up at them. He licked his lips slowly for show. On impulse Poe jumped as high as she could, ramming his chin shut with her head until the vampire's fangs pierced his own tongue.

Quickly she kicked at the howling vampire's shin and buried a wrist knife in his neck. The shorter vampire, not expecting retaliation from such a small person, was taken aback to Poe's advantage. Before he could extract a menacing 9mm Tanfoglio Force from his hip holster, Poe beat him to the draw. Two shots squarely in the face felled him to the ground next to his writhing buddy. Poe removed her knife from the tall vampire's throat and resheathed it at her wrist. With her foot she felt for the body armor on his person. The only safe place to aim for was the face. "Nobody kicks my dog!" she gritted. "C'mon, Pen."

She looked around the farm for another intruder.

"There's nothing like violence to stop a girl's tears," she pronounced angrily and picked up the Tanfoglio packing 16 rounds. "They're here!" she shouted as loudly as she could. She wiped the snot dripping from her face with her sleeve. "The motherfuckers are here!"

She plopped on her helmet and ran to the helicopter she could hear revving. *At least the propellers are turning*, thought Poe.

"Get inside! They're here!" Poe hollered over the din of the engine and propellers. The dent-studded helicopter, formerly used as a Medevac, looked like rock monsters had chewed and spit it out.

"Whoa there, Sharren," Maclemar said as he wiped his oily hands on his jeans. "This thing won't hover. The engine is running too lean. It loses compression after just a few feet in the air."

"Shit. There's no time for that. What can you do?"

"We think it's the piston. It's burnt around the edges," he said. He climbed the second ladder to join a harried Rufus. "We're replacing it now, so keep the enemy from shooting at this baby."

"Where's Michelle?"

"Up that tree yonder," said Ed, the smallest of Sainvire's fighters. He appeared from behind and startled Poe. He tossed semi-automatics and ArmaLites on the ground. "I killed six scouts just now."

"Can I have one of these ArmaLite things?"

"Help yourself, Poe," the man said. He added, "I recommend the barn roof if you're going to spot us. I'll take the rear."

"Right," said Poe, shouldering a long-range semi-automatic rifle and climbing the gutter to the roof. "Stay there, Pen. I'll get you once this is over." The dog's eyes apprehensively followed her ascent to the roof. Once settled on a spot Poe organized her weapons by size. Then she waited.

She noticed movement by the trailers. She blinked several times until she was certain at what she was seeing. "It's Maple carrying Perla," she said aloud. "I thought they would've left by now. And two jerkweeds are right at her heels."

She took off her helmet and put the rifle in front of her. With relief she found night scopes attached to the firearm. Bad elements began firing in the rear, catching Maple in the back. *Good thing she's immune to garlic bullets.*

"C'mon, focus," she urged herself and followed the little green people. She fired, taking one of them down. The second green blur ducked behind a tree. The respite gave Maple a fighting chance to reach the back of the barn. Never taking her sight off the figure behind the tree, Poe waited patiently. The moment he peeked out, she squeezed the trigger. She hit the invader in the face.

"The head's the only target," she repeated with conviction. A tad louder she asked behind her shoulder, "You okay, Maple?"

"Yes. So is Perla. Thanks to you," answered the middle-aged vampire with bludgeon arms. She tucked a drug-induced Perla into the rear of the helicopter. "Is this the only firepower we've got left?" she asked Ed.

"'Fraid so," he answered.

"How's it going, Maclemar?" asked Maple who kneeled on the ground to pick up some weapons. The vest she was wearing had deflected the bullets.

"Alright. So far. I think the new piston will get this flying machine off the ground," he answered. "Better grab your eight on board."

Rufus, silent all this time, spoke as he climbed down the ladder. He scratched at his missing ear and said, "Everyone's here except for Prentis, Joseph, Sainvire, and the woman."

"Her name's Megan, Rufus. You best remember that," Maple chided, squinting at his oil covered face and filthy overalls.

"Sorry. Megan."

The smell of kerosene blanketed the air. A flash of light followed.

"The house is on fire!" Michelle yelled from up the mustard tree.

Before Poe could scramble off the roof to pull the occupants to safety, the sight of a solitary figure watching the blaze stopped her. It was Joseph.

"He lit the fire," Poe said under her breath.

Her throat constricted. She swallowed her tears, avoiding any sentimental nonsense to claim her emotions. She saw the slowly moving puppets of darkness clicking their way toward them. The fire illuminated dozens of Revenents. They were the first wave sent to eviscerate Sainvire's holdovers.

"Revenents!" yelled Michelle from her perch. "Damn Revenents. Prepare yourselves!"

Tearing his eyes away from the burning house, Joseph calmly approached several of the walking skeletons and doused them with the canister of gasoline he held in his hand. He lit a match and watched as a handful of them caught fire. With a steady voice he asked Michelle to climb down from the tree.

"I can shoot them from here," she protested but climbed down nonetheless.

"You're getting on that helicopter, Michelle," he said solemnly, leaving no room for arguments.

For once Michelle had no smart aleck retort. She understood that the conflagration was Megan's funeral pyre.

Poe fired on as many heads until she exhausted the shots in her rifle. But they kept coming in droves.

"Mom and Dad, help us!" prayed Poe quietly. "Let my death be at my own hands."

The helicopter hovered past the barn roof during a practice run, bringing a weak smile from Poe. "Good job, Rufus!" she yelled once it landed feebly in the back of the barn. She was scared as hell at the flying machine crashing after a mile in the air.

"Not me, man," he hollered from out the helicopter window. "It's your friend, Maclemar! It was all him. Genius, he is!"

Poe's grin wavered. A few yards away flew Sainvire, burdened by a limp body in his arms. He soared low due to several Revenents latching on to his legs. The weight was dragging him lower and lower to the ground – to the grasping arms of flesh hungry Revenents.

"Hold on, Kaleb," she whispered. She took aim at the Revenent wearing a crusty tuxedo and hugging Sainvire's right leg. Another creature tugged his other leg. "It has to be the head," she said, calling on the sharp-shooter in her. "I am Bruce Lee's daughter, Jackie Chan's niece, and Xena's clone."

Pop. Pop.

As soon as the hangers-on lost their grip as they mislaid their heads, Sainvire was able to soar higher, reaching the anxious group behind the barn. Prentis, a pretty blonde the same height as Sainvire, was in his arms. Her left arm hung by a few strands of muscle and sinew. Ed swiftly took the halfdead from Sainvire's arms and arranged her next to Perla inside the helicopter.

"I can't take the opening," said Michelle apprehensively. "Give it to Poe. Or to Maclemar."

"Get in, Michelle," Sainvire ordered. "And you, too, Maclemar."

"No. Not me. Let Poe go," Maclemar said. He shook his head.

"Eight people only, remember?" interrupted Rufus. "Sorry, but this baby is unreliable."

"He can take my place," assured Sainvire. "Get in, James."

"No way," Maclemar said angrily. "Let Poe—"

"Leave her to me, man. I'll fly her away from here." Before Maclemar could further protest, Sainvire said, "Look. She's the lightest one out of all of you. Don't worry. I won't try to steal her away from you. I can't even think about such things right now."

Poe, left to use the ArmaLite because her rifle was out of ammo, was too busy mowing down Revs and the trickling vampires to notice the spectacle below her. When a gust of air nearly blew her smaller guns off the barn roof, Poe looked up in time to see Michelle and her friends shooting at creatures below from inside the chopper. That was when she noticed Maclemar's grim eyes looking directly at her helmeted face from the window. He placed his perpetually dirty hand to his heart until she could see him no longer.

Sainvire fought off two vampires that could fly. He slashed them with his sharp blade-length nails and disappeared along with the helicopter.

Her eyes watered. She couldn't help it. She was alone in a sea of monsters.

Blinking away her tears Poe concentrated on the vampires climbing onto the roof. She blasted them as she ran upon the roof frame sections undamaged by Rufus' sloppy helicopter landing. When her ArmaLite clunked empty, she picked up the Tanfoglio and Beretta and fired at the ten wily, rancid nightmares that had made it to the roof.

"Jesus, Mary, and Joseph. Mom and Dad, I need your help," she pleaded.

Poe turned to her right in time to see the thundering yellow monstrosity of a bulldozer at maximum acceleration. The vamps that saw the machine coming jumped from the roof. "Penny, you better run!" she cried.

Her left hand pulled the trigger on those still unaware of the impending destruction wrought by a giant Tonka toy while her right hand pointed the Beretta at her own forehead.

"May you all make it safely and continue the fight. Sorry I didn't get to play with you, Piper," she said. With a strained smile and a nervous cough, she prepared to die.

CHAPTER 11

THE GUN WAS YANKED away from her hand. The roof beneath her collapsed.

Before falling into the gaping hole the bulldozer had chunked, Poe felt her legs lift into the air. Bullets grazed her thigh and dinged off her helmet. But she kept flying. It was as if she was dead after all.

Old Man Death was a funny thing. He looked like the man she loved, and he carried her dog under his other arm.

"Sainvire?" she asked in a daze.

"Sorry to botch up another suicide attempt, Poe. But I can't handle you out of this world while I exist."

"I guess I'm not dead 'cause I have altitude sickness."

"No, but you will be if you don't shoot at the ancient undead on our trail," he said. He adjusted her on his shoulder like he was burping her while keeping the dog comfortable with his other arm. Penny the dog took to the air like a real trooper. Poe really was the best shooter Sainvire had ever seen.

"Right," Poe nodded. She reached for a firearm in her side sheath. "Still alive. I gotta kill."

Even in the air Poe's sure-shot skills hadn't abandoned her. A gift from God, Sister Ann had claimed more than once. *It's a gift 'cause God owes me*, Poe thought sarcastically as she shot each long-toothed gremlin that pursued them with precision. *God knows how much life sucks in vampire times, so he made me pest control.*

Sundry other thoughts floated in her mind even when she killed the last flying nasty. Two years ago she had depleted the flying vamp population in L.A. with the help of a rifle. Sainvire shifted her position once more so she could wind her arms about his neck. She could feel his disfigured shoulder bulging beneath her forearm. The moonlight emphasized the fatigue about his face. The vampire was even slightly shaking. With gentleness not known to Poe, she touched the scar above his lips.

"You know something?" she said while staring into his silver eyes. "I think you're my hero."

Sainvire laughed as he prepared to descend to a hard-to-reach field surrounded by rocky slopes. "I think you're mistaken. As far as I know I've always been on the losing side of things. I believe I've never been successful in anything, so I hope you're not serious."

Poe felt solid ground. Reluctantly she let her arms fall to her side. "Heroes don't have to be winners all the time." Penny whined and ran around in circles in praise of the land beneath her feet.

"It sure would help," he sighed. He collapsed behind a boulder. "Help me with this coat, will you?"

She pulled the dark coat from his arms and about his shoulder. It was only then that she noticed the wetness of his shirt. His back and limbs were riddled with bullets still lodged in the skin, and his left side had been cut three inches deep. Brackish blood trickled from his side. "Kaleb! You've been hit!" she cried.

"I know," said Sainvire. "I think I'm done for."

"What's your problem? Everyone and their dog's wearing bulletproof vests but you? Do you have a death wish or something?" she accused. Tears spilled down her cheek. "And don't say that. You're not gonna die. I won't let you!"

"You seem to have a magical pack," he said lightly, wincing. "Would you happen to have Plasmacore on you?"

"No. Sorry," Poe answered gravely. "You're going to be okay, aren't you?"

"Sure. Just let me sleep. With luck the bullets will pop out by themselves soon enough, and this wound on my side will solder together." Sainvire had made himself a guinea pig by undergoing garlic injections to introduce the poison into his system. Years later the vampire achieved his goal by achieving immunity to the potent vampire killer.

She brushed Sainvire's hair from his forehead. The vampire's skin felt clammy to the touch. "How about I cut myself and give you some of my blood?"

Sainvire smiled weakly. "Thanks for the offer, but your blood would weaken me even more. I might not be able to withstand the sun if I go back to drinking pure human blood."

"What about animal blood?" she asked in a desperate voice.

"Penny?"

"Shut up. Of course not!"

"Animal blood would sustain me for a few hours, but I think most creatures know to hide once the sun goes down."

Poe covered the vampire in his coat and thought about Penny, Chops, and the baby. She couldn't let any of them die, especially the love of her life. "Where can I get Plasmacore around here, Kaleb? Joseph said you've planted crates of it everywhere for emergency. And this is an emergency."

Sainvire, shivering, answered, "There's an abandoned mine about nine miles south of here. We hid some Plasmacore there."

Poe picked up her pack and nodded. "I'll go get some right now."

"Be sensible, Poe," said the vampire who was finding it harder to speak. "Scouts are all around."

Poe leaned down and kissed Sainvire's cold lips. "Just point which way is south, and I'll take it from there." Outside of Downtown Los Angeles she never did figure out her directions. "Don't worry. I have Penny with me." As if to assure the vampire, the dog placed a dirty paw on Sainvire's leg.

"You keep to the trees. Away from the green, the ground will be rock and gravel. Avoid walking on those until the very end when you see an abandoned mine shaft. Trees were planted in threes every quarter-mile or so on the gravel end. They'll let you know you're heading the right direction."

"Won't be a problem with my Skywalker night helmet."

Sainvire grabbed Poe's arm before she could leave. "Have I ever told you how much I love you, Julia Poe?" he asked in a weak voice. He was near delirium.

Poe wiped away errant tears. "Yes, Kaleb. You've told me twice before, and I'd really like to hear it again and again. Hold on for me, okay?"

244

The vampire didn't answer. He had lost consciousness.

"Help Sainvire, Great Ali," she muttered as she sprinted in the dark followed by her terrier. She prayed to anyone listening to help Joseph deal with his loss and for Perla to wake up from her cattle stupor. She was annoyed with herself for not properly thanking Michelle for backing her up. *What a great gal she is.*

Then there was Maclemar. She'd known him but a short time, but she was positive she loved him. Not the caliber of love she felt for Kaleb, but it was special all the same. He was willing to die for her, an inconsequential girl with attitude he'd met only days before.

Poe tripped on a jutting rock her helmet had failed to illuminate and skinned her elbows. She gulped for air. She was living a Twilight Zone episode. *The girl who jogged until she dropped dead.*

Exhausted having run nearly fifteen miles that night, Poe looked down at Penny. The dog was breathing erratically and panting. "I'm sorry, girl. This is a hell of a weird night. Thank you for sticking with me." She sat down on the ground and hugged the dog that smelled of soil. "Please always stay with me, Pen. I know I put you through a lot."

Losing side or not, Poe was dogged to fight on by the time the sun rose in the pinkish eastern sky. She needed Plasmacore for Sainvire. *Whoever gave me the gift to obliterate and to live this long must have a purpose for me. And that is to end the reign of corrupt, racist, and gluttonous vampires.*

"I can't die. It's not allowed," she said out loud. "I resolve to be a hero like Sainvire. I'm gonna shake the very foundation of this jacked up society. Only this time I'm winning. And you're going to be by my side, Penny Pen."

Shaky legs, screaming lungs and all, she stood up and resumed running. Her body was so tired that she felt feverish. She tracked the random trees planted on the other side of the green. They reached the mine in about two hours, longer than what she would have liked. Her knees felt arthritic, and her joints ached. She paused not too far from the mine to hydrate her dog and herself with her last bottle of water. Sitting down on the dirt, Poe stretched a leg. She took out a Ziploc full of jerky sticks from her pack and passed them to Penny who chowed them down like the end was near. As she was extending the other leg for a stretch, Penny growled in her tongueless manner. In that awkward position she found five mustached undead, high-powered rifles in their arms, surrounding her.

"What have we here?" said the burliest of the five. "Could it be Public Enemy Number Two?"

Poe inched her hand to her holster, but the burly guy said, "Hey hey. You reach for that gun, your ass is mine." He motioned for the others to disarm her. "Check everywhere, including her ankles. This little girl is slippery."

Three men dressed in LAPD blues stripped her of her pack and weapons until Poe felt naked. One of them even cupped a feel which made Poe seethe with hate.

246

"Want me to shoot the dog, Gary?" asked the runtiest of the lot.

"No!" Poe screamed, scrambling to her knees and hugging Penny to her upper body. "No one touches my dog!" Poe felt ill. Sainvire was dying and getting Plasmacore to him seemed impossible now. Her energy was so drained, and as far as she could tell, the five men were vampires.

"Sainvire is injured, isn't he, girl?" asked Gary, the ringleader. "Isn't that why you've come to the mine for Plasmacore?"

"Plasmacore?" asked Poe innocently. "I don't know anything about Plasmacore. I'm only trying to get away from Revs and vamps from the dark side."

"Don't bullshit us, bitch," a vampire named Henry with heavyset eyelids said. "You and your dog were last seen carried away by Sainvire. We have it on good authority that he was cut up by a sword laced with garlic oil and shot multiple times. And we know every Plasmacore stash location within a fifty-mile distance. The turkeys you run with left behind a map."

Poe glanced about. She looked like a tiny football player in her helmet. She saw five vicious-looking dead that would never let her escape. The price on her head was too high. She sniffed, "I don't know about Plasmacore, officer. As for Sainvire, he died three hours ago. I watched him turn to mush."

"She's lying," one of the generic mustached men accused.

"Look, asshole," said Poe. She rose and held her dog protectively like a baby. "Sainvire was the love of my life. I watched him die, and I couldn't do anything about it. I don't really give a fuck if you think I'm lying." She wiped away tears, real tears, for she knew Sainvire was as good as dead without Plasmacore.

"Why did you come here then?" asked Henry.

"I was hoping to find Sainvire's people," explained Poe angrily. "Me and Penny are alone now."

"Although I feel for your loss," a round-faced civilian said, "That's what you get for fucking a dickhead thief like Sainvire. Do you know how hard it's been for us? We've had to drink tainted black blood, Mexican blood, and Asian blood. The blood of our old janitors and bedpan cleaners. Fuck, it's just sick!"

Poe, glad that she didn't stutter anymore, laughed. "Man, you're hilarious! If you weren't flapping your mouth in semi-lucid sentences, I'd think you were a chicken flapping its wings or something."

In a blur the civilian lunged at Poe. She didn't see him coming nor did she see Gary block his way. With a shove Gary pushed him away from Poe. "I'm not going to lose my stake, Robert. You keep your hands to yourself. Trench is circling his chopper as we speak, so hold your horses." He looked at Poe. "And you. Keep your trap shut, or I'll kill your dog. Got it?"

Poe clutched Penny tighter until the dog whined in discomfort. "Got it."

———

Poe held Penny for three hours, even refusing to allow the dog to do her natural business. She wept

248

and did not care that the vampires jeered at her. Sainvire was dying or possibly dead, and she couldn't help him. His light gray eyes were blazed in her mind's eye. Life without him hurt, and her grief even eclipsed her vow for vengeance.

Lights appeared at the horizon. Gary flicked his flashlight on and off until the sound of a chopper was heard. The vampire had confiscated her helmet, and the lights of the descending helicopter, though frightening, gave her something to look at besides the stars. *I'm dead,* she thought gravely. *I don't even care to pray anymore.*

The five told their boss about Sainvire when he landed. Trench had eyes only for the girl who had irreversibly altered his life for the worse.

Traces of old tears decorated her dusty face. The child he had seen at Goss' Downtown loft was gone. Facing him was a healthier Julia Poe with some meat on her bones, and her arms clung to the ratty dog. He had expected her to look defeated. He hadn't anticipated the look of grief.

"I've waited for this moment," were the first words that escaped the master vampire's lips. "How come I'm not as happy as I should be?"

Poe shrugged. She did not feel verbally combative. She looked at Quillon Trench's face expecting to see the burnt crags she'd left on his skin when she had sprayed him with garlic water. About his face he wore a scarf that only showed his intelligent blue eyes. Rumor was he didn't leave his home any longer. The nightclub he owned at the Bonaventure Hotel shut the moment Morales had shoddily blown up the building. He never tried to open another club. Trench didn't even help defend the highly productive blood farms in Los Angeles. Only his own.

"Are you going to kill me, or are you going to torture me somewhere else?" asked Poe tiredly. Her husky voice intrigued Trench.

"I remember your voice well, Julia," he said. "Per your question, I'm going to take you back to Los Angeles. And as for you five, you will be well rewarded. Just make sure you don't get burned a couple of hours from now before dusk.

"What do you mean?" asked Gary. "Aren't you taking us with you?"

"No room, my man," he said. He gestured to Poe to step into the transport.

"Are we going to be picked up by one of the Hummers?" asked Henry who was looking with panic at his pals. None of them were sun-immune.

"The Hummers are in San Francisco with Nesbitt's battle army. Sorry about that."

"You mean to—"

Trench raised his hand. "Julia, get that dog out of my chopper." The look of alarm on Poe's face gave him the satisfaction he had been looking for earlier.

"No. Please, I can't leave my dog. She has to come with me," she said. Her lips trembled.

"No dirty rats on this chopper," said Trench adamantly.

"Sir—" began Gary.

Trench faced Gary whose bulky body seemed to sag at the scrutiny of the master vampire. "I don't like being interrupted, Gary. It's very rude." He turned back to Poe who held her dog more tightly.

"Julia, what did I just say?" he said.

Poe broke down. All the misery she'd experienced that night coalesced at that moment. Megan's death, Sainvire's death, and parting from her friends diminished her.

"Please," she cried. Her shoulders shook with every sob. "K-kill me, but don't take her away from me."

Curiosity replaced Trench's annoyance. The famous cattle rustler and vampire killer was sobbing over a dog and begging his permission. All those years he had wasted hating her for disfiguring him. Every night he had thought about the torture he was going to inflict on Julia Poe. After all, because of her he had to bind his face with a scarf when he went out in public. The beautiful people he used to surround himself with disgusted him now. Most of them he had dismissed for they reminded him too much of his flawed face.

And here she was begging him, her beautiful dark eyes inundated with grief.

"Sir, please. You can't just leave us here," said Henry.

Trench turned his head to Henry, flew at him, and grabbed his hair. He took a dagger from a sheath on his belt and slit Henry's throat from ear to ear then stabbed him in the heart. He stood beside Gary's corpse and wiped the black liquid from his hand onto the dead's shirt.

"I hate being interrupted," muttered Trench. "Do you want my men to mow you down?" he asked the four who had caught Poe while pointing out three vamps replete in S.W.A.T. uniforms. "Or do you want to hide out in the mine shafts to avoid the sun?"

"We'll hide out, sir," said Gary. The three others echoed his answer.

"Good. Now disappear from my sight."

"Sir," Gary said fearfully.

"Yes?" asked Trench with venom.

"We've worked for you for over ten years," he said in disbelief.

Trench's eyes softened. "You five have been very loyal to me, and I'm truly sorry about this. But times are different now. I can only keep the best people. I can't afford to waste limited cattle blood on unimaginative pedestrians like you." He waved his hand at them. "Shoo now and good luck."

He walked back toward the helicopter door to study Julia Poe once more. Before he could say anything, Julia Poe sniffed and said, "Let me keep my dog. You can kill me however you want. I won't protest."

Trench adjusted the scarf about his face. "Then what am I going to do with your dog afterward?"

"You don't have to worry about that," said Poe. "I'll kill her myself before you torture me."

Trench, two inches shorter than Sainvire, laughed. "Why don't you just let her go in the wilderness here? I'm sure that's better than committing doganasia?"

"Because," Poe began.

"Because what, Julia Poe?" Trench asked curiously, his brow rising.

"Because there might be a chance we'll escape from you," said Poe. She wiped her nose with the back of her hand.

Trench laughed so hard that he held on to his sides. *The impudence!* He handed Poe a handkerchief

with his monogram sewed on and said, "I'd like to
see you try."

CHAPTER 12

THEY TOOK HER DOG away. Insurance, they said.

Trench ordered her to take hour-long baths in scented oils and dense bubbles that made her slip in the overlarge tub. The master vampire now owned Downtown's most prized of all buildings, the undulating metallic Disney Concert Hall whose form flowered into what some say looked like a ship's mast or peeled-back cabbage leaves. Whatever the description, the building had no inferior photographic angles. Trench had added luxurious rooms and even more sinful bathrooms to the symphony building. Frank Gehry, the architect, would have turned in his grave at the desecration.

Janitors, or ethnic humans who were practically slaves of vampires, worked to sand down her calluses with sandstones, loofahs, and lotions. She tried speaking with them in hope of finding where her dog was being held. But none would utter a word. *Trench must've put the fear of his fangs into them.* An elderly Nicaraguan woman whose name Poe didn't know evened out the bottom of her self-trimmed hair. A morbidly thin Asian gave her a pedicure from hell while a one-eyed black woman in her late forties manicured her finger nails.

"I'm getting tortured," muttered Poe. She did not see Trench for the weeks she'd been at the symphony hall. She often thought of escaping, but they'd given her nothing but a flimsy Japanese robe and slippers to wear. Modesty itself was better than handcuffs and a ball and chain around her neck. If there was one thing about Poe, she was shy about flaunting her body. She bided her time.

The captors served Poe rich meals, but she discarded meat and wine for simpler and more vegetarian friendly offerings. Water suited her just fine, and she didn't trust herself with alcohol at the moment. The thought of Sainvire might have turned her into a lush.

On the third week she met someone familiar.

"Kawana!" she said when the pretty black police officer, paradoxically one of Trench's favorites, entered the room holding plastic shopping bags filled with horrors. Trench had personally turned the beautiful woman with high cheekbones. He punctured a hole in her skull, and biting his tongue he let blood trickle in her exposed brain. Unlike other vampires, Trench didn't discriminate when it came to beauty. Kawana had been a loyal spy for Sainvire from the very inception.

"Shhh," Kawana warned. "They can't know that you know me, Poe. I'm one of the original crew Trench hasn't gotten rid of. I need to be here."

Poe nodded and indicated a chair. Her room was pristine white from floor to ceiling from the bed coverings down to the furniture. A Campbell's Soup Can painting by Andy Warhol provided the only color. "Tell me. Have they found Morales' bus?" whispered Poe. She felt guilty for leaving her goddaughter behind.

"No. They've found no one. That's why Nesbitt is so angry. He received information from a recovered blood victim hoping to have a better life. Instead he became Nesbitt's evening meal," she said as she opened one of the boxes. "It was a good move to split everyone up before the invasion. Take off your slippers and put these on."

Poe's eyes bulged at the three-inch silver high heel shoe Kawana was holding in her hand. "What the hell?"

"He wants me to teach you how to dress, how to walk, and how to put on make-up. He said you're a plebe barbarian, and you need to become a lady."

"Um, no way. I'm not doing it."

Kawana shook her head. "Listen, Poe. This is better than torture or being turned to a blood cow. Besides, I'll be with you during the day. What I hear, you hear."

"Any word on Sainvire?" Poe said quietly for which Kawana shook her head. The young woman, unaccustomed to her hair down, swatted it away. Under orders from Trench, the janitors had taken away the six hair bands she had always brandished on her wrist.

For weeks she'd been nearly naked, and she kept to her room. If it weren't for the shame, she would have tried harder to break out. Her only consolation was the outdated plasma TV and the stacks of DVDs on the shelf. She was a movie buff. Aside from books and magazines she had learned worldly things from film.

Angrily she tossed the slippers from her feet onto the other side of the room. "I don't understand. Is he going to eat me, or is he waiting for me to break my ankles? I have pretty wide feet for being barefoot in my bunker most of my life."

"Just endure this, Poe," said Kawana. "At least your life will be spared this way. And your dog's."

"Where's Penny?" Poe asked. She placed her hand on the petite vampire's shoulder.

"Under lock and key somewhere in the Hall just to make sure you behave," said the woman who could pick up a vehicle with one arm without breaking a sweat. "Now let's see how you do."

Poe took the first twenty seconds to sprain her ankle walking on high heels, two weeks to finally be able to stand on her own without falling, and another week to walk like a runway model in four-inch spiked heels.

Within a month Poe learned how to curl her lashes, apply mascara, and bring out her features with blush and eye pencils. Kawana brought designer dresses chosen by Trench himself, but Poe adamantly refused to wear them. She opted for straight-legged slacks and silk blouses. Trench twice made an appearance to monitor Poe's progress. Both times he wordlessly left the room, and his scarf billowed behind him.

"I don't understand, Kawana," Poe complained. "What the hell does he want from me? I've mastered all this useless shit for what? When's he going to take pieces of me and make me eat them?"

Kawana brushed Poe's long black hair until it glistened. "Nesbitt stayed here last night. He was very angry that you're still alive and Barbied up. This man is Quillon's mentor, Poe. He has a lot of influence, and my boss didn't cave. He was adamant that no one touches you. Nesbitt left in a fury."

"So what now?"

Kawana opened a box full of expensive breast-enhancing brassieres Poe had never laid eyes on. "I don't think Trench knows what to do with you."

The time came when Quillon Trench summoned Poe to accompany him for the evening. He insisted she wear a red Dolce & Gabbana dress that hugged the figure and showed off the cleavage. Poe came down the escalator dressed in black slacks, black strapped high heels, and a beige long-sleeve silk blouse. She surveyed the building interior which she hadn't fully memorized. An elevator stood at the south end of the Hall, fifty feet from Trench's room. On the same floor as the escalator was the concert hall, untouched by Trench, in all its wood and acoustic glory. Five traditional vamps and two halfdeads, noticeable by their tans and inhuman speed, stood like impeccably well dressed FBI agents to guard her floor. Kawana said the kitchen was downstairs, and it had a back door if she ever decided to bust out of there.

The vampire was waiting for her in the lobby. She bated her breath for Trench to scream at her for disobeying him and choosing her own outfit, but he just shook his head and motioned her toward the exit door. Two well armed vampires held the glass door open for them. A shiny black Lincoln Town Car waited by the curb.

They drove in silence. Poe glanced at Trench just once and tried to figure out who tailored his snazzy dark designer suit. Kawana said it was important to Trench that his women know style. *But what the hell,*

I'm not one of his women. I'll never be one. He killed Goss and Sister Ann after all. And she could care less about brand names. She missed her black t-shirts, olive green army pants, and the comforts of her Adidas sneakers.

She looked out the car window at the top-to-bottom Downtown transformation. Almost all of the stranded cars had been cleared, and actual working cars drove the roads. Traffic lights had been rewired and bulbs changed to illuminate the streets. Kawana had said progress was all due to Trench who had consolidated power after the Vampire Council disbanded. The vampire had vision. Poe had to give him that.

Her wingtip eyebrows drew together as she recalled what Trench had looked like before she had disfigured his face. She'd only seen him once at the Eastern Columbia building under harrowing circumstances. She vaguely remembered that his features had been better than average compared with other vampires. His blue eyes had thrown daggers at her when he ordered his men to finish her off. For the life of her Poe couldn't picture in detail what her captor had looked like. Now he was simply Mr. Scarfman with reddish brown hair that fell nearly to his jaw.

"Why didn't you wear the dress I chose for you this evening?" Trench startled her in his deep, sensuous voice.

Poe looked at him and shrugged. "I don't wear dresses. Not even my mom could get me to wear them."

She heard him chuckle behind the scarf. "You don't know how persistent I am, Julia. In any case, why don't you like wearing dresses?"

Poe smiled against her will. "I don't like them because they make me feel like I'm naked underneath."

"One of these days you're going to wear a dress for me," he said commandingly. Before she could retort the car stopped. They had reached their destination. Poe recognized it as Warehouse Alley, the filthiest, seediest place in Downtown. There were no rules, and everything was game in that part of town.

Poe gulped down her fear. She remembered the giant-size rats and the gambling den where bored Ancient vamps anted humans for poker games. Trench extended his arm. Poe glanced at it and looked back at Trench. "You're supposed to hold my arm, Julia."

"Oh." She nodded and complied.

Even Warehouse Alley, it seemed, had received a makeover. The warehouse club they were going to was named Drip. She could already hear the music from inside. In fact her internal organs quaked from the resonating boom of the bass, the music was so loud.

"What are we doing here?" asked Poe nervously.

"It's about time you got out of the house, Julia," he said.

Poe exhaled loudly. "Is this how you're gonna get rid of me? A mass feeding?" Trench laughed, patting her hand. "You do know that I'm hated around here, don't you?"

"I do," he said in amusement. "Hence the fun."

"So that's how it is," Poe mumbled.

Drip was crawling with dead and halfdead killing their boredom away. A stage stood in the middle of the warehouse. Three extremely attractive redheads, each with her own dance pole, gyrated and pumped their hips to techno beats with the accompaniment of pulsating colored lights. The speed for which they worked the poles dizzied, and they would sexily slow down, arousing the hooting onlookers. Curiosity getting the better of Poe, her eyes roamed the club. Waiters dressed in stereotypical gothic black leather pants and red silk shirts carried cages filled with whimpering cats and dogs and handed them wriggling to patrons who liked their drink warm and fresh. Vampires bit down on their petrified meals after taking out their shavers to clean the creatures' neck areas and enjoyed the entertainment. Poe shivered.

"Trench," Poe tried to whisper in the tall vampire's ear. She finally tugged him down to her level when he didn't respond. "You haven't brought Penny here, right?"

He shook his head and patted her arm once more. "No, Julia. I promised you I would keep your dog safe. You can trust me."

Poe thought of the five vampires he had left at the mines and felt fear surge through her chest.

"Master Trench!" greeted the club owner, Breegan. He was a short man with bald head, and he resembled a St. Patrick's Day leprechaun. "It's been too long since you've graced us with your presence."

"You're very kind, Breegan," said Trench, sounding bored. "I need a table close to Shandra."

"Of course, sir. I see your beautiful date is not from around—" Breegan stopped talking and gawked at the girl. He saw the five-inch scar on Poe's face. "You're Poe! Julia Poe!"

Trench grabbed the man's collar until Breegan's feet were dangling from the ground. "You will get me that table, and you will kindly shut up. Do you hear me?"

Breegan nodded, and Trench released his shirt. "Yes, sir. Follow me, sir."

"And if I ever hear that you're selling Plasmacore in your establishment again, I will run you over with my car."

"Yes, sir," promised the vampire. His voice wobbled. Since there weren't enough rations to go around, some vampires experimented with Plasmacore which satisfied their appetites and made them stronger than when they drank blood. Even in Downtown an underground Plasmacore distribution network thrived.

The club owner's outburst alerted the keen ears of vampires. They all turned to watch Poe tensely walking the gauntlet of hissing, angry vamps. The undead population used to complain about refrigerated blood, but now they missed it like an old heirloom. All because of Poe. The cattle rustler had left the city hungry and the populace sometimes had to resort to eating vermin or dog to assuage its hunger.

Poe unknowingly held Trench's arm tighter. She watched Breegan tell a couple to vacate the table as he tossed them the remains of a kitten and an opossum. He wiped leftover fur and blood away with his own arm sleeve. "Thank you, Breegan," he said.

He handed the proprietor a card. "That's good for two pints."

For the first time Breegan's face beamed. "Yes, sir! Thank you very much."

Poe surveyed the club and had never felt such livid hate. She unhooked her arm from Trench's elbow, folded her hands together, and looked down at them.

"Never look down, Julia," said Trench. His covered mouth was inches from her ear. "Look at Shandra there," he nodded to the exotic dancer in front of their table. The dead with Jane Mansfield breasts, only larger, was spinning erotically with one leg hooked around the pole. Vee-shaped red hair peeked from under her silver see-through thong underwear. Her ass cheeks, honed like half a basketball each, impressed even Poe. The vampire winked at Trench and gestured for one of the other redheads to come over.

"Why did you bring me here?" Poe said tightly, for which he answered in a Willy Wonka voice, "Because it's the best and funnest place in town." He pointed at the smaller redhead with an Angelina Jolie mouth. "Watch this."

The C-cup vampire unhooked Shandra's over-large bra until the entire room boomed in approval. Georgia, the smaller of the two, began to lick at the giant orbs of Shandra's bosom, capturing erect nipples and massaging the neglected breast. As a finale Georgia's fangs grew two inches and buried them into Shandra's tit. Shandra moaned and groaned like she was on the verge of an orgasm.

"Shandra only does this for me," he said, staring down at a boiling Poe.

Her nostrils flaring, she looked him in the eyes. "You kill me tonight, Trench. I won't play any more of your games." Abruptly she stood up and walked toward the door. She ignored the jibes and jeers thrown her way. She just hoped she wouldn't trip wearing the stupid high heels.

He was next to her and holding her arm in a second. She could not dislodge his hold so she continued to walk outside. Straightaway his car pulled up, and the driver let them in. The silence in the car was thick. Poe imagined shooting the master vampire in the head and dousing his face with more garlic water.

When they reached the music hall, Poe let herself out and walked as fast as she could. Of course the vampire was immediately at her side. "You want to die, Julia Poe?" he asked.

"I don't. But another stunt like that, and I'll hang myself to save you the trouble," she said and climbed the escalator. Trench grabbed her wrist until she was facing him. "You will follow me to my quarters," he said, stirring her to the direction of his room. "I'll make you pay for everything you've done to me and to this town if that is what you wish."

———

Poe tried twisting her wrist from his grasp but was unsuccessful. She held onto a post with her free hand when they reached the top of the escalator, but she was yanked back. The three-inch heels didn't cut her any slack. Finally Poe was left with no other choice other than to bite the vampire's wrist. Trench's fangs elongated. She could see the outline through the scarf. Hissing, he encircled Poe's neck with his other hand and squeezed until she was near suffocation.

"You test me, girl, and you'll regret it," he promised. Tired of the young woman's antics, the master vampire swept Poe off her feet and carried her. He walked as steadily as he could under the circumstances. He had a reputation to uphold, and running like a jackass in his own home was not even a remote possibility.

Quillon Trench couldn't fly, nor could he lift multi-ton objects like Kawana and Ed. He was stronger and fiercer, of course, than average vampires. But what set Trench apart was his grand vision. The vampire always had a plan. And he was far from antiquated like the Council that was no more. Trench was a modern vampire of means. After Sainvire's citywide theft of their food source, only Trench came away nearly unscathed. He had placed his cattle all over the city and not just in one place like the other master vampires had erroneously done. He had the entire Downtown population eating out of his hands.

When they reached his quarters, a room as sparsely decorated as Poe's but multiple in scale, Trench threw her on the circular bed set in the middle of the room. Everything was white except for the four Picasso paintings from the famous Blue Period and the black satin sheets on the bed.

"Just kill me, Trench," Poe found herself saying. Her chest heaved from fear. The vampire's fangs remained sharp and menacing. She imagined the vampire's fangs to look sharp and fiendish from the indentations behind the scarf.

Trench kicked something from under the bed, and a crescent headboard rose up. "What would be the fun in that?" he said. Poe shuddered. She remembered Megan's story about how Trench drank from her through a straw attachment while Sainvire watched helplessly. Another glaringly unforgettable fact was the torture and bleeding of Sister Ann and Goss. The vampire was demented.

Poe scrambled off the bed and tried to assume a fighting stance. She was keenly aware that her ankle-strap high heels were a problem. One slip and her ankles would give out. "Do you really think you can fight me with those shoes, Julia?"

The cattle rustler wavered but stood her ground. "At least I'll die trying," she said, her voice huskier with fear.

His once angry blues crinkled in amusement. This effrontery pissed her off. Ankle breakage or no, she kicked the back of his knees until the vampire fell. A barrage of Muay Thai kicks and punches followed until her knuckles were bleeding. Trench, still on the floor, didn't even block Poe's hits. Her shins, scrubbed of calluses, hurt from his hard, dead limbs. She wasn't making a dent, so she moved away from him. By the entertainment corner she spied a heavy vase and reached for it.

"That's a rare Lalique, Julia," he said tensely. "Put it down right now."

Poe smiled. The hated vampire was a collector. A connoisseur. "You're fast, Trench. Why don't you come get it?" The moment she saw him lunge, she threw the substantial opaque vase to the wall, shattering it to pieces.

He caught her by the waist, but she had time to pick up a sculpture that looked like it was crafted of ice. With all her might she clonked the vampire over the head three times until the heavy piece cracked in the middle and fell from her hands.

Black blood trickled above his temple due to Poe's perseverance. He raised his hand as if to strike her but stopped himself. Instead he forcefully threw her until she landed in the middle of his bed. Before Poe could blink, the vampire had her wrists handcuffed to the headboard. Poe pulled at the cuffs, but her struggle only served to tighten them.

"You sociopath son of a bitch!" Poe yelled, and tears of frustration fell from her eyes. "Kill me already, you warped bastard!" she taunted him. "You fucking elephant man!"

"Keep talking, Julia," he said with razor in his voice. "That was a Gehry sculpture you just hit me with." He opened the drawer of the circular bed stand and extracted a hand-carved long-blade silver knife.

Poe's tirades died in her mouth.

"Knife's got your tongue, Julia?" he laughed. Slowly he cut away her clothes in clean lines, ensuring the silver touched her skin and elicited goosebumps. He took his time. "I've heard you were modest, Julia Poe. I was told that you didn't let anyone help you bathe or dress. You kept to your room. Could it be because you were naked underneath your robe?"

Poe looked away from him and mumbled until Trench asked, "What was that you just said?"

"Go to hell."

Trench guffawed. He looked like a deranged Rorschach. "You know what I'm going to do with you after I cut the clothes off your body? Hmm?" When Poe didn't answer he continued. "I'm going to ask you about every little scar you have. Ah yes, I've been told you've got plenty."

"What makes you think I'm going to tell you?" she said while facing him with fire in her eyes. He had cut everything off her body except for the straps of her heels, a lacy black push-up bra that made her breasts look like overripe fruit, and matching panties.

"Oh you'll tell me alright." As soon as he said those words, a knock sounded. She watched the vampire rise with elegant fluidly like he was royalty. The door opened and a handsome vampire with violet eyes and an impeccable Armani suit entered the room. He was carrying a cage ensconced in a sheet. "You can place the cage in the middle there where the lady can see it."

"Yes, sir," said the man that looked nothing short of a model.

"Joel, what do you think of the vampire rustler?" Trench asked. He narrowed his eyes in contemplation. Poe flushed all over and bit her lower lip. She tried bringing her knees to her chest but Trench sat back on the bed and clenched her ankles where they lay with an iron hand. The vampire was humiliating her, and it was working.

"She's exquisite, sir, despite her scars," the blond Adonis answered.

"Would you like to see her breasts, Joel?" he asked, cutting away at the air with his knife for effect.

Poe couldn't take the demoralization anymore. She stilled her voice and said, "I'm glad I ruined your beautiful face, and now you have to walk around like

268

the invisible man, you bastard!" In reality near-nakedness before her enemy stole her courage away.

"You're crying, my dear. How quaint," he observed, snipping away at the center of her brassiere. He pushed the cups to the side to get a better view of her full breasts. "Beautiful peach nipples, don't you think? Would you like to touch them, Joel?"

The vampire guest leaned over the bed and cupped her breasts with cold dead hands. He squeezed and pulled at her nipples. Poe forced herself to stare at Trench to show that her spirit wasn't cowed. His eyes, however, were on Joel's groping hands, and they were looking flinty.

"That's enough. Get out," he commanded without saying another word until his stooge had left. He stood by the cage. He lifted the blanket, and Poe saw for the first time in six weeks her loyal dog, Penny.

"Pen!" she said, crying silently. The dog was well groomed and looked healthy. *Please, Mom and Dad, don't let him kill Penny in front of me.*

Trench sat down next to her. He took in Poe's pleasantly plump lower lip, trembling from crying, and her perfectly shaped breasts. He pointed at the scar above her right breast. "Where did you get this one?"

Poe looked at her dog and took a deep breath. "Your man, Pengle, pierced me with his pirate hook and dangled me off the ground." Kawana had killed the vampire who had it in for Poe for cutting off his arm.

Again the master vampire's eyes burned. "Well he's dead now," he said in a barely controlled voice.

"I assume these thin scars running along your arms were acquired when you dove through the window at the Eastern Columbia?"

Poe nodded. "What about these on your left thigh?" he asked. He ran his cold hand on her thigh and traced the old cuts.

"One is from a nail wound. The other two holes are from Sainvire's nails." His eyebrow upturned in curiosity as he raised the girl's thigh. "He skewered you?" The girl nodded but said no more. "Why is that, Julia Poe?"

"I shot him in the kidneys, gullet, stomach, and the knee caps," she said matter-of-factly.

Trench laughed at this. "Lovers' spat, was it?" Poe remained silent and looked at her dog, sitting in the cage and looking worried. "I see a clean bullet wound on your arm here." He ran a hand on her left arm. "Tell me about your ear."

"My earlobe. A halfdead ate it for revenge a few days after I yanked off his ear," answered Poe robotically. "Are we done here?"

"Not in the least," he answered, pulling out his knife. He cut off her panties until she was completely exposed. "Why, you're hairless all over, Julia Poe! And you're a beautiful sight."

He rose from the bed and began undressing. He hung his coat jacket carefully on the back of a chair. Poe watched him until only the scarf about his face remained. His body was slim but muscular and oh-so-white. She thought he would unveil his face, but she was wrong. He switched off the lights and joined her in bed.

In the dark he removed her strapped heels. Poe heard them clunk noisily on the wooden floor. "Any false move, Julia," he warned, "and your dog's dead."

"I'm tied up," she whispered, fearful of what the vampire would do to her. She was the cause of his disfigurement, and he wanted revenge.

"I know," he said.

He found her mouth and sucked on her lower lips. She could feel the crags on his face as he kissed her face and inserted his arctic tongue into her mouth. When she didn't respond he ended the kiss. "You will kiss me back and enjoy it, Julia, or else I'm not going to be pleased."

When he insinuated his cold tongue into her mouth, she forced herself to kiss him back, imagining Sainvire or Maclemar making love to her. She kissed so thoroughly that the vampire had to pull back. "Easy, gorgeous. We have the entire night ahead of us." He sucked on her right earlobe, her intact ear, and licked a path down her neck to her breasts. Trench spent such a good amount of time licking and pawing her breasts that Poe found herself squirming from lust, and the feeling angered her.

He kissed her flat stomach while tightening and pulling at her nipples. The vampire only let go of her breasts when he reached her thighs which were clamped shut. "Julia, open your legs to me. Now."

Poe thought of Penny, and a defeated sound escaped from her lips. She opened her legs to the master vampire she abhorred. His tongue penetrated her once, and he spoke with triumph. "You are extremely wet down here, my dear. I'm glad that you're enjoying yourself." He resumed tonguing her slowly and expertly, and try as she might Poe couldn't help but moan. Tears streamed down her eyes as she experienced waves of pleasure. *I'm a fucking whore, and I deserve to die*, she thought.

He entered her slowly and languorously until she bit down on her lower lip to keep from making any more traitorous sounds. "You feel so tight. So good, Julia," he said hoarsely. "How many times have you made love to other men?"

Poe swallowed deeply, her throat dry. "Three and a half."

"Three and a *half* times?" the vampire asked incredulously. "Explain yourself," he ordered as he continued to thrust into her.

"Three times with Sainvire and another with a human. We got interrupted during the last bit," answered Poe without emotion.

Quillon Trench snorted. "You are delightful, my dear. I want to keep you as my little pet forever," he sighed. "Sainvire is such a monk! Only three times with this body? What an idiot!" Poe kept her mouth tightly shut. The love of her life was dead, and here was her enemy slighting him and rutting on her.

"Sorry if I'm going at a slow pace," apologized Trench. "I just don't want to hurt you. Last time I fucked a human, she bled to death."

CHAPTER 13

HE ONLY CUFFED HER when important men of the city visited.

Trench made sure she was naked to broadcast her humiliation to all. Kawana said this habit was to convince the dead of Los Angeles that the cattle rustler wasn't getting off easy. The more vampires learned about her enslavement, the more satisfied they were with Trench's handling of the situation.

Three master vampires were more particularly vengeful than the others. Charles Lamb, a striking dead with the aplomb of a Lord, lived in the Bradbury building in Downtown Los Angeles and had a thing about wrenching back Poe's hair and biting her neck without piercing the skin. He would whisper, "Someday I'm going to drink you dry, bitch."

Kato Grange, a not-so-tall barrel of a vamp, enjoyed massaging her breasts and squeezing them as if to flatten them. Trench frequently had to intercede on her behalf and pull the vampire away from her.

A bony vampire named Robert Kirlegast was the most forgiving of the three. He enjoyed her body without hurting her in any way. As so he also was the most humiliating of the three. He'd asked Trench for privacy, and in the twenty minutes granted to him, Kirlegast would undress and rub himself all over

Poe's naked body. His stale breath against her face would nearly make her vomit.

Other powerful vampires visited her to enjoy her degradation. Trench was apologetic, of course, but did little to stop the traffic to her room. Poe's mettle was losing its spark.

"Why don't you get me out of here, Kawana?" she asked before her friend was sent away to supervise one of Trench's buildings.

The vampire looked at Poe and massaged her temples. "I'd like to do nothing more, my friend, but if I leave Downtown there'd be no more information to feed the rustlers. The resistance would be in the dark. Without Sainvire the underground is already weakened. It hurts me, but I'm needed to spy, Poe, to save our people."

Darkness and despair descended like biblical locusts. Poe, humiliated over and over again, had lost her spirit. Without her guns and without her dog, she was nothing. She was locked up in Trench's room most of the time, and even if she did escape, highly trained vampires in Italian suits guarded the den like seasoned FBI agents.

Her divine talent as a sure-shot was cruelly useless. Trench, perhaps out of guilt, was unusually tender and extremely giving in bed. He never showed his face. The vampire preferred to make love to her in the dark, and by morning he would disappear. One night Poe couldn't help herself and touched his face, tracing the lines and crags with curiosity. She was surprised that he let her. She didn't know what possessed her, but she kissed his face.

"Are you going to apologize?" he asked to which she answered, "Only if you apologize for killing my friends."

Peter Nesbitt returned on her second month of captivity. As usual Trench ordered Poe to strip and cuffed her wrists on the headboard. The medium-height man with grayish brown hair looked her up and down. Trench's Obi-Wan was not as frightening as Poe had thought. He looked more like a shoe salesman in his drab blue suit next to the ever refined Quillon Trench.

"This is it, Quillon? This is what you show me," Nesbitt said. "Her lying naked cuffed to a bed isn't exactly punishment."

"The girl is modest. It kills her every time people gawk at her," Trench explained. "Why look at her. She's red from shame."

Nesbitt ran his fingers through his hair. "That's not enough, I'm afraid. This girl cost this city plenty. She has to pay. Do you know we've only caught two RVs since that costly venture in the Central Valley? Two RVs with useless cattle who didn't know anybody's whereabouts. That's embarrassing to say the least." Ire written on his face, he looked at Poe. "So no. This skin and handcuff nonsense is not enough. I will drink from her right now and turn her into cattle."

His men had braved the sun to fight Sainvire's people and retake stolen cattle. They risked getting singed by the sun and suffocation from garlic. Those who didn't die were permanently scarred. He didn't have to help Trench, but he did so out of loyalty through their long friendship.

Nesbitt's teeth elongated. Like a predator he approached the bed where Poe whimpered. Before he could bend down for a bite, Trench hurled him back. Perhaps too hard. The master vampire from Northern California was thrown to the entertainment center, destroying the 65-inch television with the impact. "Quillon, you don't want to cross me for a worthless slut like her. We have history together, boy."

"Forgive me, Peter," Trench said regretfully. "Since my face was defiled, I've only wanted to inflict pain on this girl, and that is what I do every night. I mean, look at her. She used to be fierce. Now she's like cattle."

"If she is, then why don't you just make her into a blood cow?"

"What would be the fun in that? Cattle don't get scared," explained Trench in a hardier voice. "Let's enjoy her, but let's do it my way." From his pocket he took out two silver spoons and a small surgical knife. He leaned over Poe and slashed shallow cuts into her thigh. He saw her flinch without eking out a sound. With one of the spoons he scooped up blood until the spoon was filled. He steadily handed it to Nesbitt who didn't hesitate to submit the warm blood to his mouth.

By the time they finished Poe had over a dozen slashes in her skin.

That night Poe lay in his arms, her thoughts a jumble. "Let me go, Trench," she said, her husky voice pleading. "I promise not to come back and kill you. Just let me and my dog go."

Trench didn't say anything. He touched the Band-Aids plastered all over her body.

"I'm dying inside," she said quietly, painfully.

Peter Nesbitt widely broadcasted the capture of the new appetizer in town, and Trench had no choice but to share Poe's blood with every vengeful master vampire whose cattle had been stolen. The girl lay on her back, nude and staring at the Picasso painting to her side while they feasted on her with their spoons. The painting was a portrait of Suzanne Bloch whom Poe thought looked rather like a man with a swoosh of hair. She didn't look too happy, either. *Mom would've loved the painting.* Her nakedness and the foul way vampires spoke about her while feeding on her bothered her still, but she found solace in the thoughts of the happier moments in her life.

"I want to fuck her, Trench. She looks better than that drawing you posted up all over the state. Can I get an appointment?" asked a vampire with salt and pepper hair who called himself Lord Byron.

Trench chuckled. "Sorry Byron. She sleeps only with me."

When the curious and the sated left, he would apologize to her while freeing her from her bonds. "If I don't let them do this to you, my standing in this city and your life will be threatened."

"Let them kill me then," she said tiredly. Trench would insist that she eat fried liver for iron, but she refused, just like she tried to refuse his sexual advances at night.

"You know I can't do that," he said while smoothing her disheveled hair. "I've grown too fond of you." He smiled. "I wondered what on earth Sainvire saw in you. Now I know." He kissed her forehead and walked her to the bathroom. He filled the bath with water and poured scented oils and soap, never leaving her until a janitor came to help Poe with her bath.

Trench would insist that she take a bath after serving as an appetizer. Ever since she tried to drown herself in the outsized tub, Trench never left her alone. Trench assigned the one-eyed black woman named Frieda to bathe Poe. A deep depression had taken hold of Poe. She lay catatonic while Trench tenderly made love to her at night. The old Poe, so fierce and so sure of her abilities, was gone. She was now a humiliated crumb vampires stepped on.

She remembered telling Maclemar when he held her captive that she wouldn't fall for her kidnapper. However, with Trench as her only protector, she was beginning to feel for him, especially when he finally revealed his face to her. His chiseled, handsome face was marred by crags and garlic acid lines. When he told her he loved her, she almost believed that she loved him, too. Poe had to remind herself every minute that he was her tormentor. Her pimp.

"Oh, darling. It will get better," said Frieda as she lightly sponged Poe's cut skin. "I pray for you every night so you can be bad ass again and rescue all of us from this place."

"Thank you, Frieda. I'm praying for that time, too." She started weeping. She hated that she cried over every little thing.

"You and Sainvire are all the janitors talk about. We're holding out on the hope that you'll take us to a better place." Poe sniffed out of powerlessness. The woman took her hand and patted it. "Maybe Trench will let you go. We all know he's angry that he has to parade you around like that."

Poe reached for the tissue Frieda handed her. "Trench likes his games too much. I wouldn't count on him."

To take her mind off of hellish thoughts, Poe asked Frieda about her life. "Well," the woman with the scarred eye began, "I've been cleaning up for Trench for five years now. I used to work for one of his farms, looking after leeches that did nothing but sniff glue, grow marijuana, and waste bullets on stray dogs. One of them singed my eye with heated metal out of boredom. When Trench heard he bit the leech and made him into cattle and took me to work for him."

"That was a nice gesture," said Poe with sarcasm.

The meaty woman loofahed Poe's feet and sighed. "Ever since you all took the cattle, they've made janitors like me give blood once a week."

"I heard they turned a lot of the janitors into cattle," Poe said. She sat up.

"The hardest hit farms had to, but the rest couldn't afford to stupor their help. Who's going to clean the bedpans and feed the cattle?" Poe had been so preoccupied that she had forgotten about the other poor souls trapped in the nightmare of Downtown. Frieda caught a glint of the old Poe for one second. "Will you help me with the layout of this place, Frieda?" Her embarrassment about being kept in near-nakedness had prevented her from scouting out her prison. Her only other friend, Kawana, had been sent to Parker Center to supervise Trench's police force. She'd had no contact with the policewoman for over a month.

"Only if you promise to take me with you," said Frieda.

"I promise. Find out where my dog is, and I'll take care of things," Poe said with vicious anger she hadn't felt in a long time. She needed that feeling to get riled enough to do something foolish, even without underwear in a miniscule yukata. "I can't take anymore of this, Frieda. I don't want to kill myself anymore. I want to kill vampires."

He chose the red dress he'd wanted her to wear for months. The Dolce & Gabbana sleeveless number was so short her underwear could be seen if she didn't cross her legs like a lady. The cleavage dipped down to her rib while the rest of the fabric clung to her like a second skin. Her unfettered breasts nearly peaked out when she moved. Trench was more than pleased by his woman's appearance. He was going to take her back to Drip to show off the old and unhealed scratches on her legs.

"You look beautiful, my dear. Your hair is perfect, parted to the side like that down to your shoulders. And your skill with make-up has improved. You are delectable," he said. "Do not fret. We will only stay at the club for a little while. Just enough time to show you off." He held out his hand for her.

Poe, in red spiky heels, prayed to the Great Ali and Xena to help her. *Let this work, please!* As she walked toward the vampire, she leaned her left heel a little to the right and faked a fall, hard enough to induce a bruise on her knee and bang her head against a chair. "Ooouch!" she screamed.

Trench was at her side in a second lifting her up and sitting her down upon the nearest chair. The heel had snapped where she had fiddled with it. The master vampire took her ankle and examined it with minute care as Poe cursed guttermouth at how much his probing hurt.

"What did I teach you about bad language, Julia?" he said. "It's only a sprain." He took some linen from a shelf and ripped them in strips. As gently as he could, Trench wrapped a formidable amount of linen around her ankles. "There. All better?"

"Hell no!" Poe shook her head. "Stupid heels. What's up with you wanting me to look like a streetwalker, Quillon?" She blinked crocodile tears. "You said you love me, and yet you do these demeaning, disgusting things to me!"

"My dear, there is always a reason for my madness. I wish it didn't have to involve you, but I have no choice. You stole most of the city's cattle."

"Get out!" Poe said harshly. "Leave me alone. And if I don't see my old sneakers here in ten minutes, I'll make sure to hate you for the rest of my life!"

Trench tugged at his tie and straightened his lapels. He really did feel something for Julia Poe, and for a rotten swine like him that was a miracle. He couldn't let her go, nor could he allow her to hate him. In fact he was hoping to hear from her own lips that she loved him. "I'm sorry for your ankle, Julia. I will send for more comfortable shoes straight away."

He walked toward the door. "I apologize for this, but I do have to go to the club tonight. Another master of the city awaits my arrival. I will make it up to you tonight, my love."

Poe took off the other heel as soon as the vampire had left. Twenty minutes later she heard the sound of the door unlocking. Sebastian, a halfdead, brought her sneakers. They weren't her Adidas but something Barbie would have worn – three inches tall and very glittery. "Those aren't my shoes, Sebastian!"

"I believe your old clothes have been incinerated," said the vampire with a frosty attitude. He looked like Daniel Day Lewis in his prime. "Those were the only shoes we could find in your size. Besides, they're Betsey Johnson. You ought to be thankful."

Poe shook her head. She waved the halfdead inside and hobbled dramatically like she needed help. "I know you have impeccable taste, Sebastian. More than Joel or the others." At this, Sebastian stood taller. "I want your advice." She limped over to her side of the closet and slid open the door for him to see. "Do you know Quillon's birthday?" she asked.

The daywalker shrugged. "I don't think he's ever celebrated it."

"Well it's tomorrow, and I want to wear something he'll be proud of. He said I have no taste." Sebastian's eyebrow rose in agreement. "So basically I need your help. Can you suggest which dress to wear and which shoes go along with it? I mean I'll make sure to tell him how kind you were to help and all that."

Sebastian finally smiled. Kissing up to the boss was something he never tired of. He chose a purple Prada gown with sequins that made Poe inwardly shiver. "It's between the black and the Marc Jacobs ash gray shoes, I think," he said. He wanted the ensemble to look perfect.

"Why don't you get them so I can try one shoe on?" The moment the sun-immune dead bent over to retrieve the shoes, Poe pulled Trench's silver knife from her sleeves and buried it in the back of Sebastian's neck. The dead choked from the long blade that penetrated his throat. Poe yanked the blade from side to side until she severed his head. Black blood spilled on Trench's immaculate wood floors.

Quickly she unwrapped the linen from around her ankle and put on the gaudy sneakers. She turned Sebastian's corpse over and found a 9mm Sig Sauer inside his suit jacket. Poe nearly cried at the feel of a gun in her hand. She had thirteen bullets, and she couldn't waste a single one. She headed for the elevator. According to Frieda, Penny was held in the unused pantry next to the kitchen. Her usual guard wasn't at the door to give her grief. Most of the henchmen were downstairs where she was about to go. It wasn't always so in the beginning of her captivity when about two dozen well armed guards had waited at every corner. *They think I'm broken and no threat to anyone*, Poe sadly thought.

Vamps didn't bother the kitchen staff as the smell of meat cooking for janitors and cattle was distasteful to vampires. At least that was what Frieda said. It wasn't hard to slink her way to the pantry. She heard Penny whine before she saw her. The dog was leashed and tied up, and her coarse hair was extra-groomed. The dog had gained a few pounds from too much food and lack of exercise. *Trench is a clean freak. Even my dog is fair game.*

Poe had never leashed Penny, but she was going to have to that night. Top Chefs would have been proud of the deep, gleaming kitchen she passed through. A staff of fifteen was busy cooking up a tsunami to feed the human cattle of the Hall. Trench kept thirty cattle on hand for entertaining purposes. The multicultural staff in white aprons and chef hats looked at her with shock. She put the gun to her mouth to keep them from making unnecessarily loud noises.

"Are you going to take us with you?" asked an elderly African American woman who stopped stirring her vegetables.

Poe shook her head. "Sorry. Not tonight."

"Why not tonight?" a Chinese American man asked. He wiped his hands on an immaculate apron.

"Because I can't. There's only one of me. Now, where's Frieda?"

"Frieda's at one of the farms, maybe one of the theaters on Broadway helping feed cattle," someone answered. "They're a little shorthanded there tonight."

Poe took a nylon shopping bag from a hook on the wall and began filling it with as many small knives as she could find. "You wouldn't happen to have garlic, would you?" Several shook their heads in the negative. "Didn't think so. Could you tell Frieda I'm coming back for her and for you guys, too? But right now I gotta mosey."

They showed her the back door which led to a roundabout way into the street. Poe would learn later that the entire kitchen staff was branded with a hot iron for assisting her.

The smell of freedom heated her blood. She hadn't been outside on her own in weeks. Penny, who was as excited as her companion, pulled at the leash to hasten her on. The bright moon was both a bonus and a bane. It illuminated her way, but it also made her conspicuous. She looked up at the undulating metal structure, its beauty marred by guilt, shame, and anxiety, which had imprisoned her for nearly three months. With a deep breath for courage she turned away and ran.

Her platform tennis shoes lacking arches were hell. She felt like Herman Munster trying to jog. She made it as far as a parking structure across the street before the alarm sounded. Someone had discovered Sebastian's body. With her heart thudding painfully Poe and her dog ran for it.

It was Liam who caught her scent first. Poe had never seen him because he spent most of his time in the old gift shop that had been converted into a guard post. Like most vampires, the half-black, half-Irish dead had his own special gift which was a heightened sense of smell. The moment the alarm blared he raised his nose in the air. He ran for Trench's room. He sniffed Sebastian's decapitated body then the air. Liam left the room, walked calmly to the elevator, and pressed the down button.

His nose led him to the kitchen which had nearly destroyed Julia Poe's scent. He opened the back door. He stared down the guilty-looking kitchen staff and took out his walkie-talkie. "The girl's on the loose. She's only been gone five, ten minutes tops. She left through the kitchen." He stepped out in the street and sniffed once more. "I'm guessing she's heading toward the downhill parking lot. Oh, and she's got her dog with her."

"We're on our way," the other voice on the wave said. "Careful. She's armed."

Liam followed in a swift gait. He knew exactly where the girl was. Her unmistakable scent, which Trench had inculcated in him by handing him Julia Poe's laundry items before they were washed every few days, honed his olfactory senses. Julia, the pretty human Trench was obsessed with, had a pleasant bouquet, a unique scent that if bottled would make women – human and vampire alike – gain instant sex appeal. No wonder vampires and humans desired her so.

He ran as her smell became more potent and led him to the edge of the parking structure bleeding down an incline. He could smell her dog as she had been groomed with No Tears baby shampoo. He was focusing on the dog's scent when he actually saw the animal growling at him from across the street. The dog with the coarse, dirty white fur was almost comical. Liam's preoccupation with the dog lost him footing, and the cattle rustler came out of nowhere to point her Sig Sauer at his head. Before he could say a word, Poe lodged a knife in his throat and twisted the neck meat counter-clockwise. He fell dead a few beats later.

Poe dropped the knife and wiped the black blood on her designer dress that made her look like a streetwalker. She picked up Liam's weapon, a 9mm of an unfamiliar make, and held it with her left hand. The bag of knives hung on her shoulder. She took Penny's leash and ran. That was when the first flashlight bobbing in the dark descended. Unable to see nothing but flashlight bulbs but needing to shoot the pursuer in the head as he was most likely wearing a bulletproof vest, Poe breathed in and prayed. "I need help. Let me see in the dark, Mom."

She raised Liam's weapon and pointed at the light, letting the voice in her head guide her. *Now*, it said. She fired. A flashlight clanged to the floor, and a thud followed. Music to her ears. When she reached Olive Street, a well lit part of the city, Poe found herself surrounded by men in black suits holding various types of intimidating firepower. She grabbed her dog, hid behind a parking lot column, and peeked carefully out.

"Come out, Miss Julia. We won't harm you," said one of the men. "Mr. Trench is on his way. Let's not make this any worse."

Poe blinked twice. She raised her Sig Sauer and fired at six heads in succession before anyone could react. "Let's make it worse, asshole," muttered Poe, feeling like her old self again. She spotted a figure hiding behind a painfully thin palm tree and aimed for the back of the head that peeped a few inches out. The shot shattered his skull, and she stopped herself from laughing in glee at the fallen vamp. Three more and life would be fantastic again. They shot at her from different directions – one near a parked car, the second behind a steel post, and the third by a truck. Poe unclasped Penny's leash. "You gotta run, girl. You hear me? We both gotta run like hell!"

She bolted and locked her eye on the parked car since it was the closest. Sure enough, the vamp showed himself. She took him down on the run and with her right hand fired at the dead by the post. She ducked as the farther combatant by the truck shot at her. Poe rolled to the street and shot at the vamp's foot under the truck. The old trick worked again. He screamed like fire ants were grilling his nuts, which left Poe and Penny free and clear to keep running.

They didn't scurry a block before Trench's Town Car skidded to a halt in front of them. Like a deer caught in headlights, Poe paused and wasted precious moments. She screamed, "Get outta here, Penny!" When the dog refused to budge, Poe kicked her viciously in the rump until she yelped and ran away.

Poe sprinted the opposite way toward the Museum of Contemporary Art which was a half-block away. When the driver, a balding vamp with a goatee, pursued her with superspeed, Poe glanced back and aimed for his head. The dead fell near her sneakers. Poe lost count of how many bullets she had left. The Sig Sauer was empty, and her other gun had two or three bullets at most.

She tripped on the sidewalk and painfully landed on her left wrist. Italian patent shoes that gleamed in the lamplight were inches from her hand. She looked up to find an irate Quillon Trench staring down at her and wearing no scarf to cover his displeasure. Poe's nostrils flared and she lifted her gun to shoot him, but he was too quick. He wrenched the weapon from her hand and pulled her to her feet.

He looked at her searing, unapologetic face and slapped her. Poe's head reeled, and the edge of her lower lip trickled with blood. "You killed my best men, Julia Poe," he said quietly, wiping the blood from her mouth with a forefinger. "And you're going to pay for it." He licked the blood from his finger to illustrate his point.

CHAPTER 14

HE WOULDN'T ALLOW THE other masters of the city to murder Poe. Trench said it was his men that were killed and Poe was his to intern as he pleased. He did grant concessions, concessions he regretted most bitterly, that would assuage the bigwigs of Downtown. Quillon sent for reinforcements from his many farms. He resisted the presence of boots-on-the ground LAPD thugs to mar his classy new digs, but in the end he had no choice. His brow furrowed at the thought of outfitting the undead cops with expensive suits that belonged to the truly dead.

He was considering such dire details while waiting for Poe to finish her bath. Trench had thrown her out of his room and back into her old one. He had tied her hands with rope while she lay face-down on her soft bed the past couple nights. He didn't want to see her face while he and others lashed her back with a whip cut from stingray tail.

Trench loved her, or so he thought, but she'd killed too many men to be allowed to live like his pampered princess. Every lash hurt him more than it hurt her. When master vampires came to ladle her blood, he seethed inside. The fools believed that Poe's blood was potent and gave them strength. He had no choice. Poe had tied his hands. This was the third day of her punishment. After she'd been bathed by Kawana and placed back on the freshly laundered sheets, he would supervise the roping of her hands. When satisfied he would dismiss Kawana, his beautiful and loyal ex-lover. "Why can't everyone be like her?" he muttered and looked to the bathroom.

"You've got to hold on, Poe," said Kawana, carefully running warm water infused with Epson salt onto her back. When the feverish girl didn't answer, she continued. "Help is on the way. I've been communicating with Ed. Remember Ed? The guy as strong as me? We'll he's been rounding up our old crew the past few weeks. They're going to be here soon, so be strong, girl."

Poe shrugged her eyes tearless as she held onto the slippery edge of the tub. If she didn't breathe too hard, the pain in her back didn't sting so much. "If they come, they'll die," said Poe, thinking about Maclemar and Michelle and feeling suddenly ill. "I'm not worth it, Kawana."

"Of course you're worth it! You're a symbol of hope to the resistance. We can't let anything happen to you."

"Everyone's scattered around the Central Valley, and each site is secret," Poe said, her voice huskier in hopelessness. She winced at the two days worth of lashes on her back. "Why would they want to risk their lives for me? And who'll rescue me? Some poor ex-cattle with no powers?"

To this, Kawana had no answer, and she sloshed the bloody bath water pointlessly. "I don't know who'll come, Poe, but I do know that powerful vampires and special halfdead like Ed know where each batch is living. He'll find a way to gather them all. I know it."

"My dog is free. That's enough for me," was the last thing Poe said. *Sainvire is dead. I want to die, too.*

―――――――

Trench pushed aside her hair that had grown long over the months and inspected her back. "Tsk tsk. Your beautiful back. I'm so sorry, Poe. I have limited options in this matter."

Poe didn't even grace him with an answer. She'd stopped speaking with her tormentor for the past few days. Inside she thought, *You're loving this for what I've done to your face, you asshole.*

She shut out the smell of burning candles placed randomly around the room like an offering to her. There was nothing she hated more than scented candles. They gave her headaches like strong cologne and evil vampires. And they were bad for the environment.

Three of them dressed for the opera came in. Juno Liman, a long-haired, white-skinned vamp Goth freaks would have loved, shook hands with Trench and walked over to Poe who trained her eyes to the wooden floor. He ran his hand on her rounded ass and gave it a slap, leaving a temporary imprint of his hand. Samuel Clemens, not at all related to Mark Twain, sauntered in and glanced at Poe's freshly washed back. "I can almost taste her sweetness. Her power," he said. The last dead that the came into Poe's room was a hulky master vampire named

Franco Sebastiani. "When do we eat?" he said as he took the whip from Trench's hand. Quillon bit back his annoyance and said, "You may proceed, Sebastiani."

The three vampires took turns lashing Poe's bleeding back while Trench, hidden behind his scarf, swallowed his rage. Four vampires had abused Poe two days before and another three last night. The girl was running a fever from the wounds that kept reopening with every slash of the whip. He watched Poe's face contorting with pain, her beautiful lips trembling. Yet she never made a sound. After a while the girl fainted.

"Alright. That's enough, Sebastiani!" Trench said with iron. "Have another go at that whip and I'll—"

A great boom interrupted the beginning of Trench's tirade as the foundations of the concert hall trembled. Another explosion followed by gunfire reverberated around the acoustically sensitive building.

"What the hell?" said Samuel Clemens. His blood-filled spoon shook with the foundation.

"It's not another rustling, is it?" asked Juno Liman, his mouth dripping with Poe's blood. He flicked back his long locks.

Their questions left unanswered, the door to her room flew open and a man in a long black coat with a hood entered like a typhoon, hacking off Sebastiani's arm which clanged to the floor. Before Liman could react the tall man in black split him in two at the waist and kicked his lower half out of the way. Another explosion shook Frank Gehry's architectural masterpiece and woke Trench and Samuel Clemens into action.

His incisors dripping from rage, Clemens flew at the man. He tackled the cattle rustler until they both crashed into the wall next to Poe's bed, smashing a hole from room to hallway. The intruder grunted and flew back through the hole. He slammed Clemens against the entertainment section, demolishing the sound system. Like gutting a fish the stranger sliced the master vampire from stomach to shoulder.

When the man in black turned back for Trench, the vampire was gone. The rat-a-tat of semi-automatics and the hallow boom of grenades exploding made the soothing music hall a den of chaos and disorder.

The hooded man cut the ropes from Poe's bruised wrists. He carefully turned her over without allowing her raw back to touch the sheets. An angry groan escaped his lips as he inspected the many fine scars running down her legs that had turned white. The girl was unconscious and feverish. "Poe," he said gently. "If I had known, I would've come back for you."

Poe's eyes fluttered open. "Kaleb?" she asked weakly.

"Yes. I'm here, Poe."

Poe shook her head to clear the cobwebs and touched the vampire's scar above his lip. "I'm naked. Give me your coat and get me out of here," Poe said weakly then passed out.

Morales, Michelle, and Passionada took turns looking after Poe. She'd been unconscious for three days. Infection had set in the wounds, and Morales didn't have antibiotics on hand. He made do with double doses of expired Tylenol and round-the-clock application of cold cloth on the areas of her body that hadn't been marred by a whip.

"That bastard Trench," Morales muttered angrily. The sight of Poe's raw back like it had been copiously scratched up by a T-rex made him want to land a piledriver on the master vampire who had dared treat his friend so brutally. He'd dealt with many abused cattle, but he'd never seen such purposeful torture of a human being.

Maclemar wanted to be part of the roster, but after bouts of cursing and near-hysteria at seeing Poe's state, Morales had no choice but to ban him from the sick room. Sainvire, who visited frequently, merely stood watching over the girl in his usual silence, his face contorted with rage. Dressed in black t-shirt and dark slacks, the vampire never moved from his position facing the girl's bed. Morales sometimes forgot about his silent presence.

"You didn't know, Kaleb," he had told the vampire. "You thought the Revs got her. It wasn't your fault."

To this, Sainvire said nothing. His grim gray eyes never left the pus-filled wounds on Poe's back. He had circled the mine for five days straight but could not find a sign of Poe and Penny. He had no idea that he had put the woman he loved in the clutches of Trench by allowing her to retrieve Plasmacore for his sustenance.

They'd been staying in Dogtown where they were hiding three choppers under tarps to cloak them from airborne eyes. Vampires mostly avoided Passionada's home due to the superfluous dogs that could intimidate even the ballsiest of undead, not to mention the roadway sinkholes and piles of cars surrounding the area.

Passionada had cleaned the cotton candy machine just in case the girl woke up. She felt awful for battering Poe over the head and handing her to Maclemar. As penance she helped Morales as much as she could, washing bedding, changing bandages. On the third day as she was arranging wild flowers in a vase to put on Poe's bedside, the girl stirred. Being over six feet with heels on, Passionada quickly kneeled on the floor and touched the girl's forehead for any sign of fever.

Hers was the first face Poe had seen after three days of freedom. The girl's wingtip eyebrows drew together, and she tried to push herself up. Passionada's gentle touch and the horrible pain in her back stopped all thought of standing up.

"Mija, don't move. Your back is still raw," she said. Her red puckered lips glimmered with lip gloss. She pushed Poe's hair away from her face. "Once you scab over you'll be able to move again. But for now lie still and be patient."

"Passionada," Poe said tiredly, her mouth dry. "Where am I?"

"You're in Venice. My pad. You're safe now."

"You hit me over the head—"

"I know, and I'm sorry. Kaleb's orders, you know." Passionada poured water in a glass and put a swirly straw in it. "Here. Drink up." Poe sucked on the straw until the glass was empty and stared at the woman with perfectly applied make-up. She shivered at the memory of being trained to look like Passionada. "Our friends will be glad to know your fever's broken. Maclemar and Kaleb will be especially pleased."

"Sainvire's alive?" she asked with confusion. She thought the man in black rescuing her was only a figment of her imagination.

"Well he's a vampire, so he's considered dead," Passionada winked. "But he's alive and well. It took him a few days to heal on the rock you left him. Snaring a jackrabbit gave him enough energy to get to the mine. After healing up with Plasmacore he went looking for you. He searched for a week. The poor man thought you were dead. He rejoined Morales and his crew bound for Santa Cruz."

"I wasn't dead. Trench took me," Poe said. She was barely audible.

"He didn't know until Ed scoured each settlement to find you. He met with Kawana, and she told him of your imprisonment." Passionada rose. "I better get your boys in here."

"No," said Poe, ashamed of her back and her state of undress. "I don't want to see anyone, Passionada. Especially Sainvire and Maclemar."

Her request was honored. No one, not even Maclemar, tried to see her. He'd been dying of grief in the belief that Poe had been lost, and now her insistence on being alone drew him evermore inward. He preferred to spend most of his time on a boat fishing to keep his mind off of the woman he loved. Sainvire likewise waited and drilled his crew on what to do in the event of an attack.

The only male allowed to see her was T-Doc who took his job as temporary doctor seriously. Morales opted not to put salves on her wounds to hasten the drying process. "You can sit up and walk around now, you know. It's been seven days. Scabs are already forming. By next week you'll have nothing on your skin but pink scars."

"Morales, I want you to know how much I appreciate you coming down to help me," said Poe, sincere and a little embarrassed for thanking her friend. She'd resolved to thank each and every friend who had helped bust her out of Trench's lair. She started with Michelle who had nearly wept at Poe's earnestness.

"Oh you know me. I blow with the wind," Morales said, shrugging her thanks. He was uncomfortable at the new, more somber Poe. "Besides, I got to learn a new skill."

"What's that?"

"I learned to fly a helicopter," he said with a smile. "Michelle learned, too. She was the one who flew the chopper that bore you here a week ago."

"Geez," said Poe, scratching her ponytailed head. "You're a realtor, a cattle rustler, a bomb maker, temporary doctor, a sperm donor, and now a chopper pilot. You're a Renaissance Man."

"I know, I know. It's embarrassing," he said, visibly happy with the compliments. "But seriously, Sainvire and Maclemar ask to see you all the time. They're getting on my nerves."

"I'm not ready for them, Morales," said Poe with a fearful glint in her eye. Morales sat down on the bed next to her. He wore his realtor attire and Italian shoes and adjusted her hospital gown that was open at the back. He took her pale hands in his tanned ones. "Poe. They both love you," he said quietly. "We all love you. There's no need to hide."

Poe looked up at Morales' light brown eyes and teared up. "I can't see them now, Sam. Just give me some more time, please."

Morales touched her shoulder gently and pulled her to him. He kissed her forehead and said, "Honey, after what you've been through you deserve to get what you want."

"Thank you," she sniffed.

Morales massaged her neck in a pleasant, unimposing way, which was a departure for the ladies man. "I gotta ask you, though. Would you see Joseph and your godchild?"

Poe sat up straight. "They came down here? To get me?"

Morales nodded. "Habib, the chef and babysitter, came along, too." He looked at Poe's face and noticed for the first time the change in her appearance. Her baby face had been replaced by fine lines on her cheekbones that gave her a more classic look. A woman's face. Because of Poe's different ethnic make-up, her visage had always been obscure, something he couldn't pinpoint. Whatever had happened in the last three months, no matter how horrible, Poe had never looked more beautiful and sensuous in his humble opinion.

"Joseph wants to see me?"

"Yes," he answered quickly. "You should let him. He's not over his grief from losing Megan. He still can't square Megan's final request and burning her body before Nesbitt's men came. I think you should do this for him."

"I'll see him, Morales," she said, laying her hand on his arm. "How about you? Megan was your friend, too. And you're Piper's biological father."

Morales rose, his chipper smile in place. "I'm fine, Poe. I miss her, but I got Piper, Joseph, and Habib to help me through this. Of course it's not a gay thing," he said. He winked and left the room.

Her room looked like something out of *Little House on the Prairie*. The wallpaper was floral and pink and her double-size bed draped in a colorful quilt even the Amish would have been envious of. Teddy bears festooned every single nook. Poe shifted on the bed and arranged her hospital gown. She was thankful to be wearing underwear at last. Trench's manipulation of her modesty angered Poe. *In the future if I have to run away naked, I'll do it! The hell with modesty!*

The knock on the door surprised her. She'd forgotten about Joseph while thinking about Trench's mind games. "Come in."

A grinning Joseph opened the door, and little Piper squirmed in his arms. In uncustomary black clothing the vampire entered.

"Well lookit, Piper. There's your godmother, the one who's going to teach you how to kick butt when you're older."

Poe stood up, wincing at her back that was beginning to scab over but still raw. She kissed Joseph on the cheek and peeked at the redhead baby in his arms. "Gosh, she looks way bigger than when I last saw her. Cuter, too."

"Yup. She looks like her mommy, doesn't she?"

"Yeah, except she has Morales' brown eyes."

"And my voice box," he said, grinning. "You look good, Poe. Last week you looked like crap. I've always thought Trench to be a real shit, but what he did to you takes the cake."

Poe unconsciously tugged at her ponytail. "Yeah. He is. And I'm going to kill him for it," she said.

"That's the way," he said and handed the baby to an alarmed Poe. "You gotta hate him to get rid of any phobias or humiliation he dealt you."

Poe held the baby awkwardly, and Piper could feel it, too. She wiggled and started kicking away in distress. "I don't think she likes me."

"She likes you alright. You're just not holding her right," he said and repositioned her arms. "Relax. Don't tense up. Imagine holding a teddy bear, and don't forget to rock her a little."

Joseph's instruction worked. The baby took to Poe and spit up a storm. "Listen, Joseph," she said. She stalled to glance at his brown eyes. "I really want to thank you for coming back for me, especially with Piper and all. I just want you to know that I'm in your debt."

Joseph's grin disappeared. Like Morales, he'd never seen this side of Poe before. Whatever Trench had done to her angered the vampire. "Don't worry about it, Poe. You're the closest thing I have to a sister, so don't sweat it. Just heal up and be a badass again. Sainvire's planning to hit the music hall one more time. I'm sure he wants to beat Trench to a pulp."

Poe frowned. She thought of all the disgusting, degrading things Trench had put her through. "Not if I get to Trench first."

His silver-gray eyes followed her as she walked the compound thanking every single person, day vamp, and halfdead that had helped free her from imprisonment. She stood out in the backdrop of the blue ocean as she wore a snug black Pavement t-shirt and black jeans that showed off the pleasing curves of her legs. Sainvire turned his head toward Maclemar who stood by a light post awaiting his turn. The vampire could hear the erratic beat of the Welshman's heart. The man who had taken pains to shave every day in case Poe called for him was nervous.

Sainvire, with his ability to hear from long distances, honed in on Poe's conversation with the resident head chef. "Thanks so much, Habib. I'm grateful to you for chancing your life over me. You have the baby to worry about and everything."

"Child. Ever since you feasted on my food two years ago with extreme gluttony, I have considered you a grandchild," the man with thick black eyebrows and silver hair said. "And no grandchild of mine will be harassed by trash like Trench."

Poe wiped her eyes and walked to Rufus, the pilot who had learned his flight skills through video games and passed his knowledge onto Michelle and Morales. The tall man with hazel eyes smiled down at her. "How're ya doin', Poe?"

"Alright, Rufus. Thanks to you," she said, clearing her throat. "I just want to thank you for helping me out."

"No prob. No need to speak of it anymore."

"Well," said Poe anxiously. "I also want to apologize for yanking your ear off. I was crazy back then. I'm better now."

Rufus reached for his ear that wasn't there any longer and shrugged. "I ate your earlobe, so that makes us even. Let's shake on it and promise to forget about it." They shook hands, and Poe approached and profusely thanked the team assembled by Sainvire. Her humility, though acceptable enough, disturbed him. That the girl had suffered at Trench's hand was obvious, but it was also clear that the heinous vampire had broken her spirit. When she reached Ed, the five-foot tall El Salvadoran with the strength of Superman, Poe extended her hand.

A halfdead of few words, Ed shook her hand awkwardly and smiled at Poe. He said, "Anytime. We're here for you."

Ed was Kawana's link to Sainvire. He was the one who had traveled up and down the California Central Valley and the Santa Cruz Mountains for weeks to find Sainvire and Joseph. Once the master vampire assembled his volunteers, he headed straight for L.A., stopping only to refuel three choppers. He reached Passionada's compound and began planning for an ambush at Trench's former orchestra hall. Morales took care of the incendiaries while Joseph, with his blurringly fast speed, planted the explosives in the nooks of the Disney Hall.

Trench's people didn't know what hit them when the homemade bombs exploded. That was when the rest of the team stormed in wearing Kevlar vests and brandishing high-powered semi-automatics.

Michelle, waiting her turn, smiled at Poe who kissed her on the cheek. The ex-cattle sniffed. "Glad you're here with us, Poe. There aren't too many kick-ass women left in this outfit."

Poe nodded. "You said it. I'm glad I met you, Michelle. We're as good as sisters now." Michelle nodded to the man patiently awaiting Poe.

"Better go see the Welshman, girl." He looks like he's about to have a heart attack."

Poe squared her shoulders and approached Maclemar. Sainvire could feel her heart beating faster, and a twinge of jealousy seared through his body. She had been intimate with the man until Sainvire purposely interrupted their lovemaking. It was a childish thing to do, but the thought of another man touching Poe made him furious at the time. God only knew what Poe endured in the hands of Quillon Trench.

Before Poe could speak Maclemar encircled her into his arms, making sure he didn't touch her back. He hadn't seen Poe in over two weeks and was surprised to find her outside, looking pale and saying her thanks to day vamps. His heart constricted as he waited his turn.

"No need to thank me, Sharren," he whispered in her ear before she could speak. "I'd do anything for you. And I'm sorry that dung heap Trench treated you so ill."

Poe stilled and stiffened. For some reason other people's touch, especially that of men, bothered her so. "So you all know what happened to me?"

"Yes, Poe. I'm sorry. Kawana told us," he said gravely, touching her shoulder which she shrugged away.

She wanted to cry right then and there. Her dirty secrets had been revealed, and they embarrassed her. Torture, sex, feasting, wearing make-up, heels, and dresses. The humiliation was just too much. She was glad they didn't know she enjoyed Trench's tender lovemaking even after nights of mistreatment by his vampire cronies. They would have thought she was sick.

"Poe, I've been feasted on. I know a little about what you're going through," he said. Poe remembered all the bite marks and the chunks missing from his skin. She shuddered. "If you ever need to talk—"

She shook her head.

"If I could kill him right now, I would," he said angrily.

"He'll get his moment in the sun." She looked up at Maclemar's jewel green eyes and felt love for the man. "And I want to thank you anyway. You hardly know me, and you've tried to save my life three times now."

"Three times?" he asked, cocking his head.

Poe smiled. "You could've returned to your boat instead of following me inland. You ran after me in a dark road full of Revenents. And you came with Sainvire to bust me out of Trench's lair."

"So that'd be two times that I followed you and once rescuing you. You've gotta get it straight," he said. He reached behind her head and took out her hair band. Her long black hair spilled out mid-back. Poe tensed. She remembered Trench's insistence that she wear her hair down. Maclemar sensed her distress and handed back her hair tie.

Poe took a deep breath. *Don't let Trench give you anymore phobias*. She smoothed down her hair and clapped the fisherman on the shoulder. "Thank you, James. I'll never forget what you've done for me."

Sainvire watched the interplay between Poe and Maclemar and was hit with another pang of jealousy. He noticed Poe's reticence to be handled quite yet. However, he did observe her high regard for Maclemar who got away with an intimate gesture, releasing Poe's hair. Somehow Sainvire felt he'd lost her. Keeping everyone safe had killed his sense of humor and made him cynical and overprotective of his people. Poe was the only one who warmed his cold, tired heart, and it was hard for him to hear about the pain she'd endured under Trench. He anxiously anticipated the time he could return to the concert hall and disembowel the vampire.

She left Maclemar and headed his way. Her heart beat strong and fast. Sainvire wondered if she blamed him for not searching harder for her. She looked so small and fragile. The vampire rustler and eradicator he'd met two years ago seemed to have been erased and replaced by a woman unsure of her purpose in the world. Her beautiful hair that a ponytail had always hidden cascaded like a waterfall framing her face. Sainvire had never seen her look so striking.

She nervously stopped before him and tipped her head up to take in his eyes. Her eyes caressed his face, memorizing his bright gray eyes, dark lashes, and imperfect nose. The scar on his upper lip, the one that she'd imagined seeing again so many times while a prisoner of Trench, made her smile. Dimples appeared on her light cheeks.

Poe did not speak. She merely looked at the vampire for a long time. Finally she said, "You have stubbles again. You shouldn't have them, you know. You're a vampire."

Sainvire smiled despite himself. "They only grow when I'm stressed."

"Do I stress you out?" she asked.

Sainvire shook his head.

"You're wrong." said Poe. "I stress you out the most."

Again Sainvire smiled, transforming his tired face. "You don't stress me out. Not seeing you stresses me out."

Poe pushed a strand of hair behind her ear and stared at the vampire wordlessly once more. She focused on his plump lower lip and exhaled. "I hear you're blaming yourself."

Sainvire looked away toward the terribly bright Pacific Ocean. Poe missed the contact with his silver eyes. "Don't worry. I would've left to find Plasmacore no matter what you said. So please don't blame yourself."

He kept quiet, turning his head to look at Poe's brown eyes flanked with long, straight lashes. "The problem is I do blame myself."

"Kaleb, you always blame yourself. If not me, it's for some other stiff that didn't make it," she said. "You should quit worrying, or you'll get an ulcer." She grinned until she elicited a smile from the vampire.

"I think I do have an ulcer," he laughed. "That's my problem, I suppose, and you've diagnosed it."

She reached for his hand, cold and large, and squeezed. It was the first time they'd touched since he had carried her away from Trench's home. It was an impulsive act, and she quickly snatched her hand back.

"It, it wasn't so bad," lied Poe. "They mostly did terrible things to me after I escaped and got caught. I killed a bunch of Trench's vamps, you see."

Sainvire caressed her diagonal scar with his eyes. "He will suffer for what he did to you, Poe. We are invading as soon as we get a go-ahead from Kawana. If you don't want to be a part of it, I'd understand."

Poe swallowed hard and gruffly said, "Of course I'll go. I want you to watch me kill him."

"I'll be there, Poe. But for now you've got to get your strength back, your confidence back."

Poe looked down at her new shoes, black high-top Converse. "Is it that obvious?"

"It's only obvious to me," he said. "I've known you for two years. You're fierce, Julia Poe. I watched you thank everyone who rescued you, and I saw a woman saying goodbyes and getting ready to die. You've got to snap out of it and be angry again, or I'm going to lose you."

She looked away and swallowed the rock behind her throat. She was going to lose it. Her shoulder shook, and despite herself tears began pouring. Sainvire embraced her while looking at the crowd that quickly averted their gazes. Except for one. Maclemar glared at him as if he was the cause of Poe's woes.

"I don't know what to do," she cried. Sainvre's shirt muffled her voice. She pushed him away from her. "I feel like he fucked me over and left me to wear dresses and heels in a gunfight."

"I'm here," he said. "Maclemar's here, and all your friends are here. Trust us."

"But can you trust me?" she said in a small voice.

"With my life. Or whatever's left of it." He spotted Passionada in the distance, holding a leash. He nodded to her. The giant of a woman bent over to unleash a freshly bathed Penny.

"Look who's coming," he said and turned Poe around.

Penny bounded with incredible speed toward an astonished Poe. Kneeling, Poe opened her arms to her dog and hugged the mutt to her. She cried even harder. The dog, her only family, had nearly been lost. There hadn't been a day since her convalescence that she hadn't thought of the mutt. Penny licked her face with her half-tongue. Poe held the dog at arms length to look at her. Penny seemed like she'd battled her way through Dogtown and come out the worse for it. The dog was nearly ten years old, and Poe did not want to lose her again.

The click clomp of Passionada's shoes reminded Poe they were not alone. "Thanks, Passionada. I'll never forget this."

"Don't thank me, honey," she said while resting a hand on a rounded hip. "Thank Kaleb here who was scouring the streets of L.A. day and night in his hoody to find your dog for you."

Poe stood up and faced the vampire. She extended her hand and said, "Thank you, Sainvire."

He wished, above all else, to hear Poe repeat what she'd said on the rock to him while his side oozed from the injury. He wanted her to tell him she loved him. She didn't. The vampire had no choice but to shake her hand.

"I'm going to think real hard about this attack, Sainvire, and I'm going to come up with something fierce. I hope you listen to what I have to say."

Poe turned her back to him and motioned for the dog to follow her to the edge of the sea where the surf could no longer reach dry sand. He watched both woman and dog sit in companionable silence before the flickering horizon.

CHAPTER 15

NO ONE HAD HEARD from Kawana in over a week. All twenty-two of Sainvire's team were apprehensive, and they feared ambush. They dreaded the discovery of Kawana's double-agent status. Being surrounded by nearly a thousand dogs awaiting a kill whistle from their leader jarred the nerves. They didn't dare to even to pucker their lips lest a shrill sound escape.

Poe withdrew from socializing, even with Michelle and Morales. She'd take walks with Penny for hours. She was filled with unmitigated ill wishes toward Quillon Trench. The memories evoked by smell, touch, and sound that echoed what had occurred at the Disney Hall made her want to shrivel up and hide in the sands. Shame consumed her.

She couldn't help it. Trench was a nasty thorn that insipidly raided the last of her courage she'd been trying to regenerate. He had been tender to her, making her squirm and sigh with his lovemaking. Trench hardly hurt her, yet he allowed others to do so. He would then turn around and say their attacks were out of his hands. The vampire mind-fucked her, making rehabilitation all that much more difficult. That everyone at Dogtown knew her business sickened her. And for the life of her, she couldn't look Maclemar and Sainvire in the eyes. Whenever one or the other tried to approach her, she'd run the other way.

She woke up at dawn and ran with Penny on the beach. Her body as well as her spirit needed to be in shape again. She knew Maclemar from his tent and Sainvire from the third floor of Passionada's compound watched her. The vampire never slept unlike his other dead counterparts. She overheard him explain to Passionada that once asleep he would be truly dead to the world. Vampires were hard to awaken, and he didn't want to be caught snoring when the enemy struck.

What can I say? I'm not ready to have sex with either of you or to choose between you. Or to hurt one of you because I know which one I would choose.

———

Dogtown exuded raw nerves that needed to be quelled with quick answers. How would a ragtag band of vampires, humans, halfdead, and an infant defeat the powers-that-be? In four weeks no one had developed a semi-coherent plan. Besides Trench, only the most mediocre of vampires ruled the new political and economic structure of the city. The undead who had whipped, humiliated, and partaken of Poe's blood were representative of that middling class.

Nerves were stretched like an overwound violin string. Whenever Piper wailed, three or four souls would run to pacify her fierce vocal chords. Joseph and Morales worried for their child's well-being, and they found every conceivable idea about defeating the Downtown regime to be too dangerous. They didn't want to die from a foolish plan and leave Piper in Dogtown forever with Passionada and her rancid dogs.

Michelle cultivated a habit of sharpening a skinning knife, and the sound grated on their nerves. Rufus took engine mechanics lessons from Maclemar, and they felt more rested as they buried themselves in work. Sainvire stared at the blue Pacific whenever Poe wasn't in sight. He had put forth a couple of ideas which were diplomatically rejected. He couldn't quite form a cohesive plan. Whenever he glimpsed Poe running or sitting with her dog, the master vampire would lose every lucid idea he'd been developing.

One thing he knew for certain. Trench was a dead man. He'd violated the woman most precious to him. So consumed with rage was Sainvire that nearly 24 hours a day he imagined the merciless ways he would end Trench's life. Vlad the Impaler's sadistic killing methods were nothing compared to what he would do to Quillon Trench. He swore to set those thoughts aside during their meeting because he wanted full command of his faculties. A month had passed, and it was time to make a move.

The planning session had already begun when Poe slinked inside Passionada's glitzy living room. All eyes were on her. This was the first she'd ever participated in a formal meeting. She sat down on an empty orange Ikea chair nearest the door and breathed deep, soothing breaths for courage. The time for shedding shame, fear, and self-blame was at hand.

"We've come up with nothing workable these past weeks, and we're running out of time. For all we know Dogtown is on their list of possible hiding places," said Morales after grinning at an awkward-looking Poe. "We have to get out of here."

Heads bobbed in agreement. Rufus, who was cleaning his filthy grease-stained nails with the tip of a pen knife, said without looking up, "I think we should make all kinds of noise to lure them here and have Passionada's dogs have at 'em."

"Yeah, and we can drop Morales' famous incendiaries at them from the choppers," added the usually silent Ed. "They'd most likely send a good amount of goons that will leave Downtown vulnerable."

Sainvire turned to Passionada. "Dogtown will be eviscerated, you realize, Passionada. You'll have to find a new place to stay, and your dogs—"

"They might all get killed," she finished for the master vampire. "Don't worry. I've been lucky enough to stay here as long as I have. Time to move on. Besides, wherever little Piper is, I'll be there."

Joseph grinned, but his eyes were tired. Morales smiled at the woman's generous offer and nodded in thanks.

"We can put Passionada, Habib, and the babe in one of the boats and keep them anchored about ten miles from here. It'll be safer."

"What about Downtown itself?" asked Michelle. "The big boys are there and so are the cattle. Plus we gotta think about the janitors, cooks, and custodians. And," she said with a nervous glance at Poe, "how are we going to flush out that fuckface Trench?"

Sainvire crossed his long legs with care. "Leave him to me."

"How?" asked Habib. "Security will be quadrupled Downtown. They'll be ready for us."

"I don't know the answer," said Sainvire, "but I aim to kill Trench no matter what."

"That's foolish talk," said Michelle. "You gotta think about the odds. There are only twenty-two of us here and a third of us can't fight. Downtown is crawling with Neanderthals with fangs."

"Yeah. We can't focus on one vamp when there are so many to be fought," said Joseph who rarely questioned his friend's motives. "We love Poe," he said while looking Poe in the eyes, "but it would be foolish to pool all our resources into destroying Trench alone."

Half the room nodded in agreement. "What we need is a fool-proof plan," said Morales. We need to take out two birds with one stone."

At this point Poe stood up. She made her way to the largest floral couch at the center of the room and sat between Joseph and Morales. Sitting next to good friends that were neutral was the right thing to do.

Poe feared she might not be able to speak and cleared her throat. Swallowing her nervousness she silently met every curious eye in the room.

"May I put my two cents in?" she asked. Her voice was more gravelly than usual.

"Of course, you nut," said Morales, nudging her with an elbow in the ribs. "Talk away."

"We missed hearing your alcoholic voice plenty," added Joseph whom she'd pinched.

"I'm positive we can take out two birds," she began, looking into Sainvire's eyes for the first time in weeks. "It's a good idea to lure Downtown dead here and let the dogs take care of them. It's also right to drop Morales' legendary homemade bombs on the ones who survive the dogs. Everyone here, except the ones Downtown bound, will be fighting from helicopters or boats to keep casualties down."

"How many do you need for the Downtown operation?" asked Michelle.

"Four," said Poe. She drew another long breath when she heard disbelief in their voices.

She continued. "Morales, you'll concoct something explosive for Club Drip. We'll hit the respected vamps, and that will draw attention from Downtown vamps for a little while since the club is in Warehouse Alley.

"Ed, you'll contact Kawana. Get her to organize all the janitors she can find to meet up at the convention center. Have them bring all the weapons they can get hold of. From what I've seen at Tren—at Disney Hall, they can leave the building without supervision. They have double-duties at other blood ranches." Vampires assumed that janitors were too fearful of running away because they would be sniffed out eventually and punished severely. "Without their help, cattle care will fall to pieces, and the vampires would have a hard time sustaining their food source." Poe checked around the room. They were listening without exception. "The downside is we'll have to leave the cattle behind."

She continued, "Rufus and Michelle will take the largest chopper and pick up as many janitors that can fit into the bird. If Kawana gets to all of them successfully, then they'll be waiting at the convention center."

She focused her gaze at the Welshman. "Maclemar, we need you to fix up as many boats as there are available at the marina. Pick boats that even novices can maneuver. We're all going to end up at

Catalina Island temporarily," she said. She'd been to Catalina when she was a child, and she knew it was no more than a couple of hours off the coast. "As soon as Michelle and Rufus unload and go off for more janitors, you're going to drop anchor where Habib, Piper, and Passionada wait, maybe ten miles from shore. Then come back and pick up some more people.

"Morales, you don't have to plant the bombs. Sainvire and I will take care of that. Just make sure you have enough firepower to blow up uninvited Dogtown visitors.

Maclemar's throat constricted. Poe had chosen Sainvire to accompany her that night. "And what will you be doing, Sharren?"

"Sainvire is going to fly me to the best corner buildings around so I can shoot every powerful dead in the center of their foreheads. I suggest you do the same since they'll be sure to Kevlar up when they strike here. Once we finish our rounds we'll pay Trench a visit and make him a very happy dead."

Poe swept the room with her large brown eyes expecting some dissatisfaction among her friends about her plan. They only met her with silence.

Finally Joseph said, "Sounds like a plan to me."

With minor tweaks and changes Poe's plan was agreed upon by all after nearly two hours of discussion.

Joseph put his arms around Poe's shoulder and squeezed, "Glad you're with us again, sis."

"Glad to be back," answered Poe. She meant it.

Morales kissed her on the forehead and said, "Now that you're here, I know we're going to kick Ancient ass."

She squeezed the ex-realtor's knee and said, "As long as you don't douse yourself with your yuck-face cologne, then the operation should work."

"You're such a brat!" her friend roared, tugging at her ponytail.

For the first time in weeks Sainvire tipped his chair back, laced his long fingers on his stomach, and smiled as he watched Joseph, Morales, and Poe exchange barbs. Now that the real Poe was back he could think straight again.

"Eat, eat!" ordered Habib who spread out a feast three hours before Operation Get 'Em, as Rufus popularized the mission, began. "Michelle, have some more protein. It will sustain you."

Michelle forked another Maclemar-caught fish on her plate. "I'm going to burst, Habib. This is my last one."

The vampires and halfdead passed gallons of Plasmacore amongst each other like a bootleg whiskey jug. Sainvire gulped his share as he would have to be twice as strong to transport a passenger in his arms. He particularly relished the idea.

It was an hour until sundown and the activity level at Dogtown was electric. If they were to execute the plan on point, they would lose very little life.

Poe approached the boat dock hastily built by Maclemar and his friends. Morales and Joseph had just finished saying goodbye to little Piper squirming in Passionada's lap. "Don't worry, boys. I'll protect your daughter with my life." To emphasize her point Passionada lifted a semi-automatic Spider from the pocket of her dress. Satchels full of beauty products and dresses surrounded her. Maclemar couldn't dissuade the girly woman to part with some of her belongings.

Joseph and Morales turned to Poe. Their eyes were cloudy but their smiles pasted on. "Hey, Poe. Penny going on this boat?"

"Uh huh," she answered Morales. "She'll protect the baby for sure."

"Yeah, Penny's a fierce one," said Joseph. "Never said so before, but I'm very fond of your ratty companion."

Poe smiled. "Yeah. She's the best."

Maclemar approached with Habib, carrying his pots and pans as well as provisions. Joseph and Morales winked at each other and made their exit. Poe carried Penny and deposited her in the boat.

"So many things to bring," said Habib.

Maclemar, whose eyes never left Poe's face, said, "You can't take them all, Habib. A lot of the food is distributed on the other boats. Just sit back and relax." Habib climbed the ladder and almost fell when the first explosions off of Venice Boulevard rocked the neighborhood.

"Get in, Habib. Time to go," said Maclemar urgently. He turned to Poe. "I'll take care of Penny. You take care of yourself."

"You too, Welshman," said Poe with a quiet voice. "Thank you for everything you've done for me."

Maclemar raised his right hand as if to touch her face but realized his hands were filthy from engine work. Poe, realizing this, took hold of his hand and placed the palm on her cheek. "I love both of you but in different ways. Sainvire is—"

"Your soul mate," finished Maclemar. "I know this, but I'm sticking around just in case he annoys you to death and you come running back into my arms."

Poe pulled his head toward her and kissed him deeply until the fisherman enveloped her in his arms. "You take care, Caveman," Poe said breathlessly. "I'll see you sooner than you think."

CHAPTER 16

THE VAMPIRE KILLER'S BELT, hand-tooled by Maclemar for armaments fitted with silencers of all sizes, rubbed at Sainvire's hip and ribs as Poe held on for dear life. She was clinging onto his neck like she didn't trust him to keep her from slipping. The moon illuminated rows of charred houses razed by Downtown vamps. Her heart thudded miserably at the thought that her parents' house had burned along with the others. All those wonderful photo albums she'd looked at every day, her brother and sister's tiny clothing and toys, mementos of life when it was grand. She looked up at the bright stars as they soared as high as Sainvire could muster. Her backpack full of incendiary devices banged lightly against her lower back.

Two sets of long-range rifles draped precariously about her shoulders. The girl's weapons didn't hurt Sainvire so badly since Poe insisted he wear Kevlar for the occasion. His spirit was dark. He'd witnessed the woman he loved kiss another man with palpable passion, and it floored him. Poe claimed she loved him, yet what could he say about the intimacy he'd witnessed? The master vampire could barely control his anger.

"Hey, listen," Poe interrupted his rumination. "I feel like I'm slipping. Can I snake my legs about you?"

Sainvire shivered involuntarily. The warmth emanating from the girl's lips and the sound of her silky voice caused the pain in his heart to grow more perverse.

"Do what you want," he said, looking intently at the sparsely lit skyline of Downtown Los Angeles.

Poe, who had been feeling steel from Sainvire all day, sighed. He'd been very distant with her, and she bet she knew why. The entire Dogtown lineup seemed to have seen her snogging Maclemar. Of course Sainvire must've had seen them, too. The kiss was meant as a goodbye. Nothing more. She eased her head back and tried to capture Sainvire's gaze. When she couldn't, Poe sighed again.

"If you're feeling injured about what you saw today," she began, "I apologize. I was just saying adios."

Sainvire glanced at her with irritation in his face. "I didn't see you lock tongues with Habib, Joseph, or Morales. Not even Ed got an adios."

"Maclemar thinks he's in love with me—"

"And you're just trying to satisfy his fantasies?" he said with sarcasm. He flew a hard left when a seagull who'd lost its flock headed blindly toward the two of them. Poe hugged Sainvire harder.

"Last kiss goodbye," Poe said quietly. She knew the vampire with super-sensitive hearing would hear what she'd said anyway.

Sainvire tightened his arm about the petite girl with hair as dark as his. "You expect Maclemar to die, or is it yourself you're talking about?"

Poe captured Sainvire's face with both hands and threw off the vampire's balance. She didn't utter a word until they were flying steady again, and Sainvire's eyes bore into hers. "I understand jealousy, vampire. I felt it when I saw you and Jenna together at the farm."

His gray eyes startlingly light in the dark, Sainvire cleared his throat. "We were both lonely. Besides both being deep in the revolution, our relationship stopped at sex. I loved you, and she knew that."

"Well Maclemar knows that, too," she said with pain in her gut. She didn't want to hurt the Welshman by choosing, but it was too late. She had chosen a long time ago, and Poe had wounded him. "The kiss you saw is the last between us. That is unless you say you don't want me anymore. Then he'll be my boy." She swallowed in bemusement at the last bit she'd said.

Sainvire's jaw worked angrily, and the scar on his lips looked dangerous. "Are you cold? You're only wearing a t-shirt and a vest."

"No. Not really."

"Maclemar's a good man," the vampire said. "I don't want you anymore. He can be your 'boy'."

Poe's mouth dropped open in shock. She did not expect such a reply from the man who claimed to love her. Before she could form a clear thought and express it out loud, Sainvire captured her lips with his generous mouth and kissed her so thoroughly that any memory of Maclemar or Trench's kisses vanished from her mind. Because Poe needed to gulp a breath, the two parted lips.

"I love you, Julia Poe, and I don't want you sharing your mouth with other men," Sainvire decreed. The hint of a smile tugged at the side of his lips. "It nearly killed me to hear you moan and groan in that miserable trailer with him."

Poe crinkled her nose. "So you did try to sabotage our lovemaking back in Gilroy. I knew it! I was about to have an orga—"

"Don't want to hear that, little one. The only one who's going to make you squirm and shout from now on is me," Sainvire said solemnly.

"Ditto then," she said with delight. "I guess it's official. We're going steady."

"I'm yours forever. You can count on that," the vampire said softly as he toyed with Poe's hair.

Poe sighed once more. "Forever? Hope you still feel that way when my teeth fall out and my boobs drop down to my belly."

———

Explosions desecrating asphalt and palm trees rocked the streets of Venice. Ringing silence followed. Morales, who had wired explosives in strategic sites around Dogtown, deemed thirty minutes of fireworks the perfect amount to set the bait. When the enemy helicopters came an hour later, fourteen souls were poised around Dogtown for the attack.

Joseph, the vampire with the keenest eyes, was in charge of blowing metallic birds from the sky with ancient bazookas. Though not a sure-shot like Poe in the very least, the vampire tried his best, and his best equaled extinguishing three helicopters after wasting a plethora of ammo.

Fifty Downtown soldiers consisting of halfdead, vampires, and leeches emerged from helicopters and overran the ground Most of these sentinels of the old order were the dregs with no special powers to speak of. Trench and the other master vampires were low on A-grade soldiers, and only two shared Sainvire's gift of flight.

The dark army of Downtown was in confusion, pointing their rifles and guns at the place called Dogtown. When Passionada tightened her rouged lips around a slim silver whistle and blew, a thousand dogs bore down on the enemy. The human leeches went down first, and the weaker dead who killed three dogs while screaming in horror were downed by ten.

Within the hour two more enemy choppers came to investigate to their detriment. . Morales' homemade explosives volleyed from makeshift bazookas incinerated the vampire troops aboard. Joseph, packing astonishing speed, eliminated with his bare hands the thugs left loitering on the grounds.

All fourteen revolutionaries expelled a sigh of relief at how easily they'd defeated the enemy. A roar of triumph filled the air when Michelle's helicopter returned with dozens of janitors. The plan was working so far. Ed prayed that Poe and Sainvire were as successful.

Shaking the nervousness from holding an incendiary device in her hands, Poe impulsively entered Drip alone while Sainvire was barring the exits to the rear alley. She was supposed to toss the bowling ball-size bomb and shut the door behind her. She scanned the club in search of familiar faces that had made her stay Downtown a demoralizing hell. She recognized Robert Kirlegast, the bony vampire with a fetish for scraping his nails on her back and licking them like cookie batter. Kato Grange, the short and stocky undead who loved to squeeze her breasts so hard Poe had nearly fainted from pain, made her hands shake.

"Grange!" she hollered over the din of horrific '80s music. Heads turned. In an instant fangers in the club had recognized the vampire killer.

"Poe!" Kirlegast shouted. He shot to on his feet.

"Hi, boys. The vampire executioner is back," she declared cheerfully. Poe had always wanted to make a dramatic entrance. Before any of the sneering undead could lunge at her, Poe held up the spherical kiss of death wrapped in newspaper Morales had concocted and tossed it at Grange who caught the heavy ticking time bomb sphere by instinct. Poe bolted out the door and shut it behind amidst terror-filled screaming.

She screamed as Sainvire appeared in her line of sight, taking her by the waist and launching them away. Seconds later the club exploded to cinders.

"That was foolish of you, Poe!" shouted Sainvire from the air. "Going inside with only seconds left? What the hell are you trying to do?"

"I just wanted to know who was in there," she said, surly. "I have a kill list."

Sainvire was visibly shaken. He didn't know whether to hug Poe in relief or strangle her to death. "You should've told me, dammit. I thought you were outside—"

Not the slightest penitent, Poe cut him off. "Sorry. I just needed to know. Kirlegast and Grange were in there. Two less people we have to hunt tonight."

"I told you I'd take you to their homes," he said. The dead that had despoiled Poe's body punched through his thoughts. "If you want a life together after tonight, don't take any more risks. Now who do you want to visit?"

"Charles Lamb."

"He lives at the Bradbury," said Sainvire, easing his hold on Poe's waist. Within minutes he landed them softly on the roof of one of the best regarded buildings in Los Angeles. "The glass roof used to be covered in tar during World War II in case Japanese planes invaded, but the restoration society cleaned it all up. The glass should afford you the perfect shot."

From the glass roof Poe watched a bevy of activity directed by Charles Lamb himself. He was attempting to post guards to his most valuable possessions – cattle. Slowly, without taking her eyes off the aristocratic brute who had whipped her unforgivingly harder than the others, Poe assembled her Shadow Sniper rifle. She tightly screwed on the sound suppressor.

Through the scope she saw Lamb looking as nervous as hell. She gulped a calming breath and shot the vampire in the forehead and nose. Lamb tipped over the famously crafted wrought iron banisters and landed ungracefully on the tiled floor three stories down. Before Poe could taste the triumph of revenge, she was lifted off the roof and airborne in no time. Sainvire wasn't taking any chances. He wanted to assuage Poe's bloodlust for her torturers. The vampire didn't want any ghosts haunting the woman he cared for, but he also didn't want her to get injured or perish because her mind was fixed in one-track mode.

Silently Sainvire dropped her off upon the roof of the SB Loft building across the street from Juno Liman's multi-floor home at the Spring Arcade building. The place was gilded with decorative Rococo windows that allowed prying eyes to be voyeurs. The girl spotted the goth vamp without a problem and shot him in the chest. She shot at the five vampires surrounding Liman to leave no stone unturned. *The less vamps the better*, she thought. *Bad vamps, that is*.

At their neighboring homes in the National Biscuit Company building, Samuel Clemens and Franco Sebastian were killed as quickly and efficiently as marking a checkbox. Poe's blood boiled without relief. She wasn't satisfied with the death of second-rate undead.

"Is that all, Poe? Should we move on to Trench?"

Poe clung to Sanvire's neck. She kissed his cold lips. "I love you, Kaleb. Please don't see me as a monster. I just want a clean slate. I don't want to dream about these evil monsters and know I didn't kill them when I had the chance."

Sainvire kissed her intensely. When their lips parted Sainvire said in a low, nearly growling voice, "I'll fly you all night to kill these sons-of-bitches if it means therapy for you. Put your arms around my neck and hold on tight."

"I feel sorry for the cattle," Sainvire said after a time. "There will be a mass feeding after the important undead are gone, and these poor people will suffer."

"There aren't enough of us," said Poe as she envisioned the low-rung vampires who lacked foresight to preserve their food source. "We can't do anything now.

"Take the flyers from my pockets and scatter them, Poe," he said. Ed's idea was to reproduce leaflets with the formula for Plasmacore. "Perhaps when they deplete the food supply, Downtown residents will consider making their own batch to keep from starving."

Poe released the white flyers into the darkness. She thought it was one of the most beautiful sights she'd ever seen with the moon illuminating them like ghosts.

———

Before they could land on the parking garage across the street from the Disney Hall, sniper fire whizzed past Poe and Sainvire. The shots were coming from the metallic valleys of the Gehry building. Sainvire dropped her on the rooftop of the parking structure and held her close, their heads ducked low. "Shit! You've been hit, Poe."

"No, I haven't," insisted the girl. Her heart was palpitating. The snipers were good. They were professionals. *Must be cops*, she thought.

"Check yourself, love, I smell blood," he said and turned her over. He touched her left cheek and kissed Poe's forehead. "It's only a scratch," he said while wiping the blood on Poe's cheek with the edge of his coat sleeve. "Don't get shot, alright?"

"I won't if you won't," said Poe with a grin.

"I'm wearing Kevlar, and you?"

"I'm wearing Kevlar, too, mister. Don't worry about me. I'll keep my noggin safe," she assured the gray-eyed vampire. She kneeled and laid her rifles down on the floor. She rested her head at the edge of a corner wall with tile protrusions that were perfect for cover. She raised an arm and a bevy of bullets zinged nearby. "They're good, but not that good," she said mostly to herself. "How many shooters?"

"About six," said Sainvire as he assembled the other rifle nicknamed the Varmint.

"So where do you think they came from?" asked Poe. She relied mainly on the moon to see in the night. "How about I shoot, then you take a shot when you see a spark?"

"Sounds good to me." Sainvire fired toward the second tier of the undulating building, and a dead shot back. Poe, avoiding the scopes since they limited her field of vision, relied on her eyes and instincts alone to return fire. To her surprise she heard a shout and a man in a dark suit fell to the ground. She spotted two more flashes and fired at them. Two more bodies fell on Grand Avenue.

"Three more, Poe, and we're clear," said Sainvire calmly, but his voice enthused pride.

Poe reloaded. For the first time she realized her purpose in life. She thanked whatever divine powers had given her the talent to shoot accurately and kill opportunistic vampires, and she was pleased she had avoided joining the cattle ranks. "Again, Kaleb," she said, positioning her rifle.

Sainvire fired randomly, and Poe memorized the places where gunfire originated from.

"That's it," she said. Shutting her left eye, Poe shot three times in succession at the dark. One by one, three bodies rolled down the undulating metallic walls of the Hall.

"Michelle said you're a superhero. I believe it, beauty," Sainvire said with pride. He pulled Poe toward him and kissed her. Poe kissed him back but quickly released. "There are no windows. We have to break inside Trench's home to kill him. Let's not celebrate so early."

———

Sainvire flew Poe to MOCA. The art museum was a block away from the Hall. He set her down gently and whispered, "We didn't really think this out, did we?"

Poe shook her head. "I guess I always thought we could infiltrate Trench's home through the kitchen. But I'm realizing that just might be a death trap."

"Same here," he agreed. He looked up at the massive sculpture made out airplane of scraps hovering over the museum. "Let's see. There's the ticket counter, the gift shop. The few windows the building has have already been barricaded. Fuck!" he swore.

Poe couldn't remember Sainvire ever swearing before. The past two years had altered him quite a bit. Stubble grew on his strong jaw, and instead of Zen-like tranquility in his light gray eyes, Sainvire spat out fire and deep intensity that Poe hadn't accepted yet. "There's always the front door. They never changed the glass."

Sainvire shook his head. "We'll be too exposed. Shots will be fired from the escalators, the balconies."

"We have no choice then," said Poe, dreading the thought. "We gotta go through the kitchen out back. Of course they'll be waiting for us there, but heck, it's a smaller space. We'll be able to see who we're fighting."

Sainvire looked up at the sculpture again and said to himself, "I think the artist was Nancy Rubin." He studied the hodge-podge propellers, airplane parts, and other junk. "It's a pretty good piece, don't you think, Poe?"

Poe quickly examined the artwork Sainvire was staring at. "Um, yeah. Sure."

"I think I remember this artist being influenced by the Watts Towers. She liked creating art from discarded material."

"Yeah. But what about our entryway?" prodded Poe. *Art history be damned.*

"We need our own Watts Towers, Poe. A symbol of hope," he said. He flew to the sharp edge of the sculpture. With a grunt he pulled off a chunk the size of a claw foot tub replete with propellers and airplane siding. "Sorry about that, Ms. Rubin," he apologized. He floated down in front of Poe. "Let's get to work, shall we?"

The vampire who'd been tired and angry for too long now hurled the heavy sculpture, sharp edge first, inside the dark kitchen of the Disney Hall. As predicted, a volley of bullets erupted in the dark, targeting the melded art. Poe flipped on the switch and ducked down. Steel-tipped bullets nearly clipped her. For the second time that night her mortality became the topic of conversation inside her brain. No Kevlar could stop steel. "Just keep moving, Poe. Don't do anything stupid."

The bright kitchen lights exposed five vampires also wearing bulletproof vests. One crouched like a monkey on the spice racks, another hid behind the refrigerator, two took their positions in the pantry, and one with cojones put himself near the door. Sainvire's nails elongated and slashed at the head of the vampire who was foolish enough to cross his path. The master vampire decapitated him in three spots.

Bullets hurled their way. Poe slid under the stainless steel cutting table that took over half the kitchen while Sainvire dodged death with his supernatural speed, zigzagging in the blunt space. Within seconds the table was ridden with holes. "Fuck me," she told herself as quietly as possible. Her heart thudded unnervingly. She inhaled, exhaled, and rolled on the floor to avoid bullets trained at her. *Okay, Mom, Dad. Help me out here.*

She gauged where the monkey boy on the spice racks was and shot him through one of the bullet holes in the table. To her relief, the vamp fell to the ground. "Sister Ann, help!" she cried and half-emerged from under the table. With the little courage summoned from her warrior shout, Poe raised both her hands. She fired a Glock from her left and a Beretta from the right. She hit one vamp in the eye and the other, the neck. Sainvire shot the latter behind the head to kill him forevermore.

Five down in the kitchen, thought Poe as she stood up. Sainvire took some bullets in the arms, and darkish liquid oozed from his wounds. "Okay there, handsome?"

"Yes," he said bravely. "Give it a minute or two and the holes will fuse. I hope," he added to be funny which irritated Poe to the core.

"Jerk," she said with a clenched jaw.

Sainvire handed Poe a commercial-grade iron skillet that weighed shy of twenty pounds. "Put that over your heart, alright?"

"Are you kidding me? I need both my hands for shooting. This thing is heavy as heck."

"Just until we reach the escalators, Julia. Then you can toss it at somebody's head," he said in exasperation.

"So now you call me Julia when you're annoyed with me?" she said. Her given name used to evoke passion and longing when Sainvire spoke it.

The vampire didn't answer but proceeded in front of her, his Jericho 941F in hand. Both looked wildly for snipers within the well lit performance hall. Whereas cold steel hugged the building outside of the famous landmark, the inside was effused with earthy décor and warm unpolished marble cut into rectangular tile that added resonance to the acoustics of the hall. The lobby area seemed empty enough, but both Sainvire and Poe stayed alert.

"Take the escalator, Poe. I'll check things out ahead of you," said the vampire. He looked dead serious. He soared to the second floor, and his fangs lengthened on their own accord.

Even holding the dreadfully heavy skillet against her chest, Poe did as Sainvire instructed. She remembered going up and down the very same escalator in stiletto heels, and color drained from her face. Trench's home was her horror house, malignant and sticky with nightmare. Images of Trench giving her tender pleasures and having him stand by while vampires feasted on her brought blood cursing back into her veins. *Tonight, Trench will die.*

Sainvire met her at the top of the staircase. "I circled the building, Poe. Nothing."

Afraid Sainvire correctly judged the second floor to be empty, she headed for her old room. Her findings confirmed the truth. Still unconvinced she entered Trench's boudoir and felt tremors in her stomach. "Leave me the fuck alone," she told the walls as indecent images flooded her brain.

Sainvire put a gentle hand on her shoulder. "Let's check the concert chamber, Poe."

Poe sniffed and squared her shoulders. "I'm dropping this frying pan once we're in, *entiendes*?"

Sainvire's lower lip quivered, suppressing a laugh. "*Sí.*"

They took the winding side stairs upward to reach the highest balcony doors. Both agreed wordlessly that it was better that way. They would have sight advantage at the very least if they were at the highest rung. The curvature of the auditorium was funneled, perhaps even cone-shaped.

"Take the next door, Poe, and I'll take this one. I'll open it once I hear your hand on the knob."

Poe nodded and went her way.

The concert space was lit, though nearly half the light bulbs had burned out. Poe and Sainvire entered the upper tier at the same time, thanks to Sainvire's ultra-sensitive hearing. Poe crouched low and surveyed the room. *Great Ali, point them out to me*, she prayed in hope that her hero and her instincts would lead her to the enemy.

Poe heard the sound of Santa Ana winds against cloth, and she saw a whish of black fly toward the west side of the hall. It was Sainvire, she realized, plucking from the side balcony a female vamp armed with a cross-bow. Without compunction Sainvire cracked her head and stabbed her in the heart with his finely honed nail.

"To your right, Poe," he yelled. The girl was too busy watching the killing to realize a gorgeous, leaping model vamp was speeding her way. The calm that always came at violent times blanketed Poe. She raised her Berretta and shot the vampire in the head twice. The beautiful blonde fell back, mouth open, on seat B-28.

Three more vamps burst their way out of the wall acoustic panels and blasted indiscriminately at Poe and Sainvire. From the corner of her eye Poe saw Sainvire shoot a flying vamp, but the bullet only grazed his ear. *Concentrate, Poe*, she said to herself while watching the vamps zigzag to her balcony. Exhaling, she aimed and fired at the heavy-set halfdead and followed by piercing the androgynous vampire in leather-studded clothes twice in the chest.

She looked down to witness Sainvire slicing his nemesis' neck. Poe cringed. Violence was not her way anymore, she realized. The hall was eerily still. Poe caught Sainvire's eyes and smiled.

"Is that all?"

"I think so," said Sainvire. He looked strangely at Poe.

"That was kind of easy."

"Yeah. Too easy," he said. "Poe, do you realize you're still holding that frying pan?"

Poe's right hand was indeed still holding the pan over her chest like she was about to recite the Pledge of Allegiance. The vampire hunter giggled and dropped the pan. "Stupid m—"

She imagined hearing the shot coming from far away. But what really tested her ear was when the steel-tip bullet that had been dipped in garlic oil hit her in the chest and punctured her Kevlar.

Ouch, Poe thought. She fell on a wooden bench.

"Poe!" cried Sainvire. She vaguely heard. At the stage appeared a score of vampires who prevented Sainvire from reaching Poe. Fueled by the need to see her, the vampire fought eight dead with the speed of Joseph, the accuracy of Poe, and the desperation of a man whose lover had just been shot. Within a minute all eight undead and halfdead were on the stage at his feet. Those he killed weren't clothed in designer clothes, Trench's signature bodyguard swag. They were off the streets and lacking any tangible powers. *Trench must've been hurting to hire these half-starved vamps.* Before Sainvire could take flight, the familiar sardonic voice of Quillon Trench stopped him.

"Funny, isn't it, Kaleb?" Trench said. A white and black scarf covered most of his face. He walked out to the stage. "Who would've thought that I could transform a guttersnipe like her into a lady?"

"Fuck you, Trench. Poe doesn't need dressing," said Sainvire. His eyes blazed with hatred. "She's the best out of all of us."

"She is that. It was no surprise, I suppose, that I fell in love with her like you did."

"Having her tortured by other men in front of you is not love, asshole," growled Kaleb. "It's called a fetish."

Trench snorted. "Whatever you say, Kaleb. Either way, I'm done. She killed most of my people, and those I sent to investigate the beach areas haven't returned. Even the custodians are gone."

"I'm going to kill you now, Quillon, because you're on Poe's time right now," he said. His nails lengthened twelve inches.

Quillon laughed. "I can't fight you. I have very weak powers. I'm just a brain with plans. Besides, without beautiful people and the love of sweet Poe around me, what else is there but the apocalypse?" He raised his arms and nodded for Sainvire to finish him.

Sainvire felt rage for the man who'd altered Poe forever. As he raised his sharp nails to tear Quillon limb from limb, a shot rang out and the master vampire called Trench fell truly dead on the concert hall stage with a bullet between the eyes.

Perplexed, Sainvire looked up to where Poe had lay. The girl had shot Trench to a permanent death. By the time Sainvire reached her, the Beretta had fallen between the balcony seats.

Poe's eyes were glazed with pain. "Did I get him?" Poe asked weakly.

"Dead center, love," Sainvire answered. He withheld desperation from his voice. For the first time in decades his hand shook. He gently tugged open the Kevlar and pulled it off her shoulders.

"Good. Said I was gonna kill him. Kaleb. I can barely breathe," Poe said, gasping. "Think I'm done for."

"Don't say that," said Sainvire with acid. "You're not leaving me, young lady." He had the urge to cry despite the fact that vampires could not shed tears. He lifted her black shirt soaked with blood and studied the wound above her left breast. The back of the bullet was visible. The shooter had fired from the stage. Sainvire bit his lower lip. He prayed that the bullet was of a low caliber. Otherwise he wouldn't have known what do.

"How bad?" she asked tiredly.

"Just a scrape, Poe. Just a scrape." Sainvire removed his coat and black button-down shirt.

"Why are you naked?" asked Poe in dazed. Even when dizzy, Poe could see the vampire's muscular build.

"I'm going to use my shirt as a bandage. You shouldn't talk, Poe. Conserve your strength," he answered, concealing any hint of panic. As if sweat beaded his forehead, Sainvire wiped his brow with his arms. With his index finger and thumb he extracted the bullet. Blood poured out of the tiny wound like a tipped bottle of wine. The vampire stoppered the flow with his shirt, keeping firm pressure until the blood stilled.

Poe, looking ashen, had fainted. "You have to live, Poe," he said quietly. "Our lives wouldn't be the same without you."

———

Sainvire stepped outside of Disney Hall half-naked and carrying Poe in his arms. The girl was wrapped up in her lover's clothes. The vampire cursed. Outside stood fifty vampires. "Look. I don't have time for this," he said, his hard voice carrying. "I promise I'll come back next week so you can hack me to pieces."

A bearded undead, apparently the spokesperson of the group, stepped forward. "That's not our intention, Mr. Sainvire."

"Then what do you want?" asked Sainvire curtly.

"Some of us have put guards outside the cattle farms to guard them from idiots who don't think long-term. Most everyone has tried Plasmacore at least once in this town and found it not so bad."

"So what do you want me to do?" asked Sainvire.

"Maybe you can tell us what to do. Be our master again? Without authority, we'll fall to pieces. You know that from Machiavelli and Plato, right?"

Sainvire stared at the vampire that summed up the stereotypical professor and nodded. "I'm not going to be anyone's master. I can come back or send someone here to help you organize, but my hands are full. Keep the cattle protected. Tell anyone who defies that order that Kaleb Sainvire will personally skewer them like rats if even one human is hurt. And if anybody tries to leave Downtown, I will come after them myself. Alright with you? What's your name?"

"I'm Bartholomew Hayward," answered the pragmatic vampire. "And it's alright by us, sir."

"Pleasure to meet you, Mr. Hayward," said Kaleb. He levitated slowly upward then jetted as expeditiously as he could toward Venice.

CHAPTER 17

THE SOUND OF SURF crashing against rock intrigued her enough to open her eyes. She blinked a few times to clear her vision only to come face to face with Penny looking anxious to please. She had fallen asleep on the sand again trying to avoid the island inhabitants as much as she could. She air-kissed the dog, and at once her loyal companion licked her face with sand paper tongue and lay her head on Poe's stomach. The dog knew better than to rest any part of her body on Poe's chest.

Three months earlier she had woken up in a sea of smiling faces. There was Habib, Michelle, Maclemar, Joseph, Morales, and Sainvire.

"Poe, you came back to us," said a very grateful Morales. "If I failed as T-Doc, this worthless gang of worms would've lynched me."

"Good to see you, Poe. We're all safe. Maclemar brought us all to Catalina Island single-handedly," said her curly-haired friend.

"Aye, Sharren. No Revs here. You can relax and enjoy the panoramic view when you get up and around," said Maclemar whose eyes looked misty.

"Thanks, Mister. I appreciate all you've done for me."

340

Poe's gaze rested on Sainvire who was as still and implacable as she'd ever seen him. His stubble bothered her. He said nothing.

Joseph cleared his throat and nodded at her. "Couldn't think about you being gone, sis. Not you. Our superhero."

As she gazed at the dying sun, she felt the tender love she had for her friends. However, at that moment, all she wanted was for them to leave the room and let her be. Truth was, a few months ago she would have been willing to trade her life for them. But she realized she was an ordinary girl. She was no superhero, and nothing would be the same.

Trench and his cronies had rutted on her and spooned her blood into their greedy mouths while they restrained her to the bed. There were no champions like Xena or Bruce Lee to get her out of the bind. Not even the ghosts of her parents had helped her out. *Then I got shot in the chest and nearly died. Where are you, Sister Ann? Goss?* Her pathetic belief that she was a godsend sure-shot was laughable now. Her chest hurt whenever she tried to overextend herself.

Poe tasted mortality, and it shook her enough to embody weakness and broken spirit. The guts and sass she'd honed since the deaths of Sister Ann and Goss were gone. How could she explain such a thing to her friends?

One of the bravest gestures in her life was to smile to reassure them that she was fine. Good old Poe was back.

Her chest hurt, but her courage pained her more. It was sorely bleeding, and she believed none of her friends or even Sainvire could help her.

She heard the soft padding of feet on sand. It was Sainvire. He kneeled next to her and studied her face.

"The last boat is leaving, Poe," he said with a heavy heart. "Won't you reconsider?"

Ever since Sainvire had promised to restructure Downtown, the people from Catalina Island agreed to go back if only to restore their dignity. Custodians, janitors, and ex-cattle would now have a hand in destroying the reign of the vampires for which Poe refused to be part of.

"I've done my part. Don't you agree?" she said, her voice low. "I deserve my retirement, and I can't stop thinking about Chops. Besides, the pain in my chest might foil any plans you may have of parading me around."

Sainvire sighed, and he scratched Penny's collarless neck. "You know I wouldn't do that. I just want you near me. I have to be where our people are. And we have a chance to correct the wrongs vampires have inflicted on humans. Then there's Plasmacore."

"Yes, Kaleb. I bear no ill will. I've always believed that your people come first."

Sainvire covered his face with his hands in shame for not disputing the truth of what Poe had said. Ever since Poe had woken from her near-fatal wound, she'd pushed everyone she loved at bay. She asked for her own room. He waited for her invitation and so did Maclemar, but it never came. She insisted on her privacy. To see her so haunted, so fearful that she'd rather have isolation than the company of her friends, hurt him like nothing he'd ever experienced. The old Poe was hiding behind the pain in her chest where a bullet had nearly stolen her life. Morales said that Poe had experienced the mortal coil. The pain was in her head, and the sooner she snapped out of it, the better she would be.

"You come first, Julia Poe," said Sainvire as he captured smooth black hair between his fingers. "I'll stay with you if you wish."

Poe grinned up at him. "It would kill you to stay with me, you know that. I need to heal up. I need to sleep in the sand with Penny." *The only one in this demented world who would never leave my side.*

Sainvire stood to leave as Poe rested her head in the sand. She closed her eyes and enjoyed the feel of Penny's warmth on her belly. Sainvire's dead heart was heavy. The woman he loved was defeated, and he couldn't face the sad fact. Poe was lost to everyone, and it was as if the world lost half the moon.

"I love you, Julia Poe," he said somberly.

Poe never responded, and Sainvire walked away with a barrel full of remorse on his broken shoulder.

THE END

www.ingramcontent.com/pod-product-compliance
Lightning Source LLC
Chambersburg PA
CBHW030920260626

47169CB00002B/333